Melanie Hudson was born in Yorkshire in 1971, the youngest of six children. Her earliest memory is of standing with her brother on the street corner selling her dad's surplus vegetables (imagine *The Good Life* in Barnsley and you're more or less there).

After running away to join the British armed forces in 1994, Melanie experienced a career that took her around the world on some exciting adventures. In 2010, when she returned to civilian life to look after her young son, on a whim, she moved to Dubai where she found the time to write women's fiction. She now lives in Cornwall with her family.

Her debut, *The Wedding Cake Tree*, won the Romantic Novelists' Association Contemporary Romance Novel of the Year 2016.

🐦 @Melanie_Hudson_
📘 /melhudson7171

Also by Melanie Hudson

Dear Rosie Hughes

The Last Letter from Juliet

Melanie Hudson

OneMoreChapter

One More Chapter an imprint of
HarperCollins*Publishers*
The News Building
1 London Bridge Street
London SE1 9GF

www.harpercollins.co.uk

20 21 22 LSC 10 9 8 7 6 5 4 3

This paperback edition 2019

First published in Great Britain in ebook format by
HarperCollins*Publishers* 2019

A catalogue record for this book
is available from the British Library

UK ISBN: 9780008319649
US/CAN ISBN: 9780008354282

Set in Birka by
Palimpsest Book Production Limited, Falkirk, Stirlingshire

Printed and bound in the United States of America by
LSC Communications

Dedicated to the inspirational and courageous women pilots who served with the Air Transport Auxiliary during the Second World War – the ultimate Attagirls!

Prologue

R ead Me
    This is a note to yourself, Juliet.

At the time of writing you are ninety-two years old and worried that the bits and bobs of your story have begun to go astray. You must read this note carefully every day and work very hard to keep yourself and the memories alive, because once upon a time you told a man called Edward Nancarrow that you would, and it's important to keep that promise, Juliet, even when there seems to be little point going on.

In the mahogany sideboard you will find all the things you will need to keep living your life alone. These things are: bank details; savings bonds; emergency contact numbers; basic information about you – your name, age and place of birth; money in a freezer bag; an emergency mobile phone. More importantly, there are also your most precious possessions scattered around the house. I've labelled them, to help you out.

Written on the back of this note is a copy of the poem Edward gave you in 1943. Make sure you can recite it (poetry is good for the brain). And finally, even if you *forget everything else, remember that, in the end, Edward's very simple words are the only things that have ever really mattered.*

Now, make sure you've had something to eat and a glass of water – water helps with memory – and whatever happens in the future, whatever else you may forget, always remember ... he's waiting.

With an endless supply of love,
Juliet

Chapter 1

Katherine

A proposal

It was a bright Saturday lunchtime in early December. I'd just closed the lounge curtains and was about to binge-watch *The Crown* for the fourth time that year when a Christmas card bearing a Penzance postmark dropped through the letter box.

Uncle Gerald. Had to be.

The card, with an illustration of a distressed donkey carrying a (somewhat disappointed-looking) Virgin Mary being egged on by a couple of haggard angels, contained within it my usual Christmas catch-up letter. I wandered through to the kitchen and clicked the kettle on – it was a four-pager.

My Dear Katherine
Firstly, I hope this letter finds you well, or as well as

to be expected given your distressing circumstances of living alone in Exeter with no family around you again this Christmas.

Cheers for that, Gerald.

But more of your circumstances in a moment because (to quote the good bard) 'something is rotten in the state of Denmark' and I'm afraid this year's letter will not burst forth with my usual festive cheer. There is at present a degree of what can only be described as civil unrest breaking out in Angels Cove and I am at my wits end trying to promote an atmosphere of peace and good will in time for Christmas. I'm hopeful you will be able to offer a degree of academic common sense to the issue.

Here's the rub: the Parish Council (you may remember that I am the chair?) has been informed that the village boundaries are to be redrawn in January as part of a Cornwall County Council administrative shake-up. This simple action has lit the touch paper of a centuries-old argument amongst the residents that needs – finally – to be put to rest.

The argument in question is this: should our village be apostrophised or not? If 'yes', then should the apostrophe come before or after the 's'?

It is a Total Bloody Nightmare!

It really isn't, Gerald.

At the moment, Angels Cove is written without an apostrophe, but most agree that there should be an apostrophe in there somewhere, yet where? The argument seems to rest on three questions:

1. Does the cove 'belong' to just one angel (the angel depicted in the church stained glass window, for example, as some people claim that they have seen him) or to a multitude of angels (i.e. the possessive of a singular or a plural noun).

2. Does the cove belong to the angels or do the angels belong to the cove? (The minority who wish to omit the apostrophe in its entirety ask this question.)

3. Does the word angel in Angels Cove actually refer, not to the winged messengers of the Devine, but to the notorious pirate, Jeremiah 'Cut-throat' Angel, who sailed from Penzance circa 1723 and whose ship, The Savage Angel, was scuppered in Mounts Bay (not apostrophised, you will note) when he returned from the West Indies at the tender age of twenty-nine?

As you can see, it's a mess.

Fearing the onset of a migraine, I stopped reading and decided to sort out the recycling, which would take a while, given the number of empties. An hour later saw me continuing to give the rest of Gerald's letter a stiff ignoring because I needed to get back to *The Crown* and plough my way through an ironing pile that saw its foundations laid in 1992. Just at the point where Prince Philip jaunts off solo on a raucous stag do to Australia (and thinking that I really ought to write a letter to The Queen to tell her how awesome she is), I turned the iron off (feeling a pang of guilt at leaving a complicated silk blouse alone in the basket) poured a glass of Merlot, popped a Tesco 'extra deep' mince pie in the microwave and returned to the letter ...

I expect you will agree that this is a question of historical context, not a grammatical issue.

I do not.

As the 'go to' local historian (it must run in the family!) I attempted to offer my own hypothesis at the parish meeting last week, but can you believe it, I was barracked off the stage just two minutes into my delivery.

I can.

But all is not lost. This morning, while sitting on the loo wrecking my brains for inspiration, I stumbled across your book, From Nob End to Soggy Bottom, English Place Names and their Origins *in my toilet TBR pile (I had forgotten you have such a dry wit, my dear) and I just knew that I had received Devine intervention from the good Lord himself, because although the villagers are not prepared to accept my opinion as being correct, I do believe they would accept the decision of a university professor, especially when I explain that you were sent to them by God.*

So, I have a proposition for you.

Time for that mince pie.

In return for your help on the issue, please do allow me the pleasure of offering you a little holiday here in Angels Cove, as my very special present to you, this Christmas. I know you have balked at the idea of coming to stay with me in the past (don't worry, I know I'm an eccentric old so-and-so with disgusting toenails)

True.

but how do you fancy a beautiful sea view this Christmas?

Well, now that you mention it …

The cottage is called Angel View (just the one angel, note) and now belongs to a local man, Sam Lanyon (Royal Navy pilot – he's away at sea, poor chap). He says you can stay as long as you like – I may have mentioned what happened to James as leverage.

Gerald!

The cottage sits just above the cove and has everything you could possible need for the perfect holiday (it's also a bit of a 1940s time capsule because until very recently it belonged to an elderly lady – you'll love it).

The thing is, before you say no, do remember that before she died, I did promise your mother that I would keep an eye on you …

It was only a matter of time.

… and your Christmas card seemed so forlorn … Actually, not forlorn, bland – it set me off worrying about you being alone again this Christmas, and I thought this would be the perfect opportunity for us to look out for each other, as I'm alone, too – George is on a mercy mission visiting his sister in Brighton this year. Angels Cove is simply beautiful at Christmas. The whole village pulls together (when they are not arguing) to illuminate the harbour with a festival of lights. It's magical.

But?

But … with all the shenanigans going on this year, I'm not sure the villagers will be in the mood for celebration. Please do say you'll come and answer our question for us, and in doing so, bring harmony to this beautiful little cove and save Christmas for all the little tourist children.

Surely this kind of thing is right up your Strasse?

My idea is that you could do a little bit of research then the locals could present you with their proposals for the placement of the apostrophe in a climatic final meeting. It will be just like a Christmas episode of the Apprentice – bring a suit! And meanwhile, I'll have a whole programme of excitement planned for you – a week of wonderful things – and it includes gin.

Now you're talking.

Do write back or text or (God forbid) phone, straight away and say you'll come, because by God, Katherine, you are barely forty-five years old, which is a mere blink of an eye. You have isolated yourself from all of your old friends and it is not an age where a person should be sitting alone with only their memories to comfort them. Basically, if anyone deserves a little comfort this Christmas, it's you. I know you usually visit the grave on Christmas Day, but please, for the build-up week at least (which is the best part of Christmas after all) come to Cornwall and allow yourself to be swaddled by our angels for a while (they're an impressive bunch).

I am happy to beg.
Yours, in desperation,

Gerald.
P.S. Did I mention the gin?

Sitting back in a kitchen chair I'd ruined by half-arsedly daubing it in chalk paint two weeks before, I glanced around the room and thought about Gerald's offer. On the one hand, why on earth would I want to leave my home at Christmas? It was beautiful. But the energy had changed, and what was once the vibrant epicentre of Exeter's academia, now hovered in a haze of hushed and silent mourning, like the house was afraid of upsetting me by raising its voice.

A miniature Christmas tree sat on the edge of the dresser looking uncomfortable and embarrassed. I'd decorated it with a selection of outsized wooden ornaments picked up during a day trip to IKEA in November. IKEA in Exeter was my weekly go-to store since James had gone. It was a haven for the lost and lonely. A person (me) can disappear up their own backsides for the whole morning in an unpronounceable maze of fake rooms, rugs, tab-top curtains, plastic plants and kitchen utensils (basically all the crap the Swedes don't want) before whiling away a good couple of hours gorging themselves on a menu of meatballs and cinnamon swirls, and still have the weirdest selection of booze and confectionary Sweden has to offer (what on earth is *Lordagsgodis*, anyway?) to look forward to at checkout.

And we wonder why the Swedes are so happy!

But did I really want to spend the run-up to Christmas in IKEA this year? (Part of me actually did – it's *very* Scandi-chic Christmassy). But to do it for a third year in a row, with no one to laugh out loud with when we try to pronounce the unpronounceable Swedish word for fold-up bed?

(That was a poor example because a futon is a futon in any language and I really did need to try to control my inner monologue which had gone into overdrive since James died – I was beginning to look excessively absent minded in public).

But did I want to spend Christmas in IKEA this year? Not really, no.

But the problem (and Gerald knew this, too) was that if I left the house this Christmas, then it would mark the beginning of my letting go, of starting again, of saying that another life – a festive one – could exist beyond James. If I had a good time I might start to forget him, but if I stayed here and kept thinking of him, if I kept the memories alive, re-read the little notes he left me every morning, if I looked through photographs on Facebook, replayed scenes and conversations in my mind, then he would still be here, alive, in me. But if I go away, where would that lead? I knew exactly where it would lead – to the beginning of the end of James. To the beginning of not being able to remember his voice, his smell, his laugh – to the beginning of moving on.

And I wasn't sure I was ready for that.

But still ...

I knocked back the last of the Merlot while googling train times to Penzance and fished out the last card in a box of IKEA Christmas cards I'd abandoned to the dresser drawer the week before. It was the exact replica of the one I'd already sent him, a golden angel. I took it as a sign and began to scribble ...

Dear, Uncle Gerald,

You are quite correct. This kind of thing is indeed 'right up my Strasse'. Rest assure there will be no need to beg – I shall come!

I arrive in Penzance by the 18.30 train on the 17th and intend to stay (wait for it) until Boxing Day! By which time I am confident that, one way or another, I will have found a solution to your problem. DO NOT, however, feel that you have to entertain me all week. It's very good of you but actually – and quite selfishly – this trip could be a blessing in disguise. I have been racking my brains for an idea for a new book – a history project to keep me going through the rest of the winter – and I have a feeling that hidden deep within the midst of Cornish myth and legend, I might find one.

Please thank Mr Lanyon for the offer of use of his cottage – I accept!

How are the cataracts, by the way? Are you able to drive? If so, I wonder if you could meet me at the station?

With oodles of love,

Your, Katherine

P.S. Wouldn't it be funny if 'The Cataracts' were an old couple who lived in the village and I would say, 'How are the

Cataracts, by the way?' And you would answer, 'Oh, they're fine. They've just tripped off to Tenerife for Christmas.'

P.P.S. Take heart in knowing that there is nothing simple about the apostrophe. It is punctuation's version of the naughty Cornish pixie, and seems to wreak havoc wherever it goes. There is a village in America, for example, where the misplacing of the apostrophe led to full-scale civil unrest and ultimately, the cold-blooded murder of the local Sheriff. Let us hope for your sake that the situation at Angels Cove does not escalate into a similar scale of brouhaha!

P.P.P.S. Gin? I love you.

Chapter 2

Katherine

The last station stop

It turned out that the residents of Angels Cove were expecting not one, but two Katherines to arrive in Penzance on the evening of 17 December. My namesake *Storm Katherine* – a desperate attention seeker who was determined to make a dramatic entrance – would arrive late with the loud and gregarious roar of an axe-wielding Viking. Trees would crash onto roads, chicken hutches would be turned upside down, and the blight of every twenty first century garden – the netted trampoline – would disappear over hedgerows never to be seen again (it wasn't *all* bad, then). I hoped Uncle Gerald wouldn't see my concurrent arrival with *Katherine* as some kind of omen, but really, how could he not?

Stepping onto the train in Exeter, despite the forecast weather, I was excited. By Plymouth I was beginning to wonder if it had all been a dreadful mistake – the locals would want to chat, and the woman in the shop (there was always a chatty woman in a shop) would glance at my wedding ring and pry into my life with a stream of double negatives: 'Will your husband not be joining you in the cottage for Christmas, then? No? Well, it's nice to have some time away from them all, eh? And what about your children? Will they not be coming down? No children? Oh, dear. Well, never mind ...'

That kind of thing.

By Truro, I'd decided to turn back, but *Katherine's* advance party had already begun to rock the carriages, and by the time St Michael's Mount appeared through the late afternoon darkness – a watered down image of her usual self, barely visible through the driving rain and sea fret – my excitement had vaporised completely. Gazing through the splattered carriage window, I was startled by the sight of my mother's face staring back at me. Only it wasn't my mother, it was my own aged reflection. When had *that* happened? Anxious fingers rushed to smooth the lines on my mother's face, which could only be described as tired (dreadful word) and I realised that, just like St Michael's Mount in the winter rain, I too was a watered-down image of my usual self, barely visible through a veil of grief I had worn ever since the morning James had gone.

I hadn't needed an alarm call that morning. I'd been laying on my side for hours, tucked into the foetal position, the left side of my face resting on a tear-stained pillow, my eyes focused just above the bedside table, fixed on the clock.

I watched every movement of Mickey Mouse's right hand as it made a full circle, resting, with a final little wave, on the twelve.

Mickey's voice rang out—

'It's time, time, time, to wake up! It's time, time, time to wake up!'

I'd never known if Mickey had been supposed to say the word 'time' three times, or if at some point over the past umpteen years he had developed a stutter, but I silenced him with a harsh thump on the head and lay staring at the damp patch on the ceiling we'd never gotten to the bottom of, just to the right of the light fitting.

I wanted to lay there and consider that phrase for a moment – 'it's time'. Two little words with such a big meaning.

It's time, Katherine.

How many times had I heard those words?

My father had said them, standing in the kitchen doorway on my wedding day. He'd taken my hand with a wonderful smile and walked me to the car, a happy man. We were followed closely behind by my Aunt Helena, who was frothing my veil and laughing at Mum – who did not approve of the match – and who fussed along behind us, arguing about ... I think it was art, but it might have been cheese. And now, twenty years later, the exact same words were used by Gerald, to direct me out of the house. To force me, my insides kicking and screaming for release, to slide into the long black car that waited in the yard – the car that would take us to James' funeral, the sort of funeral that has the caption 'But, dear God, why?' hovering in the air the whole day.

I turned my back on Mickey and ran my arm across the base sheet on the other side of the bed. If only there was still some warmth there. An arm to curl into, a woolly chest to rest my head on. But the sheet was cold, and like everything else in my house in Exeter, retained the deep ingrained memory of centuries of damp.

But if I just lay there and let the day move on without me ...

It's time, time, time, to wake up!

Mickey again.

I stretched. Ridiculous thought. Mickey was right. The day wouldn't move on, not if I didn't wind the cogs and drop-kick the sun through the goal posts. I threw my legs out of bed, sat up, patted Mickey, apologised for hitting him on the head and I kissed him on the face. Poor thing. It wasn't his fault James had been killed, even if he did insist in shouting at me every morning in his overly polite, American way.

It's time, Katherine.

But that was the thing with travelling alone on a train, there was simply too much time to think. Trains were just one long rolling mass of melancholy, the carriages filled with random, interconnected thoughts. Travel alone on a train with no book to read and an over-thinker can spend an entire journey in the equivalent of that confused state between sleeping and waking.

And then the guard broke my reverie.

Ladies and gentlemen, we will shortly be arriving in Penzance. Penzance is the last station stop. Service terminates at Penzance. All alight at Penzance.

It was pretty obvious I needed to get off.

The train slowed to a final halt at the station and the last of the passengers began to stir. I grabbed my laptop case, put on my winter coat, hat and gloves and trundled to the end of the carriage in the hope that my suitcase would still be there. It was time to step out onto the platform, find Uncle Gerald, and head out into the storm.

Chapter 3

Katherine

A cottage by the sea

I stepped down onto the platform and stood still for a moment, my eyes searching through a river of passengers, before catching sight of Uncle Gerald, who was waving his multi-coloured umbrella like a lunatic and working his way upstream.

My heart melted. Uncle Gerald had been a steady presence in my life as a child, and although I had hardly seen him during my adult years, the bond that was formed during those childhood visits – nothing overly special, just a kind smile and couple of quid for sweets tucked into my sticky fingers – had never gone away. It was a bond that represented the safety and easiness of family. A bond that is usually lobbed into the back of the dresser drawer, stashed away, forgotten and allowed to loiter with the unused Christmas cards, nutcrackers and Sellotape, until the day came along when you actually needed it, and you opened the drawer with a rummage saying to yourself, 'I just know I left it in there somewhere.'

Gerald rested his umbrella against my suitcase and put his arms around me.

I wasn't expecting the sudden onset of emotion, but he represented a simpler time. A happy time. A time of singing together in the kitchen with Mum. The Carpenters.

'Rainy Days and Mondays'.

I started to cry.

He patted.

'Now then, none of that, none of that.'

'Oh, don't mind me, Uncle Gerald,' I said, trying to smile while rifling through my handbag and coat pockets for a tissue. 'Train stations and airport lounges always do this to me. I swear they're the portals used by the tear fairies to tap directly into the tender places of the soul.'

Gerald handed me a folded blue handkerchief.

I opened the handkerchief and blew my nose.

He smiled. 'Still over-dramatic then?'

I nodded.

'That's my girl!'

We both laughed and sniffed back the emotion before heading out into the wind and rain. We dashed to the car and he handed me the keys. 'You wouldn't mind driving, would you? Only I spent the afternoon in the Legion ...'

The drive to Angels Cove took a little over half an hour.

It was a fairly silent half hour because Uncle Gerald slept while I battled the car through the beginnings of the storm, luckily the sat nav remembered the way. The road narrowed as we headed down a tree-lined hill. I slowed the car to a halt and positioned the headlights to illuminate the village sign through the driving rain.

I nudged Uncle Gerald.

'We're here.'

He stirred and harrumphed at sight of the sign.

'Perhaps now you can see why I asked for your help,' he said.

I failed to stifle a laugh.

The sign had been repeatedly graffiti-ed. Firstly, someone had inserted an apostrophe with permanent marker between the 'l' and the 's' of angels. Then, someone else had put a line through the apostrophe and scrawled a new apostrophe to the right of the 's', which had been further crossed out. The crossings out continued across the sign until there was no room to write any more.

'This all started at the beginning of November, when the letter from the council arrived. The average age in this village is seventy-four – seventy-four!– and they're all behaving like children. I've got my hands full with it all, I can tell you. Especially on Wednesdays.' He nodded ahead. 'Drive on, straight down to the harbour.'

'Wednesdays?' I asked, putting the car into gear.

'Skittles night at the Crab and Lobster.'

'Ah.'

We carried on down the road, the wipers losing the battle with the rain and I tried to remember the layout of the village. I recalled Angels Cove as a pretty place consisting of one long narrow road that wound its way very slowly down to the sea. Pockets of cottages lined the road, which was about a mile long, with the pub in the middle, next to the primary school which was a classic Victorian school house with two entrances: BOYS was written in stone above one entrance and GIRLS written above the other.

The road narrowed yet further before opening out onto a small harbour. I stopped the car. The harbour was lit by a smattering of old-fashioned street lamps. Waves crashed over the harbour walls. The car shook. Although Katherine had not yet arrived with the might of her full force, the sea had already whipped herself up into an excitable frenzy.

Gerald pointed to the right.

'You can't make it out too clearly in the dark,' he said, staring into the darkness. 'But the cottage you're staying in is up this little track by about a hundred yards ... or so.'

I glanced up the track and put the car into gear.

'You ready?' he asked.

'Ready? Ready for what?'

'Oh, nothing. It's just a bit of a bumpy track, that's all.' He tapped the Land Rover with an affectionate pat, as if he was praising an old Labrador. 'No problem for this little lady, though. Been up that track a thousand times, haven't you, old girl? Onwards and upwards!'

I set off in the general direction of a farm track. The car took on an angle of about forty-five degrees and began to slip and slide its way up the track. Waves crashed against the rocks directly to my left.

'Shitty death, Gerald! What the *f*—?'

A couple of wheel spins later, to my absolute relief, a little white cottage appeared under a swinging security light. We pulled alongside and I switched off the engine, left the car in gear and went to open the driver door.

'Don't get out for a moment,' Gerald said. 'I'll go in ahead and turn on the lights. It'll give me time to shoo the mice away and make it nice and homely, that kind of thing.'

'Mice?'

'Only a few, and they're very friendly.'

I wiped condensation from the window and tried to peer out into the storm. 'OK, but don't be too long,' I said. 'I feel like I've stepped through one of the seven circles of hell!'

The tour of the cottage was very short but very sweet. When Gerald mentioned that an elderly lady had left it as a 1940s time capsule, he wasn't exaggerating. There were three bedrooms upstairs, which were pretty but functional, a downstairs bathroom, a good-sized kitchen and an achingly sweet lounge. Gerald lit the fire while talking.

'I've stocked the fridge with enough food, milk and

mince pies to take you through to the New Year.' He glanced up. 'Just in case.'

'In case ... what?'

He stood and brushed down his trousers. 'This is Cornwall. Anything can happen.'

I took off my coat and lay it across the arm of a green velvet chaise longue, then crossed to the window to close the curtains. A photograph frame sat on the windowsill. The black and white image inside was of woman standing in front of a bi-plane, holding a flying helmet and goggles, smiling brightly, squinting slightly against the sun. There was a tag attached to the photo. I read it.

Summer 1938. Edward took this. Our first full day together. Two days in one – fantastic and tragic all at once. Why can we never have the one, without the other. Why can't we have light without shade?

'Juliet was a pilot,' Gerald said by way of explanation, turning to face me briefly while attempting to draw the fire by holding a sheet of newspaper across the fireplace. 'She flew for the Air Transport Auxiliary during the war. They used to deliver all the aircraft from the factories to the RAF, that kind of thing. Amazing woman.'

I nodded my understanding, still looking at the photograph.

'Juliet handed the old place to Sam Lanyon last year, but he hasn't got around to sorting through her belongings yet.' Gerald rose to his feet. He screwed up the paper he'd used to draw the fire and threw it onto the flames.

I put the frame down, closed the curtains and looked around the room ... photos, books, paintings, odds and ends of memorabilia. There was a 1920s sideboard, I opened a drawer. It was full of the same forgotten detritus of someone else's life.

This was no holiday cottage, this was a home.

Gerald turned his back on the fire a final time. It was blazing.

'Anyway, you've a good supply of coal and logs so just remember to keep feeding it, and don't forget to put the guard up when you go to bed – this type of coal spits!'

He made a move towards the door. His hat and scarf were hanging on a peg in the little hallway. He grabbed them and began to wrap his scarf around his throat.

'Are you sure it's all right for me to stay here, Gerald?' I was standing in the lounge doorway looking pensive. 'Only it seems a bit ... intrusive.'

'Nonsense! It was Sam's idea. He's happy that it's being aired.'

Gerald turned to leave and attempted to open the door. The force of the storm pushed against him. My unease at the prospect of staying alone in an unfamiliar cottage perched precariously on a cliff side, unsure of my bearings, during one of the worst storms in a decade, must have shown on my face. He closed the door for a moment and walked back into the lounge, talking to himself.

'On nights like this, Juliet always put her faith in one thing, and it never let her down.'

I followed him. 'What was that? God?'

He opened the sideboard door and peered inside.

'Ha!' He took out a bottle.

'Whiskey?'

'And there's a torch in there, too.' He put the whiskey back and walked into the kitchen. I heard him open and close a few drawers before reappearing in the lounge with half a dozen candles. He handed them to me.

'Just in case the electricity goes out. And the matches are on the fireplace so you're all set.'

The lounge window started to rattle.

He straightened his hat and headed to the door. 'This cottage might seem rickety, but it's the oldest and sturdiest house in the village. It'll take a bit more than *Katherine* to see her off now!'

I picked up the car keys from the hall table and grabbed my coat from the lounge.

'I'll drive you home,' I said.

'No, no. I'll walk back.' He pulled his scarf tighter.

'In this weather?' I asked, only half concentrating, searching in my handbag for my phone. 'Mercy, me! I have a signal!'

Gerald paused at the door.

'Put the keys down, Katherine. I'll be fine. Listen, why don't you leave your coat on and come with me to see my friend, Fenella. Poor thing. I promised her I'd pop in on my way home. She's had a bit of a bereavement and isn't coping very well.'

'Husband?'

'Worse. Dog. Her cottage is on the harbour. We can nip in and pay our respects, quick cup of tea, then make our excuses and go back to mine ... via the pub. You might as well meet the enemy straight off.'

I wanted to say, 'Thank Christ for that. Yes please.' But the curse of the twenty-first-century independent woman prevented me from throwing myself at his mercy. And I didn't fancy the pub.

'Don't be silly,' I said with a blasé shoulder shrug, taking my coat off one final time. 'I'll be absolutely fine.' (Which is the exact phrase everyone uses when they are, in fact, sure that they will not 'be absolutely fine'.)

He put his hand on the door handle.

'And how are you sleeping these days?'

I shrugged.

'Don't tell me you're still listening to Harry Potter audio books half the livelong night?'

I shrugged again.

Listening to Stephen Fry narrate Harry Potter was much better than tossing and turning all night. There was just something about the combination of the two – Fry and Potter – that made the world seem like a safe place again.

'It relaxes me. And you must admit, you can't beat a bit of Stephen Fry at bedtime.'

Gerald laughed.

'I wouldn't kick him out of bed, I suppose – but don't tell George, you know how jealous he gets. Well, if you're sure, I'll be off. Just phone me if you need reassurance. Oh, and there's WiFi here.'

Result.

'The code is ...' Gerald paused and delved into his coat pocket. He took out a scrap of paper. '... "tigermoth", one word, all lowercase. And try not to worry. I wouldn't leave you here if I thought it wasn't safe.'

Gerald kissed me on the cheek and stepped out into the wind.

'*I'll pop up tomorrow morning once the storm's gone through,*' he shouted. 'I've got a fabulous programme of events all worked out, people to meet, things to do! And lock the door behind me straight away. It'll bang all night if you don't.'

'I will,' I shouted back, down the lane. 'And, thank you!'

With the door locked and bolted, I walked into the lounge, sat on the sofa and stared into the fire, unconsciously spinning my wedding ring around my finger. The lights began to flicker, and in the kitchen, another window rattled. I grabbed my laptop from the hallway, logged onto the WiFi and – for at least five seconds – thought about doing a little apostrophe research (or any research that might lead me in the direction of a new project and take my mind off the storm). I closed the laptop lid.

Tomorrow. I'd do the research tomorrow.

I grabbed the remote control, flashed the TV and Freeview box into life and pressed the up button on the volume. The closing scenes of a *Miss Marple* rerun sounded-out most of the noise of the storm. Now all I needed to do was make a cup of tea, rustle up dinner and settle down to a spot of *Grand Designs* (the harangued couples who mortgaged themselves to the hilt and lived in a leaky caravan during the worst winter on record with three screaming kids and another on the way while trying to live off the land and source genuine terracotta tiles in junk shops for a bathroom that wouldn't be built for another five years ... they were my favourites).

With the closing credits of *Miss Marple* rolling down the screen, I walked through to the kitchen to make dinner. It was the real deal on the quintessential cottage front – not a fitted cupboard in sight – and very pretty, with French doors at the rear. A circular pine table with two chairs sat at the opposite end of the kitchen to the French doors, underneath a window. A golden envelope addressed to *Katherine Henderson, C/O Angel View*, sat on the table. I opened the envelope and took out the Christmas card.

Another angel, they were everywhere this year.

Dear Katherine

Just a quick note to welcome you to Angel View and explain about the house, which until recently belonged to a very special lady called Juliet Caron – my amazing Grandmother. You will find that her personality is still very much alive within the cottage walls. I'm sorry I wasn't able to decorate the cottage for Christmas before you arrived, but you'll find lots of decorations in the loft if you want to make the old place feel a bit more Christmassy.

Most importantly, please make yourself at home and have a wonderful time.

Yours,

Sam Lanyon

P.S. … you may find that a particularly vigilant Elf has already pitched up and positioned himself in the house somewhere. He always kept a beady eye on Juliet at this time of year. Give him a tot of whiskey and he'll be your friend for life!

Smiling, I rested the card against a green coloured glass vase filled with yellow roses and took a cursory glance around the kitchen. There he was – sitting on a shelf, looking directly at me with his legs crossed and auspicious expression on his face.

I crossed the room to take a good look at him.

'Hello, Mr Elf,' I said, cheerily. 'You needn't worry about me. As Eliza Doolittle once said, I'm a good girl, I am … unfortunately!'

A few half-burned candles were scattered around the worktop and also on the windowsill. I took the matches from the lounge and lit them. There was a notepad and pen on the worktop, as if waiting for the occupier to make a list, and a very pretty russet red shawl was draped over the back of one of the chairs. I picked up the shawl and ran it through my fingers – it smelt of lavender and contentment.

A luggage-style label had been sewn onto the shawl at one end. It read—

This was Lottie's shawl – her comfort blanket. You wrapped Mabel in it on the day Lottie died.

Feeling a sudden chill, I took the liberty of wrapping the shawl around my shoulders and began to put together the makings of dinner – cheese on toast with a bit of tomato and Worcester sauce would do. I took an unsliced loaf out of the breadbin and opened the drawer of a retro cream dresser looking for cutlery. Sitting on top of the cutlery divider was a hard-backed small booklet with a large label attached to it. Another label? I took out the booklet and ran a finger over the indented words, *First Officer Juliet Caron, Flying Logbook.*

I turned the label over. With very neat handwriting, it read:

This is your flying logbook, Juliet. It is the most significant document of your life. Look at it often (whenever you use cutlery will do) and remember the times when you were happy (Spitfires), the times when you were stressed out (Fairey Battle – awful machine), the times when you had no idea how you survived to fly another day (like that trip in the Hurricane when the barrage balloons went up just as you were leaving Hamble) and that terrible day you tried to get to Cornwall with Anna – the one entry you wish you could delete. Other than the compass, this is your most treasured possession.

My rumbling tummy brought me back to the moment. I filled the kettle, stepped over to the fridge and noticed a laminated note stuck to the door with 'Read Me' written on the top. I read it, expecting it to be instructions from Sam, or Gerald.

It wasn't.

While the kettle was boiling, I read a letter which began: *This is a letter to yourself, Juliet ...*

So that was what all the labels were for ... Juliet had been frightened of losing her memory. I took the letter off the fridge and turned it over.

Where Angels Sing, by Edward Nancarrow
When from this empty world I fall
And the light within me fades
I'll think, my love, of a sweeter time
When life was light, not shade

With bluebirds from this world I'll fly
And to a cove I'll go
To wait for you where angels sing
And when it's time, you'll know

To meet me on the far side where
We once led Mermaid home
And finally, my love and I
Will be, as one, alone

And at that moment, after pouring water from Juliet's kettle into Juliet's cup, sitting in Juliet's house and wearing Juliet's shawl, I felt an overwhelming sensation of being swaddled, that Juliet and I were somehow linked. Gerald would blame my overactive imagination, of course, but I really did feel that I was *supposed* to come to Angels Cove this Christmas.

With my dinner quickly made and eaten, I set up camp in the lounge and, trying to ignore the other Katherine who was hammering at the door to get in, I decided it was time for Kevin McCloud (such a lovely man) to transport me into his TV world of *Grand Designs*, into other people's lives – happier, family lives – where dreams really do come true (and maybe a tot or two of that whiskey wouldn't go amiss either).

Glancing into the sideboard I was mesmerised – it was an Aladdin's Cave of memorabilia, of yet more labels. Next to the whiskey was a wad of faded A4 paper held together by green string. The top sheet had the type-written words,

Attagirls!
The war memoirs of Juliet Caron
Lest she forgets

I untied the string and peeled back the top sheet to reveal a letter.

1 June 1996

My dear Sam

How is life at sea treating you? I know I say it too much for your liking, but I'll say it again – I'm so very proud of you (and a little jealous of all that fabulous flying, too!).

Anyhow, I'm sure you must be busy so I'll get to the point because I'm worried, Sam. Worried that my older memories are starting to fade and that one day soon they may leave me completely. Sitting here in my little cottage, able to do less and less each day, watching the tide ebb and flow, I have felt suddenly compelled to remember and record what happened in my life during the war. I read somewhere that if you wish to tell a story of war, do not tell the basic facts of the battle, but tell instead of the child's bonnet removed from the rubble of a Southampton street, or the smell of twisted metal from a burnt Hurricane crashed by a friend, or the lingering smell of a man, robbed of his prime by typhus, as he lays in a strange bed in a foreign land, dying. I'm not sure I shall be able to do this, but even so, I have begun to write everything down. My friend Gerald is helping me. I aim to write one instalment per month – the first one is written already and attached – and send you copies as I write them. It's an heirloom, I suppose, for you and your children (or if nothing else to give you something sensational to read during those long nights at sea!).

As you read each instalment, remember that my words will be as accurate as my aging mind allows them to be. Certain days stand out more than the rest. Just lately, I find that I can remember 1943 like it was yesterday, and yet events from yesterday elude me as if set in 1943. But what is truth of any situation anyway? I really do feel that life is made up of a constant stream of living, punctuated only by that otherworld of sleep. The fact that we choose to put a time and date to everything is merely a paper exercise. I used to think that once a moment is gone, it is gone forever, resigned only to memory. But now – now that I can no longer take my memory for granted – I realise that this is not the case. Love, for example, once thought lost, can be captured forever, just so long as someone out there strives to keep the memory of that love alive.

And so here is the first in a series of my memories that consist only of certain vivid days. They are memories of a time when suddenly, for a woman, absolutely anything (both the good and the desperately bad) became possible.

Anyway – enough of my ramblings!

Drum roll, please …

'Ladieeeees and gentlemen! Lift your eyes to the heavens and prepare to be amazed, to be wowed and bedazzled! Here she is … the fearless! The death-defying! The one and only – Juliet Caron!'

I rested the letter on my knee just as a crash outside coincided with the sudden outage of the lights and the television turned to black. The glow from the fire provided sufficient ambient light for me to reach into the sideboard and find the torch, but the battery must have been an old one because the torchlight was weak and to my disappointment, within a few seconds, petered out.

Determined to take on some of the inner strength of the remarkable woman who had written a note to herself at ninety-two years old to never give in, I surrounded myself with candles, stoked the fire and wrapped the russet shawl tighter around my shoulders. And despite knowing that I shouldn't waste my phone battery on a little light reading, not tonight of all nights, I got myself cosy on the sofa, abandoned Harry Potter, enabled the torch on my phone and began to read.

Chapter 4

Juliet

1938

A Cornish Christmas

Newspaper Cutting: *The Bicester Herald*

FREE AEROPLANE FLIGHTS FOR TEN LUCKY READERS!

AIR DISPLAY EXTRAVAGANZA!

Reach for the stars with the one and only

LOUIS CARON FLYING CIRCUS!

Old Bradley's Field

1st July (for one day only)

2.30 p.m. till dusk

Star Attraction

JULIET CARON

The daredevil darling of the skies and Britain's finest
child star & aerobatic pilot

Admission 1s. Children 6d.

My name is Juliet Caron and although it would be difficult for anyone to believe if they saw me now (age has a dreadful habit of throwing a dust sheet over the vibrancy of youth) I was once the celebrated flying ace and undisputed star of the one and only *Louis Caron Flying Circus*.

I do not say this to boast, well, maybe a little bit, but to explain how it was that my father taught me to fly almost as quickly as I learned to walk and how, on a bright winter's afternoon just a few days before Christmas 1938, I found myself soaring one thousand feet above Cornwall in my bright yellow Tiger Moth, looking for angels. It was a simple time in my life. Simple in the way that only those brief years before we know the agony of love, can be. My lungs were exploding with the exuberance of youth and my face was tight against the freezing air. In sum, I was living a life that was just about as alive as it is possible for a human life to be.

But first I must tell you a little of the flying circus, because my childhood *was* the circus, it moulded those formative days when the personality begins to take shape. My circus years were wonderful years. They were the years I had my parents with me, parents who were – and always would be – my inspiration, my warriors, my rocks.

When I was fourteen a journalist asked me to describe what being part of a flying circus was like. My father stood by me while I thought of my answer. We were in Sam Bryant's field near Bicester, Oxfordshire, our aircraft lined up side by side, waiting to display. The crowd was arriving and the buzz of expectation bounced in the air while a cornflower blue sky kissed by a soft, silky breeze heralded the chance of a wonderful display. Tongue-tied, I looked at my father, who knelt next to me, and stalled as to what to say. He said to close my eyes and imagine how it *feels* to fly – to say the first thing that came into my head. The answer I gave was the answer of a child, but I would have given exactly the same answer as an adult, because the euphoria of flying – that feeling of absolute freedom – never left me.

'Imagine heaven on earth,' I said, 'or rather, heaven in the skies. Imagine you're in a dream and in that dream you somehow shrink down to the size of a doll and strap yourself onto the back of a golden eagle. You cling on to his feathers while he swoops and dives and soars and loops. And then you realise that if you're very gentle with him and pull lightly on a feather here and there, you can control him a little, and then you're flying too, every bit and just as naturally as the bird, and every element hits you with a freshness that can't be matched, every sense is bright and alive. And then the bird dives towards the earth, barely missing the ground, before turning on a hairpin and soaring away. You are not in control at that moment, I think, but you are not in danger either, not so long as he – you – pull up in time. But that's the best thrill of all – the not completely knowing if you'll pull out of the dive in time. You simply have to trust, have faith in your judgement and let go of all fear. But you do pull out, because instinct and survival and an understanding of how to fly and how to move through the air kicks in, and you climb higher and take a breath, but not for long, because then you jump off the bird and into your father's arms and cling on while he spins you around and around and the whole world is no more than a line of spinning colour. And your hair and skirt and legs are flung out at ninety degrees and you know that if he lets you go, you'll fly out of the dream and into oblivion. But again, you have to trust, to become a part of the motion, to know that he will never let you go, you're safe.' I glanced up at Father and smiled. 'I suppose I just feel full of joy and completely free. That's all, really.'

An hour after the interview, my Father and mother died. Father was flying and mother was his wing-walker, her long hair and scarf trailing behind her. She was waving at me just before she died. I was standing next to my Tiger Moth, my performance coming later. I waved back at her, proud and happy. But then Pa lost control somehow and didn't pull up in time, and I was no longer waving but screaming and running, not believing such a thing could possibly be true, already aching for a feeling I would only ever know once again – that feeling of unquestioned security and unconditional love.

But back to Cornwall and Christmas 1938.

The little Tiger Moth, its Gypsy engine humming a familiar tune, clung to the Cornish coast as I peered over the side, my face tight against the freezing slap of the winter air. I was looking for my final navigational landmark – three small craggy mounts known locally as the Angels – that sat a few hundred yards out to sea next to a little fishing village called Angels Cove. All I had to do was to find the mounts, then a mile or so further along the coast I would find my destination, a rather grand-looking house called Lanyon and in turn, my landing strip.

I took a moment to glance down again and cross-reference the river arteries on a map before turning at Lizard Point to follow the coast northbound. If my calculations were correct, the mounts would be on the nose in two minutes exactly. They were, and looked exactly like stepping stones plopped into the sea for the convenience of a Cornish giant. After circling around the Angels a couple of times to take a closer look, I headed inland and descended, slowing to almost stalling speed looking for Lanyon – a large, red-brick manor house, with four gables and twelve chimneys. And suddenly it was there, sitting above a little patch of sea haze, in majestic reverence, on the cliffs above the cove.

The landing strip was nothing more than the lawned area in front of the house, but drat it all, a downdraft from the cliffs pulled at the aircraft's little wooden frame as I approached, dragging me far too close to a line of very tall cedar trees as I turned finals. I powered on, overshot the approach and climbed away, waving cheerily at a couple of gardeners just a few feet below, who were leaning on rakes, open-mouthed, watching. The performer in me not dead but simply sleeping, couldn't resist throwing the Moth into a tidy little barrel roll, before disappearing off over the horizon, to find pastures new and within these pastures, hopefully, a safe place to land. Within a minute I had found a stretch of level grass on the cliffs, directly above Angels Cove. There was a large barn in the corner of the field, too, which, if empty, could act very nicely as a store for the Moth. I turned into the wind, began my final decent and moments later, to my great relief, landed safely.

With the propeller slowed to a stop, I tore off my goggles and wool-lined leather helmet, unclipped the harness and jumped out to gather my bearings. A minute later found me jumping back into the wing's stepping plate because a dozen or so cows approached at speed with a collective air of indignant and inquisitive over-confidence.

From my position of height, I attempted to shoo.

Shooing proved fruitless.

Help appeared almost immediately in the form of two men and a dog. They were walking towards me from the direction of the barn. The first man was wearing a long coat, his collar turned up against the wind. On closer inspection he was frowning. Definitely frowning. The second – the stockman by the looks of things – was shaking a stick in my direction. Even the dog seemed to walk with an air of peeved annoyance.

The men slapped fat sashaying backsides as they walked towards me, saying things like, 'Get on with you,' and 'Away, away.' On seeing the younger man's face more clearly, and suffering from sudden and complete amnesia regarding the existence of Charles, my fiancé, who was waiting for me at Lanyon, I attempted to tidy my hair, which was beyond redemption. I quickly glanced down at my clothes. I was wearing a flying jacket (my father's, far too big for me and ripped on the right sleeve) and, over thermal long-johns, men's overalls, covered in oil, rolled up at the ankle and pulled in at the waist with a wide belt. The icing on the cake was my footwear – muddy, fur-lined flying boots.

Taking a cloth from my pocket, I gave my face and hands a quick wipe. The two men were only a few steps away now. The younger one paused out of earshot to speak to the other man, who snorted in my direction before turning tail and heading towards the barn, using a long stick to usher the cows with him.

The man approached. His expression did not soften.

'Well, hello there,' I said, cheerily.

He stood there for a moment, not speaking. A kind of apoplexy seemed to have set in (this often happened to a man who found himself unexpectedly face to face with a female pilot. It was the shock, you see). I decided to wade straight in with an apology. Farmers could be ever so touchy about aircraft landing in their fields without invitation. It was best to take the wind out of their sails with a smile.

'I'm so sorry for the …' I glanced towards the cows. Their backsides lumbered from side to side as they began to disperse. Tails flicked with annoyance '… disturbance. I meant to land in front of a large house, up the way there.' I paused to look in the direction of the house. 'It's the one with the four gables and twelve chimneys ... or is it four chimneys and twelve gables, I can never remember ...? Do you know it?'

'Lanyon?

'Yes.'

'Of course. But look here ...'

My bright smile and humble apology fell on blind eyes and deaf ears. He began to chide – *really* chide – something about the utter irresponsibility of landing an aircraft in a field full of cattle ... could have killed myself, etc. etc. He went on for quite some time about all kinds of things that might possibly have happened had luck not been on my side, but I really couldn't concentrate because he was just so damn gorgeous and to top it had a slight American twang in his accent, too, and I had a very definite soft spot for a soft American accent on a man, probably because of all the movies we watched in those days.

I was just trying to work out what an American was doing working on a Cornish farm when he stopped preaching and returned to his preoccupation of staring at me. I realised he was waiting for me to respond to his disciplinary lecture, but not knowing quite how to respond, and rather than answer and annoy him further, I simply kept quiet and ran my fingers through my tangled mop of thick hair, just as the cold wind nipped at my face and turned my nose into a dripping tap. I wiped my nose with the cloth and we stood in a kind of 'what now?' silence while the Tiger Moth rocked on its wheels in the wind. He was obviously going to wait it out until I spoke. There was nothing left to do but to shrug and apologise again.

'You're absolutely right, of course,' I said, adding a suitably big enough sigh. 'Landing on a cliff in a field full of cows was not my finest spot of airwomanship, but to be fair, I didn't see the cows and if you think about it, nothing bad actually *did* happen so I wonder, could we start again because, you know, 'tis done now, and what else can I do but say to that I'm so very – *very* – sorry.'

I tried my best to look remorseful.

He took a deep breath. His eyes were cold, steady.

'I'd say that was a perfunctory apology.'

'Perfunctory?' I repeated.

'Yes, perfunctory.'

He had more.

'You think that because you're a beautiful woman you can do whatever you want – gallivant around, hither and thither ...'

Hither and thither? An American saying 'hither and thither'?

I let him rant on again, completely unaware of what he was saying because frankly, he could say what the hell else he liked. No person on the planet (other than my parents) had called me beautiful before – even my fiancé had never called me beautiful.

'Listen,' I interrupted, eventually, 'we seem to have got off on the wrong foot.' I turned towards the cows again who were quite a way away now. 'You're absolutely right in everything you say. Perhaps we could shake hands on the matter and start again – shall we?'

I removed my right flying glove and held out my hand. He hesitated, as if some kind of trickery might be involved, but then my hand was in his, being held for what seemed to be a couple of seconds ever so slightly longer than necessary, despite the chiding.

He pulled away.

Silence again, except for the whistle of the wind across the cliff tops. The void needed to be filled.

'And hey! As a thank you, how about I take you flying this week sometime?'

He tilted his head to one side. He was suppressing a smile, I was sure of it.

'A thank you? A thank you for what?'

I glanced towards the barn.

'Well – and I know it's ever so cheeky – but for allowing me to store my aircraft in your barn for the week.'

He turned to look at the barn.

'The thing is, I can't leave the old girl out here all week. I'm a guest at Lanyon for Christmas, you see, and I'm sure they would vouch for my good character – although it seems you've made a decision about that already.' I added, with a side-eye towards the dog, who looked unconvinced. 'I'll pay for the inconvenience, obviously, although you'll probably simply accuse me of throwing money at the problem ...'

He braced his back against the breeze. His expression was unreadable. Was that a smile, though?

'Which one?' he asked, finally.

'Which one, what?'

'Which Lanyon are you the guest of?'

'Er ...'

Now, I know I *should* have said, Charles, I'm his fiancée, but the angel sitting on my right shoulder went into all-out battle with the devil on my left and the devil won. I should also have added, 'We're getting married this week, on Christmas Eve in fact. Do you know him?'

But I didn't. Instead I went with ...

'Oh, I went to school with the daughter of the house. Lottie Lanyon?'

He nodded a kind of understanding.

'The cove was the most perfect navigational landmark, what with the mounts ...' I touched my hair far too often as I spoke. 'But the lawn at Lanyon – where I was expecting to land – was not at all suitable – trees, you see – and then there was the most terrible downdraft from the cliffs. So, it was either put down in your field or bust the old girl up in a hedge. And as I said. I didn't notice the cows. I'm so very sorry.'

Just how many times would I need to apologise to the man?

He sniffed, considering. I wasn't sure quite just what he was considering, exactly. We glanced in unison at the cows again, who were slowly being funnelled through a gateway into the next field.

'Are they very upset by it all, do you think?' I asked. 'Is that what the problem is? Should I go and, I don't know, pat them all and apologise or something.'

Finally, he laughed. Even his dog glanced up at him with an amused eye roll.

'I shouldn't think an apology is necessary.' He patted the aircraft, visibly relaxing. 'They would have eyed this machine of yours as an excellent scratching post. They're most likely annoyed to have missed a good look-see. Cows are inquisitive beasts. Don't you think so, Miss?'

'Caron,' I answered brightly. '*Miss* Caron.'

What the hell was I doing? The man was a rude and sanctimonious ass. And, oh, yes – I was getting married.

'Caron,' he repeated, softly. 'Is that a French name?'

'Yes. My mother was the Caron. She was French. She insisted that Papa took her name. Papa was English through and through, though.'

'How very ...'

'Modern?' I offered.

'I was going to say, "good of him". They sound like a progressive family.'

Gaining just a little of the sense I was born with, and not wishing to talk about my parents, I took control.

'But back to the barn,' I said. 'I know it's such an imposition, Mr ...' I paused and waited for him to finish my sentence.

'Nancarrow – Edward, Nancarrow.'

A Cornish name? But the American accent? Intriguing.

'... Nancarrow, but as I said, do you think I could put my

48

aircraft in your barn overnight. Only, the wind's getting up and an aircraft like this isn't very sturdy – it's not much more than a few planks of wood nailed together, really – just a wing and a prayer, as my mother always said. And the thing is, I'm here for the whole of Christmas week – I think I told you that already – so I'll need somewhere safe to stow her and I'd be ever so grateful if I could pop her into the barn, really I would.'

Edward tightened his scarf against the wind. 'I should think that would be all right,' he said, turning towards the stockman who waited by the far gate, looking back at us, probably still scowling. 'But you'll have to check with Jessops over there, first.'

He glanced across to the stockman. I took the opportunity to examine Edward's face. The afternoon light highlighted golden flecks in his hair and the wind reddened his cheeks to a marvellous healthy glow.

He noticed you looking at him. He bloody-well noticed.

Edward returned his attention to the aircraft and stroked it this time, rather than patted.

'But you shouldn't call this lovely old Tiger Moth a few planks of wood, she's beautiful. Absolutely beautiful.'

I adopted an expression of surprised amusement. 'You actually know what type of aircraft it is?'

'Ah, you think I don't know one end of a magneto switch from another?'

Handsome *and* a flyer ...

'But seriously. You fly too?' I pressed.

'Now and again, a bit of joy riding. Nothing much more

than that. And there's the feed to consider ...' The change of tack confused me.

'Feed?'

'For the cows. Jessops may have to check with your Mr Lanyon first, before you put the aircraft away. This is Lanyon land and they're his cows, after all. But as you're their guest ... I'm sure it will be fine.'

I wanted to say, 'Don't be silly, he's not *my* Mr Lanyon,' but then remembered that, of course, Charles was exactly that – *my* Mr Lanyon.

'*His* cows? I thought they were *your* cows.'

He shook his head. '*My* cows!? No. I was walking my dog along the cliffs and I'd stopped to talk to Jessops when we saw your aircraft coming in.'

He glanced around, realising the dog had wandered off while we were talking.

'Speaking of your dog, where is she?'

He whistled. Moments later the red-and-white Collie dog appeared from behind a Cornish hedge. She had one ear up, one ear down. Edward ruffled her head. His face was a picture of fatherly pride. I knelt down to fuss the dog who jumped backwards and had absolutely no interest in me, just as Edward decided to turn tail towards the far field in the direction of Jessops.

'Wait here a moment, will you ...?' he shouted back, already dashing across the field.

The dog ran after him. I shivered. The breeze really was

frightfully cold, and I hadn't been able to warm up since the flight. I danced on the spot and waited for Edward to come back.

'All sorted,' he said, slightly out of breath having run across the field with the dog, whose name I would later learn was 'Amber', barking at his heels. 'You can leave it in the barn for the week. No need to check with the big house. But perhaps you could arrange for some kind of gift to be sent to Jessops – some beer or cider perhaps, as a thank you. It's quite an inconvenience for him.'

You'd have thought the man was my father!

'Of course. I'm not a completely inconsiderate oaf, you know!'

Edward's face fell.

'Fine. If you're all sorted, I'll be on my way.' And with a curt nod of the head, he began to walk away.

'Wait!' I said, running in front of him, forcing him to stop. 'Sorry, sorry to impose – again – but if I show you how, could you turn the propeller for me to get her started?' I spun my arm in a clockwise direction. 'I would do it myself, but it's much easier with two, and it would be better to taxi her across to the barn under power than to push her all the way.' I glanced down at Amber. 'You might want to tether the dog first, of course.'

Edward took a deep breath. For a moment I think he considered walking away – it seemed he also had a devil and angel on each shoulder, too!

The angel won.

He changed his mind.

'I know how to spin a propeller.'

He strode back to the Tiger Moth ahead of me.

But then, from nowhere, his face softened and his eyes danced when he noticed the paint work on the side of the aircraft.

'The Incredible Flying Fox?' He turned to me, smiling. 'That's never you?'

I shrugged. 'Once upon a time, yes.'

'You've got to be kidding? But you're too young, surely.'

He was genuinely shocked. My heckles started to twitch.

'Kidding? Not at all. I'd take you up, take you through my routine, but I doubt you've got the stomach for it. Few do.'

My 'I dare you' expression set off a further glimmer of amusement in his eyes. He took the bait and ran with it.

'Oh, I've got the stomach for it, but only if you truly know what you're doing. I've no wish to die young.'

'Ah, I see.' I turned away and knelt to duck under the aircraft to remove the chocks while talking. 'You're one of *those* men.' He followed me.

'Those, men?'

'Yes, the type who can't believe – or cope with – a woman doing anything outside of the ordinary drudge they're usually stuck with. I grew up with a thoroughly modern and fair father – progressive, as you said – and I'm simply not used to being around men like you.' I glanced up at him.

He raised his brows into a question mark.

'Dinosaurs,' I said.

I expected a smirk. But he smiled. A soft smile. He stepped towards me.

'I was joking. Truly. I'm not at all one of those men.'

It was my turn to take a deep breath. I'd been overly nice to this man long for enough. I put on my helmet, goggles and gloves with sharp snatches.

'So, will you help? Because I can manage on my own if not.'

'I'll help,' he said.

'And you've started a propeller before, you say?'

He nodded. 'A few times, yes.'

'I'll jump in and leave you to it, then.' I paused. 'But only you're sure you know what you're doing?'

'Of course, I do.'

'Good.'

'Good.'

I climbed into the back seat and prepared the Moth for taxi. He turned the propeller and then ...

'Contact?'

'Contact!'

And off the little Tiger Moth went.

Chapter 5

Juliet

Lanyon

I grabbed my bag and ran away from the field, *sharpish*, arriving at Lanyon half an hour later to find a concerned Charles on the drive pacing outside the grand front door.

'Oh, hello, darling,' I said, blundering my way into the hallway ahead of him. 'Sorry I'm late. I had to put down in a field and ended up having a bit of commotion with some cows, but it's all sorted now.' I pecked him on the cheek. 'Where's Lottie,' I asked, taking off my flying helmet while glancing in the hall mirror. God! Had I really looked like that in front of Edward? I quickly tidied my hair and tried to rub a smudge of oil away with the back of my hand. 'Only I'm desperate to catch up.'

Charles didn't answer but took my hands.

'But ... Darling,' he paused. 'Before you see Lottie, I really

do think we need to talk about, you know, the arrangement ... only, Pa wants to iron a few things out. Details,
you know.'

I shook him off with a peck on the lips.

'Yes, I suppose we do. But not now though.' I smiled my
brightest smile and patted him on the arm. 'I'm desperate
to get in front of the fire and warm up, it was absolutely
freezing up there today. Oh, and I'm afraid I rather upset
those cows when I landed. Do you think you could send
a thank you to your man ... Jessops, is it? Perhaps some
cider or something? He was ever so helpful, moving the
cows to another field. And I've left the Moth in a barn.'

Charles laughed.

'Poor Jessops. Yes, of course I can. I'm visiting him
tomorrow. I'll take something to him then.'

I kissed Charles again, with a little more enthusiasm
this time, before striding across the hallway and placing
my hand on the sitting room door handle. 'Is Lottie in
here?'

Charles nodded. Smiling, I slipped off my muddy flying
boots and turned the brass knob on the large panelled door.

Lottie was dozing on a large sofa by the bay window.
A King Charles Spaniel lay by her feet. An embroidered
shawl, the most perfect shade of russet red, was wrapped
around her shoulders.

'Juliet!'

Lottie, stirring at the sound of the door, threw her legs
off the sofa and crossed the room to hug me. 'I've been

waiting for you all afternoon. We saw you fly past ages ago. Charles imagined you dead in a ditch somewhere, although why a ditch always has to be involved whenever anyone goes missing is beyond me.' She took a step backwards to look me up and down. 'But looking at the state of you, I think you really have been in a ditch!' She turned to Charles who had followed me into the room. 'Do leave us to catch up in peace, Charles! And perhaps arrange for some tea?'

Charles shook his head in mock disapproval, crossed the room to kiss me once more before turning on his heels to leave us alone. Lottie returned to the sofa while I mothered around her, straightening her shawl around her shoulders. It was Lottie's comfort shawl from school, the thing she always turned to in moments of distress (that and a book of Christina Rossetti poetry). This wasn't a good sign. If the shawl was out, before you knew it the poetry books would also be out and Lottie would spiral into a depression that could last for weeks. The door clicked shut.

'Good, he's gone!' Lottie said, lounging back into the sofa. 'So, tell me, what have you *really* been up to all afternoon?'

I was just about to sit down myself and launch into a watered-down version of the truth when the door clicked open again and Charles' mother rushed into the sitting room carrying a bed sheet.

'Ah, Juliet. You made it. Jolly good ...' She glanced at my clothes and then at the bed sheet. 'It's because of the oil, dear,' she said kindly, before laying the sheet across a chair.

'Sorry, Ma,' (Lottie insisted I called her this, although Mrs Lanyon and I both seemed to wince every time I said it) 'But I *did* take my muddy boots off in the hallway.'

She glanced at my stockinged feet – men's stockings – and patted me on the head as I sat down – 'Thank you, Juliet. Most considerate.' She pulled the bell for tea, sat down and started to chat, leaving Lottie to roll her eyes with annoyance at having had her confidential catch-up delayed.

The late afternoon passed pleasantly. Charles reappeared with the maid, Katie, who brought tea and a few eats, and we all caught up in the civilised manner befitting gentle folk who lived in a house like Lanyon. Final plans for the wedding were made, and it was only when Ma and Charles retired to dress for dinner that Lottie and I finally found a few moments to be alone. We sat in a delicious silence at first. I was perched on the end of her sofa, having dragged the sheet with me to tuck underneath my oil-stained clothes. We stared out into the darkness of the garden, which in daylight had uninterrupted views across the grounds to the ocean beyond, but at night was one long expanse of black, except for the moon, which was almost full and served to back-light a line of cedar trees perfectly, the moon shadows throwing glorious patterns across the lawn and river of silver through the sea.

'I don't know why I'm asking,' Lottie said, breaking the silence. 'But have you given any thought to what you might wear to the wedding?'

'Oh, I've brought a warm woollen suit that belonged to Mummy. That will do, I suppose.'

Lottie shook her head in frustration. I pressed on.

'But it's winter, Lottie! And it's very smart, too. Truly it is.'

'But it's your wedding day, Juliet. I can't understand why you're keeping it so simple.'

I began to play with a tassel on Lottie's shawl.

'Charles and I agreed – no fuss. And your Ma was relieved on the "no fuss" front, too. There might be a war. It doesn't do for the big house to start being extravagant in front of the tenants. And I've got no one to invite, no one at all. I'd much rather spend Pa's money on a new aircraft ...' I sat up. 'Oh, did I tell you? There's this fabulous little monoplane coming out soon and it's ...' Noticing Lottie glance down at her very slightly swollen belly, I stopped. 'Well anyway, that's just a bit of a dream. But what about you.' I tried to buoy her up. 'What will you wear?'

She shrugged, disconsolate.

'I know!' I said, not waiting for an answer. 'You should wear your cream cashmere two-piece. The one I bought in you in Paris.'

Lottie shook her head.

'I was going to. But Katie can't do the zip up anymore. And anyway, I want *you* to wear it.'

'Me! But ... look at my hands, Lottie! I'll never get them clean enough to wear cream.'

'I thought of that. I've told Katie to scrub them. No buts. It's been laid out on the end of your bed. I knew you wouldn't have brought anything suitable.' She glanced at my clothes. 'Just look at you, Juliet. I mean to say, have you even brought *any* decent clothes? You do know there's a party here tomorrow evening? In *your* honour, I might add.'

I went back to the tassel.

'I managed to pack a few bits and bobs. But truly, Lottie, it's difficult to fit anything in the old Moth, what with the tools I carry and so on ...' My voice petered out.

Lottie wasn't listening. She stirred herself sufficiently to leave the comfort of the chaise and cross to the fireplace to ring the bell. Katie appeared.

'Katie, please escort Miss Caron to her room – via my room. Do not allow her to deviate. Wash her hands and help her to pick out a dress for dinner this evening, and for tomorrow evening, too. And when she finally steps out of the dreadful clothes she's wearing, wash them and when she's not looking, give them to the poor, although the poor probably won't want them so you might as well burn them.'

'Lottie!'

Katie tried to hide a smile. I made tracks towards the door.

'Oh, and Katie ...' Lottie added, forcing Katie to pause at the door.

'Yes, Ma'am?'

'Tomorrow's dress should be something stunning for Miss Caron. And don't forget to take that tweed suit I pointed out for yourself, too. I don't need it anymore and it will be nice for you to wear it over Christmas ...'

Katie's eyes widened.

'Thank you ever so much, Ma'am.'

Lottie batted us off, but as we left the room, I took a moment to look at Lottie from the doorway. She had turned to face the moon shadows again. There was something in the way her head dropped and in the way her right hand was reaching to her cheek that told me she was crying. I wanted to rush her, to hold her and tell her everything was going to be all right. But if I did, Lottie would want to discuss the inevitable – *her* inevitable – a topic we had been skirting around all day, the topic Charles wanted to discuss when I arrived. The topic of a baby – and a promise, too. And if we did that, I wasn't entirely sure that my previous resolve to help my friend would hold true, and the problem was, it had to.

Instead, I grabbed my boots, flying helmet, coat and gloves from the hallway, followed Katie to Lottie's room and asked her to lay out a couple of evening dresses – but not to worry too much about what she found, any old thing would do.

Chapter 6

Juliet

The compass and the coddiwompler

18 December 1938

Dear Juliet

We said our goodbyes without arranging a time or date for the flight you offered me. Is today too soon? I can get fuel if necessary. I'll wait at the barn at one p.m. in the hope you can make it.

Yours,

E. Nancarrow

Edward's letter, handed to me by Katie a little after breakfast, caught me by surprise. I would usually run to Lottie with this kind of thing, but I didn't tell her about the letter because ... well, because I didn't want anyone to know. I spent the morning walking the grounds with

Lottie pretending E. Nancarrow did not exist, but later, with Charles busy paying Christmas good tidings to tenant farmers (including Jessops who would receive extra cider this Christmas for his inconvenience with the cows) and with Lottie resting, I felt restless and bored. Persuading myself that I really should go and make sure the aircraft was safe and sound, I pulled my flying jacket over a shrunken Argyle jumper of my father's and tucked Oxford bag trousers into my flying boots before striding out and heading down the road. This Edward Nancarrow chap may well have been what might generally be regarded as quite a dish, but still, summoning me to take him flying when he had behaved so dismissively the day before really was taking the biscuit.

No, I would go to the barn and explain that I could not fly today, but as a woman of my word I would take him flying at some point that week – but at my convenience, in a day or so perhaps, weather permitting.

When I arrived at the barn Edward was already there, sitting on a hay bale and engrossed in a literary supplement – *The Beano*. I stood in the doorway and watched him. He tittered to himself while reading, seemingly a different man from yesterday – a happy-go-lucky, relaxed man. I coughed to attract attention and hoped that the midday winter sun backlighting me in the doorway would highlighting the copper (my mother called it red) hair in just the right way. He looked up and smiled.

'Hello, there,' he said, putting the comic down before

making his way around the wing and stepping towards me. His greeting had the casual air of an old friend about it.

Who was this new man with his relaxed airs?

Whoever he was he was dressed in layers of warm clothes.

Ready for flying, no doubt.

The presumption!

'I thought I'd check the aircraft over for you,' he said. 'Make sure she survived the night. She seems perfectly fine, though – not a cow scratch in sight!'

Humour, now? I didn't smile but sniffed out a kind of thank you. He followed me around the aircraft as I checked her over for myself.

'You got my note, then?' he asked.

I paused by the propeller and looked him in the face. 'Note?'

His expression was perfection – there is nothing more satisfying than witnessing the sudden onset of self-doubt in an overly-confident man.

'Yes, note,' he repeated. 'I delivered it to Lanyon myself, this morning. I asked the maid to take it to you directly.'

I shook my head before unclipping the stowage door. I removed my tool bag and a spare set of overalls and dropped them onto the barn floor.

'I received no note this morning.' I glanced up at him again, pulling the overalls on over my flying boots. 'What did it say?'

'Say?' Edward was rubbing his temple now.

'Yes. The note?'

He considered this.

'Well, it, er ... it ...'

I rummaged unnecessarily in the bag before taking out a spanner, stood to my full height – all five foot five inches – and looked up at him.

'It said that I'd ...' He glanced around the barn, still considering his next sentence.

'That you'd?'

'Well, that I'd be here – waiting for you – in case you were free to take me flying this afternoon. You did offer. I'm sure you did.'

I walked around to the engine housing and lifted the casing away.

He followed me.

'Pass me my tool bag, would you?'

He sighed, picked up the bag and joined me by the engine. I took an oil-stained scarf out of the bag and tied my hair back before finding another rag to check the oil.

'So, how about it?' he said, watching me.

'How about what?'

'The flight you offered – *my* flight. How about it?'

I paused to look at him.

'Today?' I asked. 'Right now?'

'Yes.'

I shook my head and returned to the engine. 'That's not possible. Today is a day for essential maintenance.

She was a bit sticky in the rudder on the way down and I want to sort it out.'

'*You* do?' he said, his voice playful. '*You* need to sort it out? *You're* doing the maintenance?'

Not this again.

'Yes, Mr Nancarrow. *I'm* doing the maintenance.'

'But, how ...?'

'My father wouldn't allow me to fly solo until I knew how to fix her. He'd say, "There's absolutely no point galli-vanting off around the countryside if you can't fix your own kite, you know, Juliet, no point at all!" I know exactly what I'm doing, but if you aren't happy with that state of affairs then I suggest you find someone else to take you flying – a man, perhaps. Now, if you'll excuse me, I'm very busy and I suppose you'll be wanting to be on your way.'

I turned back to the engine.

He smiled then and his shoulders relaxed. I didn't see the smile or the relax, but I felt them. And then a hand rested gently on my shoulder.

'You misunderstand me,' he said. 'I think it's wonderful that you know how to maintain her. Truly. And I'd be honoured to fly with you. Today, tomorrow, the next day. Whenever you're free.' His hand fell but I didn't turn around. 'Perhaps, like you said yesterday, we can shake hands and start again. I have a feeling that I was a bit of a pompous ass yesterday. It's just, at the time I thought you were very lucky not to crash, and that would have been a terrible waste. I don't like waste. I've seen a lot of unnecessary waste in my life and I over-reacted, I'm sorry.'

I turned to face him, the spanner still in my hand. I eyed him as a mouse would eye a smiling ferret. 'Start again?' I asked.

His eyes flashed brightly. 'Exactly! Let's pretend this is the first time we ever met, right here, right now ...'

I hesitated.

'I suppose I can do that. You were ... quite, helpful yesterday, after all. But I still can't take you up today ...' I softened 'no matter how sweetly you smile ...'

He laughed. I laughed. It was nice. Too nice. I remembered Charles.

'But I really must get on. I have the engine to finish and then I really do need to take a good look at that rudder. Let's say ... same time tomorrow, and if the weather is fine, I'll take you up.'

He visibly deflated. I turned back towards the engine.

'Sorry, yes, I'll leave you too it,' he said to my back. 'Till tomorrow, then?'

I nodded without looking around. I didn't want to be rude or play with him, truly, but there was something in his smile, in the touch of his hand on my shoulder. He interrupted my thoughts by turning at the barn door.

'I don't suppose you're free later this afternoon. Say, in a couple of hours, or so?'

I bent to glance at him under the wing.

'Today?

'Today.'

'This afternoon?'

'Yes. They're putting on an afternoon tea and an early Christmas party for the children in the village hall. I've been asked to help out – organise games, play the guitar, that kind of thing – and I thought you might like to come, if you've finished here, that is.'

I considered the afternoon ahead. There was no sticky rudder. I made that up. Charles was out with his father and Lottie was sleeping. There really was no reason for me to say no, and yet, there was *every* reason for me to say no.

'I don't understand this change in you,' I said. 'You were quite ... shouty, yesterday.'

'Shouty?'

'Yes, shouty. And now you seek my company, even though I'm an irresponsible and spoiled little rich girl.'

He tilted his head to one side.

'I didn't say that.'

I waited for him to think about it.

'Well, not those exact words.'

'Thank you for the offer,' I said, suddenly coming to my senses, 'but I'm not really dressed for ...'

'Nonsense! You look perfect!' His eyes were so bright. So alive. So blue. 'Come on, it will be fun! Come coddiwomple with me.'

Now, that got me. I smiled.

'Coddiwomple?'

He nodded. We were still communicating through the gap between the two wings of the Tiger Moth.

'I never heard of such a word.'

'Oh, it's a word,' he said. 'And I'll tell you what it means if you come with me. How about I treat you to afternoon tea? Look, I'd love to know all about the flying circus, and I'd love to talk to you about flying, that's all. I want to know about the flying fox. You, well, you fascinate me, Juliet.'

Fascinate? Well ...

I knew I should walk away, stride out of the barn, open the gate, march up the hill and not look back. But the fire in his eyes was just too bright. It's always the eyes that get you. He drew me in and I so desperately *wanted* to be drawn in.

'All right,' I said, in as nonchalant a manner I could muster. 'Why not? But I'll have to finish up here, first.'

He dashed around the wing and joined me by the engine, talking off his heavy overcoat and placing it on an obliging hay bale before appearing by my side, full of enthusiasm.

'In that case, think of me as your apprentice. How can I help?'

'No one works on my aircraft but me, I'm afraid.' I nodded towards the comic left abandoned on the bale. 'Perhaps you could carry on reading your newspaper ...'

He laughed and returned to lounge on the hay bale while I worked away.

'But *why* don't you want to know what coddiwompler is?' Edward asked as we sauntered, arms swinging, down the lane to the village, my hair still held back with a rag. I'd taken off my overalls but my flying jacket was a must. Yes, it was far too big and smelt of a mixture of fuel and cigars, but it was like being wrapped in Pa's arms again, and I treasured it.

'Because you made it up.' I flashed him a quick smile as we walked down the lane.

'Well, I'll tell you anyway, because I think you're a fellow coddiwompler, you just don't know it, and that would be terrible.'

'What would?'

'To be one, and to never to know.'

We arrived outside the village hall. He'd got me now. I stopped

'Go on then,' I said. 'Tell me.'

He shook his head.

'It's too late. We're here.' He leapt up the steps to the hall. 'You've missed your moment. I'll have to tell you later ...' He winked and opened the door for me to step inside. 'Or tomorrow, when we go flying.' I stepped through the door and as I did so our hands brushed, and not quite by accident, I thought.

We spent the afternoon helping with the teas and making paper chains and Christmas cards with the children. Edward had a natural manner and was clearly the darling of the ladies' committee. It was light. It was easy. It was fun. And as the afternoon moved on, I had the distinct feeling that E. Nancarrow was exactly the sort of man my mother had warned me to steer clear of.

When the children began to disperse, we took a moment to wander away from the hubbub of the hall to sit on the harbour wall. We sipped whiskey from Edward's hip flask and talked of flying. The inevitable moment came when we began to explore into each other's lives more purposefully, to tentatively probe, to edge-in sideways.

Edward began. He wanted to know the ins and outs of how a young woman, barely twenty years old, had spent her formative years as the child star of a flying circus, able to nip about the country in her own aircraft.

I explained some, but not all, of my story ...

My father, Louis Caron, was a philanthropic and yes, a wealthy, man. He was the proud owner of the *Caron Flying Circus*, which meant that I had rarely spent more than half a day straight with my feet on the ground. On my twelfth birthday I was strapped to the wing of a Gypsy Moth and told to smile and wave at the crowd. I loved it.

My mother was a descendant of French Romany Gypsies, albeit two or three generations removed, but she retained that air of exotic adventure about her and was a tigress of a woman. I didn't take after her very much, I explained, except for a genetic disposition for slender ankles and copper hair. On my thirteenth birthday, Father argued the case with Mother that it was time for me to join the circus as a pilot – I had been flying duel-seated for years and could handle an aircraft as well as anyone he knew. I'd be wonderful, he said, and an asset to the show.

Mother asked father to leave us alone for a moment. She sat me down in the garden and took a while searching under leaves until she found what she was looking for – a caterpillar. She held the caterpillar in her hand and began to talk of butterflies, explaining how caterpillars are happy enough, to begin with, with their little caterpillar bodies and caterpillar feet, because they don't know any better, but eventually, there was an awakening within them – a realisation that it was time for a change, to evolve into a completely new being – to blossom, to fly. She said that the caterpillar, quite wisely, chose to spend some time alone before it flew – to cocoon itself in its own thoughts for a while – and then, when it was ready, it shed the trappings of adolescence and transformed itself completely by growing wings and, at just the right time, took to the skies and flew.

She said, 'Juliet. Your father has kept you a boy for far too long. It is time to shed your boy-like caterpillar frame, let go of those clumsy feet, hunched shoulders and flat-framed body. It is time to chrysalis into the woman your body is aching to become, which is why I have decided to send you to school – yes, there is no point arguing – for two years, with other girls your own age who can teach you how to become a woman. Join the circus now, by all means, but only on the proviso that, at fifteen, you will go to Paris and become a butterfly. Those are my terms.'

I said nothing. There was no point arguing with Ma.

'But listen to me, Juliet, and listen hard,' she added. 'When you do blossom into a woman, remember that there are two types of man in this world – the non-predatory and the predatory. With your gypsy looks and wild-hearted spirit I know that you will attract the latter, but you must promise me, my love, that when you marry, you will marry the former. Oh, toy with predatory men if you must, make love to them, tease them for your own entertainment, but never – never – marry a charming man, and remember ...' she tipped my face upwards from the chin at this point '... are you listening to me, Juliet? If you ever fall properly and desperately in love, remember that the first throws of love are nothing more than obsession, they are not love, not really. And *never* let a man know how deeply you love him, because once he has the upper hand, he will break your heart in a single moment and not even pause as he steps over your broken body to move onto the next.'

Then, when I was fourteen, came the crash. Bereft, and dependent on Pa's solicitor who was intent on carrying out mother's wishes, I was sent to school in Paris and that's where I met Lottie Lanyon, who took me under her wing and helped me through the darkest days of my life, never leaving me alone during the holidays, always taking me home to Cornwall, to Lanyon, and sharing her family with me, which is how I met Lottie's brother Charles, the most non-predatory young man I had ever met. After a short courtship, I agreed to marry him.

Edward listened while I told an abridged version of my story. At no time during the course of the whole conversation did I admit to my engagement or to my mother's warning about fast men. Was this a deliberate omission on my behalf – absolutely.

'On my fourteenth birthday – which is also Christmas Day, by the way – Pa took me into the little club house we had at our landing strip in Oxford and he gave me a good luck charm, to keep with me, always.'

Still sitting on the harbour wall, I took my lucky charm out of my pocket and handed it to Edward. It was a compass, cased in gold.

'It's the most special thing I own – will ever own,' I said, smiling at the thought of Pa.

'It's lovely,' he said. 'It's a compass you say?'

'Yes.'

'But it looks like a pocket watch.'

He pressed a catch on the side to open the lid, revealing the compass.

'Yes, it does, rather. But look ... if you flick this tiny little lever, like this, and *then* turn the catch, the back of the compass casing opens rather than the front ... see? And then you find that it's not just a compass at all, but something else entirely.'

Edward looked at it, confused. A needle was centred on the face, but rather than pointing to North or South, the only words written on this side were, *Oui* and *Non*.

'It's an heirloom from my mother's side of the family,' I

explained. 'They were travellers. This side of the compass acts as a kind of fortune teller's trinket.'

'How does it work?'

'Well, let's say you have a pressing question you desperately need an answer for, you open the compass, ask the question, then press the catch to spin the needle and see where it lands – yes, or no. When Pa gave it to me, he said, "Here is your real inheritance, Juliet. But remember, if you ever need an answer to an important question, know that in your heart, you already know all the answers, and most often, if you are in doubt about something and are looking for an answer, then whatever it is that you are considering doing – don't. Pause, wait, consider. There is much more time around than anyone supposes."'

'Have you ever asked it a question?'

I shook my head. 'Never.'

Edward closed the compass and handed it back.

'It's wonderful,' he said. 'He must have loved you very much.'

I felt tears sting my eyes. Dear, darling Pa.

'He did.'

'You never thought of giving it up, after the accident – flying, I mean?'

I thought about my answer.

'Have you ever thought of giving up breathing?'

He shook his head with a smile.

'There you go then. It's who I am. When I'm in the sky,' I looked up with a sigh, 'up there, I'm in heaven. I don't blame aeroplanes for my parent's death and have no intention of stopping flying because of it. It was a moment's misjudgement on Pa's behalf, and as devastating as it has been, I know he would want me to keep going, whatever the consequences.'

We sat in silence for a while, our shoulders touching, before turning our thoughts to Germany and the heartbreaking possibility of war. I talked of my grand plan – a plan I had not revealed to anyone, least of all to Charles – that being my determination to fly for the RAF, perhaps even join as a fighter pilot, the first woman ever. I just needed to work out a way to persuade them to have me. Edward did not mock. He accepted my dream as an equal, saying that if I dreamt hard enough, anything could happen. And I liked that. I liked that very much indeed.

'Anyway, your turn,' I said, returning the compass to a pocket. 'You're obviously not local, so why rent a cottage here? Why has E. Nancarrow come to Angels Cove?' I took a quick slurp of whiskey. It was Edward's turn to pause before answering. I filled the gap by answering my own question. 'No, wait! I bet you're an artist. It'll be the light. Are you in with the Newlyn set?'

Edward shook his head.

'I'm not in with any set. I just thought I'd come and stay for a while, take in the sea air. Enjoy the view.'

'How very leisurely of you. But what do you do for a living – other than walking your dog on the cliffs and getting in the way of women trying to land their planes – what *are* you?'

A wry smile drifted across his face.

He rubbed his chin in thought. 'I told you. I'm a coddi-wompler.'

I laughed. 'That again.'

'Yes, that again.' He took a sip of my whiskey. 'Does that answer your question?'

I kicked my legs against the harbour wall.

'Bearing in mind I have no idea what a coddiwompler is, I would say that you have in no way answered my question. So ...?'

'So?'

'So, go on then, what is one?'

Edward sniffed and shook his head.

'Oh, well, this is quite awkward, because I'm not really allowed to say.'

He looked away, pretending to be interested in a couple of men who were sitting on a boat, supposedly mending their nets but really just chatting at the far end or the harbour wall.

'Not allowed to say? But you were going to tell me earlier ...'

'We coddiwomplers are members of a top secret club – I was going to tell you before because I thought you must be one, too' – he turned to me – 'because it hit me last night that you seem to be exactly the sort of person who would love to live her life as we do ... but now, I'm not so sure. You might be a bit ...'

'A bit?'

'Sensible.'

'Nonsense. You've seen my aircraft – Daredevil is quite literally my middle name. Tell me!'

He shook his head. 'No. We'll just have to play I spy, instead. I'll start.' He glanced around the harbour. 'I spy something beginning with B.'

'Boat?'

His eyes lit up.

'Yes! Say, you're real good at this! I'll give it another shot ... I spy something beginning with S ...'

'The sea.'

'No, that would be T S. Try again ...'

The time passed far too quickly and without even noticing it, the sun began to set beyond the islands. I jumped off the harbour wall in a wild panic. Edward had a definite look of satisfaction on his face when I chided him for keeping me talking for so long.

'Before you go, let me just ...' Edward surprised me by taking a folded handkerchief from his coat pocket. He wrapped a corner of the cloth around his finger and lifted his hand towards my face. 'You have a smear of oil across your face, that will never do at a house like Lanyon. Far too proper.' I didn't move away, but allowed him to wipe my cheek.

'How long has that been there?'

'All day. I let you run with it.' He stepped back to admire his handy-work. 'There, all gone. Although, I actually preferred you as you were, with the warrior stripe – it really suited you,' he added, softly.

A cloud passed over our fragmented bits of conversation. We had had our moment, both of us knowing I should have dashed back to Lanyon much earlier, but we had already taken on the selfish attitude of lovers and from the ambivalent view of the naïve observer – the men working on the fishing boats, for example – we would have appeared to have had nothing more than a pleasant afternoon enjoying the polite interaction of two friends. But Edward and I knew differently, and we knew it from the first, 'Hello'. Because that was the thing with love at first sight, it was like the birth of time – the big bang of the universe itself. It was the ignition of a silent understanding exchanged in body language – in the blink of an eye, the angle of the head and the positioning of the body. It was that first spark of a silent understanding that set in motion an unstoppable series of events. A motion that creates a kind of energy that forever links two people in an impenetrable and invisible connectedness. A connectedness that almost always brings a heady emotional mix of absolute joy and unbearable pain.

Mother would not be happy.

As I waved goodbye and dashed up the hill, I felt like Cinderella running away from her Prince Charming. And just like Cinderella, I knew that the road would not lead us apart for very long, but would curve all the way around our respective destinations in the shape of an interconnected heart, and that we would stand in front of each other again, smiling, not wanting to walk away. And yet, at that very moment, I still didn't know what he did, where he was from, why he was here – and most importantly, I realised dashing up the road, smiling – I still had absolutely no idea what a coddiwompler was!

No one at Lanyon knew what a coddiwompler was either. Pa Lanyon thought it sounded like 'old English' and after a rebuke from Lottie for being gone all day and a strange side-eyed glance from Charles, Pa pointed me in the direction of his library where I would find a miscellany on old-English quirky words. Sure enough, between cockamamie (ridiculous; incredible) and codswallop (something utterly senseless) I found coddiwompler: someone who travels in a purposeful manner towards a vague destination.

How very vague, and elusive, and exciting, and myste-rious ... *and*, he was an American, too ... just dreadful!

Chapter 7

Katherine

A moment's pause

I lay the manuscript down on the sofa and stoked the fire before selecting the search engine on my phone.

Several sites popped up on the search feed associating themselves with coddiwompling, including a webpage dedicated to the written ramblings of free-spirited bloggers who shared their adventurers on the internet.

One particular blogger – *The Last Coddiwompler* – caught my eye. He was a man who occasionally travelled with no real agenda other than to seek out one thing and one thing only – fun. He aimed always, he said, to simply 'stumble' across adventure, rather than to seek it out, genuinely believing that if he kept his eye out, even in the most mundane on places, adventure was only ever a heartbeat away. It seemed that in the process of hitting the road aimlessly, this blogger regularly found himself spending time in the most amazing places and meeting the most fascinating people – and not necessarily in exotic locations from glossy magazines, he stressed, but absolutely anywhere – Spain, Mexico, Hull ... As I read this tale of modern-day adventure and stared in admiration at his photographs, I couldn't help but be drawn in, and all the while a clearer picture of Juliet's mystery man began to take shape, because if Edward Nancarrow was anything like the man staring out of the screen in front of me, he would have been a fun, free, sexy, enticing kind of a man. And yet wasn't this exactly the sort of person Juliet was, too? An adventurer, a dare devil, a coddiwompler? Edward clearly thought so, and he knew it from the moment she landed her Tiger Moth on the field in front of him.

But it was only when I scrolled to the bottom of the webpage that I noticed and recognised the name of the blogger–Sam Lanyon.

My head tipped to the angle of a questioning puppy.

Sam Lanyon? *The* Sam Lanyon, Juliet's grandson? It couldn't be, could it?

With my interest in this family suddenly piqued to even greater heights, despite the early hour of the morning and itchy eyes, I huddled closer to the fire, wrapped the shawl tightly around my shoulders and read on.

Chapter 8

Juliet

19 December 1938

Flying with Edward

The morning after the pre-wedding party I woke with a desperate desire to jump into my Tiger Moth, fire up the engine and fly right away.

I had behaved foolishly. I'd begun to flirt, to toy, and what good ever came of that kind of shenanigans?

What happened?

I was unmasked, shown to have behaved like a fool, and I deserved it.

Having been standing in the hallway with Charles, welcoming guests to the Lanyon Christmas party, I was utterly gobsmacked when, of all people, Edward walked in. I had no idea that he was at all acquainted with the Lanyons. He hadn't said he was attending the party that afternoon. Perhaps, thinking me single, he had wanted it to be a surprise.

He arrived at eight. I saw him before he saw me, walking through the door, smiling, naturally at ease, a happy and contented man. I wondered momentarily, as I stood there, my heart in my shoes, waiting to greet him, if Edward had known I was Charles' fiancée all along and if the attraction between us had been on my part only. That I had misunderstood his interest in me.

But when Charles introduced me to Edward as the future Mrs Lanyon, my heart broke to see that he had not known. Edward tried to hide his confusion, before quickly walking away and disappearing into the gathered crowd. He spent some of the evening with Lottie before retiring back to the village early, with the excuse of a headache and an early start the next day. We did not speak that evening, which was both a relief and an overpowering disappointment.

The following morning, having arranged with cook to breakfast before the house had risen and having previously arranged with Jessops for fuel to be delivered to the barn, I dashed to my aircraft, desperate to fly.

I was not surprised to find Edward there, waiting. He was sitting on his adopted hay bale, a blue and white striped scarf wrapped tightly around his face, no dog with him, no *Beano* and he'd clearly been on no more than nodding terms with sleep.

'Why didn't you tell me about Charles?'

Because I've fallen in love with you ...

'I'm not sure. Does it matter?'

Edward didn't answer.

I busied myself around the aircraft, avoiding eye contact. We fell silent, unsure how to behave, how to speak. A few jerrycans of fuel were hidden at the back of the barn, exactly where Jessops, now amiable thanks to the cider, had left them.

'You're going flying?' Edward jumped down from his lofty position on the bale.

'Yes ... I needed to clear my head and I knew ...' I stopped pouring fuel into the tank for a moment.

'You knew I'd be here.'

'I thought you might be.' I put down the can smiled up at him. 'I promised you a trip and I'd like to honour that promise, if I may.' I glanced out of the barn. 'And it may be cold, but it is a beautiful day, after all.'

He smiled too. 'It is indeed a beautiful day and I'd love to go flying with you.'

We spent another ten minutes preparing the aircraft before pushing my beautiful yellow Tiger Moth out of the barn.

'Put these on,' I said, handing him goggles and helmet before showing him where to place his feet on the wing. 'It will be very cold up there and the clouds are bubbling out to the west, so it might be a bit bumpy.'

I leant across him to tighten his straps and secure him

in the seat. He took me by surprise by taking my bare hand in his gloved one.

'Listen, I think you're amazing and beautiful and fascinating. But I know you're spoken for. We can we be friends, can't we. Just for a little while? I'm not a reckless fool, Juliet. Not really.'

I finally looked him in the eye which was, as I suspected, lethal. A naughty Cornish pixie must have jumped my shoulder just then, because I suddenly realised that there really was only one way to go ...

'Not a reckless fool?' I said (with a very definite flick of the hair and twinkle in the eye) 'how very disappointing. I have a sudden fancy to run through my stunt routine today, which is why I'm making sure your straps are nice and tight, and only a reckless fool – or maybe a true coddiwompler – would even begin to consider jumping on board for that kind of a ride ...'

His face came alive. His whole body sparked with energy, with life.

'I lied,' he said, putting on his helmet. 'Show me what you've got, Miss Caron! If we're going to go down, let's do it in style!' He snapped on his goggles with a flourish. 'I'm ready!'

For the next twenty minutes Edward was taken on the ride of his life. The chill from the wind was fierce, but as we flew low and slow over Angels Cove, children ran out to wave at us, racing the little aircraft as we flew parallel with the road. I flew half a mile out to sea and performed only part of my stunt routine – a tick-tock stall and a few loops – but not too much, it wouldn't do to turn Edward's stomach and embarrass him.

On landing back at the field, I taxied the aircraft to just outside the barn and cut the engine. I jumped out once the propeller had stopped and leant across Edward to unstrap him. The cheeks on his face burned red but his eyes were as bright as shiny new pins.

Edward jumped out, ripped off his goggles and helmet and just stood there, looking at me and smiling – half madman – before picking me up, spinning me around and finally placing me, very gently, on the ground again.

'That was incredible, Juliet. Thank you. Thank you so very much.' He handed me the goggles and hat. Still on a high from the flight, he babbled on about the joy of flying while we pushed the Tiger Moth back in the barn.

'I wonder, do you have time to come to the village again for tea? They're having a Christmas lantern parade on the twenty-third and I seem to have been roped in again to make lanterns and decorate the church, and you seemed to enjoy our afternoon in the hall. I have a feeling you'd love it. What do you say?'

I wanted to go. I wanted to go so very, very badly, but I shook my head, leant against the wing and sighed.

'I'm sorry, Edward, but I can't.'

He stepped in, too close for mere friends.

'Why can't you?'

I shook my head and smiled resignedly.

'I think we both know why.'

He stepped closer still and leant in to brush my cheek with his lips. 'In that case, thank you for the flight,' he whispered. 'It was wonderful.' He stepped back. 'Consider the debt paid, Miss Caron.' And then, without looking back, to my absolute surprise, he walked away.

Chapter 9

Katherine
18 December

Poor George

The candles were half their original size and surrounded by pools of wax when I place the manuscript on the sofa beside me, disappointed at Edward for walking away, and cursing Juliet for letting him go.

But it was time to stop reading. Not just because I needed to sleep (although, what did I know of sleep any more? Sleep had become a fitful irrelevance since James had died) or because my phone battery was down to ten percent and I wanted to save a little just in case the roof really did blow off, but because now that I was engrossed in Juliet's story, I wasn't sure about the — what to call it — moral correctness? — of reading someone else's private memoirs, even if that person was no longer around to care. The only answer was to email Sam, the grandson

– the coddiwompler? – and ask his permission to read on. I had ventured to Cornwall looking for a historical story to tell and it looked like I had found one, but that suddenly didn't seem important, because looking into the lives of these strangers tonight had led me to throw side-glances towards my own story which, as Gerald knew, had not just stagnated, but stopped. Juliet was leading me somewhere – I just didn't know where that somewhere was.

I poked my head out of the candlewick bedspread at about ten a.m. the following morning and promptly ducked under again once my nose had direct contact with the cold. I had two options, stay warm under the bedcovers but starve to death, or face the cold and risk hyperthermia. The second option won by a narrow margin leading me to jump out and dance on the spot while throwing open the curtains – a bright, wintery, sunshiny glow flooded the room. I stopped dancing and stared. What a difference a few hours could make, and what a view.

James would have loved this.

Wall-to-wall ocean broken by three little granite islands that sat in the bay.

So here were the famous Angels, splattered with tiny flecks of white, as if God had gone on a paint flicking frenzy. I put my glasses on and realised the white flecks were actually seagulls, presumably taking a well-earned rest after the stress of the storm. The sea was a little swollen still, but it seemed *Katherine* had moved on to terrorise pastures new, leaving a bright winter morning in her wake.

I turned on a wind-up radio that sat on the windowsill at the top of the stairs and tried the bedroom light. Still no power. Allowing as short a time as possible for my bare skin to feel the sharpness of the cold, I dressed in the previous day's clothes and headed down the stairs, pausing to sit on the bottom step to check my phone for messages and contact Gerald regarding the day's agenda.

Uncle Gerald had beaten me to it.

Terrible news. George has had a heart attack. Have rushed to Brighton in Land Rover – used the spare key as didn't want to disturb. Have spoken to Fenella and she's going to look after you – you are not to sit home alone moping! Will text when I know more about George as there is talk of a stent being put in. So very sorry to love and leave. Have a fabulous time. Don't forget about the apostrophe, will you? Oh, and best keep a beady eye out for Percy and Noel who will no doubt try to cajole – they are leaders of opposing camps! X

My first thought was obviously, 'Poor George ...' but my second thought was very definitely ... 'Bollocks!'

'Bollocks, bollocks, bollocks.'

And, 'Bollocks to the bloody apostrophe, too!'

Sitting on the bottom step of the stairs I stared at the

door, just as *Have Yourself a Merry Little Christmas* came on the radio. Alone again for Christmas after all.

There was only one thing for it – I'd go back to bed for an hour and bury myself in both the snuggly covers and the embrace of my new friends – Juliet and Edward. Hoping that their paths would surely cross again.

Chapter 10

Juliet
22 December 1938

The promise

*D*ear Juliet
On second thoughts, I'm not entirely sure the debt is paid completely. The children are making lanterns in the hall from eleven and as the future lady of the manor, I thought it probably your wish – your duty – to help out. Lunch on the beach afterwards as a thank you?
Yours, the incorrigible coddiwompler,
E. Nancarrow
P.S. If you come, I'll tell you what a coddiwompler is.
P.P.S. Wrap up warm!

The Christmas Card was hand-delivered by a young boy shortly after breakfast. I was having coffee with Lottie in the lounge when Katie handed it to me. I recognised the card. Edward had made it in the village hall during our afternoon together, when we sat with the children, in a moment of perfect happiness. I dare not open it and yet to leave it unopened would draw suspicion from Lottie.

Lottie glanced up from her book. I opened the card and feigned a smile.

'It's from Jessops,' I said. 'To thank us for the cider.'

I returned the card into the envelope, both gleefully happy and torn apart, made my excuses by explaining to Lottie that I really must return to servicing the aircraft—that sticky rudder came to my rescue again – and I explained that I would be out for the day. No one batted an eye at this. All they had ever known me do was walk for miles along the Cornish coast and tinker with my aircraft. As the Lanyons were neither walkers nor flyers, I had often spent much of my time during the day in Cornwall alone gathering my thoughts and healing my broken heart.

I dashed to my room to read the card again – slowly this time, drinking in every word. There was such a cocky confidence about his invitation and a secret intimacy, too. If Charles were to read it, he would think nothing untoward, but what Edward was really asking was to be alone with me one final time before I married.

There was only one thing to be done.

Without a moment's hesitation, I pulled on my flying jacket over my best trousers, blouse and cardigan and headed, as fast as my feet could carry me without actually running, down the road to Angels Cove.

I lost the final piece of my heart to Edward that day. And yet, the very next day found me standing on a small table in the garden room at Lanyon, with Katie fussing around me with pins in her mouth adjusting Lottie's cream cashmere suit. Lottie and Ma Lanyon looked on. I tried my best to smile, but my mind was a whirlpool.

I have often wondered if human attraction works in the exact same way as magnetic attraction and if this is why it is so utterly impossible to repel someone you are deeply attracted to. I knew I shouldn't see Edward again and yet the pull towards him was beyond my control. If the universal law of magnetism was involved, then it really wasn't my fault.

It was weak excuse but all I had.

And here was another – just as the north pole of one magnet will attract toward the south pole of another, so will the same polarity force each other apart, and I wondered if, with the introduction of Edward, Charles and I no longer attracted but repelled each other. In the evenings at Lanyon I tried my utmost to be near to him, to hold onto him, to be in love with him, but I couldn't. And the more I thought of Edward, the more Charles became pushed away. The physics of magnetism then, was my feeble excuse for my behaviour that day, my excuse for dashing to Angels Cove at the first possible moment, hoping to find Edward in the village hall.

But Edward was not in the hall. He was, I was told by a lady trimming the Christmas tree, most likely at his cottage, Angel View, a whitewashed cottage up a little track to right of the harbour. *And it's got the best view in the village* – said another lady who was hanging off a ladder hanging paper chains in the hall.

I had not yet been to Edward's home. Our meetings, although inwardly intimate – certainly intimate inside my thoughts and dreams, and I'm certain intimate inside of his – had been kept purely on a friendship footing, which meant keeping away from the privacy of his house. There had been no talk of love, no snatched kisses, no hand holding, just lots and lots of fun. Which was why, as I approached Edward's cottage, I felt nervous. I stood there for a moment, just short of the cottage and stared out to sea, at the islands, my confused thoughts bouncing around my head. The tide was out and the Angels – the three granite mounts I had used as a navigational aid just a few days before, when life had been so much simpler – stood proudly in the bay. They were larger when the tide was out and it was odd, but as I stood there and looked out to sea, with my coat fastened tightly against the freshness of the Cornish breeze, I wondered how on earth they had been given such a name and thought that 'angel' was far too beautiful a word to have been adopted for these ragged-looking islands, which seem to hide in every nook and cranny, some dark and foreboding secrets.

My thoughts returned to the present and to Edward and also to a story that Edward needed to be told. And yet it was a story I couldn't possibly tell him – a story I had promised never to tell. It was a story that promised to tie me to the house – to Charles and to Lottie – forever. And there was absolutely nothing I could do about it.

From the moment Lottie and I met, we were inseparable. We were for each other the sisters neither of us had ever had and despite my early misgivings, I loved my time in Paris and even felt the tug of my French ancestry calling me home. I spent every holiday with Lottie at Lanyon and became a welcome member of the family. Ma and Pa could not have been kinder and I became, without question, an accepted and loved member of the family. Those holidays at Lanyon were days of a privileged, gentrified youth – sailing on the river, a game of tennis, riding, croquet on the lawn – and although the loss of my parents could knock me sideways into a deep depressive abyss without a moment's notice, bit by bit, although the weight didn't lift completely, the grief became lighter as the months and years passed on.

My dream of flying as a career was not forgotten, but very definitely put on hold while I reluctantly did exactly what my mother had wanted me to do, transform into a lady. Ultimately – inevitably, perhaps – Lottie's brother, Charles, became part of the package. I suppose it was expected from the get-go that Charles and I would marry, and so when Charles kissed me one balmy June afternoon in 1938, I kissed him back with the mechanical acceptance of a woman who had known for some time that this moment would come and accepted it.

This, I said to myself, was love.

Love was two people who got along and, after an appropriate amount of time, kissed, and after a further appropriate amount of time, married and perhaps had children. It was a steadier romance than Lottie and I had imagined during our nights reading novels a school, but I didn't mind. My passion was reserved for flying and unlike Lottie, I had never actively looked for romance or expected anything other than that one day, I would perhaps marry the kind of man my mother had instructed me to marry – the non-predatory kind, the kind who would adore me to eternity.

Charles, very definitely, fit the bill.

Lottie, by comparison, was desperate to find the opposite kind of love, one that burned with the raging heat of a thousand furnaces and was determined not to settle for anything less until she found it. In late September 1938, while I took myself off on a flying tour around France with an old flying club friend, Lottie disappeared north to spend two months in Scotland on an estate belonging to friends of her parents – the son was deemed to be a suitable match. Bored by the son, Lottie found passion elsewhere, with another house guest, an eminent one, who was not only a married man and a charlatan, but also a high-profile politician, close to the Prime Minister himself. By November she knew she was pregnant and with her tail between her legs and her heart well and truly broken, Lottie dashed home alone.

There were no histrionics. A plan was hatched. A promise made. I would marry Charles earlier than planned and we would leave immediately for Oxford. The child would, after Lottie's confinement with an aunt in Yorkshire, be passed off as mine. My only proviso was that I would continue to fly. The child would be kept in the family at Lanyon. Lottie would be the doting aunt and everyone would be happy. And I had, until the moment I met Edward Nancarrow, in a breezy Cornish field just before Christmas, been, if not happy, then resigned to this arrangement. I owed it to them.

Determined to do the right thing for everyone concerned, I took the final few steps up the lane towards Edward's cottage and knocked on the door.

Edward sat in a chair across from me next to the fire and listened as I told him – not Lottie's story, I could never tell him that – but how I loved the Lanyons and how, no matter what, I intended to marry Charles. I explained that I was marrying not just the man, but the family – my family. I explained how well they had treated me and how much they relied on my substantial fortune to save the house and estate from ruin – relied on me to save the hard-working tenant farmers like Jessops from ruin, too.

When my story reached its natural end, he reached across the fire and took my hand.

'Are you in love with him?'

'I love him,' I answered without hesitation, and it wasn't a lie. 'He's a good man. And until recently, I believed myself to be in love.'

Edward released my hand and stepped over to the window.

'Your silence says everything there is to say, Edward.'

He turned to face me. 'I'd rather say nothing at all than say the wrong thing. With people like the Lanyons, I have found that it's generally best to keep one's own counsel.'

'The Lanyons? That's so dismissive. They're good people, Edward. Truly they are.'

Edward took a deep breath.

'All I know is they will stop at nothing to keep their house – their name – in order.' He sat down again. His voice was kind. 'Why are you here, Juliet, in my cottage, right now?'

Because I've fallen in love with you. Because you're my every waking thought …

'I wanted to explain.'

He stared out to sea before suddenly sitting forwards in his chair. He took my hands.

'What are you doing for the rest of the day?'

'Nothing much. I'm supposed to be working on the Moth. Charles is in Penzance making some last …' I

stopped, not wanting to speak about wedding preparations. 'At any rate, I shan't see him until dinner, I
suppose.'

'In that case, spend the day with me. Let's take one last
day just for us – one wonderful day together – a day to
last a lifetime. Let's coddiwomple together, one last time.
What do you say?'

I laughed at this.

He knelt by me and took my hands again. 'You know
why I said I'm a coddiwompler, Juliet?'

I shook my head.

'Because I've never wanted to become focused on any big
goals or aspiration. I've seen too many men forget to live
in the moment because all they can see are the goalposts
ahead of them. I live for today, right now. No promises.
No expectations.'

My mother would definitely have despised him ...

'Say you'll spend the day with me. I'll show you the
cove – the best bits – and you can take me flying. I'll grab
my camera. Do you like lobster?' His bright smile was
intoxicating. I nodded, my eyes swelling with tears.

This was how it was supposed to be, being in love.

'I love lobster.'

Edward took a handkerchief from his pocket again and
dabbed away my tears that now flowed freely. 'And we can
even sail on the river this afternoon,' he added, 'if it stays
fine. Did I tell you I have a little boat here? The Mermaid.
She's lovely. What do you say?'

I smiled perhaps the broadest smile I had ever smiled in my life. I should have said no. I should have run away as fast as my legs could carry me – I *still* knew absolutely nothing about him. And yet, I knew him as I knew my own reflection. Which is why I didn't say no.

Of course, I didn't say no.

'Oh, Edward,' I said. 'One wonderful day just for us? I'd absolutely love it.'

Chapter 11

Juliet

Magnetism

Oh, the impetuosity of youth!
   Scratch that.

Oh, the impetuosity of being in love, whatever the age of the lovers. I would have trampled my own mother to spend time with Edward that day. Why is it that we turn into foolhardy, live-for-the-moment and 'to hell with everyone else' children the very moment we fall in love?

Magnetism, again?

Whatever the answer, it was a wonderful day. But a great many things can happen in twenty-four hours ... in fact, not just in twenty-four, but in an hour or two, or even just in a minute. And by Christmas Eve everything in my life had changed in a way I could not possibly have imagined when I said yes to spending the day with Edward.

Our 'one wonderful day to last a lifetime' had proven

worthy of its name. We spent the morning as Edward had planned – exploring the cove, taking a trip in the Tiger Moth, lots of photographs and then lunch. It felt like the first day of a honeymoon – that carefree, selfish time of pleasing only ourselves. After lunch the weather closed in suddenly, as is its want in Cornwall, and we did not head down to the river as planned, but stayed indoors, resting by the fireside in the cottage. We read, we talked, we listened to the gramophone and bit by bit, the light that had shone brightly through the kitchen window in the morning – a light that held all the promise of a fabulous day in its fiery glow – faded, only to be replaced by thick fog that shrouded the Angels in a heavy and oppressive blanket of gloomy murk. The perfect flicker of candles and the glow of firelight only served to continue to wrap us in romance, and I loved every single moment of it.

The little Art Deco clock on the mantelpiece chimed four times when, with a heart made of lead, I rose from my place on the rug in front of the fire and began to gather my things. Edward took a vinyl from his collection and placed it on the gramophone. Standing slowly, he took me in his arms and without words we danced to Peggy Lee, *Linger In My Arms A Little Longer*. It was at that very moment, while resting my head on Edward's shoulder, that I was at my most happy and most sad, right then and there, in a little cottage called Angel View, with a man I had known for less than a week.

The song ended.

I stepped away from his embrace and in the firelight Edward said just four words, 'Don't marry him, Juliet.'

I kissed him then – the perfect kiss to end the perfect day – and answered in the only way I knew how.

'I won't.'

Holding my father's compass for luck, I dashed upstairs to find Lottie. Pa's motto, after all, was, 'when in doubt, don't!' And so, I wouldn't – I wouldn't marry Charles. I would call off the wedding. But I needed to find Lottie first. She would have to find a plan B.

I turned the door knob and stepped inside to find the shutters closed and her bedroom shrouded in darkness. Lottie's frame was highlighted from the light of the hallway. She was laying on her bed, her back to the door. I didn't turn on the light but crossed to the bed and shook Lottie gently.

'Lottie,' I whispered. 'Lottie ... there's something I need to talk to you about. Something I need to tell you.'

Lottie stirred.

'Juliet?' she murmured, in that confused, barely awake state. 'You've been gone all day. Where on earth have you been? Ma is starting to get a bit cross with you disappearing off all of the time, you know.'

'Never mind that now. Listen, about Edward Nancarrow. How well do you know him?'

Lottie raised herself up and rubbed her eyes. She turned to plump a pillow against the wooden headboard.

'Well, let's say I know him well enough to wish I wasn't pregnant so I could persuade him to take me out to dinner sometime. Why?'

'He's a good man, then?' I pressed.

'He seems so, yes, although no one seems to know much about him. He's rented that old cottage by the beach from Pa for about a year now. Pa knows him quite well, I think. He's quite old, though. At least thirty! But sexy as anything!' She giggled. 'But he's a bit of a charmer if you ask me, not that Edward Nancarrow could ever be in the running if you're thinking of pairing us up' – she glanced down at her belly – 'even if I wasn't in this damn pickle ...'

'Why not?'

She sat up further, more animated now.

'There's rumour that the American accent is fake. That he's actually German!'

'German?! No, not really?'

Lottie nodded.

'Really! And he's married, too. But it's an odd carry on if you ask me.'

And at that moment, with Lottie's words bouncing around the room like a stray bullet, my world fell apart.

Edward. Married.

Spend the day with me. No promises. Today, right now, that's all that matters ...

And then I turned to see Charles standing in the doorway, and when I saw the desperate expression on his face, I felt certain he knew about Edward. That's it then,

Juliet, I thought. The game is up. You're left with nothing and you deserve it.

But Charles didn't know about Edward. His anguished expression concerned another issue entirely.

Charles walked into the bedroom with his arms outstretched and directly behind him, Pa Lanyon appeared at the door, his face wet with tears.

Ma Lanyon, Charles explained, was in hospital, fighting for her life, and so was Katie. A car crash returning from Penzance, they said.

Taking in the scene as if watching from above, I saw my new family gathered around me in the darkness. They were people who had supported me through the worst news a young woman could ever have, the premature loss of her parents. I saw Lottie, too, asking frantic questions about her beloved Ma. Lottie, who was being forced into hiding in Yorkshire after Christmas because her illegitimate baby was beginning to show. And I saw Charles, trying to be brave standing side by side with Pa Lanyon, who was driven half-crazy with the worry of how to financially maintain an estate that since the end of the First World War had been unable to support its tenant farmers and staff. This family needed me as much as I had once had needed them.

Which was why, on Christmas Eve, while Ma Lanyon and Katie fought for their lives, I stood with Charles, Pa and Lottie outside a nondescript room in Penzance Town Hall, in my old tweed suit, waiting for a clerk to come and escort us in.

The clerk appeared at the door. 'It's time,' he said with an encouraging smile.

With no other friends or relatives around me, through silent tears I listened vaguely to the registrar as he talked us through the vows and eventually whispered the only words that were left for me to say ... 'I do.'

Chapter 12

Katherine

Finding Fenella

With the bubble caption of 'Don't marry him, Juliet!' floating above my head, I decided that I really did need to put down the manuscript and spend a part of the day out of bed. Reaching the bottom of the stairs, I noticed vaguely that a note had been pushed under the door. I meandered into the kitchen with the note in my hand and smiled at the elf – at least I still had *him* for company, even if he did wear the expression of an edgy sociopath. I picked him up, gave him a little kiss and sat him on the chair opposite. He smiled. I read the note.

Dear Katherine
My name is Fenella and I'm friends with Gerald. As there is no smoke coming out of your chimney, I assume

you must be freezing and possibly hungry. Come down and warm yourself by my Aga. A full breakfast is waiting for you in the bottom oven. Mine is the pink thatched cottage by the harbour on the corner. It's to the left of the shop (don't go in unless you want to spend a tenner on a tea towel. Tourists only).

Yours, F

Thank you, Lord!

I pulled on my boots, hat, coat and gloves and was out of the door and running down the track before the elf on the shelf (or the chair) knew what had hit him.

A ruddy-faced woman – the top of her head just about reaching my nipples – opened the door. She was wearing hair rollers, slippers and a blue tabard apron over Jazzercise leggings and a Christmas jumper (at least, I guessed it was a Christmas jumper, what with the shimmering antlers popping out of the top of the tabard). Her eyes shone with the unsquashed enthusiasm of an eager puppy.

'Hi,' I said, waving the note in my hand as if handing in a winning raffle ticket. 'I'm Katherine? Gerald's niece?'

She beckoned me in. 'Yes, yes. Of course, you are. Of course, you are. Come on in! Come on in!'

I ducked to pass under the door frame and stood in the hallway, being disrobed. Once shot of my coat, she took my hands in hers and blew on them. Her breath was like dragon breath on ice.

'Like two little blocks of ice, they are!' she chided. 'Never mind, we'll soon get that sorted out. Go on through to the kitchen. Terrible news about George, although what on earth Gerald was doing rushing off in the middle of the night – in the middle of the storm – to get to him, I will never know. But ...' she sighed, 'I suppose that's love for you. I'd have been the same if it had been the dog.' She shooed again. 'Go on through, go on through. You'll soon warm up in there.'

Stepping into Fenella's kitchen was like a re-entering the womb – swaddled, cosy and ever-so-slightly claustrophobic. She bustled towards the Aga, grabbed a mitt and bent – her rear end in the air – to open the bottom oven door. I pulled out a pine chair with a padded cushion on it, sat down with a contented sigh and tried to look around but couldn't as my eyes were fixed on a small, intricately carved wooden box sitting in the middle of the table. The brass nameplate on the front read:

My Beloved Monty
Rest in peace old friend

Ah.

I decided to leave Monty as the elephant in the room and looked away, only to notice a dog's bed by the Aga, which matched the empty water bowl sitting by the door and the lead hanging on a peg with a pair of battered walking boots abandoned underneath.

'Gerald said you need feeding up,' she said, placing a full English breakfast in front of me. She paused to take in my physique. 'But by the looks of you, you're not going to waste away any time soon. Tea?'

I looked down at my breakfast – the fried egg was utter perfection, and that's not easily done – and sighed yet another contented sigh. 'Ooh, yes please. That would be lovely.'

After five further minutes of bustle, Fenella eventually sat herself down across the table and watched me polish off my breakfast with the obvious delight of a woman who takes great pleasure in feeding people up.

'How was your first night in the cottage?' she asked, taking the wrapper off a Wagon Wheel.

I dabbed runny egg off my bottom lip with the back of my finger and tore off a piece of kitchen towel to use as a napkin. 'Oh, it was fine. Windy, but fine. Lovely place.'

'Best house in the village, most say. Best view, anyway. Not sure what Sam Lanyon's going to do with it, but there's not rush.'

'It was very good of him to let me stay.'

Fenella snapped the Wagon Wheel in half and dunked it in the tea before swallowing her first bite. My eyes narrowed in concentration as I watched the biscuit make its precarious journey from cup to mouth. Surely Wagon Wheels were not designed for dunking.

'Such a lovely man, Sam Lanyon.' The Wagon Wheel hovered by her lips. 'The ex-wife was an absolute dragon. Buggered off with another sailor, and all while Sam was away at sea, too. Horrible woman. He came back to an empty house. Kids gone. Just a note. Dreadful.'

She took a bite.

'How awful. How long ago was that?'

She swallowed. 'Ooh, ten years, give or take. Juliet was ninety then, but still going strong. Sam fell apart, but she kept him going, wouldn't let him give in. Got him to go travelling for a bit. He'll be home for good soon. After Christmas, according to Gerald.'

'Oh?'

'He's leaving the Navy and taking over his estate. Big deal round here, the Lanyons. But it's time he settled here, I think. The old house sold years ago, but the estate still carries on. Sam is the sole inheritor. It was always the plan that he'd have his time in the Navy then come home and run the estate. That's why Juliet insisted he spent time with the tenant farmers when he was young – learn their ways, you know. But she taught him how to fly when he was just a nipper, so I suppose he was always going to go off and spread his wings first. But he loves it here, though, so he does.'

Fenella silenced herself for a moment to dunk her Wagon Wheel again while I considered telling her the truth about my first night in Angel View – that I had sat up half the night reading Juliet's memoirs. But I didn't. I wanted to keep Juliet private for a little while and not risk her ruining the story for me with any little titbits here and there. We moved onto the apostrophe issue instead.

'The cove is nothing more than a village of old folks and holiday cottages now. All the young ones have left or been priced out. Such a shame. And I don't suppose the old folks have got anything better to do than argue. But not to worry,' she said, taking my plate and emptying the dregs of the teapot into the sink, 'because *you've* come to sort it all out for us, haven't you, lovely?'

'Hmm?' I took my third slice of toast and started to butter. 'Oh, yes, I suppose I have. Gerald wants me to come to some kind of dramatic conclusion at a meeting in the village hall, but now that he's gone to Brighton, I've no idea what will happen.' I twisted the lid off of a pot of home-made marmalade and spoke into the pot while scraping off a little mould. 'I suppose all I can do is make some notes during the next couple of days, chat to a few people and then offer my hypothesis to anyone who wants to hear it ...'

Fenella put the kettle back on the Aga and stood waiting for it to boil.

'Hypothesis?' She sniffed. 'That won't do. You need to be firmer than that or they'll eat you alive. No, you need to *tell* them what to do, no argument. That's what Gerald wanted. And they'll listen to you if you're firm – you should act a bit prissy. Gerald said you're a history professor ...'

Ah ...

'I'm afraid I'm not actually a professor as such. Just a teacher. Gerald has a tendency to ...'

'Play things up?' She grabbed a tea towel and began to wipe some plates.

'Exactly!' I laughed. 'My husband is ... *was*,' I corrected, '... the actual professor.' I smiled thinking of James. 'He'd have known exactly what to do. I gave up academia years ago when we got married. I think Gerald just wanted to add a bit of weight to my credentials with the professor thing.'

I glanced at the urn on the table. Fenella followed my eyes to their resting place. I smiled to show my silent understanding and noticed her eyes mist over. I swear I saw tiny little velvety strands of sadness seeping from her heart and winding their way across the kitchen into the little wooden box. The silence hung heavy. Fenella took a very large intake of breath through her nose and, try as she might to hold them back, within a few moments, the tears began.

'I just can't seem to able to pull myself together,' she said, leaning her back against the sink and dabbing her eyes with the tea towel. 'He's been gone for two weeks, but I just can't get over it – he was my best friend.' She took a photo frame from the windowsill and handed it to me. 'There he is, you see ... my perfect little man.'

A more ragtag of a dog the world had never seen, but you could tell in his eyes he was a sweetheart, and I swear he was smiling at the camera.

'Always there for me, he was' she said with a sniff. 'Always. Thick and thin, day and night, either sitting on my knee or by the side of the chair or the end of the bed.

Dogs only know love – how to love and be enthusiastic – that's all they know. And I keep on hearing his little footsteps padding around the house, then I hear him scratching at the door to get in, and I open it and he isn't there, just like my own little Cathy from *Wuthering Heights*. And I worry about him being all alone, you know ...' she glanced up and her voice broke revealing the deep and desperate outpouring of a broken heart. She dabbed her eyes again. 'And he hates to be on his own, hates it. He's never been left on his own, never.' She blew her nose on paper towel. 'Sorry, love. You don't need to hear all of this.'

'Don't be silly. I don't mind. Not a bit.' I sat immobilised by the impotency of the listener and began to finish my toast but then realised that eating during such a discussion was a bit ... irreverent. Fenella pointed to a pine shelf to the right of the kitchen window.

'See those boxes on the shelf?'

I twisted my neck to look. Three boxes (that looked remarkably like the one on the table) sat on top of a bigger box – which also looked like the little wooden box on the table.

'That's my life, that is ... my life in dogs. Every single one of them loved. And that's not all of them, either. The earlier ones were buried in the garden, bless them.'

The kettle began to whistle on the Aga. Fenella busied herself making a fresh pot of tea while talking. I stared at the boxes with the words, *my life in dog*, ringing in my ears. But I couldn't get my head around the bottom box. It was massive. What the hell kind of horse-dog needed a box *that* big?

Fenella read my mind.

'The bottom box isn't a dog, mind you ...'

'Oh?'

'It's my mother. She liked to have a dog sitting on her lap. And there they all are, sitting on her lap in heaven. How about a biscuit? Blue Ribbon? Rich Tea?'

Despite my enormous breakfast – and extra toast – I couldn't refuse a biscuit and it was definitely a Blue Ribbon kind of a moment (actually, it was more of a Jaffa Cake moment but I didn't want to be picky at a time like this).

'Oh, go on then.'

She jumped up and opened the larder.

'But to get another dog now ...' she said, finding the biscuit barrel, closing the door, placing it on the table and sitting down. 'I don't think I've enough time left. I'm eighty next and I'm not as steady on my feet as I used to be.' She let out a laugh. 'It'll be my own box up there soon, and I wouldn't want to go before the dog ... wouldn't be fair. No, it's time to put my walking boots away. I'll give them to charity.'

Charity? They were falling apart.

'Actually,' she crossed the room to pick up the boots. '– what size are you? *You* could have them. There's loads of miles left in these little beauties.'

'I'm a six.'

'Perfect! Take them with you when you go.' She put the boots back on the floor under the lead. 'But listen to me, moaning on ...' She poured the tea. 'Happy bloody Christmas, eh? Oh, by the way. Did Gerald say anything to you about the gin?'

Now we were talking!

The teapot was returned to the table.

'Gin?'

'Gin.'

I remembered Gerald's letter.

'I think he said there would be gin. Why?'

Fenella pressed her hands on the table to push herself up. I swear the woman never sat still for two minutes straight. She nodded her head towards the door.

'Follow me.'

I put down my biscuit and followed on. Fenella's small back garden was blessed with a twee stone barn. She took a flowerpot off the top of a milk pail and delved inside the pail. Having found what she was looking for – a key – she turned the key in the lock and opened the dilapidated barn door (which was so rotten the key was almost an irrelevance) and stepped inside. With a pride on her face usually associated with a new mother at a Christening, she pulled an old bed sheet away and revealed, of all things, a copper gin still and behind it, a small-scale bottling plant.

'Meet Maggie ...' she said, patting the shining copper still with affection. 'She's the crankiest old boiler in Cornwall, but I do love her.'

I shook my head. Amazed.

'You make gin?'

'Every year – *Christmas Spirit*, I call it.' She tapped her nose. 'Made from a secret family recipe. Not allowed to sell it, a course. Special friends only.'

'How much do you make? How many bottles, I mean?'

She hunched her shoulders and stuck out her bottom lip, thinking.

'I suppose I usually clear about ... five-hundred bottles?'

My eyebrows shot through the barn roof. Good. God. Just how many friends did she have?

Fenella threw the sheet back over Maggie, walked out of the barn and closed the door behind us.

'Can't be too careful,' she said, glancing around furtively before snapping the lock shut and leaning into me with a whisper. 'There's folk in this village would literally kill for this gin! Been desperate to get their hands on the recipe for years!'

Fully in cahoots with the village bootlegger, now, I nodded. 'Oh, I bet they would!'

We ambled back into the kitchen just as the fridge whirred up and the kitchen light came on.

'Ah, finally. It's back on. Thing is,' she said, not pausing to take a breath, 'There won't be any gin this year if I can't get a fresh supply of ...' She sniffed and her nose twitched.

'Of?'

She tapped her nose again. 'My secret ingredient.'

'Which is?'

She looked over her shoulder out of the kitchen window (you clearly couldn't be too careful in this rogue part of Cornwall) and then glanced back at me.

'Promise you'll keep it a secret?'

I crossed my heart. 'I promise.'

She grabbed the kettle again. The tea just never stopped.

'It's Seaweed. Now then. What do you think of that?'

I was pretty sure seaweed was put into other several, quite trendy, gins but chose to keep that little morsel to myself.

'Seaweed?' I confirmed, my eyes wide, playing along.

'Not just any old seaweed, mind you. I use a special kelp that's only found around here, on the other side of the Angles.'

'Ah, I know all about them,' I said, feeling like a local. 'They're the little islands in the bay.'

Fenella nodded.

'Thing is, I can only harvest my ...' she winked '... special ingredient, on the night of a spring tide, because it grows deep. Doesn't lay around on the beach like your common or garden kelp. Gerald normally takes out his canoe and gets it for me – I need to use it fresh, see, that's the secret.'

'And when is the next low tide – the spring one?'

'Tonight. And with Gerald away ...'

'With Gerald away?' I asked.

'He said you would go.'

'I would go?'

'When he dashed off, he said, not to worry, Katherine's done lots of canoeing, she'll do it.'

Lots? I'd done a five-day course in the Lake District ten years ago with James and his students and hated it.

'Well, it's got to be done by someone,' she said (quite forcefully I thought, considering I was a guest). 'I make a batch for the old folks' Christmas party every year, and I wouldn't want to let them down. It's for the forgotten ones.'

'The forgotten ones?'

'Those with no family, or family that don't bother with them. I sometimes think it's only my gin that keeps them going. It takes three days to make, so ...' She tailed off – literally – by disappearing into the hallway and returned holding a wetsuit. 'This should fit you.'

Holy crap.

I looked into Fenella's watery eyes. They didn't meet mine but travelled towards the little box on the table. If she hadn't nailed it with the story about the abandoned elderly, then she definitely had me with the dead dog. I glanced at the harbour through the window. There was still a bit of a swell going on, even in the shelter of the harbour.

'Oh, don't worry about that ...' she said, following my gaze. 'You'd be amazed at how quickly the sea calms down – with a southing breeze and a calm moon, she'll be as flat as a fart by teatime!'

I sighed. Defeated.

'OK, I'll give it a go.'

Fenella was about to make more tea but I stood up to leave. She followed me into the hallway and handed me my coat and the walking boots.

'Thanks so much for the food,' I said with a smile. 'You're an absolute life saver.' I put on my hat. 'What time shall I come back, later?'

'Seven o clock all right for you? The rest of the village will be tucked up in front of the telly or at the pub by then! Stray tourists don't matter, not that there are many around this year, what with not bothering with the light festival and everything.'

'Seven is fine.'

I stepped towards the door and put on my gloves.

'Oh, before you go,' she said, suddenly less bright. 'You wouldn't do me another little favour would you?'

I looked at her, standing there in her tabard and Christmas jumper. She really was such a sweet woman. I felt like I'd known her for a year, not an hour. I smiled.

'What?'

'Put Monty on Mother's knee, will you? I haven't had the heart to do it, but I think it's time.'

I crossed the room, picked up Monty and placed him in his final resting place, on the kitchen shelf.

'There you go, Monty,' I said, 'Time for a little rest.'

I turned to look at the dog bed by the Aga.

'What about everything else ... the bed, and the lead and everything. Do you want me to tidy them away?'

Fenella looked around and fought very hard to hold back the tears.

'Not just yet, love,' she said, glancing towards Monty's photograph. 'One thing at a time, eh?'

I thought of James and the things I had left littered around the house. I put my arms around her.

'Absolutely,' I said. 'There's no hurry. No hurry at all.'

Feeling my arms around her, Fenella began to cry – big heaving sobs of grief. Because that's the thing with grief, it's like the sand that gets stuck between your toes after the beach, you can never brush it all off in one go. And just when you think you got rid of it all, a little grain will still be there, catching on your sandal. One minute you're dunking a Wagon Wheel talking about gin, and the next thing someone unexpectedly puts their arms around you and you feel a bit of sand rub your toe and it's back to square one.

She set me off.

'I'm so very lonely,' I suddenly confessed, still leaning forwards, not sure whether I was holding Fenella or if she was holding me.

Fenella nodded into my chest and stepped back. She grabbed the warm tea towel off of the Aga rail and dabbed my eyes and then hers. It was quite a congested tea towel by this point.

'You're too young to be a widow. Far too young. But listen ... we might be a bunch of cantankerous, argumentative old so-and-so's hereabouts, but you've come to the right place. No one is ever on their own at Angels Cove, Katherine. Never. You'll see that I'm right. Now why don't you go for a good walk and clear your head a bit. You've got your new boots now.'

I found a stray hanky in my coat pocket and blew my nose.

'Walk? I wouldn't know where to go?'

'Any path out of the village will take you somewhere lovely, and anyway, it doesn't matter where you go, any dog will tell you that. Just sniff the air and enjoy it.'

As I turned the door handle and prepared to step outside, I realised that the moment I rested dear Monty's ashes on the shelf, something inside both of us had clicked, the energy had changed. There was a sudden feeling of ... of moving forwards. The door opened and as I took two steps out of the house the sun took two steps in and flooded Fenella with light. She looked just like an angel, and, in a way, she was. Stepping away from the cottage, in this strange village miles away from home and a little unsure of where to go, I thought suddenly of Edward and realised Fenella was right. It didn't matter in which direction walked, all that mattered was to walk with purpose, even if the destination was a vague one. And as I walked away from the house not really sure of where I was headed, I felt the eyes of Juliet looking down on me and wondered if she was with me, somehow, and if – just perhaps – in the passing of that moment in Fenella's kitchen, I, too, had taken a step towards becoming a coddiwompler.

Chapter 13

Katherine

Noel and Percy

I walked up hill, past the school, the village hall and the pub, half-expecting one of the apostrophe vigilantes to dash out of an alleyway and offer me a bribe, but I didn't see a single soul. I couldn't help but glance – OK, stare – though the cottage windows as I walked (stick a tree in your window and you're asking to be ogled, is my opinion) but most of the cottages seemed to be holiday lets with *Cornish Secrets* or *Cornish Hideaways* written on a plaque by the door and were empty. There were a few twinkling trees but absolutely no *Santa Stop Here!* signs in the gardens and no fake snow daubed round the edges of the windows. The website for Angels Cove I had googled the week before portrayed a different village entirely, one of sparkling lights, mulled wine and lots of people wondering around, smiling inanely. For a village that was famous for its Christmas Eve lights festival and all-round festive spirit, the whole effect was a bit of a damn squib. They really had thrown the towel in this Christmas.

I was just about to turn tail and head back to the cottage when Juliet flashed into my mind. I looked down the street and imagined her, walking to the village hall with Edward at Christmas. The view of the village from the top of the hill would have been more or less the same then as it was now. She would have walked with the same image painted in her mind. I liked that, it peeled away the years. The field where she landed the Tiger Moth would be just up the road, too, and I suddenly wanted to stand there, in the place where she stood, to find the exact place she met Edward, the place she fell in love, to absorb myself in someone else's love story for a while.

I marched up the road (Fenella's boots really were very comfy) which was tree-lined, meandering and steep. After ten minutes the woodland gave way to a wide expanse of fields. I stopped for a moment to catch my breath and take in the panoramic (if breezy) view of several miles of grazing land that gave way to the sea cliffs and, ultimately, the sea. The fields were ordered to perfection by a patchwork of Cornish stone hedges. A five-bar gate with a stile next to it appeared to my left. A signpost for the coastal path pointed over the stile into the field. I climbed over the stile and followed a well-worn groove in the grass. After backtracking towards the coast for a few minutes, the footpath began to follow the cliff edge. Veering away from the path

I crossed the field to a dilapidated barn in the far opposite corner. Could this have been Juliet's barn? Enormous doors banged in the breeze. Large round bails covered in black plastic had been stacked at the back of the barn. I leant against one of the bails and thought again of Juliet and Edward, how they had pushed her Tiger Moth in here that day in December when an unstoppable process began. The process of falling in love, an involuntary, nonsensical occurrence unmatched for its utter loveliness in the whole spectrum of human emotion.

Suddenly overcome with a wave of tiredness, with my eyes closed and enjoying the shelter of the barn, I decided to have a little lie down across the hay bales. I awoke some time later to the sound of the barn door banging in the wind and the feeling of a very wet nose resting on my face. I opened my eyes and found myself looking straight into a large and shiny brown eye.

I shrieked, which startled the cow who jumped backwards, which isn't easy when you're on four legs not two and weigh roughly the same as a small car. Having brought a few of her friends into the barn with her, the cow snorted before glancing at her pals as if to say, 'We've got a right one here, ladies!' I stirred myself, patted my new friend on the head, pushed past the lot of them and stepped out into the field.

An elderly man with a purposeful stride, wearing a red waterproof jacket with a white fur-lined hood and a woolly hat was crossing the field and heading towards me. I stood with the cows and waited as we watched him approach, our heads cocked collectively to the right. His beard was fluffy and sparklingly white. He stopped a few feet away to pat one of the more inquisitive cows before kissing another one on the head, which I thought was possibly edging towards over-friendly. He turned to me while continuing to fuss the cows as if they were a pack of Labradors. To be fair, they loved it.

'Hello,' he said. His smile was warm – genuine – the sort of smile you save for an old friend that's been out of your life for a while. He was the spitting image of someone I recognised ... someone famous ...

'You must be Katherine,' he said, slightly out of breath and smiling. 'Fenella phoned and said to look out for you on my walk. She knows I like a good stretch of the legs at this time of day. I'm Noel.' He shook my hand with a firm yank. 'Terrible news about George.'

I nodded in agreement and we made pleasant chatter about the weather until a cow from the back of the pack moved forward and nudged his arm.

'Hello, you,' he said, rubbing her head with both hands. 'Did I leave you out? I'm very sorry.'

'Are you heading back to the village?' I asked. 'Because if you are, would you mind walking across the field with me? These cows are lovely, but a bit ... over-friendly.'

'I'd love to,' he said, offering me his arm. 'And how do you fancy a spot of late lunch at mine, it's only cold meats and a bit of Christmas chutney, but there's something quite particular I'd like to talk to you about ... something Gerald said you might help me with ...'

I paused and thought of Gerald's warning – beware Noel and Percy!

'And would that particular something having anything to do with a rogue apostrophe, by any chance?'

Surprisingly, he shook his head.

'No, no. Not that – although it is very important to me, obviously. No, this something else, completely different issue – quite, delicate, if you know what I mean ...' He stopped walking. The cows and I stopped too and waited for him to carry on, which he did, after about thirty seconds, which a long time to stand waiting for a man to take his turn in conversation in an exposed Cornish field with the wind on your face. 'It's ... well, I've got a favour to ask ... something a little bit ... sensitive.' His eyes brightened. 'And Gerald did say you'd be happy to help. Didn't he mention it?'

I shook my head.

'No, I'm afraid he rushed off rather suddenly.'

His countenance fell. 'Of course, of course. Dear George.'

I took his arm again.

'But that doesn't matter. How about we head back to the village and you can tell me all about this favour over a nice cup of tea.'

He pulled a sleeve back to check the time on his watch.

'Or ... as it's over the yard arm. How about a tot of something more festive?' He winked and leant in. 'Gerald said you like a tipple, and I saved some of Fenella's gin from last year ...'

Gerald was in for a bit of a chiding on his return. Was nothing sacred in Angels Cove?

'... and I've got some of that new-fangled, trendy tonic water to go with it, just for you!'

Sold.

'So, tell me Noel,' I began, feeling like Dorothy when she'd picked up the scarecrow at the beginning of her own holiday in a strange land, before linking arms and heading down the yellow brick road (albeit with a few more cows in tow). 'Has anyone ever told you, you look exactly like Father Christmas ...?'

'A Tinder profile? That's what you want help with?'

Noel nodded and handed me a tumbler of gin.

'I'm struggling to upload a photo. Could you take one on your phone, perhaps of me laying on the sofa ...'

'But, Tinder? Are you sure, because Classic FM have a dating site that's, well, perhaps more suited ...'

He cut me short.

'I'm younger than I look ...'

I doubted it.

'Ok, well ...' I grabbed my phone. He combed his beard and draped himself across the sofa. 'Say cheese!'

Noel and I had a lovely couple of hours drinking gin while completing his online dating profile. When I asked what his accepted age bracket for his prospective partner was, he said, 'Eighteen to forty-five' which I thought a little wide, and perhaps optimistic for a seventy-eight-year old man, even if he did have elves and a red nosed reindeer. After a little polite persuasion, he eventually agreed to upping the age limit to fifty-eight – 'but no higher!' he said. 'Women go downhill rapidly after that. And I need someone young enough to keep up!'

And so, with a smile on my face and a gin-infused spring in my step, I clicked Noel's door behind me and carried on down the hill, only to be quickly seized upon by Percy, (who, if Noel was my scarecrow, must, therefore, be my tin man) who leapt out of his front garden gate as I passed by and invited me into his cottage for a festive glass of sherry and to meet his wife, Cherie.

A batch of tasty canapés had, quite coincidentally, just come out of the oven, he said. Seeing this as a perfect example of seizing on an unexpected opportunity and making the most of it (aka coddiwompling), I allowed him to guide me in.

Drinking sherry with Cherie was surprisingly enjoyable, but the arrival of a couple of apostrophe vigilante neighbours soon marred the experience. The conversation turned to the positioning of the 's' and I realised that my company had been sought for unscrupulous means. I was just about to pop my second prawn vol-au-vent into my mouth when, realising I was impervious to bribery (and possibly edging towards a conclusion that the apostrophe should go before the s), Percy saw that he was getting nowhere, took my glass from my hand and announced that I must be wanting to be on my way and I was man-handled out of the door moments later without much more than a bye or leave.

I never did warm to the tin man as much as the scarecrow.

I carried on down the hill, warmed a little by the gin and sherry and stopped by the harbour wall to assess the state of the swell. As Fenella predicted, it seemed the sea was now sleeping off the mother of all hangovers and had adopted a flat, calm, comatose, couldn't be arsed, state.

I really shouldn't have had that drink.

But I wasn't needed at Fenella's until seven, which meant I had plenty of time to sober up before foraging for seaweed. I settled myself at the kitchen table, flashed up the computer and was just about to email to Sam Lanyon when my phone pinged.

Uncle Gerald.

George stable. I've told him a thousand times to cut back on the port and cigars, not to mention the truffles he ships in from Harrods. Hope you're having a good time. Feel terrible to have left you on your own. I'll make it up to you. Any joy with the apostrophe? Did Fenella mention the seaweed? X

Blooming seaweed.

I opened my email and selected 'compose'. It was a fairly easy letter to write:

Dear Mr Lanyon

My name is Katherine Henderson and I'm the lady who is staying at Angel View this Christmas. Thank you so much for allowing me to stay in your beautiful cottage (I love it!), but I'm afraid I have a confession to make(and I may as well tell you before the elf grasses me up).

There was a shocking storm last night and to calm my nerves Uncle Gerald pointed me in the direction of whiskey in the sideboard and said that I was to help myself. The thing is, I stumbled across your grandmother's memoirs while taking out the whiskey and I'm so sorry but I'm afraid I started to read them, and now that I've started, I'm afraid I don't want to stop. I think I've fallen a little bit in love with Juliet, and was wondering if you would be kind enough to allow me to carry on reading her story. I know it sounds odd, but feel as though she is very much still alive within the cottage – like she could walk back in at any moment – which I know makes no sense at all now that she's gone.

I know you must be very busy, what with being at sea and everything, but it would be wonderful if you found the time to email back giving the green light for me to delve into your grandmother's fascinating life.

With very best wishes,

Katherine

P.S. Are you the same Sam Lanyon who writes the travel blog? I've been reading it.

P.P.S. I'm not a mad stalker, honest.

Sam's Christmas card was sitting on the table, resting against the vase. I opened it to find his email address – sam.lanyon459@mod.uk.gov

I pressed Send on the email and a grain of sand caught my toe.

My shoulders dropped about two inches and my poor damaged heart, held together with not much more than a bit of frayed garden twine, broke into yet more fragmented pieces. My longing for James, as ever, was triggered by the most obscure of things ... a photo, a song, a place or, in this case, a number – number 459.

James always left the house before me in the morning. He would often leave a post-it note stuck to the kitchen table with a random message written across it using text speak, which he knew I despised. On the morning he died, a bright pink note was stuck to the table with the numbers '459' written across it – no words just, numbers. Utterly confused and smiling to myself, I sent him a text:

459?

An hour later, he replied:

It means, 'I love you' x

On the day of the funeral, I still had no idea why 459 meant 'I Love You', but learned later from a student that 459 transposes to the letters 'ILY' on a telephone keypad. I loved it.

I grabbed my phone, meandered through to the lounge and did something I'd done at least once a day since James died – I scrolled down the messages list until I found James' name and opened up a long line of his old messages – his loving one-liners sent every single day. They were all committed to memory by now, and yet I still scrolled through them, smiling, aching, remembering. I sat in the lounge, warming my hands on the electric radiator by the window and glanced through the messages while looking up now and again to watch the sunset over the islands. My thoughts wandered from James to Juliet. This was the very window she looked out on that last day with Edward ... the same window, the same view, the same sun. I thought of the letter she had sent to herself, the letter on the fridge – a reminder to never forget him – and I knew exactly what she meant. But perhaps, living this way, with one foot in the past, was not quite healthy, not anymore. It was one thing to remember, and to remember with happiness, but another entirely to stick a pin in the world and stop it. Had Juliet sat at this window, whiling her life away remembering, scrolling through old letters, or had she gone out and grabbed life and left her time for remembering to the later years?

Desperate to read on and discover how – if – their relationship had developed, and half-hoping to find the permission to grab my life back again from within the pages of Juliet's story, I glanced at my watch and decided that one more excerpt from Juliet's story without permission from Sam wouldn't hurt, surely? After all, the elf was stuck in the kitchen and he would never need to know ...

Chapter 14

Juliet

Along came 1940

Mabel Juliet Lanyon was born on 18 July 1939, less than two months before the start of the war. I was in Yorkshire at Lottie's side during the birth and knew from the moment Lottie held Mabel in her arms that she would never let her go, which was, for me, an absolute and blessed relief. Lottie argued (rather macabrely) that with the war with Germany practically unavoidable now, even if it lasted just a few months, by the end of it, lots of young women would find themselves widowed with fatherless children, and Lottie could easily be just another one of them. Her calculated approach confounded her mother, who had survived the accident and was convalescing at Lanyon, but was far too weak to argue.

It was decided that Lottie and Mabel would continue

to lie low with the maiden aunt for a couple of years, and eventually the story would be passed around that Lottie had married in Harrogate after a whirlwind romance with an Army officer who had died in the war, and she would eventually return to Lanyon, legitimately – if fictionally – widowed.

After Charles and I wed, a significant part of my inheritance was handed to Pa Lanyon, which left Charles free to follow his own dream – to join the Royal Navy as a warfare officer. In September 1939, at the very beginning of a war no one could guess would be even longer than the last, I drove Charles to the British Royal Naval College Dartmouth and waved him off at the start of, what Charles and Pa Lanyon believed, would be a sparkling military career. I did not for one second find difficulty saying goodbye. Despite trying to force the memory of Edward out of my mind, he lingered on – in replayed conversations, in a remembered smile, a walk or a song.

But with Charles gone, I had no intention of returning to live at Lanyon, as was expected, because I did not want to risk seeing Edward in the village – so desperate, in fact, that immediately after the wedding I had insisted we begin our married life in a rented house near my old family home in Oxfordshire.

By the Autumn of 1940 I was living alone at an absolute loss as to what to do to pass the time. Helping the war effort was paramount in my thoughts, but in what capacity? I was qualified to do one thing – fly. But the War Office remained insistent that women would not be allowed to fly in combat, or in any capacity within the RAF or the Fleet Air Arm. I could join the WAAFs in a non-flying capacity, but to sit at an air station and watch all the men fly while I polished their shoes? Never!

I had lunch in Southampton with an old friend from the flying club my father patronised. I chomped my gums throughout the meal, moaning with venom about my utter frustration at not being allowed to fly in the RAF, despite being more qualified and a better pilot than most of the men. Janie, whose father was in the War Office and was well up on opportunities for women, offered solutions, and they didn't include polishing shoes.

There were many opportunities open to women, she explained, but if I was determined to fly, then the options were limited – limited, but not none existent. For a start, I could volunteer to fly a target-towing aircraft over the Solent.

'It can be a bit hairy,' Janie said, 'what with the aim of the trainee gunners being a bit off-centre to start with, and you'd need to fly your own aircraft, but the pay's jolly good and at least you get to fly. Have you still got that darling yellow Tiger Moth?'

I did. It was in the barn at Lanyon.

'Next?'

Janie scratched her chin.

'Well, you could always join the Free French. The French are more like the Poles and the Russians – you know, not sniffy about women pilots – but it's a bit radical, Juliet. Better off as a target tower if you ask me. But the absolute best thing you could do ...' Janie paused to scrape the frothy milk out of the bottom of her coffee cup, 'is what I'm thinking of doing ...' Janie paused again to add just the right amount of dramatic effect.

'Go on ...'

'Join the ATA,'

'The ATA?'

'Air Transport Auxiliary. They deliver aircraft from the factories to all the air bases – move aircraft around the country for maintenance, that kind of thing. They're letting a few women in as pilots now – I suppose they've got to, there simply aren't enough chaps around to meet demand, these days.'

Janie grabbed her clutch bag, snapped open the fasteners, took out a newspaper clipping and rested it on the table in front of me.

'There you go.'

Wanted

Women pilots to fly for Air Transport Auxiliary
Salary £400 per year
Further details write to: PO Box 410

I sat up straight.

'But ... this is incredible, Janie! Where are they based? When do you think I can start? Oh, Janie.'

'Steady on, old girl. They haven't let you in yet.'

I thought of something – the excitement of which I could barely contain. 'Oh, my God! Are we going to be allowed to fly the Spitfire? Because honestly, Janie. I would do anything – anything – to fly one of those.'

'I'm not sure, maybe,' Janie answered, pouring the last of the coffee. 'The first tranche of women have only just joined – they're at Hatfield. There's around, oh, I don't know, a thousand or so men dotted about the different delivery pools – they're all the chaps who are either too crock or too old to join the RAF. I'll bet the women get stuck delivering the old Tiger Moths – the RAF use it as their training aircraft. I know yours is a little beauty, but in the winter, they really are cold, breezy old things.'

'Moths? But I wouldn't mind that in the least! And at least we'd be flying again, Janie. That's all that matters, surely?' I ran a finger over the advertisement. 'Being grounded is damn well killing me!'

Janie tipped her head sideways.

'What will Charles make of it, do you think?'

I shrugged. Charles wouldn't give too figs.

'He'll be fine about it. Definitely. He's quite a modern man, you know.'

'But what about his family? Didn't you say they're a bit straight-laced. They might not be impressed. You're a married woman now – lady of the manner and all that. It was one thing to fly under the banner of your dear old Pa, but they might not like this, Juliet ...' Janie took the advertisement out of my hand and looked at it. 'It's all so very ...'

'So very, what?'

'Well, it's very ... I don't know, masculine, I suppose.'

I laughed.

'Oh, Janie. There's a war on. Absolutely everything women do these days is masculine. It's the only upside of having this damn war in the first place!' I took the advertisement back.

'Can I have this?'

She shrugged. I took it as a yes and tucked the scrap of paper safely into my handbag.

'Mark my words,' I said. 'Pretty soon, they'll realise just how much they need us.'

'Us?'

'Women! Janie. Women! WAAF, Land Army, factories ... you name it, women are doing it all nowadays, and doing it well, too.' I leant in and whispered. 'And I for one fully intended to make the most of it!'

Chapter 15

Juliet

Attagirls!

Some days come along in life that are so significant they stay with you for eternity. Such days remain as bright and clear in my mind's eye now as on the day itself and usually fall into two categories – days so terrible I would rather forget them, or days so wonderful I want to remember them forever. The day I flew a Spitfire for the first time fell into the latter category. It was the day I fell in love all over again and it was made all the better for sharing the experience with my wonderful new ATA friends, the ultimate Attagirls, Anna and Marie.

'I don't think I can do it,' Anna said, her right hand to her forehead, shading the sun. We watched Marie as she completed her first circuit of the airfield. Anna's left hand still in mine. I squeezed her hand gently.

'Yes, you can. I know you can. You're every bit the pilot I am.'

She looked at me. Her face puce.

'All right,' I admitted, 'perhaps you're not *quite* as confident as me, but you haven't had the same amount of experience in the seat, that's all.'

We'd met several months before, Anna, Marie and I, in London at Austin Reeds Taylors. We were being kitted out for our ATA uniforms – navy worsted suits and forage caps. Anna and I were to be based at the all-women ferry pool at Hamble, but Marie was set for White Waltham, which had male pilots too, much to Marie's delight. We cut quite a dash in our gold-trimmed uniforms, a uniform guaranteed to provide limitless male attention and a seat at the best tables in town.

Anna was Canadian. A more practical, kind, straight-talking woman you would never meet. We had a great deal in common, Anna and I. Her father had taught her how to fly on the family farm and had also died suddenly just a few years before. Marie was American. When we asked her where she was from, she simply answered, 'Money'. She placed everyone she met into one of three categories – a Honey, a Hottie, or a Sonofabitch. Her family originated in Texas, where she learned to fly, but she had spent a great deal of time in Manhattan and socialised with the kind of people a woman of her wealth and status was attracted to. Bored to death with her life as a socialite and desperate to do her bit in Europe, from across the Atlantic she had heard the cry for ATA pilots and, sensing the adventure of a lifetime was just an ocean away, had jumped aboard *The Beaver* bound for Liverpool and risked a perilous journey across the Atlantic, dodging German U-boats, in order to join the cause.

Marie was something of a celebrity in certain flying circles (mainly due to an episode crash landing her Gypsy Moth in the African bush and spending a night with a Masai herdsman) which was an image that did not quite ring true with her perfect coiffure and manicured nails – always painted pillar-box red ('because you never know when the next hot guy might happen along'). Anna and I were both a little in awe of her when we bumped into her that day at Austin Reeds, but we soon found ourselves scooped up under her protective wing, heading, right there and then, in fact, to her flat in Chelsea for cocktails before venturing out into the blacked-out London night dressed in our new uniforms.

And now, here we all were, together again at the Central Flying Training School, RAF Upavon. The three of us having been selected for a flying conversion course to learn to fly the most iconic and beautiful flying machine ever created – the Supermarine Spitfire. Edward was right, if you dreamed hard enough, the very best things really could happen.

For the first few days our feet were kept firmly on the ground, spending time in a classroom or in a hangar listening to our RAF instructor, learning the basics. But there was no substitute for the real thing and today – 21 March 1941 – was one of the best and most important days of my life, because today was the day I would fly the Supermarine Spitfire for the first time. I could not wait to jump into that wonderful little cockpit, start her up and hear the sound of the Merlin engine purring through my soul. But Anna's nervousness was not without merit. The first flight was to be a solo flight because all the aircraft at Upavon were single seat, which meant that there was no room for an instructor in the back, which meant there was no room for error, either. Going solo would require a strong nerve and absolute confidence.

Carrying our parachutes over our shoulders while walking out to the line, we met our instructor on the apron. He was a dour and aging Squadron Leader called McCormack (or to Marie, 'that damn, condescending sono-fabitch') who was afflicted with a dodgy limp and an eye for Anna's more than ample bust. I couldn't work out if he was simply a miserable and disillusioned old man, or if he had taken a disliking to us as women pilots. We were, after all, driving a coach and horses through what had been a bastion of manhood. Whatever his problem was, we didn't care, because McCormack was nothing more than a means to an end to us. This was our moment and we were going to make the most of it.

A Spitfire sat on the line, shimmering in the sunshine, waiting. Marie and I danced with excitement while listening to a final chat from McCormack. We were to take turns to get airborne, fly two circuits of the airfield, then land – that was it. He glanced pointedly between myself and Marie – no heroics, he said, and no showing off. I stood between my two friends and took their hands in mine while we listened. Anna's hand was shaking.

At the end of the chat, we were left to decide between us the order in which we would fly. Anna had no intention of going first, but Marie and I (who had eyed each other with a good-natured but steely competitiveness since the day we met) spoke over each other volunteering to go first, neither one prepared to back down. The instructor took a shilling out of his pocket and flipped it. Marie called heads. She won.

She *whoopee*-d, tapped me on the backside and walked towards the Spitfire with a wink and a wiggle that left the ground crew drooling. Marie paused by the port wing, taking out her Ferry Pilot's notes, before completing her outside checks. With a final salute in our direction, she climbed onto the wing, slipped into the cockpit and started her up. With the sound of the iconic Spitfire engine echoing through the station, Marie taxied across the grass strip, turned the aircraft into wind, opened the throttle, hurtled down the runway and was airborne with her wheels retracted before the paint on her fingernails would usually have had the time to dry.

The sun glinted off the airframe, highlighting her curves in all the right places, and just like Maire on a Mayfair dance floor, the Spitfire glided around the sky with a style and panache guaranteed to turn every head in the crowd.

'I honestly don't think I can do it.'

I took Anna by the shoulders as Marie turned downwind to land.

'What is that you're frightened of? Crashing?'

'A little, maybe. But it's not just that, Juliet. What if I messup, make a fool of myself and ruin it. This is such a big deal, you know, for womankind, I mean.'

'Womankind? Isn't that a bit ... dramatic?'

'No, I don't think it is.' She nodded her head in the direction of the ground crew. 'Just look at that pair, over there, sniggering, waiting for us to fail. And it's such a powerful machine, Juliet. I've never flown anything anywhere near as fast as a Spitfire.'

'Neither have I! None of us have. But you aren't going to open up the throttle and dash off into the sunset. We have to stick to 250 mph in the cruise, remember, and you aren't even going to get anywhere near that in the circuit. And honestly, Anna, all you really need to know for the sort of flying we do is the take-off speed, the stalling speed and that landing speed. That's it.' I turned to face the airfield to watch Marie land. She bounced a bit and we both laughed.

'It's just another aircraft, Anna.' We both knew this was a lie. 'It has an engine, two wings and wheels. Come on, give it a go, what do you say?' I nudged her playfully, 'I'll let you have my chocolate ration next month if you come back alive ...'

Anna smiled and sighed.

'Oh, all right. I'll give it a go. But you go next. I need a little bit longer to pull myself together.'

Marie taxied in and cut the engine. She was buzzing when she jumped out.

'Jeez Louise, that was fantastic!' she said, throwing her arms around the instructor, who balked and blushed. Despite his gruffness, I was surprised to see that he was pleased that Marie had cracked it, and maybe even a little proud, too. Maybe we were beginning to break through?

'They're right when they say she's a bitch on the ground and a babe in the air,' Marie said, taking off her helmet. 'And watch the rudder, it's a bit over-sensitive, and there's a hell of a kick back when you let off the brakes, but oh my, Juliet, the power in that thing! And she's a talkative gal, too. She'll shudder just before she stalls so watch for that, and that damn nose is heavy on the ground, so steady on the brakes after landing. But just wait till you feel the power – the power, Juliet—'

Marie stopped talking then, suddenly speechless. 'Well, what you waiting for, honey. Off you damn-well go and see for yourself ...'

I kissed Marie, hugged Anna who was still puce, and walked into the best dream of my life, just as Marie turned to McCormack and said, 'Say, Sweetie, can I do that again?'

From the very first day of flying for the ATA I knew I'd found heaven. Working with women of my own ilk, fellow women pilots, most with wild and sometimes quite notorious flying and socialite backgrounds like Marie, who simply wanted to continue to fly, was wonderful. Yes, we wanted to help the war effort, of course we did, but it was pretty obvious that the initial group of women ferry pilots were flying addicts, every last one of us. I at once gave up the house in Oxfordshire and took out a lease on a pretty cottage by the river in Hamble, inviting Anna to lodge with me.

Hamble sat on the neck between the Solent and the Hamble river, conveniently close to the Spitfires that were built at the Vickers Supermarine works in Southampton. Despite the horror of the Luftwaffe bombing campaign just a few miles away in Southampton, living at Hamble was a little like holidaying at a seaside resort and sometimes, just for a just moment during the day, it was possible to sit by the river and watch the birds and the occasional boat go by and pretend that all was well. But then the barrage balloons would go up, which were a frightening blot in the skyline for a pilot, or we would hear the ack-ack target practice on the Solent, or worst of all, a Luftwaffe raid on Southampton would hit, and we were catapulted straight back into the nightmare again.

But despite all of this, the atmosphere at Hamble was calm, professional and buzzing with the excitement of a group of women who were finally being allowed to show their metal. We were a fabulous band of sisters – the Attagirls. British, Polish, Canadian, American, Dutch ... women pilots from all over the globe who had responded to the call to arms (or if not 'to arms', then 'to fly', at least), and although our monthly pay cheque was considerably less than our male counterparts for quite some time, I don't believe any of us really cared. They could have cut our pay entirely and we would still have flown.

My friend Janie had been quite correct when she guessed that we would spend the first few months delivering the Tiger Moth to RAF air stations around the country. I didn't mind. I loved the Moth. Yes, one winter I had to be lifted bodily out of the cockpit due to having frozen into a solid block flying to Scotland, but at least the aircraft had been delivered – that was the important thing. One moment I might be landing at an air station like RAF Brize Norton and then, quick as a flash, I would be jumping into the taxi Anson, which was a little transport aircraft used to ferry the ATA pilots around, and dashing back to Hamble before jumping in another Moth and heading off somewhere else entirely. It was wonderful to finally have purpose all of my own and not be defined by the rank and status of a husband, or even worse, a house.

Trips to Scotland or the North of England sometimes required an overnight bag and a long, cold train trip back trip to Hampshire the following day, and there had been a (quite significant) degree of chauvinism to deal with initially. The ground engineers would occasionally jibe, 'where's the pilot, love' when looking up to see a woman take off her flying helmet, and then there was the issue of a lack of ladies' lavatories at many of the air bases to contend with, but we were all just so ecstatic to be flying again. And there was something else that pushed us on too – an absolute determination not to let the side down – of not wanting to ever make a make a mistake and give ammunition to those – and there were many of both sexes – who objected to women being employed as pilots.

But flying for the ATA didn't come without a significant amount of danger. We flew with no radio and no navigational equipment to guide us to our destination, only a map and a compass. Instruments were fitted in the panel in the cockpit, but we were never taught how to use them which meant flying hundreds of miles across the country, dodging cloud, skimming trees and – unable to get weather updates while airborne – hoping the weather stayed with us.

Should we have been taught how to fly on instruments? Yes, I do believe we should, but such training would have taken time and money – the ATA had neither. Which left us to deliver our aircraft navigating by the seat of our pants, using rivers, roads and railway lines to guide us to our destination.

We were sitting ducks for the Luftwaffe and for friendly

ack-ack units (who occasionally got their aircraft recognition wrong), both of which led to the shaky return of many an ATA pilot who had been taken aback to see a friendly tracer flash past a vulnerable wing. It was only our sense of adventure combined with bloody-minded guile and resilience that got us from A to B and kept us going.

It was amazing!

With a last look at my Ferry Pilot Notes I took a tour of the Spitfire, talking my time, drinking her in, admiring her, sitting as she was with her nose in the air, snootily checking out the competition. But she knew she was in a league of her own and in terms of simple beauty, could never be matched. The men who had gathered to watch our first flights – pilots and ground engineers, mainly– still loitered, but it didn't bother me, I was used to performing in front of a crowd, part of me even revelled in it. With a quick step onto the wing I climbed in and felt at home immediately. The cockpit was no wider than my shoulders – it was the glass slipper to my Cinderella foot, the feel of a perfectly fitting glove on a delicate hand. Aircraft were not generally designed with women in mind but we all knew that the Spitfire was a much better fit for a woman that a man. I was in a cocooned haven of total harmony and synchronisation. She was heaven on earth and I loved her.

I started her up. Once awoken, like me, she trembled with an urgency to be in the air. Leaving the canopy open as we always did for take-off in case of the need to bail out,

I gave the signal to the ground crew to remove the chocks and excitement had to be replaced by a steely nerve and calm practicality. Taxiing was tricky. Her long nose, pointing upwards, meant the need to weave right and left to check that that the taxiway ahead was clear – and by goodness, she got into a strop if she had to sit on the ground too long – but I didn't keep her waiting. The runway was a simple grass strip which meant, with a lean out of the cockpit to have a quick check ahead of me, after a short taxi, I turned the aircraft into wind and prepared myself for the most significant moment of my life.

Letting off the brakes, the kick Marie warned me of threw me back into my seat, and after a gentle pull back on the stick, moments later I found myself airborne, the iconic curves now invisible to me. All I could see was the black, curved instrument panel and a whole heap of sky around me – but my goodness she was responsive. Given half a chance, I really would have opened her up and burned off into the sunset, but not today. As McCormack had said, today was not about heroics. Today was for two perfect circuits and a landing.

There have been times in my life when I have needed to go to a happy place – to cheer myself with a memory – and the memory that always comes back to me is this one. If the day ever comes that I can no longer remember my first flight in a Spitfire, that is the day I want to die. Unlike any other love affair, the Spitfire has never broken my heart and the memory has never been bittersweet – her love was reciprocated and equal in every sense – it was just me, the machine and the sky, flying in harmonious perfection, together, as one.

Anna was no longer puce, but a sickening shade of grey/green when I climbed out of the Spitfire and crossed the grass – beaming – to join her. It was clear that McCormack – who was beginning to doubt Anna's ability to go solo – was arguing the toss with Marie who was asking for the crowd to be dispersed before Anna took to the skies. It took us half an hour to persuade her to fly, but finally, after many deep breaths and a 'You're a damn Canadian, for Christ's sake! Show these Brits what you're made of and pull yourself together,' sharp slap from Marie, the shaking Anna, mustering every ounce of courage she would ever need in her life, climbed into the Spitfire cockpit and started her up. Despite our bonhomie, Marie and I were also shaking while Anna weaved her way across the grass to position herself for a take-off run. She seemed to sit there, considering her take-off, for an age.

'Come on, Anna ... get that sonofabitch into the air, you damn Canadian woozy!' Marie shouted across the airfield.

I wasn't sure that would help.

But Marie was right, Anna did need to get going. We knew the Spitfire hated to sit on the ground once the propeller was running and could over heat if the pilot dallied for too long. It was a tense and uncomfortable couple of minutes, but the stoic Anna finally rallied, let off the brakes, powered through and took to the skies like a beautiful, graceful swan. And when she landed ten minutes later and the propeller had stopped and the chocks were in, Marie and I dashed to the Spitfire, lifted Anna into the air and bounced her around the airfield like a conquering Olympian. I have never, in my life, been so proud, of anyone. Every part of Anna's body and soul had been petrified of flying the Spitfire alone that first time, and she knew that she carried the weight of responsibility – for womankind, no less – to prove that women could fly every bit as well as men.

And by God, she did it, too.

From that moment on the three of us called ourselves the Spitfire Sisters – true Attagirls. We were bound together for eternity in the way that only those lucky people who have experienced an incredible moment together can be. On completion of the course, Anna and I returned to Hamble and Marie to White Waltham with a promise to meet as often as we could in London. No longer restricted to flying the Tiger Moth but qualified to fly all aircraft of a similar type, including the Hawker Hurricane, we felt that we had finally earned our ATA golden wings.

Chapter 16

Katherine

Seaweed

She flew a Spitfire! A bloody Spitfire. I lay the manuscript down with the realisation that Juliet Caron was nothing short of a wonder woman – a true heroine, a goddess!

But Juliet's story would have to wait, because a little adventure of my own awaited me. It was time to head down to Fenella's, have a quick lesson in how to tell my bladder wrack from my three cornered leek, jump into a wetsuit and go foraging for seaweed, and all because the residents at the local home for the elderly wanted to get smashed off their tits on bootleg gin this Christmas (even as the sentence formed in my head, it seemed ludicrous). Also, I was pretty certain there were laws against collected sea weed, which made me a potential criminal in anyone's book. But if Juliet could fly a Spitfire for the first time solo, surely, I could paddle a few yards out to sea to grab a bit of seaweed ...

The door clicked shut behind me and I headed down the lane. The cloudless sky allowed the moon to act as my flashlight for the evening, albeit a flashlight equipped with a low-watt, energy saving bulb. But there was something very special about the sea tonight, lapping in moonlight, and I was just about to take a few seconds to imagine canoodling with James on the harbour wall (I knew it was self-harm but the thoughts would come) when my moment was smashed by Fenella, who was standing at her front door and beckoning me to hurry up while furtively glancing up and down the harbour, looking for all the world like a silent movie villain.

It took ten minutes to yank the wet suit over my thighs. Fenella tried to help but gave up and disappeared off with a chunter, muttering something about too many biscuits. She wandered into that dark place she often retreated to – not the deepest recesses of her mind, but a place shrouded in awe and mystery nonetheless, a place also known as 'the back room'. I was standing in front of the Aga (a bad idea) jumping up and down trying to get the crotch of the wetsuit to marry-up with my own crotch when Fenella re-appeared from 'the back room' holding, not just a life jacket, but fisherman's socks, wellies, a head torch, Gortex gloves and an elf. The elf, who was the size of a human toddler, was tucked under her right arm. She put all her accoutrements down on the table, sat the elf on a chair, opened a drawer and took out some scissors.

She moved towards the elf and positioned the blades against his throat. I swear his little eyes widened in terror, but I could do nothing to help. My arms were trapped inside the wetsuit which was only half-up.

'Stop, Fenella! In the name of all that is Christmas, stop!'

She looked up, nonplussed, the scissors remained only a fraction away from the elf's terrorised face.

'What?'

'You can't dismember an elf ... it's ... it's ... well, I'm not sure what it is, but it's not right, especially this close to Christmas.'

'But I need his hat.'

Don't ask why. It will be nonsense.

'Why?'

'Gerald always canoes to the island wearing a hat with a bell on it. But it's his own hat. I haven't got it.' She nodded towards the elf. 'So, I thought we'd use this one.'

I was definitely going to need Botox. My whole face was crunched into the shape of a question mark.

'Again ... why?'

It seemed perfectly obvious to Fenella. She sighed and spoke in the tone a teenager uses when explaining how to use the iPad to his mum. 'When I do this with Gerald, I stand in my front bedroom with the window open and listen for the bell ... when I hear it, I know he's on his way back, which is when I dash down to the harbour to grab the bag of seaweed. Gerald calls it a ... what's the word ... a *covert* operation.'

Utterly ridiculous.

157

'Tell me Fenella, just a thought, but has Gerald usually had quite a bit of gin to drink by the time he canoes off into the moonlight.'

She shrugged.

'He might have had the odd tipple, here and there. It *is* Christmas.'

I managed to yank the wetsuit over my left shoulder and wriggled around a bit in an attempt to persuade the whole thing to rest in a more comfortable position. 'Ok, fine,' I said. 'But just leave the poor thing intact and I'll take him with me. I'll shake him as I paddle back.'

I put on the socks and wellies (I was pretty sure wellies and canoes didn't usually mix, but I was well-past the point of caring) and five minutes later saw me ready for my mission and standing at the door with a life jacket over my shoulder and an elf under my arm, not quite an Attagirl, but not so very far off, I thought.

I was so right. Wellington boots do not mix well with a canoe. Not one bit. They were full of water by the twenty-metre point. The good news was that the moon was so full and so bright, I could easily see where I was going without the head torch and had harvested a bag of seaweed (the special kind my arse!) in less than half an hour.

We didn't waste any time on pleasantries when I brought the canoe alongside the harbour wall and with a sudden outburst of Herculean strength, Fenella hiked the canoe and paddle out of the water, stowed it next to a gig boat and had grabbed the bag of seaweed out of my hand (with a swift backwards glance over her shoulder) before I had time to remove my life jacket. She dashed into the house leaving me to follow on behind.

I walked into the kitchen to find a very large pot of water boiling on the Aga. She tipped the seaweed onto the kitchen table and took two pairs of scissors out of the drawer.

'Get snipping,' she said. 'Small sections, like this ...'

She cut a piece of seaweed roughly two inches square and held it up for me to examine.

Seemed simple enough. A pile of freezer bags sat on the worktop. She grabbed one.

'Put two pieces of seaweed into each bag, squash the air out of the bag, seal it and put the bag in the pot – we'll weigh the bags down later with a tin of beans.'

'How long do the bags stay in the pot?'

'About twenty minutes,' she said, already processing the seaweed like an automaton.

I put the scissors down and removed my life jacket.

'Ok. Just give me minute to get changed,' I said, moving towards my clothes that lay over a kitchen chair.

'No time for that!' She waved the scissors in my direction absently. 'You're fine as you are. Time's money!'

Now, I didn't know where the dear old lady I met that morning had gone, but she seemed to have been replaced by a mafia don. I took a stand by sitting down.

'Well, at least give me time to get out of these wellies,

Fenella.' I began to remove my right boot. 'My feet are like ice and I'm sorry, but my hands couldn't actually hold a pair of scissors properly at the moment even if I tried. I'm frozen through.'

She put down her scissors and shuffled into the back room, reappearing almost immediately with a knock-off pair of Ugg boots and a gin bottle with *Christmas Spirit* written on the label.

'Put them on then,' she said, a little brusquely, I thought, 'and stand by the Aga for a moment. But don't heat up too quickly or you'll get chilblains.'

My feet slipped into the wool-lined boots like they'd been given a first-class ticket to heaven – a really fluffy heaven. A heaven where little feathery angels fed you chocolate and selected the best programmes on Netflix while massaging your shoulders.

Fenella put the bottle on the table.

'Last year's gin,' she said with a wink (what was it about Fenella's particular brand of gin that led everyone who drank it to wink) before filling a small pan with milk and placing it on the Aga top plate. 'But first,' she said, opening a cupboard and taking out a purple container with Cadbury written across it, 'let's get something warm inside you. Cream and a flake, do you?'

My eyes widened to dinner plates.

'Cream and a flake would do me very nicely, thank you, Fenella.'

Feeling warmer just at the notion of hot chocolate I

picked up the scissors and, like the obedient worker bee I'd become, started to snip.

It was one a.m. when, still buzzing with the night's shenanigans, I turned the key to Juliet's cottage. It was cold inside (those old-style Economy 7 heaters never did cut the mustard), but after the heat of Fenella's kitchen (Did I say kitchen? I meant sweatshop!) and two glasses of *Christmas Spirit*, I was happy to cool down a little. Needing to take a moment to calm my brain before heading upstairs to bed, I flashed up the laptop to check if Sam had written back. He had.

Hi, Katherine
Thank you for your email. I'm so pleased you got in touch because I'm afraid I need your help, but more of that in a moment, because, to put you out of your misery straight away – yes, I am happy for you to read Juliet's memoirs.

A bit late now.

Reading your email, I had the feeling you believe Juliet to be dead … this is not the case.

What? Never!

Juliet will celebrate her one hundredth birthday this Christmas Day. She lived at the cottage with increasing amounts of help until a couple of years ago when finally (kicking and screaming) she moved into a local care home for the elderly. The care home is called Lanyon, which is a name you will no doubt recognise from her memoirs. Lanyon House is our ancestral home, but was sold by Juliet in the 1970's. In returning to Lanyon she has gone full circle, which far from being wonderful, is, I fear, the last thing Juliet would have wanted to do, but there was no other workable solution.

I received an email from the manager at Lanyon this morning explaining that Juliet has become agitated. She is desperate to find a particular item that belonged to her father – a compass that looks like a pocket watch. It seems she has mislaid it. I wonder … could you please have a good nosy around to see if you can find it – I'm sure you will. It's probably got a label on it, knowing Juliet. If you find it, would you mind nipping up to Lanyon (someone from the village will give you a lift, although it isn't too far to walk), explain who you are – Juliet is aware that you are staying at the house for Christmas – and take it to her. Also, would you mind sitting with her for a while?

Not at all. I'd bloody love it!

Her body has been frail for some years, but her mind has remained as sharp as a new pin and you should find her excessively good company, depending upon the extent of the reported agitation.

Please tell her that I'm trying my best to get back for

162

Christmas. I was only supposed to be temporarily detached to cover for a crew member who left the ship due to an unexpected bereavement, but three weeks later, I'm still here. Juliet and I made a pact several years ago that if she managed to live so long, I would reward her by taking her flying in the Tiger Moth on her one hundredth birthday – Christmas Day – and she is holding me to it. The aircraft in question is the very same yellow Tiger Moth her father gave her for her birthday, all those years ago. It is stored at an old airfield called Predannack, just down the road from Lanyon. When I made the pact with Juliet, I thought the chance of her living to one hundred unlikely, but this is Juliet Caron we're talking about and I should have known better. The thought of taking her flying at her age petrifies me, but she is absolutely determined to go.

Do carry on reading her story. Gerald told me you're a professor of history and once wrote a book. Perhaps one day you could do something with Juliet's story, too?

Best wishes,

Sam

P.S. Gerald said you're going to find an answer to the apostrophe question (poor you!). You could do worse than to ask Juliet … she believes in angels, by the way.

P.P.S. Yes, I am The Last Coddiwompler. What did you think to my blog?

My mind whirred. Not only was Sam the same Sam Lanyon who had written the blog, but most importantly,

Juliet was alive! And I would actually meet the lady whose story had begun to mean so much to me.

I slid happily into a lovely bed, warmed by an electric blanket and for the first time in two years of bedtimes, didn't need Harry Potter to help me drift away.

Chapter 17

Katherine

Troubled angel

Pulling back Juliet's lounge curtains the following morning revealed a damp and grey day. I remembered Sam's email and decided to turn the house over in the hope of finding Juliet's compass.

For three hours I searched. I emptied every drawer and opened every cupboard. I looked in boxes stored under the bed and scrambled with my arse in the air into deep packing boxes stowed neatly in the loft. In the course of my search, I stumbled across many of the little notes Juliet had written in order to remember her life. I began to collect them on the kitchen table, but no matter how hard I looked, the compass was nowhere to be found.

At lunchtime, after a final frisk of the elf to see if he was harbouring it within his stuffing, I flopped onto the chair with the elf on my lap and accepted defeat. I was thrilled at the prospect of meeting Juliet and had wanted to appear at Lanyon like an old friend and conquering hero, brandishing the compass, thereby ingratiating myself with her immediately. Now I would have to appear at her side as an empty-handed stranger.

With a disappointed sigh, I put the elf back on the shelf, grabbed my coat and hat and headed out of the door.

I was halfway up the street when, a hundred yards up the hill, a man that wasn't Noel or Percy dashed out of a cottage.

After being accosted by the scarecrow and the tin man it was safe to assume that this must be the lion. He raised a finger as if to say, 'Ah, just the very person.' But I wasn't in the mood for Oz today, and so took on the vague expression of a woman who had just remembered she had something really quite important to do, made a swift exit to the right, which happened to be into the churchyard, darted into the sanctuary of the church and adopted the type of countenance my surroundings promoted, reverent.

I am not a religious woman (correction, I am not a religious woman unless circumstances are such that I find myself required to pull out the Church of England card – weddings, christenings, funerals) but I took a seat in the second to front pew and decided to take a moment to look around. It was lovely little church – cold, but lovely – and unlike the village, was decorated for Christmas in the most beautiful, understated, traditional way, with swags of winter foliage and a simple tree. But the aspect of the church that interested me most was the stained-glass window that sat to the right of the alter. It depicted a young man with blue eyes and long golden hair who was surrounded by animals. He had the most enormous angel wings tucked behind him and was looking up into the clouds questioningly – troubled – presumably asking God a question.

My phone pinged in my pocket.

Gerald: *George is on the mend! Any luck and we'll be home for Christmas. Keep your chin up, lovely. Hope you're making friends. Any decision on the apostrophe yet?*

Me: *Brilliant news. Stop nagging about the apostrophe. It's all in hand, sort of.*

I put the phone back in my pocket, looked at the window again, took the phone out, and sent another text.

Me: *Why didn't you tell me Juliet is alive?*

Gerald: *I never said she was dead.*

Me: *Just asking – no particular reason. Do you believe in angels?*

Five seconds later ...

Gerald: *Yes, I bloody well do! Doctors and nurses. Surrounded by them here. Why?*

Me: *I'm popping up to see Juliet. Sam Lanyon wrote and said she believes in angels. I was just wondering if everyone except me knew about angels and I was the only one who didn't, like a secret I've not been included in.*

Gerald: *I think you're spending far too much time alone – it's unhealthy. And I hope you've bothered to put a brush through your hair today, you never know who you might bump into. Ooh, doctor just walked in. Got to go*

Me: *This is the twenty-first century! You can't say that kind of thing to women anymore. Who cares if I look like rat shit?*

G: *Smarten up, buttercup!*

Well, that was helpful.
He wasn't quite finished.

P.S. *I just had text from Geoffrey (Parish Council chap – not Noel or Percy). He says you're avoiding him! Have told him you are deep in research and cannot be disturbed. He's arranged the village meeting for 2pm Boxing Day – you can deliver your verdict then.*

I knelt at the altar, looked up at the angel and said a little prayer for George (and for a miracle answer to the apostrophe question to appear). I've never been sure what to do on leaving an altar, but on films they always seem to sign a cross across their face and chest and reverse out, so I copied that. I raised my coat collar to avoid detection, felt my stomach growl and rather than head to the care home at lunchtime (surely the worst time to pitch-up) I slunk down the hill and knocked on Fenella's door (she was bound to feed me up). Twenty minutes later I was sitting at the table enjoying yet another hearty meal and listening to a Christmas CD.

The conversation consisted mainly of me asking questions.

Yes, Fenella did believe in angels – hurrah – but then clarified this by explaining that they usually came in the form of dogs. But to be very clear, *not* Chihuahuas, who were the spawn of Satan. She refused to explain why.

She had no opinion regarding the apostrophe and had decided in bed the night before that she cared even less about the issue. I was to forget about it until Boxing Day then make up the first thing that came to my mind (those idiots on the council would never know the difference!).

My questions turned to Juliet.

I confessed that I was reading her war memoirs and explained about the email from Sam asking me to look for a golden compass, which I had failed to find. Fenella shook her head.

'Sorry, Lovey,' she said, shaking her head. 'I've known her for years, spent lots of time up there having a good old chinwag, but she never mentioned any compass to me. I'm sure you'll find it, though. You'll just have to have a good look see.'

I studied Fenella across the table. I wondered if she was alive during the war. She looked like she might be old enough. How old was she? Seventy? Eighty? Hard to tell. She was fresh faced though, whatever her age. Must be all that gathering of the seaweed over the years ... it was either that or the gin. She read my mind.

'I was just a kiddie during the war, you know.'

My eyes widened. 'Never! You don't look old enough, not even nearly.'

She stood to turn on the radio because the CD had started to stick, took the boiling kettle off the Aga and made a fresh pot of tea

'Well, they always did say I had the best complexion in Cornwall,' she said, 'and the best legs, 'o course ...'

Legs? She was tiny!

'Did you live here during the war,' I asked, standing to take the milk jug out of the fridge.

'Yes, in this house.'

I sat down while Fenella delved into the biscuit tin.

'Really? You've lived here all that time?'

'I have. Mother lost both her brothers – they were a bit younger than her and she'd always mothered them – on the same day at Dunkirk, but she'd been told they were together when they fell, so she had that to comfort her, at least. Father worked on the farms.' Fenella glanced out of the window. 'He worked for Juliet's crowd up at Lanyon – reserved occupation, you see, farming – so he was saved from all the fighting, thank goodness. But Mother never got over losing those two boys. Never. Poor woman.'

Her eyes misted over and she stared up at the dead dogs, just as *Have Yourself a Merry Little Christmas* came on the radio. That bloody song (not the Chihuahuas)

really was the spawn of the devil! I stood and crossed to the windowsill.

'Do you mind if I change the station, Fenella?' I asked. 'I can't abide Christmas songs. The happy ones remind me that I'm on my own, and the sad ones are just too bloody depressing.'

'Of course, you can, lovey. How about a bit of Radio 3?'

'How about I just turn it off?'

I sat back down and picked up my teacup. The newfound quiet in the room harder to listen to. It needed filling. Fenella tipped her head to one side and smiled.

'It's a difficult time, Christmas,' she said. 'Gerald was hoping you'd buck up a bit this year. Shame he had to go away, and I'm not much company for you, not really.'

Now I just felt bad.

'But you are! You're the best company I could wish for, honestly.' I fixed a bright smile across my face. 'And I've met Noel, too, and Percy and his wife ...'

She didn't look convinced.

'I *am* cheery – honestly! I'll find my Christmas spirit this year, you'll see!'

She leant forward and winked.

'Lucky for you I can help out on that front ...'

She rose slowly and shuffled sideways to the back room, returning with Christmas spirit already bottled in her hand (I should have known from the wink). 'Let's get some of this down you with a nice bit of grapefruit tonic and you'll soon be singing along to Christmas songs.'

I doubted it, but who was I to argue. I looked at the clock. The sun was just over the yard arm ... I poured the gin into two large glasses.

'What was Christmas like back then?' I asked. 'During the war, I mean.'

Fenella took a frozen piece of grapefruit out of the freezer and popped it into my glass, it fizzed.

'Well, I was born in thirty-seven, so I only remember the tail end of it.' She took a sip of gin, the tea now abandoned, and smiled. 'I do remember the kiddies' parties up in the hall, though. Christmas has always been a good time in Angels Cove, we all pull together, you see. Did you know this village has done a lantern festival on the harbour wall every year at Christmas since 1918, except for during the war, a course – blackout, you see. But this year ...' she tailed off.

'This year?'

She shrugged. 'Well, I suppose what with all the goings on with the council and that blooming Storm Katherine pitching up (why they have to go putting a name to a storm these days I will never know) we haven't even got the lights up, yet. And with half the cottages used as holiday lets now, and not so many kiddies around the village, it all seems to be dying away – first time since the war, too. Tragic really. And with Gerald away, no one's had the *umpf* to grip it. It's such a shame, but there you go.'

She was right. It really was tragic.

'Not to worry,' she added brightly. 'There's still my gin

tasting for the old folks to look forward to. Do you think you could drop by tomorrow evening and help bottle it up, we'll have a nice old sing-song – no sad Christmas songs, promise.'

'Of course,' I said. 'I'd love to.'

I sipped on my gin and thought of Gerald's original letter – *save Angels Cove for all the little children this Christmas.* In all honesty, I was yet to see any children, but that was academic, because Fenella's face was so full of disappointment, it broke my heart, and when combined with her occasional glances towards the empty dog bed, I couldn't not want to help – genuinely – and realised that, for all of Gerald's nagging, Dorothy needed to run back up the yellow brick road, grab her wing men, and take this apostrophe business a bit more seriously, because maybe Gerald was right. Maybe I *could* save Angels Cove in time for Christmas ... but there was one very special lady I needed to see first.

Chapter 18

Katherine

A Promise

I stood by the gates to Lanyon, chewing my bottom lip, feeling odd. Through Juliet's memoirs I had immersed myself in this place and my imagination had conjured a Lanyon of the 1940s, but the house standing before me was not quite as I imagined. I arrived during a busy moment involving an ambulance and an elderly gentleman. He was wrapped in a red blanket and strapped to a stretcher and was being loaded (such a dreadful word for the movement of a human being and yet it fitted the scene perfectly) into the ambulance. A woman, perhaps in her sixties, walked alongside, fussing. I continued down the drive and looked on just as a care worker, wearing not only a Christmas jumper but also reindeer antlers, said her quick goodbyes to the gentleman and turned towards the front door. The house, the ambulance, the man – it didn't seem to all fit together, somehow.

The care worker was called Yvonne, her badge said so. After signing in, I was led beyond the entrance hall with its tinsel-strewn notice boards, to Juliet's room past open doors that led into all the other resident's rooms. The residents were all much older and more infirm than I had imagined. Some were sleeping, some were watching the TV and some were just sitting in the corridor alone. Yvonne explained that some of their more active residents sat in the lounge during the day, to chat and take in the view. But Juliet wasn't one of them. She kept to her room, which was – Yvonne was quick to add – a corner room with the best view in the house, and where Juliet spent her days, looking out to sea while listening to audio books. We paused at the end of a corridor.

'You've never met Juliet before?' Yvonne asked.

I hesitated. It seemed odd to say that I hadn't.

'No, I've never met her before in my life. I'm staying in her house in the village. I was asked by her grandson to look for something she's desperate to find.'

'Yes. The compass? Did you find it.'

I shook my head.

'Sorry. I didn't. I came to tell her. Sam thought that perhaps I might stay for a chat, if she wants me to.'

'A bit of advice then,' Yvonne said, putting a hand on my shoulder. 'She looks younger than she is but she's frail, *really* frail, not that she wants anyone to know that. Also, if she thinks you're talking to her like a child she'll boot you out.' Yvonne put her hand on the door handle and lowered her voice. 'This is a woman who listens to TED talks every day and exchanges emails with the Arch Bishop of Canterbury and that science chap on the telly.'

'Science chap?'

'Can't remember his name. She's been trying to argue the case that quantum physics can actually prove that heaven exists ... or something like that.'

Yvonne knocked and without being beckoned we walked into a beautiful, baking hot room. I took off my coat and draped it across my arm. A large chair sat with its back to us by the corner window, the kind that has wings for resting the head. Juliet was sat in it, her eyes closed, her body so small inside a chair so big – a beautifully dressed, tiny, white-haired doll with perfect skin. She was wearing an indigo blue cashmere jumper with a contrasting wrap draped around her shoulders. A blanket rested on her legs.

Here she was. The fearless. The death-defying. *The* Juliet Caron. The woman who dashed around the country flying Spitfires and Hurricanes. The woman who fell in love with a stranger in a field a couple of miles away. The woman who once owned this large stately house. I could have bowed down at her feet and kissed them.

Yvonne leant forward and moved as if to wake her. I placed a finger to my lips and shook my head. 'Let her sleep,' I whispered. 'I'll wait.' I sank into a matching and equally deep, high-backed chair, the arm of which touched the arm of Juliet's and was set to a perfect angle for conversation. I looked out across the lawns to the sea. A line of cedar trees framed a view of the sea to the west. I watched as the pink/blue hues in the sky deepened as our little bit of the Earth slowly turned away from the sun. I felt swaddled and cosy. My eyelids, feeling heavy suddenly, closed. I rested my head against the wing of the chair and slowly, very slowly, drifted away.

Goodness knows how long I slept, but it was completely dark outside when I woke up. I glanced around. The room was lit by a scattering of lamps. Juliet was awake. She was smiling at me.

'Oh, Lord. I'm so sorry,' I said, stifling a yawn and shuffling to sit up straight. 'It must have been the heat. I never normally sleep during the day.'

Biggest lie of my life.

'I'm Katherine,' I offered, still shuffling and trying to sound bright. 'I'm staying in your cottage for Christmas. How rude of me.'

She smiled.

'Not at all.'

I began to babble.

'Your Grandson asked me to have a good look in the cottage for the compass, but I ...'

Juliet reached across and patted my hand with long, knotted fingers. Her watery eyes were so very bright.

'Don't worry about that just for a moment,' she said, her weak voice narrowly betraying her years. 'Give yourself a second to come to and I'll ring for tea.' She picked up a wire with an orange button on the end that was tucked down the side of her chair. An alarm began to sound. Yvonne appeared in front of Juliet's chair, breathless. She was still wearing the antlers but now sported a tabard that had the words, *I'm doing the drug round. Do not disturb me*, written across the front and back.

'Ah, Yvonne,' Juliet began, putting on glasses that were draped on a chain across her chest. 'Could you arrange for tea for two, please, and on the silver set with the china cups.' She glanced at Yvonne over the top of her glasses. 'And make sure we get the pink wafers this time, not that dry shortbread you've been pawning around all week.'

I saw words that were perhaps not quite Christian forming in Yvonne's headspace. She buttoned them in.

'But what about your dinner? You've not had a bite yet what with this one ...' – a pointed look in my direction – '... falling to sleep.'

Guilt splashed over me like a soggy flannel.

Juliet waved a dismissive hand.

'Life is full of meals, Yvonne. Missing one won't kill me.'

Yvonne looked at me with a frown and said, 'I'll tray it up, then,' before managing a weak smile and disappearing out of the door with a chunter. I'd never been to a home for the elderly before, but I was pretty sure the care workers didn't tend to do on-demand silver service tea trays when visitors arrived. Juliet turned to face me.

'I hoped you'd come,' she said, her demeanour having returned to sweet older lady status. 'Sam emailed and told me all about you.' She patted my hand again. 'What a time you've had of it. But, you're here now. That's all that matters.'

I made a mental note to text Gerald and find out just how much all these people knew!

'That's Sam's chair,' she said, a glow of absolute pride across her face. 'I ordered it for him especially, for when he visits. Comfortable, isn't it?'

I let out a deep and relaxed sigh.

'It certainly is. I could live in it!'

'People never spend enough money on mattresses and chairs,' she added. 'But they're so important. Get you mattress right and your day will be better from the get go. So, tell me,' she began in earnest. 'How do you like my cottage?'

I smiled.

'I love it. Thank you so much for letting me stay.'

She nodded her agreement and we made polite conversation about Angels Cove until the tea arrived, which was when, once settled with my teacup in one hand and pink wafer biscuit in the other, I tried to turn the conversation back to the missing compass. She stopped me again.

'All in good time,' she said. 'I'd like to hear about you first.'

I was about to protest but her eyes were so kind and her body so frail, it really did seem I must.

'But it's *your* life we should be talking about,' I said, twenty minutes later, having given Juliet a quick rundown on the past few years of my life.

'Sam said in his email today that you're reading my memoirs.'

'Yes. I hope you don't mind?'

'Of course not. Nice to know someone else other than Sam will remember the old days once I'm gone. I'm glad I wrote it all down. My memory isn't what it was, which is why I simply cannot remember where the compass is ... and it's so very important.' She glanced out of the window. 'So very important.'

Juliet turned her attention away from the view to glance beyond me. She was looking at a photo on a side table. It was a picture of a woman, I guessed in her thirties, standing by a car on the drive, in front of Lanyon, something from the 1950s perhaps, a young girl stood with her. The woman had her arms around the girl. They were smiling. Happy. She seemed to study the photo before sitting back in her chair and closing her eyes. She was so very tiny. I finished my tea and stood. It was time to go.

Sensing my departure, she opened her eyes and held out her hands to take mind. Her hands were cold.

'Love doesn't have to last a lifetime, to last a lifetime, does it?' she said, kindly.

I smiled and shook my head.

'But as I said to my grandson after his heart was broken,' she went on, 'there comes a point when it's time to ...'

'Believe in love again?'

She smiled. 'That's it. See, you're half way there already. Don't go yet,' she said, still holding my hands. 'There's something I want to ask you. I would ask Sam, but he's still away. We were supposed to have a few days together before Christmas, he was hoping to be back to take me flying for my birthday, but ...' A cloud crossed Juliet's face before she rallied. 'There's a picture of him, over there. He's the man with the ridiculous beard ...' she rolled her eyes playfully. 'Pass it to me, will you Katherine?'

I handed her a photograph of a man wearing a Royal Navy uniform. He was standing next to a fighter jet, his flying helmet in his hand. Juliet stroked the man's face, kissed the photo and handed it back.

'You'll know what he looks like now, when he pitches up.'

'Yes,' I said, thinking of Sam's blog. 'I suppose I will.' I returned the photograph to its prime position before being despatched with a conspiratorial whisper to close the door.

'Loose lips sink ships,' she said, as I lowered myself back into the chair. 'The thing is,' she began in a semi-whisper, '... and I know you might find this a bit odd – but Gerald said you wouldn't mind helping out with something while you're here ...'

I had to smile. He'd clearly pimped me out to the whole village.

'Of course. Just ask. Anything at ...'

'I want to escape!'

'Escape?'

She nodded.

'It's impossible to get the staff here to take me out, but there are a few things that I need to take care of, before I go.'

Go?

'I was going to ask Sam to help, but what with him being detained, and Gerald *did* say you'd be the perfect person to help me ...' she widened her eyes, 'to help me go out with a real bang!'

Go out? My eyes narrowed to help my confused brain attempt to understand.

'I'd like you to drive me around – just to a few places nearby. I'll tell you where I want to go tomorrow, when we set off.'

My eyes betrayed my concern. She was practically one hundred years old and so very frail. What if she fell? What if she ...

'Oh, stop fretting and relax,' she added with a sniff, reading my mind. 'I'm asking you to take me for a run out in the car, not strap me into an abseil and throw me off Gunwalloe cliffs!'

I laughed.

'Trust me,' she went on, 'I'm stronger than I look. I just want to go on a little trip down memory lane, that's all. There are some things I need to ... let's just say, retrieve.' Juliet nudged my arm. 'Just two days together before Christmas, you and me. What do you say?'

I smiled. Hadn't that been exactly what I had wished I'd had when I thought Juliet had died already? Hadn't I wished that I had been given the opportunity to get to know this incredible woman in person, before ...

'And if you don't have a car, we'll take Fenella's,' she

added firmly. 'She never uses it and she'll be too busy with her gin this week to need it.'

Her eyes pleaded now.

'Please, Katherine, stop seeing me as an old lady and see me as I really am. The body you see before you does not represent the mind or the soul. I have things I need to do. It's so very important ...'

I rubbed my forehead. Would it really be too bad to give this amazing lady the gift of freedom for a few hours?

There was nothing left to say, other than.

'I'd love to spend two days with you. Of course, I'll take you out.'

Juliet relaxed into her chair with a smile. I stood one final time and grabbed my coat.

'Have you ever felt that you were guided somewhere for a reason?' she asked as I pushed an arm through a coat sleeve.

I sat back down, coat half on half off.

'It's funny you should say that, but when I found your memoirs, I felt that maybe ... oh, it's silly, I suppose, but I felt that maybe I was *supposed* to read them.'

Juliet nodded her agreement. 'I know exactly what you mean! When Gerald told me you were coming and staying at the cottage, I had such a feeling that we – you and I –would get along. And when Sam was delayed at sea, I knew for certain that you were the one who was supposed to help me to move ...' She paused. 'Well, to help me. That's all.'

I knelt beside her and tucked the blanket down the sides of her legs.

'I'll see you tomorrow,' I said, standing up. 'Shall we say ten 'o clock?'

'Perfect.'

I went to leave. Juliet grabbed my hand.

'And would you keep looking for the compass,' she said. And then quieter. 'It's so very important, you see.'

Chapter 19

Juliet

Oh, Marie!

May Day 1941, I remember, was the first day that year we didn't wear a coat as we cycled to work. I also remember that particular day for another, more important, reason.

Anna and I began our day by going through the usual motions – checking the programme next to our names on the chalk board and glancing into the pigeon holes for the day's flying delivery chits. Then came the met brief, then the planning of our navigational routes and if there was time, a quick cup of tea before take-off. Taking advantage of the fact that neither of us planned to be airborne before eleven, Anna and I sat outside of the mess and took in the sunshine. We were just chatting about everything and nothing when a sleek, black car rolled up. The first thing we saw were two very long, shapely stockinged legs appear from behind the driver door. The voice gave the driver away before the blonde hair or the face did.

'Hey, what's all this laying around in the sunshine, you damn work-shy, British – oh, and Canadian – assholes!?'

Anna jumped up.

'Marie! It's Marie!'

We ran towards her like she'd just landed from a Battle of Britain dog fight.

'What on earth are you doing here?' I asked, watching Anna throw her arms around Marie.

'And it's wonderful to see you too!' she chided, before turning to Anna with a smile. 'Get me a coffee, will ya, honey? And a cigarette, too. I'm all out.'

Anna trotted off. She turned suddenly to shout back.

'All right, but don't talk about anything until I get back. I want to hear *everything*!'

I took Marie's arm and we walked together towards the mess.

'It's fabulous to see you! But, come on, tell me, why are you here?'

Marie paused at the door.

'I just wanted to work get the old gang back together again – the Spitfire Sisters – my best gal pals in the whole world. That's OK, isn't it?'

I tilted my head to one side and took her in. This was Marie – Marie who wanted to live as close to London as possible, despite the relentless bombing during the Blitz.

'Hamble is two train rides away from town. I don't buy it.'

'All right,' she said with a shrug, taking off her hat. 'I may have ruffled a few feathers ...'

That was more like it.

'How?'

She sniffed, took a cigarette and lighter from Anna – who had rushed back at light speed – lit the cigarette and inhaled.

'I took a Spit somewhere I shouldn't have ...'

'Oh, Marie!' said Anna, her shoulders dropping. 'Where to this time?'

Marie exhaled and shrugged.

'Only to St Athan.'

'St Athan. As in RAF St Athan, in Wales?'

Marie shrugged again.

'But we go there all the time,' I said, confused. 'Why was it a problem?'

'Because I should have been at Biggin Hill.'

We burst out laughing.

'You never did!'

Maire laughed, too. It was a throaty laugh, a laugh full of cigarette smoke and seductive misadventure. She threw an arm around each of us.

'You bet your ass I did!'

It turned out that Marie had met a cute RAF pilot in town the week before and having been given the whole day to deliver a Spitfire from White Waltham to Biggin Hill, she had decided to 'nip' to Wales en route Biggin Hill to pay a surprise visit to the said pilot and allow him to buy her lunch.

'And you should have seen his face – all of their faces – when I – a broad – jumps out of the cockpit. Priceless. I was sex on legs ladies, sex on legs!'

We shook our heads, still laughing. Marie had a tendency to represent everything the women of the ATA were repeatedly briefed *not* to represent – a world of the sexy, show-off, aviatrix! But Marie simply didn't care.

'So anyhow, some asshole at St Athan blew the whistle and I got my ass hauled in front of the commander when I got back.'

'Back from St Athan?' Anna asked again.

'What's with you and St Athan, you *doozy*? From Biggin Hill! I still made the delivery. I'm not *that* much of a chump!'

'What happened then?' Anna and I said, simultaneously, before turning to each other and laughing.

'Happened?' Marie took a drag on her cigarette. 'They tried to sack me for a misappropriation of fuel. So, I told him – the boss guy – socked it to him straight. I said, "You damn sonofabitch, I'll pay for the fuel myself if it makes you feel better. And if wasn't for my daddy – who's working his ass off to make damn sure fuel *and* aluminium keeps on being delivered to this smoggy, soggy shithole of a country, with badly organised rationing and silly men with even sillier moustaches,' She paused to look at me, '– no offence, Juliet – then the Nazis would have rolled in months ago."'

Anna and I eyed each other.

I let Anna ask the obvious question.

'And what did he say to that?'

'He said to get the hell out of his office.'

'Jeez, Marie!' Anna said, following on with a suitably drawn out whistle. 'You've been sacked!'

Marie stepped a few paces across the room to stub out her cigarette.

'I haven't, as it goes,' she said, her cashmere two-piece hanging from her hips in all the right places. 'I'm a damn good pilot. I went back in, told him he'd be a damn fool to lose me and offered to come here – a new start, I said, just with the gals. Once he'd calmed down, he saw sense and agreed. I knew he would. I *know* people, if you know what I mean, and he knows I know people.'

'So, you'll be flying from here, with us?' I said, hardly containing my excitement.

'Sure will. I just need to find myself somewhere to live and a place to park the Bentley – a good hotel, maybe?'

Anna looked at me. I knew what she was thinking and nodded.

'Why not live with us?' I said. 'It's not the Savoy, but it's homey. And you could leave the car here. We always cycle in – you wouldn't get the fuel ration to drive a car to and fro everyday anyhow.'

Marie mocked a shudder.

'Cycle? With my hair?' But then she beamed. 'Well, smack me on the ass and call me a hootie dootie! You just

189

got yourselves a roommate! How about we celebrate by going up to town tonight ... we could go to the bar at the Dorchester first, and maybe move on to the Landsdowne at Hyde Park Corner for dancing? But then there is the Plygon ...? Or how about the 400 Club at Leicester Square? Gerry hasn't bombed it yet, has he? What do you say?'

Marie's eyes burned with excitement, but with only two days off in ten, we didn't tend to burn the candle at both ends. Anna frowned and rubbed her chin nervously.

'Ah, come on, Anna,' Marie persisted. 'Live a little!'

'But what about sleep?' Anna asked. 'We're flying tomorrow.'

'We'll sleep on the way back, on the milk train! Then it's just a short trip to Eastleigh and we're home. I've looked into the whole thing. I'll drive us to Eastleigh and leave my car at the station. We'll be back by dawn, fresh and ready for another day. Ah, come on. What d'ya say?'

Marie had obviously done her homework and got the whole thing worked out.

Anna and I smiled at each other.

What else could we say, but ... yes!

Chapter 20

Juliet

An explosive evening

We gathered in my bedroom after work – hair, lipstick, nails – just the usual preparations for a girls' night out, except for the uniform, of course (Marie insisted we wear our uniforms into town) and there was also the minor issue of the chance of being bombed, and the gas mask holders slung over our shoulders ...

'I wouldn't normally wear this colour for a night out,' Marie said, slipping on her skirt over her stockinged legs and turning to me with a wink, 'but you bet your sexy asses this little baby' – she put on her chip hat at a jaunty angle – 'will get us a date with any hot guy in town tonight, too.' She turned to Anna and threw a lipstick in her direction. 'Honey, you look too pale. Try this ... it's called Passion Blush!'

Anna opened her compact, applied a little lipstick and clicked it shut.

'Listen, Marie ...' Anna began, handing the lipstick back. 'I want to talk to you.'

'What about, honey?' Marie stood in front of the mirror, taking in a last admiring look.

'It's just ... we need to be careful tonight ...'

Marie rolled her eyes in my direction before placing a hand on her hip and turning to face Anna.

'Here we go. What's the buttoned-up Canadian prissy missy gonna preach to me now?'

'That's not fair, Marie. Not fair at all. I just don't want you to get in trouble. And don't pretend you didn't get the brief about how to behave, because I know *all* the Americans did ...'

'Brief,' I asked, buttoning up my ATA tunic and glancing down at my wings with a smile. Marie waved her hand dismissively.

'Oh, she means some bullcrap we all got – just after we got off the boat – about fitting in with you guys. Some buttoned-up suit read us the riot act – how to behave in Britain. No showing off, no flashing our American dollars around and absolutely no annoying the natives. A damn cheek, if you ask me. If not for the U-boats I'd have jumped right back on that ship and sailed home!' Marie turned to Anna. 'I don't give a damn what those po-faced prudes say, and neither should you! None of us knows what tomorrow might bring, and if I'm going down, then I tell you now, honey pie, I'm going down dancing ...' She softened and linked arms with Anna, who was looking more than a little apprehensive. 'Oh, stop your fussing and worrying. You're gonna have a fabulous time tonight!'

We grabbed our cardboard gas mask cases which were hanging on the pegs by the door. 'Oh, I meant to say,' Marie went on, 'The Billy Townsend band is playing at the Empire, how d'ya fancy meeting up with some old friends of mine at the Savoy, first ...'

'Friends?' I asked, closing the door behind us and placing the key under a cracked tile.

'Just some Navy guys, and Dirk might be there ...'

'Dirk?' I asked, stepping through the door.

'Bogarde. You know. The actor.'

Anna and I stopped. Our mouths gaped.

'What now?' Maire asked, genuinely surprised at our incredulity. 'I know him. He's a nice guy. A bit annoying when he's drunk, but aren't they all? But listen, one of the Navy guys is a real hottie and I need you gals on my wing tonight, just don't let me flirt too much.'

Anna sighed again.

'If you sigh one more time, Anna Beatrice Moore!' Marie chided, linking her arms through ours and marching us down the road towards her car. 'It's only dancing – except maybe the sirens will go and we'll all get blown to kingdom come, then maybe – *finally* – you'll both listen to me about having a good time!'

The air raid warning did sound that night, but not before we had spent a couple of hours settling into what promised to be a fabulous evening. The 'Navy guys' Marie had referred to were not simply junior officers, but men of high rank and great significance in the War Office, with a great deal of gold visible on their jacket sleeves. Marie had been right when she said that wearing our uniforms into town would guarantee us the best tables and heaps of attention. The women of the ATA had caused quite a stir in the press and, much to Anna's annoyance (and my amusement and Marie's delight) once settled into the dancehall we became celebrities of sorts, but my wedding ring acted as a significant enough buffer to keep some, but not all, male attention at bay. I spent the evening sitting at a table chatting happily to a happily married RAF pilot. He was flabbergasted to find that ATA pilots were expected to fly in some fairly dodgy weather, without any understanding of how to fly blind – in cloud. Seeing it as his moral duty to correct this, we spend the evening conducting an impromptu lesson on instrument flying, which I loved.

The surprise of the evening was Anna, who – much to Marie's delight – had an absolute humdinger of a time. I was sitting quietly for a moment, watching her swirling around the dance floor with yet another suitor in tow, when the air raid warning sounded. The sad, monotone drone of the siren was all too familiar to us now, and although unnerving, did not send us into a frenzied scramble towards the shelters as it once might have done, although perhaps, tonight, it should have.

Billy Townsend silenced the band and announced that

we should all make our way to the exits and head to the nearest tube station, which was only a street away, to take shelter. Anna made her way towards me from the dance floor and I glanced around to find Marie. I couldn't see her anywhere, but I did see someone else, standing across the ballroom as if freeze-framed in space and time, the crowd ebbing as one continuous movement past him.

It was Edward, and he was staring at me.

Anna pushed me forwards towards the exit, but I couldn't move.

'Come on, Juliet,' Anna shouted above the hullaballoo and the sound of the siren. 'Grab you gas mask. We need to go.'

'But what about Marie ...' I asked, suddenly pressed against a table and losing Edward's face in the crowd. 'I can't see her. You go out, Anna. I'll just go take a quick look for her, won't be a mo.' I turned towards the dance floor, straining to find Edward's face in the crowd.

Anna grabbed my arm. 'Oh, no you don't. She's a big girl, she's probably out already. Come on, this way. There's another exit down here, see?'

Reluctantly, I followed Anna, her hand in mine, to the exit, the crowd gaining momentum now. We were just stepping out onto the street when a bomb pierced through the high domed ceiling of the ballroom and landed with a direct hit on the dance floor, sending a tsunami of debris – glass and walls and chairs and tables and band instruments and doors – flying through the air. Anna and I were knocked off our feet into the road, having had moved away just enough to avoid being buried (dead or alive) by the debris. I lay there in shock for a few moments. Anna's hand reached across the void and squeezed on mine. We lay for what seemed like an eternity but must only have been seconds, waiting for the noise of the collapsing building to stop. Two words – two people – flashed through my mind: Marie and Edward.

The first sound to penetrate the silence once the rubble had settled was the bell of the Fire Service truck as it worked its way through streets to reach us, which was tricky as access was barricaded by the detritus of other collapsed buildings flattened by the bombing. The bell acted as a call to arms, leading the able-bodied survivors to clamber over the rubble in a desperate attempt to find friends. The Fire Service attached a hose to the hydrant and sprang into action against a fire that was now taking hold behind the stage, which seemed utterly surreal now in its new, open-air status, completely visible to the street.

We searched for Marie before being dragged away by members of the Auxiliary Fire Service. We looked on at the devastated scene as the bodies of the men and women we had just been dancing with – bodies of those who hadn't rushed to get out quickly as Anna had made us do – were pulled from the rubble and laid to rest on the side of the road.

We heard Marie before we saw her. She was sitting on her knees on the road behind the bombed-out dance hall and through a cascade of tears she was singing Anna's favourite song – *Over the Rainbow*. A man's head was cradled in her lap, his Army uniform shredded by flying glass, a bright red line trailed from his open skull across Marie's skirt and pooled on the road.

I rested a hand on Marie's shoulder.

'Did you know him?' I asked.

She shook her head. 'No, but he was just left here and I didn't want him to be alone.'

Come on sweetheart,' I said, at the arrival of the stretcher bearers. 'You need to leave him to the auxiliaries now.'

Marie sniffed, nodded, took a deep breath of the dank air, rested the man's head on the floor, stood, attempted to brush down her tattered, blood-stained uniform and – as only Marie could at such a time – asked Anna for a comb to run through her dust-covered hair. We began to edge away but didn't get very far before Anna stopped in the middle of the road and threw her arms around Marie.

'We thought we'd lost you,' she sobbed.

Marie used her thumbs to wipe away Anna's tears.

'Lost me?! *Me*? You gotta be kidding, honey. No Gerry bomb is gonna stop this Yankie-doodle-dandy from having a good time!' She looked down at her uniform again and then at us. Our uniforms were our pride and joy. It was heart-breaking to see them in tatters.

'Sonofabitch Gerry bastards!' she said. 'Look at the state of us! We'll head straight into town next day off and buy new!'

'Yes, let's do that,' I said, brightly, trying to help Marie bolster Anna who had begun to shake. 'Looks like it's back to Austin Reeds for new togs, eh, Anna?'

'Austin Reeds?' Marie scoffed, incredulous at my choice of tailor as we continued down the road. 'Not this time! This time we'll go to my own personal tailor, and hey,' she nudged Anna's shoulder, 'how about I treat us all to a fabulous silk lining in the jacket, a matching one just for the three of us? The Spitfire Sisters. How do you fancy silver? Too obvious?'

'A silver lining!' I repeated. 'Oh, yes, that's a fabulous idea!' I threw my fists in the air, shouting out. 'Spitfire Sisters, forever!' We stopped at the entrance to the tube. Marie turned to Anna who was still shaking and put a big-sisterly arm around her shoulder. 'And afterwards, how's about we get dressed up and have a few drinks with some pals of mine at the 400 Club, and then off to the Plygon for some dancing – if it's still standing, that is. We'll spend the night at my place in Chelsea, make a real good night of it, whad'ya say?'

Anna turned to me and shook her head with a resigned smile.

'After tonight, I'd say you're barking mad. But yes, thank you. I'd love to!'

We boarded the train at Waterloo Station, utterly dishevelled. Despite Marie's desire to rouse spirits, as she rested her bruised head against the blackout blind and closed her eyes, I noticed several stray tears escape from her long lashes and ebb down her beautiful face. Anna rested her head on my lap and smiled up at me before closing her eyes. I stroked her light chestnut hair as the carriage helped to rock her to sleep. And as the night train headed west and left a broken but not defeated London in its wake, my heart seemed to be finding it a strain to simply keep on beating, not just because of the tragic events we witnessed tonight, but at the not knowing ... the not knowing if Edward Nancarrow, whose face I had glanced briefly across the crowd at the Empire, was dead or alive.

Anna woke just before Southampton and glanced up at me.

'Who's Edward?' she asked in a whisper, trying not to wake Marie and wiping sleep and dust from her eyes. 'You were shouting for him, when we were searching for Marie, you kept shouting his name.'

I looked away, further down the carriage, anything rather than to catch her eye.

'Oh, no one in particular,' I lied. 'Just someone I used to know. I thought I saw him in the crowd.'

At which point Marie stirred.

'I've made a decision,' she said, stretching her long arms skywards. 'The Bentley's a bit of a gas guzzler and I can never get enough coupons to fuel it.' She raised the blackout blind, causing us to blink but allowing the morning sun to fill us with light. 'So, I'm going to buy me a motor bike! A real beaut of one, too.' She looked from Anna to me. 'Whad'ya think?'

Chapter 21

Juliet

Summer 1941

A surprise communication

I was in the Met Office at Hamble, self-briefing the weather for a delivery to Scotland when Marie, sidled in. She nudged my shoulder and handed me a note, folded into four.

'What's this?'

Marie leant her back against the map table and smirked.

'What's this, my ass! You're the dark horse, no mistaking, Third Officer Caron ... or should I say, *Mrs* Lanyon. No wonder you use your maiden name in the ATA. I would too with a man like *that* on my tail.'

I didn't understand a word Marie said. Then I read the note.

Dear, Juliet

I'm writing in the hope that you are safe. It was a shock to see you in London at the Empire last evening. I became trapped with some of the bandsmen behind the stage area. Luckily the fire did not spread and we were rescued, but it took a couple of hours for the building to be secured enough to get us out.

I looked for you afterwards amongst the injured but obviously didn't find you. I'm hoping that you escaped unharmed, but until I know for sure, I will not rest. Seeing you was surreal. Only that morning I had read an article in The Times about women in the ATA. The article led with a (very glamorous) picture of you. You were stepping off the wing of a Spitfire with your hand running through your hair. You looked extremely happy. I couldn't believe it was you at first, but then I could believe it completely, because flying Spitfires in the ATA is exactly what I should have realised you would do. I have done a little digging and traced you to the Hamble Ferry Pool – sorry if this is intrusive, but I need to know you're safe. I am in Hampshire for a few days and was hoping we could meet one evening – this evening, perhaps? I will stay at the Bugle pub in Hamble until Friday and eat there each evening in the hope that you might join me.

Yours, as ever.
Edward.

I stood motionless.
'How did you get this?' I asked.

'A chap – a very good-looking chap, by the way – stopped me at the gate as I cycled in. He asked me if I knew Juliet Caron – Caron, you'll note, not Lanyon – and handed me the note, which of course I read. I'm guessing by the tone that this Edward fellow is not your brother, more's the pity.'

'I don't have a brother,' I whispered, still looking at the note.

Marie stopped joking around and shuffled me to the mess for a cup of tea. Anna had just landed and was walking in from the flight line. She was grabbed and told to meet us in the mess hall in five minutes – urgent conference required!

'But you're obviously going to meet him, whoever he is,' Marie said, taking a slurp of weak tea and then looking into the cup with despair. 'Jesus Christ, I hate this shit!'

'I can't. I'm delivering a Spit to Turnhouse this afternoon. It's a priority one. I won't be back until tomorrow.'

'Tomorrow, then?' Marie pressed.

'Marie!' Anna chided. 'Stop encouraging her. She can't meet him, she's married!'

Marie sat back in her chair with a scoff. 'Oh, poopdie-doo to that!' She lit a cigarette, took a drag and handed it to me. I didn't usually smoke, but today ...

I took a drag and rested the cigarette on an ashtray, folded the note and placed it in my pocket. There was only one way to deal with this.

'Anna. I don't suppose you would do me a very big favour, would you?'

'Go on ...'

'Nip down to The Bugle tonight, find Edward and tell him I'm very sorry but can't see him. And tell him ...' I thought for a moment. 'Tell him that I'm safe – thank you for asking – but I'm married now and that I know he's married, too, or better still, just tell him I've run away with the circus. The flying circus.'

Marie sat up straight. 'What!? You're never gonna pass on dinner with a hot guy like that? Are you nuts?!' She turned to Anna. 'And he's desperate to see her, I could tell. There goes a man very definitely in love. It's in his eyes.' She turned back to me. 'Hell, it's only dinner, Juliet ...'

I took the note out of my pocket and read it again.

'It isn't though, is it?'

Marie sniffed while Anna just smiled, comfortingly.

'Well,' Marie began, standing up and stretching. She was always stretching – or exercising – it was her thing. 'I'll leave you two to it, then! I'm flying the Anson this afternoon.' She leant in and whispered in my ear before she left. 'Honey, make damn sure you're certain before you let him go, because I'm not sure that phoney marriage of yours ...'

I scrunched my face in disapproval. Marie backed down and stopped whispering.

'... look, we could all be dead tomorrow. I'm just saying, meet the guy and have dinner. We work hard, why not play hard, too?'

She kissed me on the head and left.

Anna smiled. It was a 'that's Marie for you?' kind of a smile.
'Do you still want me to go see him for you?' she asked.
I nodded.
'Absolutely I do, yes.'

The flight to RAF Turnhouse was a turbulent one.

Navigating to Scotland in a fighter aircraft with no instruments or radio to fall back on required a fresh and concentrated mind. I usually adored any trip in the Spitfire – sleek, powerful, edgy on the ground but an angel in the air – but today ... today there was no joy to be found in the flight. I could only see Edward's face ... in every field, in every river and every town. The look he gave me across the Empire ballroom was a look of absolute surprise mixed with longing, confusion and disappointment.

The one plus point was that the weather stayed fair for the journey and somehow, even though my mind had been elsewhere for the majority of the flight, I touched down safely at RAF Turnhill with the satisfied knowledge that another vital delivery had been completed. I threw my parachute over my shoulder, grabbed my overnight bag and caught a lift into Edinburgh. If I was quick enough, I'd be in time to catch the sleeper to London and from London – if luck was on my side again – the Milk Train to Southampton, arriving back at Hamble the next morning, tired but pleased with the delivery and ready for another day's work.

Luck was with me. The following evening, I fell,

exhausted and still thinking of Edward, into my cottage. Marie was out, which was a relief. With my resolve to keep away from Edward fading, I didn't need any extra encouragement tonight.

Anna was asleep on the sofa when I walked into the lounge and flopped onto a chair. She stirred.

'Hello, you,' she said, sitting up. 'You must be dead on your feet. There's some Carnation in the kitchen, just opened, if you fancy one of my special bedtime brews.'

I closed my eyes. 'Thanks, maybe in a moment.'

Anna grabbed Marie's cigarettes and a box of matches taken from the Bugle and lit a cigarette. Her daily smoking rate had gone up significantly since flying the Spitfire. She inhaled and sat back in her chair.

'I delivered your message, by the way.'

I kept my eyes closed.

'And?'

'And, nothing. I passed on your message and he said, 'Thank you' and I left. That's it, more or less.'

I opened my eyes and sat up.

'Didn't he ask where I was or ... or anything about me at all.'

Anna exhaled a long, slow breath and flicked ash into an ashtray.

'He seemed upset – you know, disappointed – if that's any help.'

I closed my eyes again, sat back in the chair, took a deep breath and sighed.

Anna sat forward and tapped me on the knee.

'So?'

She wanted details. Who wouldn't?

'So ... what?'

'So ... what's the story? This is the man you were shouting for at the Empire the other night, isn't it?'

'Yes. I saw him across the room at the Empire, briefly, just before the air raid warning went up.'

I stretched and walked to the French windows that, on nicer days, were open. But today the weather had closed in just has I landed from my final flight, and as I watched the rain dance on the river, I couldn't help but wonder if Edward had stayed on at the Bugle. If so, he was less than half a mile away. I glanced at my watch. Half past six.

Anna rested her cigarette on the ashtray, joined me at the window and put an arm around my shoulder.

'We've still got some gin stashed away in the kitchen. How about I make us a little snifter and you tell me all about it?'

I shrugged. 'There's honestly nothing to tell.'

Anna didn't believe a word of it.

'Oh, yes there is. You looked like death when you read his note yesterday. And your shoulders are tense as hell.'

I allowed my shoulders to drop and smiled.

'I'd love a glass of gin.'

I told Anna the story of Christmas 1938 and how I fell in love with a man called Edward Nancarrow during the week before my marriage to Charles. When I finished the story, Anna didn't say anything but went straight to the hallway and grabbed my best woollen coat.

'Now, I know I'm going to sound like Marie,' she said, 'but I think you should brush your hair and put this on.' She handed me the coat.

I waited for an explanation.

'He told me to tell you that he'll be in the pub for two more days, that he'd wait for you – forever if necessary, should you change your mind.'

I bit my lip.

'Oh, Anna. You don't know how I felt about him – still feel about him. I have to be faithful to Charles – to all of the Lanyons. They've done so much for me. You can't know how much I owe them. It's risky.'

Anna shook her head.

'You owe them nothing. And as for risky? Bullcrap, as Marie would say. What we do at work – *that's* risky. This? This is just meeting up with an old friend. I'm not saying you should jump into bed with him, but dinner might be nice.'

I allowed Anna to help me into my coat. She dashed into her bedroom to grab a hairbrush, face powder and Marie's lipstick. I drew the line at the lipstick.

'But I'll regret it tomorrow,' I whispered, walking to the door.

'Tomorrow?' Anna took me firmly by the arms and stood in front of me. 'Now then, Juliet Caron, just you listen to me. Marie might be a bit over the top sometimes, but she's right about one thing. Which one of us knows if there will even be a tomorrow? Do yourself a favour and just go. It's only to the bloody pub.'

'Bloody?' I laughed. 'Next thing we know, you'll be calling everyone a sonofabitch and then we won't know if you're Canadian, English or American!'

Anna laughed. 'Canadian, Polish, Czech, English, American ... we all feel exactly the same to me.'

I smiled, kissed Anna on the cheek, grabbed an umbrella from the rack and opened the door.

'I'll see you later,' I said. 'Wait up for me!'

And with my final words hanging in the air, I stepped outside, put up the umbrella. And turned towards the pub.

Chapter 22

Katherine

The unlikely quest

Having wheeled an excited Juliet out of Lanyon (past a scowling Yvonne, who believed our big day out to be utter madness) we soon settled into Fenella's very old and very tiny car, ready for the big day out. Juliet looked like a model for Paris Vogue, wearing a pretty cashmere jumper – this time pastel pink – and a contrasting Chanel neck scarf. A little make-up highlighted her porcelain skin. I draped a blanket over her legs and my mind flashed to the photograph of her standing in front of the Tiger Moth. Even in flying overalls, with her hair blowing in the wind she had been a striking woman and still was.

I put the car into gear and started down the road. Juliet asked me to head towards Land's End but still didn't explain why or what it was she wanted to do. I had been told to bring walking boots and a good coat as we were going on a little adventure down Memory Lane, and Memory Lane could get a bit muddy, apparently.

'Did you have time to look for the compass again?' she asked, placing her handbag in the footwell besides her feet.

'I searched again first thing this morning.' I took my left hand off the steering wheel to touch her shoulder. 'I won't give up. If it's in the house, I'll find it. I know I will.'

She turned to stare out of the window, taking in the bare hedgerows and trees. 'It's Samuel's inheritance, you see.' She said softly.

At Heamoor, we turned onto a country lane that led up to the moors. It was an eight mile stretch of winding road that linked the north coast with the south one, in this very narrow, final stretch of Cornwall. I was to drive through the small village of Madron and she would give me further directions after that. Classic FM played quietly in the background and I allowed Juliet to drift into her own world as I drove through the winter sunshine.

Juliet stirred as the road ventured upwards, high above Penzance, onto open moorland. A derelict tin mine stood silhouetted on the horizon, adding a perfect dash of sinister to the sensational ambience of the place. In the far distance, a crag of towering rocks stood proudly, puncturing the skyline, adding a Neolithic permanence to the landscape. Ahead of us, easily one thousand feet below, beyond a patchwork of stony fields, lay a carpet of deep blue – the Atlantic Ocean. It was all so ancient, so wonderfully atmospheric, like nowhere else on earth (and also just a little bit unnerving, as if early-man wielding a flint axe might pop up at any second).

Juliet's smile was wide and bright as I pulled off the road and parked in a small lay-by. She wound down the window, took a very deep breath and sighed.

'Isn't it wonderful?' she asked, her watery eyes a picture of happiness.

I continued to take in the landscape while Juliet took an ordinance survey map and reading glasses out of her handbag. It was cut into a small section and folded neatly. She tapped me on the knee.

'Look at this. It shows you where you need to go.'

Go?

'It's not far,' she added, noticing my surprise, 'and you don't really need the map, it's just for reference while I explain. You brought your walking boots like I said?'

Fenella's old things ...

I smiled, overly brightly. 'Yes. Show me where to go. Have boots will travel.'

'I used to come here, quite often, and there's something I need you to get for me – to look for. There's a couple of Bronze Age monuments down the lane here,' she pointed to the map. 'One is a circle of stones, like Stonehenge but smaller and without the horizontal capstones, and the other is, well, I'm not sure what it is – *was* – but it's called Men an Tol and it's basically a circular stone that sits on its side. If you crawl through the stone you can make a wish, so I used to come up here to get my head together and make wishes, and Sam did, too.' Juliet took a cotton embroidered handkerchief out of her handbag and dabbed her eyes. She wasn't crying, just, happy.

'We'd bring picnics and make a day of it. Climb through the stone, head up Carn Galver – that's the crags up there, see? – and then run down the hill to the sea. There's a cove near Pendeen lighthouse that hardly anyone goes to, although, I suppose more people know about it now. The thing is, I used to bury things – offerings – near the stone (you can't make a wish without offering something in exchange to the Gods) and I'm wondering if I've left the compass there, in my special place.'

'Special place?'

'When I sold Lanyon and money was tight, I created a few places scattered around the countryside that I used as my own special ... I suppose you'd call them savings deposit boxes. I always liked to have a secret escape fund, you know, just in case ... I couldn't bear the thought of ever not having enough money to fly, so I used to hide a bit of cash away, in ammunition boxes buried in the ground. I always liked to have a plan B, if you know what I mean. Was that terribly bad of me, do you think?'

A secret stash of cash?

'Not at all. It sounds like a perfectly sensible plan to me. I wish I'd had a plan B on quite a few occasions in my life, I can tell you.'

'The thing is, I'm pretty certain I have a ring put away

in this one, and I'd really like to see it again. And there's the compass, too. I always thought the compass was in the house, but now I'm not so sure, maybe I put it with the ring ... my mind is so jumbled. Maybe I left it in one of my deposit boxes, and I just can't remember?'

'And when was the last time you went to this ... box?' I asked.

Juliet took a deep breath and tried to think.

'The early eighties?'

Ah.

'Well, it sounds like a fun quest. A ring and a compass – I can do that!' I reached to the back seat for my coat and Fenella's boots. 'Show me exactly where you want me to go and I'll totter off, but won't you get cold sitting here alone while I'm gone? Shall I leave the engine running?'

Juliet shook her head.

'There's a tearoom just down the road in Morvah. Shuffle me in there and I'll be perfectly fine for an hour until you get back. I know the owner. It'll be good to say goodbye.'

Goodbye? Was that how it was to be one hundred years old? Was every hello a possible goodbye?

Having waved au revoir to Juliet, I returned to park at the lay-by, donned my boots and followed a farm track sheltered by high Cornish hedges, until I came across the sign for Men an Tol. I climbed a stile and followed a well-worn path to three desolate stones – two uprights and a holed-out circular stone sitting on its side, between them.

Juliet had said that I should stand next to the circular stone with my back to the relic of a tin mine which was away in the distance, look to my right – two o clock – and find a lone hawthorn tree, its branches shaped to follow the prevailing westerly wind, roughly a hundred yards away across the moor. Amazed that the tree still stood there alone, after all these years, I crossed at a ninety-degree angle to a stone hedge. In the pasture field directly behind the hedge was a flat stone, under the stone I would find a small green ammunition box. I followed the instructions to the letter and by some minor miracle, there the box was.

Having been instructed not to open the box, I set off at a pace back to the car, but not so fast that I didn't pause to touch the megalith. Juliet had said that there was a theory that the capstone had originally sat atop a burial mound, to act as a portal to the otherworld – a passage to find the final sleep. I imagined Juliet climbing through the hole in the stone to make a wish and burying an offering close by. I decided to make a wish of my own, but what could I offer to the Gods in return? I delved into my coat pocket and found a tissue, my phone and car keys. All I had to offer of my own that the Gods might be remotely interested in was a single band of gold, my wedding ring. No, I wouldn't let that go, and I had nothing to wish for anyway – even the God's can't bring someone back from the dead. But as I picked up the ammunition box, I realised there was something I desperately wanted to wish for.

I fell to all fours, climbed through the stone and wished, with all my heart, for the compass to be found, with a promise – an I Owe You – to return before I left Cornwall with an offering.

The next stop was the Minack Theatre for lunch, which meant heading back over the moor to the south coast. I had never been to Minack, but knew it to be a steep amphitheatre high on the cliffs overlooking the beach at Porthcurno. I wasn't too sure about taking an elderly lady to a wind-blown rocky precipice, but Juliet was determined to go.

I needn't have worried. The café was at the entrance and easily accessible by wheelchair. We manoeuvred our way inside, the ammunition box perched on Juliet's knee, and took a seat at a table looking out to sea. I draped a blanket over Juliet's legs, sat down and from nowhere began to laugh. She looked questioningly at me from across the box which sat on the table.

'I just can't believe this is real,' I said, shaking my head. 'When I started reading your memoirs, I would have given anything to meet you. And suddenly, here you are, the woman who flew Spitfires. I'm so in awe of you Juliet and I feel so ... lucky. And I have so many questions, so much I'd like to know.'

'Such as?'

I thought about it. What pressing issue would I like this wise woman's opinion on?

'I know ... would you ever have considered Botox?'

She laughed out loud and shook her head in amusement. 'Let's have a look inside the box, shall we?'

It opened easily. I glanced inside, smiling up excitedly to Juliet, whose eyes also sparkled with anticipation. I slowly emptied the contents – a tiny teddy bear, four freezer bags stuffed full with old-style twenty-pound notes and, to Juliet's absolute delight, a ring box, covered in mould. She opened the box and there it was still, a very pretty gold band with a large ruby set inside.

Juliet slid the ring onto her bare engagement finger, put the ring to her lips, closed her eyes, took a deep breath and exhaled, happily.

On a roll, I felt through the plastic money bags to see if the compass was hidden within the money. Please, God, let it be there. It wasn't. I shook my head.

Juliet smiled.

'Never mind,' she said, 'you'll find it for me, I know you will.'

She looked down at the ring again.

'I take it that's a special ring to you?' I asked, wanting to know the story but not wanting to pry.

Juliet nodded. 'Oh, yes.' She admired it on her finger. 'I needed to move on from it for a while, which was difficult, but it's time to wear it again now, I think. Tell me,' she began, looking up, 'how far have you got?'

'Got?' I swallowed a mouthful of quiche. 'With your memoirs, you mean?'

She nodded.

'Let's see ... you're just about to meet Edward at the Bugle. I can't wait to find out what happened next.'

Juliet's eyes sparkled.

'I'll tell you now if you like.'

'Now?'

Juliet glanced around. 'We have the time, why not?'

Why not, indeed!

Chapter 23

Juliet

Twenty-four hours in Cornwall

Edward was nowhere to be seen in the Bugle when I arrived. With the phrase, 'let sleeping dogs lie' floating around in my mind, I smiled at the barman, explained that the person I had hoped to find wasn't in the bar and turned to leave. Which is when I saw him – Edward – standing in the doorway. His left arm in a sling and a deep, angry-looking gash across his jaw line. His expression reflected my own – a perfect mixture of adoration, longing and fear.

It was this particular expression, as if captured forever in a photograph, that my mind's eye would return to the most in later years. It was a snapshot of a moment, unplanned and instant, that sealed my fate irrevocably. When Lottie had said he was married, I had placed Edward firmly in the category of one of those men my mother had warned me about – an opportunist, a coddiwompler – who lived in the moment, without thought of the consequences. I had locked him away as the sort of man who could – who would – move on to another woman without pause, never able to develop a deep, lasting, emotional connection, and I had made that assumption, pushing Edward away, in the flash of a moment without thinking it through. But as our eyes locked in the doorway of the Bugle and the energy between us ignited in an undeniable moment of truth, I knew that Edward was deeply in love with me. It was in his eyes, in his shortened breath, his smile. It was a love that could not be mimicked, not at such a spontaneous moment.

The owner of the Bugle, Mr Palmer, walked into the lounge bar from a private room. He handed Edward a suitcase with a smile.

'Your car has just pulled up outside, Sir,' he said.

If Edward heard Mr Palmer, he didn't respond. Mr Palmer looked in my direction and put the suitcase down on the floor.

'Hello, Edward,' I whispered, motionless.

'Hello, Juliet. Poor timing seems to be our nemesis.'

I didn't respond, mainly because I didn't know what to say, until ...

'Why did you come here?' I asked.

He led me by the arm to a corner of the bar.

'I wanted to know you were all right, after the Empire bomb. I was out of mind with worry. I couldn't find you and ...'

'You shouldn't have come,' I whispered. 'Everything is different now. *I'm* different now. I'm married. And so are you.'

'Who told you I'm married?' His voice was tired, strained.

'Lottie Lanyon.'

'When?'

'After I left your cottage. On that last day.'

He shook his head. Mr Palmer coughed by the door.

'I have to go, but it isn't – wasn't – what you think. But I can't tell you about it now – not here. I wish you'd come to see me, to ask.' He rubbed his forehead, frustrated.

I sighed with the sadness of it all. The lack of sleep, the strong measure of gin and not to mention the war, was starting to take its toll. I was so very tired.

'None of that matters now, Edward. I should never have told you that I wouldn't marry Charles. I couldn't tell you the whole story, but at the time I had no choice. And now, what with the war. Everything is different. I'm not the girl you knew.'

He shook his head.

'May I write to you?'

I didn't respond.

'*Please*,' Edward persisted. 'It's important. If I write to you at the ATA, at Hamble, will you get the letter?'

'Yes, but really, there's no—'

Edward interrupted. 'There's *every* need.'

'You have a wife,' I whispered.

Edward didn't answer but walked to the door and picked up his case. He turned to face me.

'There is no wife, Juliet.' His shoulders sagged with sadness. 'I'm no longer married and I wasn't when I met you. When I arrived in Angels Cove, Lottie would sometimes come to the village and seek me out. I was invited up to the big house a few times, she jumped to the wrong conclusion one day and I let her run with it. It was easier, somehow.'

He crossed the room and kissed me on the cheek before whispering in my ear.

'I've never met anyone like you and I know I never will.'

A moment later, he was gone.

A week later two letters arrived on the same day. They could not have been more different. Edward's was short, but said everything I needed to know.

Dear Juliet,
Say you'll see me again.
Yours.
E x

Charles' letter was longer. He wrote to inform me of changes that had taken place at Lanyon and he was concerned that I had not been consulted or made aware, it was my inheritance, too, now, after all. Charles explained that the east wing had been commandeered by the Foreign

Office for their own particular use during the war. Charles asked if I might be able to find the time to visit Lanyon to check the old place over, explaining that Pa seemed excessively stressed in his letters. Organising the estate in terms of managing the tenant farmers – many of whom had taken on city children – and organising the Land Army was, Charles thought, perhaps a little too much for him, especially since the accident.

I read the letter as if I were reading about people I barely knew. I had corresponded with Ma, who had recovered, albeit a weakened woman, and I kept in touch with Lottie, too, who was based at RAF Leeming in Yorkshire, where some of the Canadian squadrons were holed up. Lottie, it seemed, had discovered a renewed life-purpose in the WAAF, and was working tirelessly as a driver for the Mechanical Transport Section while Mabel was looked after by her aunt.

But to go to Lanyon now?

The note from Charles ended with a postscript which confused me. He wrote that one of the men in charge of the comings and goings at Lanyon was none other than our old acquaintance, Edward Nancarrow. It was odd, wasn't it, he said, how things were able to change so significantly within a fleeting moment. He went on to say that such moments should be grasped with both hands – that the war had taught him to run *at* life, not away from it. He concluded by asking again that I go to Lanyon for a few days and if I felt lonely, I could always seek out that chap,

Edward, and perhaps go for a walk or something, *just like the old days*. Then Charles had signed off, *wishing you all the very best in the world, my dear Juliet*.

I held the letter for some time, staring at the wall, thinking. The tone hadn't been like a letter from a husband at all. No, we had never had the time to develop our marriage and deep down, even though I couldn't help but desire another man, a man – let's be clear – I barely knew, but the taking away by the war of my first years with Charles had saddened me, because how on earth could we ever pick up where we left off, when there was no 'leaving off' place to pick-up from? It would be like trying to keep a child sitting on a knee it wasn't familiar with. It would keep sliding off – *we* would keep sliding off.

But what to do about Lanyon?

I was sitting in the mess at Hamble darning a pair of flying socks listening to the radio with Anna when I paused to consider this question. We decided that I really should pay Lanyon a visit, and not just because of the chance of seeing Edward (we both reiterated at exactly the same time) but because of the great piles of money I'd sunk into it. Like it or not, Lanyon – in all its dilapidated but splendid glory – was beholden to me, and I was tied – for better for worse, for richer for poorer – to it.

But how, and when? It wasn't like the old days, the days of endless summers when I could jump into my Tiger Moth and nip down to Cornwall for a day's excursion. Private flying was not permitted and fuel rationing for private cars was fierce, not that I'd ever learned to drive. I could, of course, catch the train.

Anna had a different solution.

The South West of England had become increasing vulnerable to attack by the Luftwaffe and so a number of airfields had been built in Cornwall, one of which was RAF Predannack, about five miles from Lanyon. Anna knew this because our Polish friend, Leska, had delivered a Hawker Hurricane to that air base the week before and had complained about the chauvinism she found there. All I had to do, Anna suggested, was explain my personal circumstances to the boss and ask if I could take the next delivery to Predannack. There were bound to be lots of deliveries headed that way, how else would the new squadrons come up to strength?

Within three days, my wish was granted, which was how I came to find myself flying to Cornwall again – in a Hurricane this time – heading into the afternoon sun, checking off major towns and rivers en route. This time I kept inland, away from anti-aircraft gunners who monitored the south west approaches, and smiled at the wonder of it – me, in a Hurricane – and with a sudden flashback to my stunt-pilot days, decided not head straight for Predannack but threw the rule book out of the window and headed towards Lanyon, where Ma and Pa had been told to watch out for me. I did not fly by the house sedately. No, this time, I – Juliet Caron, the celebrated star of the Caron Flying Circus – paid homage to my parents, and with the speed, aggression and fury of a fighter pilot with a Nazi on her tail, opened up the throttle and roared past Lanyon like a bat out of hell, darting over the cedar trees before turning the fighter on its wing and heading back towards the house, slower this time, waggling the wings as I passed the back terrace.

No one on the ground who saw the aircraft would have believed the pilot was a woman and as I turned away from Lanyon, glanced down and saw Angels Cove, I couldn't help but smile remembering one particular day during Christmas week 1938, when I sat on the harbour wall with Edward, swinging my legs and telling him how – as God was my witness – one day I would find a way to fly for the RAF, and in a way, I had (and the fact that Edward may have looked up from Lanyon and seen me showing off, even if he didn't know it was me at the time, was the icing on the cake).

After handing over the aircraft and signing the paperwork, I grabbed my overnight bag and headed across the airfield towards the Operations Room in the hope of finding a phone, which is when I noticed a man leaning against the passenger door of an open-topped Morgan.

It was Edward and he was smiling at me.

'Hello, you,' he said as I approached.

It was too familiar. Too intimate. I tried to change to hide my joy and excitement at seeing him again. But I was still buzzing from the flight. He nodded towards the Hurricane.

'Still making a dramatic entrance. I saw you from the house. Is that kind of flying allowed in the ATA?'

I stopped by the car and put my bag and parachute on the ground.

'I wrote to you,' he said.

'Yes.'

'You didn't write back.'

'No.'

He touched my cheek.

'Oil on your face, again.'

I glanced around to see if anyone was watching us, took a deep breath, stepped away and picked up my things. Being near Edward – talking to Edward, seeing his face, his hands, his mouth – was magical. It was the most alive I ever felt with my feet on the ground. But I'd made my bed with Charles and now I had to lie in it – alone, seemingly.

'How long have you got?' he asked, picking up my parachute with a groan.

I looked him in the eye.

'Don't, Edward. Please. I should be heading straight to Lanyon. I promised ...'

'Just tell me. How long?'

'Twenty-four hours.'

He placed the parachute in the boot of the car.

'Now, I know you normally like to walk home from your aircraft, but I told the Lanyons I'd give you a lift. They aren't expecting you until later. How about we drop by Angels Cove ...'

'Edward, stop and listen to me. I can't.'

'Just for afternoon tea? And it's a lovely day, we could go out on the river afterwards.'

It all sounded so perfect and a million miles away from real life – from barrage balloons and rationing and bombs and bullets and the whole utter bloody nightmare of it, all of the time.

'Afternoon tea?' I repeated, standing in complete impotence, watching him load the car. 'There's no shortage of butter and cream in Cornwall, then?'

'There is. But when old Pa Lanyon told me you were planning a visit, I saved my ration coupons and, well,' he shrugged, 'there are usually ways to get a little extra. And I managed to make some scones, too ... and little sandwiches ...'

'*You?*' I laughed. '*You* made scones?'

He nodded, brightly. 'I sure did!'

He was so damn sexy. But I didn't want my resolve crumble. I didn't want to dishonour Charles. And above all else, I *did not* want to be a sure thing.

'I'm sorry, Edward. But I really should go straight to Lanyon. Ma will be waiting for me. I haven't seen her in such a long time, and what with her accident, and as I told you in Hamble ...'

Edward opened the passenger door.

'I told them not to expect you until dinner ... you're a busy woman. Log books to sign, chits to hand in, that kind of thing ...' He leant in and whispered in my ear. 'Just one more day. That's all I ask.'

I was nothing more than putty.
'Let me change out of my flying garb first ...'

And that was when it began – really began. On a boat.
On the Helford River. On a sunny Wednesday afternoon
in early August 1941. It was the beginning of knowing for
definite that this was the only man I could ever consider
loving. Ever truly give my body to. Ever feel this connected
to. The fact that I was already married to Charles and that
his family were just a couple of miles up the road seemed,
at that moment – despite my half-hearted excuses – utterly
inconsequential.

Afternoon tea in the cottage was fun and charged with
an increased sense of flirtation and expectation. I did not
mention Edward's wife – or ex-wife – and Edward did
not mention Charles. We placed ourselves firmly inside
a bubble.

And yet we didn't kiss. But does that mean that our
day together was an innocent one? No, it does not. How
could it when our hearts had already become so irrevers-
ibly intertwined? To unravel that tangle of emotion would
have been impossible. I'll never forget the joy in Edward's
tanned, bold face that afternoon as we pootled down the
river and out to the islands on his boat, *The Mermaid*. He
was so completely happy. It was like a firework had gone
off inside his heart. And it was the same for me, too – that
same honeymoon feeling. As if, with two previous false
starts under our belts, we were both determined to make

the most of every moment together. I'm sure that, if it hadn't been for poor Lottie's unexpected arrival at Lanyon that evening – with Mabel in her arms, declaring that her new husband (yes, husband. A Canadian whom she had secretly married after whirlwind romance) had been shot down, presumed dead, over Germany the week before – then, like a thief in the night, I would have dashed down to his cottage after dinner and spent the night. But it seemed that other people – other priorities, other consequences – would continue to get in the way of our taking the final step, of the giving of ourselves to each other and being able to set the affair, irrevocably, in stone.

Chapter 24

Katherine

Be more Marie

Juliet sipped on water and turned to glance towards Logan Rock, across the beach.

'Oh, Juliet. What a life you've led,' I said, looking up from my empty coffee cup. 'It was all so very ... romantic.'

She smiled. 'Yes, I suppose it was. But tell me, what do you think of Anna and Marie?'

'Oh, I absolutely love them. How could I not? And the job you all did? It was amazing.'

Juliet put on her reading glasses, opened her handbag and with stiff fingers, unzipped an inner compartment. She took out a black and white photograph.

Three women wearing the same ATA uniform I had seen hanging on the outside of the wardrobe in Juliet's spare bedroom – a knee length skirt and smart buttoned jacket – were standing in front of what I believed to be a Spitfire. Across the top of the photo someone had written *Attagirls*. They all looked so incredibly happy.

I leant in so we could look at it together. A perfectly manicured finger as gnarled as a twig pointed shakily towards one of the women.

'That's my Anna,' she said. 'And there's Marie.'

Tears edged onto her lower lids – sand between the toes again. I pointed to a vibrant-looking woman with chin length thick hair standing to Anna's left. 'And is that you?' I asked, certain that it would be.

She nodded. 'It all seems like yesterday,' she said, returning the photograph to its safe place. I sat back in my chair and we both took a moment to stare out of the window and sip tea. Juliet turned away from the view to smile at me kindly. 'Gerald said you've given up a little, since your husband died.'

'Given up?' That was the last thing I wanted Juliet, the ultimate Attagirl, to see me as. 'Not ... given up, so much, as pressed the pause button.'

Juliet nodded her understanding.

'And when do you intend to press play?'

Her response surprised me and I floundered, because it sounded so simple, and the truth was I had become exhausted by my grief, playing Queen Victoria to James' Albert. But like a soldier living on the edge of no-man's-land, I had dug my trench of grief deep enough to keep me safe from the stray bullets life could send ricocheting in any direction. Life in a trench is a stale, stagnant, half-life, however. And having in dug-in so well in the first place, it now seemed nigh on impossible to clamber out, which is why I stayed there, in the gloop, because it's easier, safer.

'And that's how other people start to see you,' I explained, 'as the widow. So you stay in that image, partly out of worry that if you're seen to be happy ...'

I paused, uneasy at suddenly feeling able to be so completely honest.

'They might think you didn't care,' Juliet finished, understanding.

'Yes, I suppose so.'

'And I do see that no one would see it that way, at least, no one of importance, and all this self-imposed restriction is suffocating, and not at all what James would have wanted. Gerald has been worried, I know he has, and I do see that it's time for the widow's garb to be thrown on the fire, but it's ... it's odd, reinventing a life. I wish I could be more like ...' I glanced around, thinking. 'Marie! More like Marie.'

Juliet laughed. 'You'd be arrested inside the week!'

I widened my eyes – 'But it would be one hell of a week!'

Juliet's eyes were so kind, so understanding. But how could I explain that part of the problem was that even before James died, I had dug another trench, not so deep this time, but a trench all the same – it was the trench of James' life. I had buried myself in his career, his city, his friends, and all at the tender age of nineteen, and I'd done it willingly, too – I'd taken the easy route. And now, having had no adult life without him, if I climbed out of the trench, as I knew I must, where would I go?

Juliet read my mind. 'It must be difficult, reinventing your life from scratch, but all you really need is for someone to pass down a ladder. Trust me, it's much more simple than you think, once you set your mind to climb out.'

I smiled.

'And when I get to the top, where would – will – I go?'

Juliet took a deep breath and gestured towards the wide expanse of sea.

'Coddiwompling,' she said with a wink. 'That's where.'

When no performances are scheduled, it's possible to explore the terraces and the stage at the Minack, and so I wrapped Juliet in enough blankets to survive a polar expedition and wheeled her out to the upper viewing area. The winter sun shone its faint, watered-down glow onto Juliet's silver hair. I knelt next to the wheelchair and we remained in silence, taking in the theatre and sea.

'I always fancied myself performing here,' Juliet said, her face so frail against the cold breeze, nodding down towards the stage, which was a significant way down a myriad of stone steps, below us. 'Sam and I used to visit here during the quieter times, jump on the stage and give it a go. He sang a whole song for me once. Didn't give a damn who was listening!'

'Really?' I asked, delighted. 'What did he sing?'

'We'll Meet Again.'

She glanced up – coquettishly.

'I don't suppose ... you could ...?'

I quickly leant back as an automatic reaction.

'*Me?* Down there? No way! People will think I'm nuts.'

Juliet shrugged. 'I thought you wanted to be more like Marie. She would have loved it here. And those two over there,' Juliet pointed to a happy couple who were exploring the terraces, 'were just a second ago singing and having fun on the stage. You didn't think badly of them.'

But that was exactly the point, *two* people had been prancing on the stage, together. When two people arse about it's fun, when it's just one, it's not fun, it's lonely.

'And don't forget to really belt it out so I can hear you up here.'

'But I don't know the words.'

'Of course, you do, everyone knows that song.'

'But ...'

Juliet took my hand. 'You were just saying it was time for a change, to be more optimistic. I'm handing you the ladder, Katherine. Don't you think it's time to put a foot on the first rung?'

'Couldn't you hand me the ladder another way? Like ask me to wrestle a tiger, or something? Something I little bit ... easier.'

Juliet shook her head.

'It's time,' she said.

I sighed, tottered down the steps to the stage and looked back up at Juliet sitting in her wheelchair, waving at me.

My voice would never carry all the way back to her, for goodness sake, she was miles away. The couple who had been frolicking on the stage stopped their steady climb out of the theatre and turned to look at me, smiling.

'Be more Marie,' I whispered to myself, standing on the stage. '*We'll meet again, don't know where, don't know when, but I know we'll meet again some sunny day …*'

I was dreadful. Croaky. Out of tune. But it didn't seem to matter. The fun couple dashed back to the stage to link arms with me to join in. Competing with the elements to throw our voices into the amphitheatre was not easy, but Juliet was right, who the hell cared, certainly not the handful of other people milling around the theatre who, by the second verse, all joined in, too. Two further women joined me on the stage while others flashed up the torches on their phones and swayed side to side as we all sang.

'*So, will you please say hello, to the boys that I know, tell them I won't be long...*'

By the second rendition someone from the café put on the stage lights and we were all really rocking it – legs kicking in unison, the lot. It was my very own flashmob Vera Lynn moment, and I loved it.

'*Keep smiling through just like you always do, till the blue skies drive the dark clouds far away … We'll meet again, don't know where, don't know when, but I know we'll meet again some sunneeee day.*'

As we closed the final line, I waved up at Juliet who was clapping much more wildly than I'd imagined a woman two days from her centenary should be able to manage and feeling a sudden jolt of electric energy – of determination – I realised that it was time to start looking forward rather than constantly glancing over my shoulder trying to keep a focused view of the past in sight. I would help Fenella tonight with the bottling of the gin and if it wasn't too late, I would persuade the village mafia to put aside their differences and hang the Christmas lights – if only for the sake of all the little (non-existent) children.

But first, there was another ammunition box to find, near the Helford river this time, and as we drove away from Minack, I hoped more than anything that my wish at the monument would come true.

Chapter 25

Juliet

A visit to Lottie

I began my story by saying that there are certain days in life that are printed, for good or for bad, more indelibly into our minds than most. Such was that day with Edward, when we played like children on the river, in his boat, in the sunshine, in love.

My promise to Charles to spend the day at Lanyon, checking on Ma and Pa, had been thrown out of the window completely. How easy it is to go back on one's word when the alternative is spending time in the company of a new and exciting love.

But it was only during the train journey back to Southampton that I began to consider how little I knew about Edward and wondered what the exact nature of his work was for the war effort at Lanyon.

He was, he had finally explained, of Austrian origin

– the American/English accent developed as a by-product of travelling the world with his father, a diplomat. In his work for the Foreign Office it had been suggested he adopt the Cornish surname, Nancarrow, while living in England. His real surname was Gruber, first name Felix, and was far too Germanic-sounding to sit comfortably for a man living in a country on the brink of (and now firmly ensconced in) war.

I did manage to spend a little time at Lanyon during my stay. When probed about the changes at the house, Pa Lanyon had explained, simply and straightforwardly, that the chaps who had taken over the other side of the house kept themselves to themselves and that we were encouraged not to ask questions.

Edward (it was too late to think of him under another name) when asked directly, had been matter-of-fact. He shrugged and said, 'I can't tell you. It's a Foreign Office type of affair. And it's best you don't know.'

When I pressed, 'But is it dangerous, Edward?'

He simply said, 'No more than your job.' Which meant nothing.

On returning to Hamble the next day, I went straight to the mess and sought out Anna and Marie. Anna was airborne but Marie was preparing for a flight to Prestwick in a Tiger Moth.

'A sonofabitch Tiger Moth!' she moaned, walking out of the Met Office to get her kit together before departing. 'And Scotland will be damn cold, too!'

'In August?'

She ignored me. 'I bet I get pneumonia. There are polar bears in Scotland, right?'

I laughed.

'You've been spoiled lately, with all the Spitfire deliveries. It will do you good!'

She stopped walking and turned around excitedly.

'Hey, tell me. How did it go in Cornwall?'

I shrugged and tried to feign coy. I could never feign coy.

'Cornwall? Oh, you know. Same old same old. But honestly, Marie, flying the Hurricane down there was an absolute peach!'

Marie frowned.

'Hurricane? What the heck? I'm talking about Lanyon! Did you see Edward?'

I smiled. My smile betrayed me. Marie turned towards the operations room.

'Walk with me while I prepare, and *keep talking*.' She took her pilot's notes out of her flying bag and skimmed through the start-up checks for the Tiger Moth. 'I want to know *everything*!'

Over the planning table I gave an abbreviated account of the last twenty-four hours.

'Then we had a picnic on his boat – *The Mermaid* – such a lovely thing. He flirted relentlessly, I batted him off, and then he tried to quote Burns, putting on a Scots accent, you know, but he failed – at both the poetry and the accent. He was so funny!'

Marie couldn't resist an eye roll, which I ignored.

'We sailed, we walked, we talked and eventually ... well, I headed back up the hill to Lanyon. I promised to make my excuses with Ma and Pa and head back down to the village, to Edward, to spend the evening together. But then Lottie arrived at Lanyon, out of the blue and in tears.'

'That damn Lottie!' Marie said, looking up from her map. 'She's always in the background, messing things up. Damn woman.'

'She doesn't mess things up on purpose. Her husband is dead!'

'Husband? A real one?'

'What other kind is there?'

'Don't make me laugh, honey. No one even knew she was engaged let alone married. She can't have known the guy for more than two minutes!'

'Does that matter? I've only known Edward for the briefest of time, but still, I ...'

'So, you *are* in love with him. I knew it!'

I sighed, defeated.

'What's he doing in Cornwall, anyways, this mysterious stranger of yours?' she asked, pouring over a map.

I dashed around the table to stand next to her.

'No one seems to know, exactly. It's all very hush-hush. Foreign Office thing. But get this, his name isn't Nancarrow at all, it's Gruber!'

Marie raised her brows.

'He's a spy, I'll bet! Shall I do some digging?'

I narrowed my eyes and nodded.

'Sounds like a plan, Marie. Sounds like a plan.'

It turned out that the organisation Edward worked for was the SOE – Special Operations Executive, which was part of the Special Intelligence Service, also known as MI6. It was an organisation established to conduct espionage, sabotage and reconnaissance in occupied Europe. Contrary to Edward's quip about his job being no more dangerous than mine – it was. Significantly more dangerous. The SOE employed and trained special agents. But what the SOE – also known as Churchill's Secret Army – were doing in Cornwall, at Lanyon, was not information Marie (or Marie's contact) was party to, that information I would discover later, and very much first at hand.

The hand of war can deal the most agonising and downright cruel turn of fortune, and none more so than for Lottie Lanyon. When Lottie had holed herself up in Yorkshire after Mabel was born, she declared that she would return home a couple of years later with Mabel in tow as a war widow – albeit a fake one. But poor Lottie had not reckoned on karma, and on the day of her return to Lanyon – the day I had spent with Edward on the river – she finally confessed to her elopement with Canadian officer, Jim Reece, who, ten days later, was killed when his bomber was shot down over Germany.

With a wedding ring on her finger and the pretence

that the wedding had occurred quite some time before, however, Mabel could now be passed off as legitimate, but would remain at Lanyon with her grandparents and keep the surname she was given at birth – Lanyon – for ease of inheritance, it was explained. Frankly, it was all a bit of a mess, and Ma Lanyon needed quite a bit of a lie down after all the details had been discussed, but somehow, it worked.

Pa deemed it best all round if the confused and despairing Lottie, who by her own admission was not capable of caring properly for the child at this time, returned to her life as a WAAF with a new posting wangled, by hook or by crook, to RAF Predannack, just five miles down the road. Pa knew people who could make this happen, and he did.

And as for me? I was promoted to First Officer Caron and was now qualified to fly all RAF and Fleet Air Arm aircraft with the exception of the heavy four-engines bombers.

Life in the ATA was exhausting but exhilarating, and not, as Edward had said, without a significant degree of danger. It wasn't long before female friends in the ATA lost their lives to accidents caused by pushing the envelope by flying in poor weather conditions, and it was heart-breaking to see names of our co-workers rubbed off the chalk board in the operations room, one by one, as they passed away. But the pressure to deliver to the squadrons, who lost aircraft on a daily basis, was immense. As women pilots in the ATA, we possibly felt the pressure greater than our male counterparts. Determined to prove anyone who questioned our capabilities wrong, we pushed on.

Early one summer morning that year the Spitfire Sisters cycled to the airfield from our home by the river. We headed straight for the ops room to pick up our flying chits for the day. Anna and I were programmed to fly two Spitfires to RAF Dishforth, in Yorkshire. The taxi Anson would arrive at RAF Leeming, ten miles north of Dishforth, the next day, to bring us back to Hamble. Which meant we would have an overnight stay in Yorkshire. Marie was peeved to be missing out, but didn't mind too much because she having a trial run out on a motorbike that evening.

'But that's brilliant,' I said to Anna, once Marie had walked away. 'We can fly up there together, in formation, and stay with Lottie and her aunt nearby, rather than in the mess.'

Anna, despite being desperate to meet the notorious Lottie, wasn't so sure. She began organising the maps we would need on the table.

'I think we should fly separately,' she said, having studied the route. 'I've never flown in close formation before. I don't think I can do it.'

I could understand this. Formation flying could be tricky.

'How about you take the lead and do all the navigation,' I suggested. 'I'll sit on your wing. I used to do it all the time with Pa. I loved it.'

Anna glanced at me.

'You'll let me navigate – the whole way?'

I nodded. 'Of course, I will!'

'I don't believe that for a second,' she scoffed. 'But all right. If you're happy to sit on my wing. Let's do it.'

I had yet another idea.

'Don't you have an uncle near Oxford?'

Anna looked up from her selection of maps.

'Yes. Why?'

'What say we give him a bit of a flypast, pop into Brize Norton for a suck of fuel and he can bring us some lunch out to the airfield?'

Anna's eyes burned bright as a flame.

'Oh, Juliet. He would absolutely love it! Imagine both of us turning up in Spitfires ... jeez, Louise, that would be the business! He'd die and go to heaven, right there and then!' She leant in. 'But we'll get in terrible trouble if anyone ever finds out we beat up the village.'

I glanced around the ops room.

'But no one is going to find out, are they, so don't worry!'

After a rather marvellous lunch, we arrived at RAF Dishforth around six p.m. to find that Lottie had wandered into the Officers' Mess the night before and declared that two of the most beautiful women in England were flying into Dishforth the next day and would require a lift to RAF Leeming. She was inundated with offers and an hour after telephoning the RAF Leeming Officers' Mess to announce our arrival, Anna and I were sitting in the back of a Canadian Air Force Jeep being escorted up the road by a couple of airmen from Montreal.

Lottie was waiting outside the Met Office when we arrived, wearing her WAAF uniform. She hugged me as if she had just that second discovered the whole world would end tomorrow.

'Oh, Juliet,' she cried, not letting go. 'I was so relieved when you said you could come. I can't tell you how desperate I've been to see someone from the old place since I got back here. I miss Mabel so much and everything here is just ... hellish.'

'Hey, hey,' I said, not minding as she wiped her tears on the shoulder of my flying jacket. 'It's all right. It's all right. It won't last forever. Everything is going to be fine, just wait and see.'

But in the late afternoon sunshine, with the sound of a heavy Canadian bomber landing on the airfield, Lottie continued to refuse to let me go, and I knew at that moment that I needed to get Lottie home to Lanyon.

I stepped back and held her at arms' length to take her in before nodding towards Anna.

'Lottie, meet Anna.' Anna held out her hand. 'Anna, this is Lottie, who's a bit overwrought just now. But we'll soon sort that out, won't we Anna?'

Anna shook Lottie's hand and took an oil cloth out of her pocket to dry Lottie's tears.

'Darn right we will!' She put an arm around Lottie.
'You're with the Attagirls now, don't you know. If I can fly
a Spitfire in formation to Yorkshire, then trust me, anything
is possible!'

'You know what?' she said, smiling. 'I really think you
might be right.'

We spent the evening not in the company of a bar-full of
Canadian airmen, but at Lottie's aunt's house, which was
an impressive double-fronted Edwardian town house, situ-
ated on the high street in the local market town of Bedale.
Lottie's Aunt Pru – a women's rights lobbyist and gardening
expert with a penchant for orchids – proved heavenly. But
it was after dinner, when Anna and Pru went for a stroll in
the garden, that I discovered the extent of Lottie's despair.

'The thing is,' she said, linking her arm through mine as
we stepped out of the front door and headed to the park
for a stroll. 'I've got this terrible feeling of dread hanging
over me. I can't seem to shift it.'

'It's the war, Lottie,' I said. 'We all feel that way.'

'No, I know, we do. But it's more than that. It's a very
definite feeling that, pretty soon, it's all going to be all
over for silly old Lottie, and I'm worried about what will
happen to Mabel.'

I stopped walking.

'Oh, Lottie,' I said, embracing her once more. 'Which one
of us can know if we'll still be here tomorrow?' I looked
her firmly in the eyes. 'But if any one of us is most likely

to survive, it's you.' I took her face in my hands and smiled. 'You're ... what's the word? Indefatigable. You always have been, Lottie, truly you have. You need to find your spark again, that's all.'

She shook my hands free of her head.

'Truly, Lottie,' I persisted, 'I think you should look at things realistically. You're off to RAF Predannack in two weeks' time, and you'll be living at Lanyon with Ma and Pa again and dear little Mabel. You're just missing her, that's all, and it must have been a terrible loss, to lose Jim. I'm so sorry I didn't get the chance to meet him, by the way.'

She began to cry.

'You would have liked him,' she said, dabbing her nose with the back of her hand.

We entered the park but she stopped walking again to face me. 'But if anything should happen to me,' she said, 'you will look after Mabel, won't you? I know I asked you before – which was so wrong of me and I'm sorry. But when Charles gets home, if I'm not there, you'll bring her up as yours, as your daughter, with your own children?'

I hesitated. Lottie took my hands. Her eyes were bordering on wild-looking.

'Promise me, Juliet.'

I wanted to say, 'I'm sorry but I can't promise that.' I wanted to say, 'I am not in love with Charles and it was unfair of me to marry him, just as it was unfair of him to marry me, just as it was unfair of you to ask me to raise your child. But all these things were done at the time with the best, if somewhat naïve, intentions.' But most of all, I wanted to say, 'I'm in love with Edward Nancarrow, who is in my thoughts and dreams and prayers every second of every day. He is my future, not Lanyon.'

But I couldn't.

Standing in front of her now, I saw that motherhood and the war had done for Lottie. She had nothing left. And all I could say was, 'Of course I'll look after her. But please, Lottie, try not to worry.'

Lottie calmed.

'And when she's older, read our poem to her ...'

'Our poem?'

'The Christina Rosetti one, you know, the one I read to you to help you to feel better when your parents died. It's called *Remember ...*'

'*Better by far to forget and to smile, than to remember and be sad?*' I asked.

Lottie nodded. 'Yes, exactly. I want her to be happy.'

'But you aren't going to die, Lottie.' I said. 'This is madness. Truly. You're not in danger, so stop worrying, please.'

For the rest of the evening we played cards and rationed out a bottle of whiskey Aunt Pru had hidden in the back of the larder in 1938 and had been waiting for a special occasion to break out. Anna eventually persuaded Lottie to take to the piano and we sang Jo Stafford songs until the early hours of the morning, ending with a song that one day would mean more to me than any song had meant before or any song would ever mean again – Anna's favourite and the song Marie sang with the naval officer's head resting on her lap, *Somewhere Over the Rainbow.*

Back at Hamble the following day, we picked up our delivery programmes before heading into the mess to grab some late lunch. A letter with a Cornish postmark sat in my pigeon hole. It was from Edward and it was a proposition.

Darling, Juliet
Spend the weekend with me?
Let's have two days just for each other – two days to last a lifetime, to remember each other by, whatever happens.
I'll meet you anywhere.
London, Southampton, the moon?
Say the word and I'll make it happen.
Yours, as ever,
The kindred coddiwompler.
E x

I read the letter twice before hurriedly pushing it into my jacket pocket. Marie noticed my flushed face.

'I won't ask you right now what's in that letter,' she whispered through the side of her mouth, having sidled up to me at the planning table. 'But by the colour of you, I would guess that has something to do with a certain chap in Cornwall, am I right?'

I bit my lip. I couldn't look her in the eye.

'He wants to spend a whole weekend with me,' I whispered.

Marie's face lit up.

'Where?'

'Anywhere I like. He thinks we should have one weekend, just for us – two days to last a lifetime, he called it.'

Marie turned her back on the table and rested against it. 'So ...?'

'*So*, what?' I opened out a map of South Wales.

'So ... are you going to meet him? Because if you are ...' she whistled and another pilot glanced up and smiled from across the table. Marie lowered her voice. '... if you are, that means spending the night together. And you do know what that—'

I cut her short.

'Yes, thank you. I know exactly what that means. But there's no way I could get two or three days off work.'

Marie sniffed.

'But if you *could* get away, if you could meet up with him, say in a hotel, or even better, at my flat in Chelsea, just for a night ...'

'It's not possible ...'

'But if you could,' she persisted. 'Would you?'

I took a deep breath and looked her in the eye. My eyes must have shone.

'Yes,' I said before laughing out loud. 'I do believe I would!'

Ten minutes later, as I was about to enter the Met Office for a brief, Marie put a note in my hand.

Spoken to Anna. We have a plan and it's a hootie! See you tonight. Fly safely, my beautiful friend.

And I wondered at that moment, truly, what would I do without them?

Marie got her way.

It was arranged that Edward and I would meet in London at Waterloo Station on Friday evening. I had been given the Saturday off, but would need to catch the Milk Train back to Southampton on Sunday morning and from there the early morning district train to Hamble. I knew by now that there was no problem getting the Milk Train to be back in time to fly the following morning. Yes, you were a bit tired, but it was worth it, and anyhow, that's how we all lived then, from one adventure to another, grabbing every moment, at least, that's what I kept telling myself as stood in front of my dressing table and turned a photograph of Charles away from me, before packing Marie's lacy negligée into my overnight bag, a negligée so fine it could pull through a wedding ring.

But I needn't have turned the photograph around because Fate, that overly-sensible overlord, would once again take me under his control, and as I stood on the platform in a hedonistic haze, pushing Charles from my mind and waiting to begin my 'two days to last a lifetime' I saw Anna and Marie running toward me, out of breath, just as the train arrived. Anna was waving a telegram.

```
Charles   injured  Stop  Hospital  ship
docks Southampton Monday Stop Operation
on  Tuesday  Stop  Can  you  be  there  Stop
Love  Ma
```

'I said we shouldn't come,' she said, shaking her head. Anna talked over her. 'But I thought you'd be even more desperate when you got back if you didn't know. The guilt would hurt you too much, it would ruin whatever time you'd had.'

The guard blew his whistle. Train doors slammed shut. I stood with the telegram in my hand. My friends stared at me, waiting for a decision.

Marie took hold of my arm. 'Go!' she urged. 'You'll still be back in plenty of time to support Charles. This is your moment for happiness, Juliet. For passion! Edward said as much in his letter – two days to last a lifetime, remember?'

I thought of opening my clutch bag and taking out my father's compass. Was this to be the first time I would ask it a question? I glanced questioningly – desperately – at Anna, my moral compass, who's face told me exactly what I really ought to do. Leaving the compass where it was, and mute with disappointment and guilt – disappointment of having my chance with Edward taken away, and with guilt for not being heartbroken about Charles' injuries, because God only knew what they would turn out to be, I stepped away from the train.

'No!' Marie persisted. 'You were far too young and naïve

when you married Charles, you know you were. It was all a ridiculous mistake – even Charles knows that! What if something happens to Edward and you miss this chance. *Please*, Juliet. The train is starting to move. You can still jump on. Go to London! I'm begging you, go!'

I felt my wedding ring through my glove, leant towards her and kissed her on the cheek before turning to hug Anna, just as the steam from the engine engulfed our embrace.

'It's no good,' I said. 'I can't have a wonderful time with Edward now, not knowing the extent of Charles' injuries. I can't.'

The train picked up momentum. Even if I had changed my mind, it was too late to jump on now. Marie's shoulders slumped.

'We should never have brought the damn telegram!' She threw a bitter look in Anna's direction. 'We should have let you go to London with the innocence of not knowing.'

I picked up my small suitcase with a protracted sigh.

'Innocence?' My dejected exhaustion at the whole sorry mess now echoing in my voice. 'Nothing about that trip would have been innocent, Marie. You did the right thing.'

We walked down the platform.

'But don't you think Edward deserves an explanation in person?' Marie asked. 'You could catch the next train to town, go to the Savoy and explain. Have dinner and catch the last train home ...' Her eyes were pleading.

I shook my head.

'If I go to London, I won't have the strength to come

home tonight. I know I won't. I'll get caught up in the moment and Edward will too.' We began to walk again. 'I'll telegram Edward at the Savoy. Try to explain, somehow.'

'Maybe he knows already?' Anna said, suddenly brighter. 'He works at Lanyon. He may have bumped into your in-laws, they would have told him about their son, surely.'

I shook my head.

'Edward hasn't been at Lanyon this week. I don't know where he's been.'

'Do you think he'll understand?' Anna asked. 'It'll be a terrible blow. Do you think he'll ask you to meet him again?'

Tears pricked my eyes and I thought of Edward on the Helford River, trying – and failing – to quote Rabbie Burns, *my love is like a red red rose*, while he sailed across the river, laughing.

'No,' I said. 'I don't.'

Edward did not answer my telegram.

Sitting next to Charles' hospital bed four days later, I wept. I wept for Charles, whose ship had taken a direct blow leaving him fighting for his life with internal injuries and needing surgery to save his life, but mostly I wept for my lost love. Being at war was no different to being in the first throws of a desperate love affair, because it brought nothing but extremes. On the one hand I had known nothing but pure joy in my work and had been given a flying experience that would never have been open to a woman just a few short years before, but it seemed that if we were given such bright, beautiful, joyful light, then it must be at a price – if the joy is extreme, then so must the darkness be – the blackest of black. And when I thought of all that had happened so far – the lives lost, the ships sunk and the cities destroyed – I realised that I was tired of living a life of wild emotional ups and downs and all I wanted was for something in my life to feel settled. Although I was not, and perhaps never had been, in love with Charles, I did love him, and sitting by his hospital bed I knew that he represented an easier, more secure time, and that I simply had do the right thing and stay by his side to support him and at least try, for the first time since my marriage, to be a good wife.

Charles survived his operation and stayed in hospital for a month. I was given compassionate leave to visit as often as I could. We were lucky that he had been sent close by to Southampton, but the demand on ATA pilots to deliver great swathes of aircraft every single day had never been greater. Which meant that as Charles grew stronger, I returned to full time flying and once again, barely saw him.

After six weeks in hospital Charles was discharged. But where to send him to recuperate?

With Marie on leave and staying in London, Anna and I spent a week agonising over the problem. The options were quite straight-forward. I could leave the ATA, bring Charles home to Hamble and tend for him myself, or I could still bring him home to Hamble, but continue to fly and hire a nurse – I did not relish this option, as the girls would have to move out. There was a third option, of course. We could both go back to Lanyon and I could care for him there. But the thing was – and Charles felt it, too – our marriage had been in its infancy when the war began and I really didn't know him well enough – on an intimate level – to nurse him.

In the end, Charles made the decision for both of us. I was sitting at his bedside and was about to launch into chapter four of Lottie's copy of *Gone With the Wind* when he reached over and put his hand on my knee. I put the book down and took his hand.

'I've decided,' he said, not looking at me but facing forward. A scar ran from his right eye across his temple and down to his ear. 'I'd like to go home, to Lanyon.'

His kept his head facing forwards. It was a distant kind of communication.

Charles' wish to return to Lanyon was the worst possible news for me. I would definitely have to leave the ATA, but most importantly, I would run the risk of seeing Edward and I wasn't sure how on earth I could cope with that. But if it was what he wanted, everything else was simply not important.

'All right,' I said, slowly. The last thing he needed was a row. 'I can sort that out for us.' I tried to be bright. 'And with Lottie there it'll be just like the old days and who knows,' I added, 'it might even be ...' I stopped myself. Charles's mental health had gone into decline and 'fun' wasn't something he would consider at the moment. And who was I kidding, life at Lanyon could never be like the old days so I finished with, 'Well, it might be for the best, that's all.'

Charles squeezed my hand.

'You misunderstand me. I don't want you to come with me,' he said, 'not right away.'

I didn't know what to say other than, 'Why?'

'It's difficult to explain,' he said, 'but I think, first of all, it's best if Ma and Lottie sort me out, you know, until I find my feet.' There were tears in his eyes. 'You love flying and the ATA need you. That's a good feeling – to be useful. If you come to Lanyon, you'll be unhappy. Pa has said he'll come up for me ... in a couple of days ...'

It had all been sorted out without me, then.

Charles let go of my hand.

'I say, old thing, I'm awfully tired tonight. Do you mind if we give the next chapter a miss?'

I closed the book, kissed Charles on the top of the head and took my coat from the back of the chair.

'I don't mind at all,' I answered, holding back the tears and trying to show a bright smile in my voice. I grabbed my coat and turned to leave, but thought of something, suddenly. 'The thing is, Charles, I've got a busy flying schedule tomorrow, I'm going all the way to Prestwick ... and if Pa is coming for you on Tuesday ... I ... well I won't get to see you before you go ...'

He nodded and waved his hand to dismiss me.

'You're busy, don't worry. I'll see you at Lanyon, whenever you can get down. No hurry.'

'But, Charles,' I said, sitting down and taking his hand again. 'You're more important than any of that. Why don't I see if I can ...'

He didn't let me finish. His expression hardened.

'Don't see about anything. You've got an important job to do. Lottie is at a loose end ... she can help.'

'Loose end? Hardly, Charles. She's still a WAAF, you know, and there's Mabel to consider ...'

'You should be getting along now. Last train and all that.'

There was nothing left to say. And as the ward door closed behind me, I felt that I had just said goodbye to a distant relative, not my husband, and for so many reasons, with the train carriage blackout blinds pulled down low, I leant my head against the rocking carriage, and wept the whole way home.

Chapter 26

Katherine

Never email tipsy!

*D*ear Sam
   I'm sitting in Fenella's car in the car park at Lanyon having just escorted Juliet back to her room. We've had the most wonderful day together, touring the local area. She asked if I could take her on a couple of outings – looking for buried treasure, no less! I'm sure Juliet will tell you all about it when she sees you, so I won't steal her thunder, needless to say, despite scouring most of the Penwith peninsular, we did not find the compass.

   I can assure you that I am keeping her well wrapped up and trying my hardest to hold her back from exerting herself too much. There is a very definite feeling of 'swansong' about the trip – many last goodbyes, last looks, which is understandable but occasionally unnerving. She's a remarkable woman, *but then you know that already, and I can't tell you how grateful I am to have met her.*

With very best wishes,

Katherine.

P.S. I'm still reading Juliet's memoirs. She has just missed out on a passionate weekend away with Edward, and now Charles has pushed her away! Nightmare. I'm reading your blog, too. I particularly enjoyed the one about your exploits on Orkney. Did you really dance naked with the Hairy Bikers on the summer solstice?

I put the car into gear and headed down the familiar road to the village, past the school and the pub and down to the harbour. It seemed that Angels Cove had transformed itself into hotbed of activity during the day and a heavenly host of snowflakes, candles, angel wings and a whole manor of Christmas-themed lights had sprung up all over the village, with lights now pinned on every building, lamppost and harbour wall.

I bumped into Fenella who was standing on the pier wearing a Day-Glo tabard and acting as foreman to two men, one of whom was dangling from a ladder attaching an electrified elf to a telegraph pole. It seemed that Fenella had taken a little speech I made to heart – a tipsy one proffered while snipping seaweed, or eating a full English. I couldn't remember, but anyhow, a speech about how it was the civic responsibility of the modern-day villagers to rekindle Christmas spirit – and she had taken off to the pub to hunt down and enlist the vicar with an offering (bribe) of gin. Once settled at the pub she had called an extraordinary meeting of the village elders to discuss saving, albeit at the last minute, the Angels Cove Christmas lights festival, and according to the man at the top of the ladder (who really did need to focus a little more on what he was doing rather than look down at me) she had given quite a rousing speech during the meeting which, when combined with her threat of keeping her gin to herself this Christmas, had led to a temporary truce between the two warring parties (Percy and Noel) which was similar, now he came to think of it, to the famous Christmas Day truce between the Germans and the Brits when they had temporarily lain down their weapons in 1914. Fenella had further swayed them (Percy and Noel, not the Germans) by saying that, as the matter of the apostrophe was soon to be cleared up by 'The Professor' (a title that refused to be shaken off) who was busy – as she spoke – carrying out crucial research on the issue, it was time to let bygones be bygones and get into the Christmas spirit once and for all, if only for the sake of the children (I was still yet to see any) not to mention the need to keep the tourists happy (ditto) and businesses booming.

They agreed.

She also got them to agree to a reinstatement of the Boxing Day party in the village hall, where (again, inspired by our little chat) they would re-enact a wartime Christmas party and make a tidy profit in the bargain by charging gullible visiting Londoners a tenner for entry. She handed me her clipboard and pen through the open car window and said, 'Write this down – trestle tables, a bit of dilute pop for the kiddies, cheap hock for the adults, wartime songs and paper chains. That's all we need. Nip down to mine later and we'll iron out the details. You can drop a flyer through all the letterboxes tonight, the exercise will do you good. And then we'll get bottling! Park up for now and we'll go to the pub.'

Two gins later, determined to search the cottage once again for the compass, I made my excuses at the pub, turned the key in the door and went into the kitchen to say a quick 'hello' to the elf, who was spending far too much time alone this Christmas.

My phoned pinged once the WiFi cut in.

Hi Katherine.

Thanks for taking the time to look for the compass and to visit Juliet. It's wonderful to see that you're enjoying yourself and I hope we will get the chance to meet before you go. I have heard so much about you from Gerald, not to mention Juliet, who has also emailed to say that you spent the afternoon together and how delightful you are.

You mentioned the notion of sensing an atmosphere of things coming to a close for Juliet, of final goodbyes, perhaps? Maybe you will understand a little more of her state of mind once you have read further along in the memoirs.

All the very best,
Sam
P.S. I can't believe she got you to sing at the Minack!!
P.P.S. Strike that. I can!
P.P.P.S. Yes, I really did dance naked with the Hairy Bikers.
It was surprisingly liberating. Orkney is a very special place
for me. I hope my blog has inspired you to visit there sometime.

Two hours later, with the compass still elusive, I put my coat on and snuggled the elf into an inside pocket (he'd been on his own all day and I didn't have the heart to leave him again) trundled down to Fenella's, ate a massive shepherd's pie dinner, drank and bottled copious amounts of gin, put on a ridiculous Christmas jumper (a present from Fenella) tolerated Christmas songs and made enough paper chains to wrap around Cornwall, before retiring to the pub to talk about the apostrophe with Percy, Noel and Geoffrey, who all seemed to be flagging with the thing. Fenella, with clipboard still at the ready, persuaded the local band who were performing in the pub tonight to put on an impromptu performance at the Boxing Day village party. She then wrestled me into my coat before sending me out to deliver one hundred flyers through one hundred letter boxes, before dragging me back into Percy's house, wrestling me out of my coat and handing me a glass of homebrew cider.

Sometime later, at a very hour of the early morning, I found myself turning the key to the cottage once more, drunk, tired and happy. Which is when I made the barking-mad decision to return Sam's email and went on to empty my heart onto the computer screen.

I told him everything – about my enforced isolation, about the past two Christmases at IKEA (for the love of God, why did I mention IKEA) – and how my life had become a black hole of nothingness until now, when Juliet had persuaded me onto the first rung of the ladder. I told him all about my lovely new friends Percy, Noel and Fenella (the feeder-upper) who had forced me to canoe to the islands (which was a nightmare on account of the fact that my thighs were far too chunky to look good in a wetsuit). But my crowning moment was when I told him Juliet had shown me his photograph and that I wasn't at all sure about the beard.

For three sorry pages I rambled on, my fingers tip-tapping on the keyboard as I poured out the random threads of my pinball mind, before concluding that if he managed to get home for Christmas then he must stay at home, at Angel View – there was more than enough room (and food) for the both of us. After pressing 'send' (an action I regretted three and half seconds later), far too engaged with Juliet's story to contemplate sleep, I decided it was time to make myself a sobering coffee and return to Juliet's memoirs, but this time I began by sending out a little prayer that Edward and Juliet would be given the happy ending they deserved.

Chapter 27

Juliet
Christmas 1942

News spread around the ferry pool that a select number of women were to be chosen to be trained to fly the four-engine bombers, such as the Wellington and the Lancaster.

This was fabulous news. Other than the battle for equal pay with our male counterparts in the ATA, who earned, in the modern-day equivalent, £300 per month more than the women, we had achieved parity in our work, and being allowed to fly the big bombers would mean that the last male stronghold had fallen. I was determined to be one of the women chosen to fly them.

Before too long, my wish came true, and I returned to Hamble after a successful multi-engine conversion course to discover that I had been awarded for my passion and commitment by being granted a little leave for the holiday season.

But to return to Lanyon at Christmas?

I wasn't sure I wanted to, wasn't sure at all. Charles' letters were short and perfunctory and when I telephoned the house, the majority of the phone call was spent talking to Lottie or Ma Lanyon, rather than to Charles. While at Hamble I was able to put my disastrous marriage out of my mind, keep going and carry on! And besides, how could I think about Charles, when Edward was always in my thoughts and prayers, scorched into my brain like cattle branding.

I asked Lottie once, on the telephone, if she ever bumped into that chap, Edward Nancarrow. She said she didn't, come to think of it. The chaps from the other side of the house kept very neatly to themselves. A lock had been put on the adjoining door with the message to the Lanyons (except Pa) being a very clear, keep out!

This was both a relief and a huge disappointment to me. If Edward was seen at Lanyon, at least I knew that he was safe and, if I should ever want to get in touch with him, I would know where to find him.

But if Edward had left Lanyon, then goodness knows if I would ever see him again – if he was alive or dead, even – and the thought of either not seeing him again was beyond anything my poor broken heart could deal with.

In the end, I decided to go.

I flew to Lanyon and took Anna with me. Two Spitfires were to be delivered to RAF Predannack on the twentieth of December and knowing the location of my family home, the duty programmer for that day gave the flights to us. A taxi Anson would collect us at eleven a.m. on Boxing Day – Anna was to be awarded leave too. Marie didn't mind missing out too much. She would stay in Hamble and hold the fort (while also cavorting with a new squeeze she had met in Southampton the month before).

The flight to Cornwall was heavenly. Anna, still under-confident about flying in formation, insisted I stay on her wing. With a cloud base of about three thousand feet, we were able to skim underneath the cloud layer and follow, for the most part, the Great Western railway line the whole way down.

Lottie was waiting for us at Predannack, wearing her smart WAAF uniform and – I was thrilled to see – a vibrant bright new smile. She waved madly at us from her perch on the balcony of the control tower as we taxied in.

'She's cheered up then,' Anna whispered as walked towards the operations room. Lottie, who despite being a WAAF was still completely oblivious to correct military protocol, ran wildly towards us, tripped over my parachute and fell straight into my open arms.

'Oh, Juliet!' she shouted. 'It's so wonderful to have you home for Christmas! You, too, Anna!' She leaped forward to give Anna a hug. 'Welcome to Cornwall!'

Anna responded by ruffling her hair. 'Steady on,' she said, 'I need to pee, and then I need to eat. Do me a favour Lottie and point me in the direction of somewhere I can do both!'

We ate lunch in the airman's dining hall. It never failed to surprise me just how much the wearing of our Sidcot flying suits could rouse such a stir. Lottie was getting glasses of water when one young woman dashed up to Anna – as Anna was about to spoon rice pudding into her mouth – with a pen and a notebook and asked for her autograph. Anna shrugged, put down her spoon and scribbled her signature across the book. The young woman, looking at the name, was clearly disappointed.

'Oh,' she said with a sigh. 'I thought you were Amy Johnson ... she flies for the ATA, doesn't she?'

Anna bit her lip in an effort to remain polite.

'She did. But I'm afraid she's dead. It was in the papers, didn't you see?'

The young woman's shoulders dropped.

'Dead? That's terrible. But how?'

'Flying accident, delivering for the ATA as it happened. She crashed into the Thames, I'm afraid.'

Anna tapped pointedly on the notebook in the girl's hand. 'But trust me, that signature will be worth a fortune one day, so I'd save it if I were you!' (Marie was having a definite influence on Anna's increased confidence).

The girl smiled, tapped her nose, tucked the notebook into her pocket, gave Anna a sudden hug and went on her way.

Lottie returned to the table with the drinks.

'I've just been chatting to one of the girls,' she said. 'There's a Christmas dance in the mess hall tonight. I know you won't want to come, Juliet, what with just getting back to see Charles and everything, but you'll come with me, won't you, Anna?'

Anna turned to me. She knew I was dreading seeing Charles. Despite my letters and phone calls home, we had become almost entirely estranged, and anyway, a party at Predannack would be great fun.

'I'm not sure,' Anna said, uncertainly, glancing un my direction. 'Wouldn't your parents think it was a little rude if I disappear off, first night and all?'

'Don't be silly! And you don't mind do you, Juliet.' They both looked at me.

I shook my head in answer, trying to feign excitement for them both. Anna noticed my disappointment, Lottie didn't.

'How is Charles, by the way?' Anna asked, diverting Lottie's attention away from the party.

Lottie scrunched her nose.

'Oh, you know. He's getting there. Some days good, some days bad.' She nudged me. 'You can always tell when he's been on the phone to Juliet, though. It cheers him up no end.' I glanced at Anna, confused. Charles, cheered up? 'Speaking of which,' Lottie went on, 'you must be desperate to see him, Juliet, and here we are chatting away.' She stood and glanced around the dining hall. 'I'll just nip and see if I can tee us up a lift with one of the chaps on the squadron. Pa doesn't let me use the old Rover anymore, so I have to cycle everywhere, or walk, worst luck! Back in a mo—'

She turned to leave but seemed to remember something and turned back quickly.

'Oh, I almost forgot!' She perched herself on the arm of the chair next to mine. Her face was on fire with excitement. 'Remember that chap, Edward Nancarrow? The one I took quite a shine to before the war?'

Anna's ears pricked up.

'Well he's back at Lanyon and you'll never guess?'

'Go on ...'

'He's not married at all! I've no idea where he's been lately, but I was chatting to him in the garden yesterday and ...'

I swallowed.

'Sorry, what did you say?'

'I said ... Ma and Pa are having a drinks party on Christmas Eve and he's coming along as my guest!'

Lottie let out a little excitable shriek and dashed off. I glanced up at Anna who lips were moving but the sentence was taking a while to form. I put my hand up.

'You don't need to say a word, Anna. Not one word.'

I went to the party at RAF Predannack that night, and I went because Charles urged me to. From the moment we said our forced, 'Hello's' in the lounge in front of Ma, it was obvious that Charles was as uncomfortable as I was at the thought of acting out the part of married couple within the close confines of a much-reduced household and the anxious gaze of his parents. It was with a resigned and weary acceptance that we played our parts, knowing that Christmas at Lanyon would prove, once more, to be nothing short of an odd, displacing and emotionally exhausting time.

The only person Charles would allow to fuss around him was Ma, and as for sleeping in the same room together? Charles suggested it was probably best if I slept in the guest room as he was suffering from insomnia and anyway his valet – who wasn't a real valet but rather Pa Lanyon's old retainer who worked at the house for practically nothing – needed to have easy access to him to help with dressing and washing and so on. I was, in all honesty, relieved at this, and thanked God for Anna's encouraging spirit around the house. Something had changed with Anna recently. I didn't know if it was the indomitable Marie having a super-charging effect, or if flying the Spitfire was spurring her on, but her confidence and sense of joy had gone from strength to strength.

But there was another reason for Anna's exuberance this Christmas and the source of the joy could be found at the Predannack party. I sat in a corner for most of the night, catching up and reminiscing with Lottie, while Anna was serenaded by a pilot who asked her to dance – and had continued to ask her to dance until the final number – *I'll Be Seeing You*, sung by Jo Stafford.

Until now, Anna had been happy to keep herself to herself on the man front. Yes, she had occasionally agreed to a date rigged up by Marie and gone up town from Hamble

271

with some chap from the Navy or the Royal Marines. Men were not usually looking for a real date, just a bit of fun on a Saturday night, which suited Anna. Being a practical soul, the last thing she wanted to do was fall desperately in love with someone who, in Anna's words, 'might not make it past the final furlong'.

'I do not,' she said, '*ever* want to be like Lottie!'

But Anna hadn't reckoned on Bill, the RAF pilot, who had flown in the Battle of Britain and who, within less than an hour of meeting Anna, had fallen madly in love with her. The feeling, much to Anna's dismay, was mutual.

And as for me? My Christmas was spent with that unsettling feeling of nervous turmoil bubbling around in the pit of my stomach, the sort of turmoil that is the curse of the anxious lover. I roamed for miles around the local area with Anna, showing her our haunts – the Tiger Moth stored in the barn, the village, the church and even (from a suitable distance, of course) Edward's cottage.

Like any close female friend who is supporting a pal who has suffered heartache, Anna spent hours listening to me ramble on as I went over and over questions buzzing around in my head, the most important one being, why on earth Edward would agree to go to the Christmas drinks party with Lottie if he knew I would be there? Did he have designs on Lottie, after all? Was it revenge for not meeting him? Did he even think of me now? Was my mother right? Had I been fooled by this charmer, this coddiwompler, all along? These were all questions that we couldn't possibly know the answers to, but as any woman who have ever been desperately in love will know, talking about him endlessly to a patient friend – even in a negative way – made him real.

And so, it was with a sense of both dread and excitement that we prepared for the party by putting up the blackout blinds, lighting the candles on the tree and gathering the house party together in the hallway to welcome the men from the other side of the house into our home. The guests were a sullen bunch, but it wouldn't be for several months more that I would discover just how risky and complicated their operation was. I would also learn that Pa Lanyon had known the true nature of their work all along, but none of this information came to light tonight. Tonight was for sharing the significantly reduced and somewhat meagre feast from our Christmas table and, in so many ways, making the best of a bad lot.

Lottie had pulled out all the stops in terms of choice of outfit and was looking fabulous – if on tenterhooks – waiting for Edward to arrive. Charles chose not to stand in the hallway but to sit in the lounge by the fire, with the family's' King Charles Spaniel by his side. My heart went out to Charles, but it seemed that every single time I tried to get close to him, he pushed me away. I was a prisoner in a marriage neither party wanted and Charles wasn't even trying to mask the estrangement any more, which meant my disastrous marriage would be laid bare tonight for all to see – for Edward to see. And yet, would he even care? Edward was expecting to spend the evening with Lottie and with the way Lottie looked tonight, who could blame him.

Anna – at my insistence – had brought Bill to the party, but she stood by my side as we welcomed guests, offering drinks. Eats did not match up to pre-war standards, but Ma Lanyon and Lottie had done us proud with the little they had and as the guests filtered in, just for a moment, one might almost – almost – have forgotten about the war. Edward was the last to arrive. I saw him before he saw me. I took Anna's hand and gave it a squeeze.

'He's here!' Lottie squealed, rushing to the door to welcome him.

'She'll never get him to fall for her behaving like that ...' Anna whispered in my ear. 'I can see why you like him though. Quite the dish!'

With her widowhood seemingly forgotten, Lottie – dear, sweet, naïve Lottie – ushered Edward towards the welcoming party for introductions.

'This is Edward,' she said to us all, beaming. 'Edward – from left to right – this is Anna, Bill and finally, my brother's wife, Juliet – oh, I forgot, you already met, didn't you? *Years* ago!'

Edward looked directly at me.

'It was four years ago almost exactly,' he said.

Anna held out her hand, despite having met him briefly before. 'Pleased to meet you, Edward.'

Edward did not look at me for a moment longer than

is usual during an introduction. We shook hands but it was too much for me. I couldn't maintain the pretence. 'I'm sorry, you'll have to excuse me, Lottie. I really should see if Charles is all right.' I turned to Edward. 'Have a good evening, Edward. It's ... good, to see you again.'

He nodded and for a moment I thought I saw a flicker of ... warmth?

I sat with Charles on the periphery for a while. At times he was almost tender and I wondered, not unkindly, if this tenderness was something of a show on his behalf, to save face for both of us, but who on earth could tell what Charles was thinking anymore. The whole evening was a confusing mess.

By nine-thirty Lottie decided to fill the house with music and established a make-shift dance hall in the dining room. Anna appeared by my side at ten o'clock. She had left Bill in the lounge, talking to Charles.

'How's tricks?' she asked, watching Edward and Lottie move around the floor to a catchy big band song playing on the gramophone.

'I'm fine.'

'Really? I wouldn't be.'

'Charles is behaving like a husband – well, almost. Edward has clearly forgotten me and I'm happy playing out the role of the dutiful wife. And in two days' time you and I will go home. It's all fine and exactly how it should be, truly.'

She took a deep breath. '*Fine* is how people describe a

situation when in reality they are feeling awful. You deserve better than "fine".' She squeezed my arm. 'I want you to be wonderful, not fine'.

We stood in silence and watched the dancers.

'What's he playing at, do you think?' Anna asked, nodding towards Edward.

It was my turn to sigh and shake my head.

'I doubt he's playing at anything. I don't think "playing" is Edward's style. Do remember that I consistently walk away from his advances and I am married. Why shouldn't he have a good time with Lottie?'

'Because he's in love with you, that's why.'

I linked my arm in Anna's.

'Maybe one upon a time, but not anymore.'

During the whole evening – perhaps because there were far too many guests gathered in too small a space – Edward and I managed to behave like two independent planets, circling in the same orbit, but always a million light years apart.

At ten, Charles had excused himself and expressed a wish to go to bed. I offered to sit with him in his bedroom a while but he reached for my hand, pulled me close, kissed me on the forehead and declined. It was when I followed him into the hallway, where Lottie was dancing with Bill, that my heart finally broke in two. On seeing Charles retiring, Lottie had broken away from Bill and rushed over, offering to escort him around the dance floor before he went to bed. I had, on a number of occasions, offered to do the same thing, but Charles had refused to dance every time. But now, asked by Lottie, he accepted. And it was at the moment Charles stepped onto the dance floor with Lottie that Edward caught my eye. He was across the room, standing in the entrance to Pa's study. His head tipped slightly to the side. Noticing Charles on the dance floor, Edward crossed the room towards me. He held out his hand.

'Would you care to dance, Juliet?'

Anna kissed Bill goodnight just as the clock struck twelve. I waved off the last of the guests and joined Anna on the sofa in the lounge. An exhausted but happy Lottie had already said her goodnights and gone to bed, which left the two of us alone in the semi-darkness, with only the embers of the fire and a last flickering candle for company. We slouched side by side on the sofa, my cold left hand tucked into Anna's warm right one.

'He's definitely not in love with her, you know,' Anna began, staring into the fire. 'I watched them all evening and, honestly, he made every possible excuse to get away from her at every possible moment. It was quite sad for Lottie, really. I don't think Edward even knew he'd been invited tonight as Lottie's particular guest. I think she's a bit ... delusional.'

I said nothing. What was the point of analysing the thing? I was married. Edward was single. The end.

'Charles has upset you again, hasn't he?'

I nodded, just as the tears I'd buttoned in all evening spilled over my lower lashes.

'At first, I thought he was actually being quite husbandly towards you,' she said, dabbing my eyes with a handkerchief, 'quite sweet, in a way, but to dance with Lottie and then with that other woman at the end of the thing and not with you ... it was cruel, Juliet, not to mention bloody humiliating, especially in front of Edward.'

I was too tired to argue. Anna didn't let up. She took my hands firmly in hers.

'Listen. It sounds to me like this marriage happened for all the wrong reasons at a time when you were excessively vulnerable. I know he's been injured, but I really do think you should leave him, Juliet, for your own sanity, if not for his. I hate to say it, but the man seems to resent you.'

This one-way conversation carried along the same path for some minutes until Anna suddenly stopped.

'*Ssshhh*,' she whispered. 'I can hear someone ...' We quietened a moment. 'Is that Charles' voice?'

It was.

We tiptoed to the door and listened.

'... I know, darling,' we heard him whisper into the phone, 'and I feel the same way too, it's all a wretched, blasted mess. But what can I do? She put bags of money into the house and we're her only family. I can't just walk away, not at the moment ... yes, I love you, too ... yes, yes, I know, but just give me some time ...'

Anna and I turned to face each other in the firelight. She leant forward and whispered into my ear.

'Get your warmest coat. I'll see you at the kitchen door in ten minutes.'

It was one a.m. when I arrived at Edward's cottage. The moon, just like a reliable old landing light, shone a path from across the sea down to Angels Cove, guiding me home. I freewheeled down the hill through a wind so sharp it cut into my face like a dagger and by the time I pushed Lottie's bicycle up the track for the last hundred yards from the harbour to Edward's cottage, my face burned bright red with a mixture of wind-burn and exhilaration. I didn't care.

Despite the blackout, a low candle burned in Edward's lounge window. I propped Lottie's bicycle against the cottage wall and glanced through the window. Edward was sitting on the sofa, a whiskey glass in his hand and a slow, melancholic tune echoed through the glass. Without hesitation, indifferent to the time of day, I knocked on the door.

There were so many questions to be answered, but as we looked into each other's eyes across the doorway, the need for explanation faded away. Edward glanced at his watch and whispered just three words.

'Happy birthday, Juliet.'

I smiled, took his outstretched hand in mine, stepped through the door and – the devil be hanged – stayed the night.

Chapter 28

Katherine

A return email

'You go, girl!' I thought (not being able to think of anything similar, a little more English, just at that moment).

I lay the manuscript down on Juliet's bedside table, smiling, and thought of her – a beautiful, frail, enigma of a woman, who sat alone in the care home every night, living through her memories, living a life of perpetual last goodbyes.

I turned off the light and tried to sleep, but my head was full of contradicting, bizarre images and in my dreams my own story was mixed with Juliet's, making for an unpleasant cocktail of drama and death. At three a.m. I grabbed my phone and typed a text:

Are you out there, James? Can you hear me?

I was about to press send, but then, letter by letter, pressed delete. I had just deleted the last letter when the phoned pinged.

An email, from Sam.

Hi, Katherine.
I just read your email. I'm so sorry about your husband. I do, kind of, understand, but it certainly looks like you're beginning to have a lovely (and lively) time, which is great. I just wanted to say, I wouldn't worry too much about the size of your thighs. Men are never as bothered about these things as women think they are.
Yours,
Sam
P.S. Call it a wild guess, but have you been drinking Percy's cider this evening?
P.P.S. I'm on my way home! Thanks for the offer to stay, but as I'll be back late I'll crash down in the wardroom and probably get to Angels Cove on Christmas morning, for Juliet's birthday. I don't suppose you would like to come flying with us, would you? To be honest, I could do with the support. See it as a bit of an introduction to coddiwompling, perhaps?

Dear God, why had I mentioned my thighs?

But flying? On Christmas Day? The old Katherine would have shied away, but the new one ..? The one who was on the first rung of the ladder?

I hit reply.

Dear Sam
As a converted coddiwompler I can confirm that I'd love
to come flying with you!
See you soon!
Katherine

I closed the lid of the laptop and it hit me that, in her own story, Juliet had stridden out beyond a kind of crossroads tonight, and if I, too, was going to start dying to live rather than living to die, I would need to get my skates on if I was ever to catch up, because the world had not been waiting to move on without me.

Chapter 29

Juliet

A day to last a lifetime

I spent the whole of Christmas day with Edward. It was the most selfish, inconsiderate, downright rude thing I had ever done and yet I didn't care a jot, because that crisp, sunny December day at Angels Cove was the most perfectly put together passing of time of my entire life.

Within the ten minutes it had taken me to grab my things the night before, Anna had devised a cover story to explain my absence on Christmas Day. At breakfast she would say that a message had been delivered to the house just as we had gone to bed instructing me to report to RAF Predannack the following morning to do a test flight on an aircraft that was possibly required back at the factory for deep maintenance. It was all nonsense, of course. Any number of RAF pilots could have carried out such a task and we weren't even qualified to carry out test flight. The only person at Lanyon other than Charles who may have smelled a rat was Lottie, and she wasn't working that day and wouldn't surface till gone midday. But as it happened, I really didn't care what Charles or anyone else thought of my absence. To hell with them.

Dawn brought only a little sleep before we eventually, reluctantly, rose to make something of the day – Christmas Day, my birthday. Edward dug a rusty saw out of the shed and we went on a hunt to find the perfect Christmas tree, but I felt a desperate pang of guilt. There was so much destruction in the world, why harm a little tree? Instead, we knocked on the door of a chap Edward knew in the village and borrowed the man's wheelbarrow and spade. I watched while Edward dug up a tiny little fir tree we found in a copse at the back of the school and placed it carefully in the barrow. The little tree was placed into a pot and given pride of place in the lounge.

'It's not quite finished, though,' Edward said, frowning from the doorway as I turned the pot to offer the tree's best aspect to the room. 'There's a box of decorations in the loft. Back in a second.'

We sat in front of the fire and took great delight in rummaging through a box of decorations Edward had saved from the festivities of Christmas 1938. Most were bits and bobs made by the children in the hall – dried orange peel on string and paper chains. In 1938, Angels Cove had seemed far removed from the real world and the prospect of war, and even now, with the war raging on – not just in Europe but via the Luftwaffe on our home front, too – Angels Cove still seemed separate from the rest of the world, an escapists paradise, where all the right elements came together to promote nothing but harmony and an inexplicable feeling of peace and contentment.

But there were two particular items in the box which, when I saw them, filled my heart with joy – a Christmas tree ornament and a Christmas card.

I recognised the Christmas card, which had a hand-drawn angel on the front. I opened it up to read the message.

Dear Edward.
I have loved my week at Angels Cove and it's been an absolute pleasure to meet you.
Here's wishing you the very best of Christmases.
Yours, with love,
Juliet

Edward smiled as I read it. My eyes misted over.

'You saved it?' I whispered, still looking at the card in my hand.

'Of course. Although, once you married Charles, I put it away with the decorations ... too painful.'

I glanced up at him adoringly.

'When did you know?' I asked.

'That I was in love with you?'

I nodded. 'It's a school girl question, I know, but answer it anyway.'

'I suppose it would have been that day on the cliff, when you jumped out of the Tiger Moth with oil smeared all over your face, trying to shoo the cows.'

We both laughed at the memory.

'The very first day, then?' I pushed.

He touched my face tenderly and nodded.

'The very first day.'

I placed the card on the mantelpiece and delved back into the box. The second item – the Christmas tree ornament–had a sliver of a red ribbon attached for hanging and was, in fact, a tiny oil painting set into a silver frame. The painting depicted a winter snow scene of Edward's cottage, painted from the side aspect when looked on from the tiny pebbly beach which was down the path, just beyond the cottage, around our secret corner.

'This is lovely,' I said, holding the ornament in my hand.

Edward looked on tenderly.

'It's yours, actually.'

'Mine?'

'I painted it as a Christmas present that first year – the night you left. But when you married Charles, I ...'

My heart melted. 'I'm so sorry, Edward. More than you can ever know.' I stood and crossed to the sideboard to hang the ornament on the tree. 'We'll have to make sure it's always on show at Christmas, won't we?'

He joined me by the tree.

'Always?' He took me by the hand and we crossed to the velvet chaise.

'I'm leaving Charles tonight and heading back to Hamble in the morning. It's over, Edward. No more lies.'

He nodded and stroked the back of my hand.

'I'm not going to ask you if it's the right decision because I'm sick of doing the right thing. I want you in my life, Juliet, whatever it takes. For ever.'

He kissed me then.

'But what about Lottie?' I asked, his mouth exploring my neck.

'Lottie?'

He pulled away slightly.

'She seems to have designs on you again. And what with you having escorted her to the party last night ...'

'Escorted? What on earth?' He let go of my hand and pulled away. 'Listen to me, once and for all, Juliet. Mr Lanyon invited all of us – all the guys who work there – to the house for Christmas drinks. I only went because I thought you might be there. I don't understand why Lottie keeps coming into this. She's recently widowed, for goodness sake. She's got a baby to the man – if, indeed, he *is* the father, which I doubt – and she's a pal. That's it. The only woman I will ever – *ever*– love, in my entire life, is you. I know you're married and know I shouldn't have asked you to meet me in London, but you are never out of my mind. When you married Charles, I was devastated. But the fact that we might actually have a chance now ...'

His smile was suddenly wide and bright. '... I can't tell you how happy that makes me feel.' He took my hand again. 'Somehow, the two of us need to survive this war. And when we do, we'll come back to Angels Cove and the rest of the world can go to hell – forever!'

We kissed, we made love, we held on.

We played on the beach, touching each other with the carefree jostle of children mixed with the magnetic body-language and sexuality of adulthood, and in the late afternoon sunshine, we sat quietly on the beach, kept warm by a combination of thick clothes and happy thoughts.

'Edward,' I began, scrunching my shoes into the pebbles. 'I know you can't give me any real detail about your job, but my friend Marie, well, her friend is quite a big wig in the foreign office and she was telling me about the SOE ... and I was wondering ... is that what your set up is, here? Can't you please tell me something – anything – if only so I know how to communicate with you, how to get in touch, that sort of thing?'

'You're not far off the mark,' he said, pausing to throw a pebble into the sea. 'We plan certain operations ... and I travel around making sure those operations go to plan.'

'You go to Europe?' I asked.

'Yes.'

'By boat from the Helford?' I pushed.

'Sometimes.'

That was enough. He was an operative for the SOE, that

much was clear – one of the most high-risk jobs of the war – but it wasn't until much later that I would find out that Edward Nancarrow – or Felix Gruber – codenamed Savage Angel, was so much more than that.

I looked across to the islands. It was high tide. The sun created low shadows across the sea.

'Those little mounts led me here,' I said, resting my head on his shoulder. 'They're the reason I found you.'

'Ah, but they're not actually mounts,' he corrected, placing an arm around my shoulder and tucking me in closer, 'they're angels. They watch over the village and keep it safe – have done for centuries. They do a fabulous job keeping fisherman from peril, playing home to the mermaids, that kind of thing.'

I smiled.

'Mermaids? Really?'

'Oh, absolutely. The mermaids live on the far side, though, where only the fisher-people can see them. They protect us, too, of course, the mermaids, when the angels are busy, but only if we're very good. They're picky.'

I took a pebble out of Edward's hand and put it in my coat pocket to save as a memento.

'Good?' I sighed. 'Oh, dear. They'll send me straight to the devil, then, especially after last night.'

Edward turned my face towards his.

'Don't feel that you owe Charles – or the Lanyons –any kind of guilt, because you don't. They've got your money and that's good enough for them. You'll end the marriage tonight?' he asked, more as a statement than a question.

'I will.'

Charles was in the lounge sitting with his mother listening to the wireless when I arrived at Lanyon.

'Oh, Juliet! Happy birthday!' she said, turning to face me. 'You must be absolutely exhausted.'

I took my flying boots off at the lounge door and glanced inside. Lottie and Anna, who had been playing cards in the kitchen with little Mabel, dashed through the hallway to welcome me home.

Anna raised her eyebrows in my direction but said nothing, while Lottie fussed around me like a mother hen.

'You absolute poor thing, having to work today! I don't understand why one of the squadron chaps couldn't have done the rotten silly test flight, really, I don't. And look at the state of you. You look like you haven't slept a wink!'

Anna pursed her lips and tried to suppress a laugh. I glanced across the lounge at Charles and noticed him frown.

Ma Lanyon pushed herself up out of her favourite, if saggy, floral-covered armchair.

'Come on in and warm yourself by the fire, dear,' she said, taking my coat and giving orders to Lottie to rustle me up a little supper. She glanced at Charles. 'On second thoughts, why don't we *all* go to the kitchen and make supper for everyone and give Juliet and Charles some private time.' Lottie began to protest but Ma insisted. 'No,

Lottie ... give them some space. Juliet disappears off to Hampshire tomorrow and they've hardly had any time alone.' She scooped Mabel up. 'Come with Grandmama, little one. Show me what you've been baking!'

'But we haven't been baking, we've been playing cards,' Mabel said, confused. 'Anna taught me poker!'

'Oh, well, show me how to play, then.'

Charles rubbed his forehead, anxiously, as they left.

'Would you close the door, please, Juliet?'

With the door closed I returned to sit next to Charles. He got straight to the point. I was expecting a blazing confrontation about my day-long absence. I didn't get one.

'I spoke with Anna,' he said, softly. 'The telephone call last night ...'

I couldn't believe it. Anna must have taken the initiative and told him he was rumbled. What an angel.

'Yes, it was quite a shock.' I said.

'I ... I don't even know where to begin. I met her last summer, in Singapore. She's a nurse. I ... it's a cliché, I know.' He wrung his hands before taking mine in his. 'I can't be without her, Juliet. I'm so sorry that such a thing should happen. Truly.'

'Don't be sorry,' I began. 'I understand, and much more than you know. You know I do.'

He nodded. 'Nancarrow?'

'Yes.'

It was time to tell the truth, finally. Time to discuss our

marriage in the cold light of day – the light of Christmas Day. When the conversation was over and I had confessed my feelings towards Edward (and Charles had asked me to pour us both a stiff drink) we hugged each other with a closeness we had not known since the war began. It was a hug that conveyed the absolute relief that the pretence was over, but it also expressed the real love and affection we had always felt for each other – would always feel. But a sibling kind of love was not enough for either of us, not anymore, and no amount of wishful thinking from Lottie or Ma and Pa Lanyon would ever be able to turn it into anything else.

Chapter 30

Katherine

About time

I looked out of the window on Christmas Eve morning to be met by a curtain of dank drizzle. It would have been a duvet day in Exeter, but here in Cornwall, gazing out of the lounge window at the calm sea as it lapped against the islands, I felt drawn to taste the salt on my lips and feel the crunch of pebbles under my boots before driving up to Lanyon to escort Juliet on her penultimate day out.

Meandering across the beach I replayed Juliet's story in my mind. I crossed to where I imagined she had sat with Edward and looked through the sea fret towards the tiny islands she had used to navigate her way to Lanyon. Once upon a time, I realised, stories from history had fascinated me. I loved to pick through the eye-witness statements of the past – the stories, the rumours – to try to gauge some idea of the truth of what had happened at one particular time and place, while the Earth tumbled through the universe at sixty-seven thousand miles per hour, always seeming to repeat itself in its seasonal, patterned way, day after day, year after year, and yet in reality, never really doing exactly the same thing twice. With each moment in a particular time a space gone forever the very second after it happened, the only way of knowing anything about anything that had gone before was either through memory or the recording of historical data. And as I stepped on the sands of time and the droplets of mist that had soaked previous faces and curled other stray strands of hair, I remembered, what had interested me the most during my own years as a student – one of James' students, in fact – was that, without humans on Earth, without the human brain and soul to see it all, nothing really existed. Not the sun, nor the moon or the stars – nothing. Because without our distinctly human ability to see it all – to pause, to consider – none of it, nothing that existed in the whole of the universe and beyond, was really there at all.

Once the human race was lost, there would be no one left to wonder at life and all that was amazing and wonderful and frightening, would be gone. The whole universe would no longer exist, simply because there would be no one around to look up and see it. Humans were the most important part of the universe, because they were the only thing that made it real.

And this was why, once upon a time, a young woman called Katherine Henderson (or Jones, as I was then), a free-thinking history student, had wanted to write books about 'then and now' and make television programmes and inspire children. But that was all before she fell desperately in love with her university professor, married him, moved into his house, and absorbed herself into his life, at which point there had been no room for two sparkling careers behind the green door of that leafy Exeter street. Love had persuaded me to take a seat on the reserves bench – supporting my husband, promoting and encouraging his ideas (which were sprinkled with more than a smattering of my own) – and I had never regretted walking away from my own chance to make my own history.

Until now.

Until a woman called Juliet had brought me back to life, handing me a ladder.

Juliet.

I suddenly wanted to see her. To make the most of her, while I still had the chance.

I ran back to the cottage, jumped into the car, shot up the hill and drove through the pillared gates for Lanyon, all the while wanting to take a pin and stick it in the earth, to slow it down in its relentless journey through the universe or even to spin it backwards a few marching paces, to be given just a little more time. And as I jumped out of the car, my pace began to speed even quicker, because Time, it turned out, was so very precious indeed.

Chapter 31

Juliet

Over the Rainbow

'I've been fired.'

Marie was laying on the sofa in the dark. The blackout blinds up even though it was early afternoon. She was chain-smoking and listening to the wireless when Anna and I, having dropped our bags in the hallway, walked in the living room.

'Fired?' I repeated, putting on the light and taking off my coat. 'From the ATA? Never!'

Marie sat up and stubbed out her cigarette. She looked utterly dreadful. It was the first time Anna and I had seen her in anything but a perfectly put together state.

'Sonofabitch from the Home Office got an eyeful of me and Jimmy at the 400 Club. He blew the whistle to the newspapers and before we knew it flashbulbs were going off in our faces and guess what? I'm being *encouraged* to move on.'

'But that's crazy,' Anna said, taking a seat next to Marie. 'They're desperate for good pilots, how can they even think of letting you go? Why should anyone care if you were out with Jimmy at the club? I don't understand. You can do what the hell you like, surely?'

Marie glanced up at me. I knew exactly what she was going to say.

'Jimmy's married.'

Anna dropped her head.

'Oh, Marie.'

'Oh, stop your chiding Miss Prim! They've been looking for a reason to get rid of me since I flew under that bridge.'

Anna and I looked at each other. 'Bridge?' we said in unison.

'Oh, it was nothing, not to me anyhow, but you Brits are always so damn straight-laced all the damn time ...'

We waited for an explanation. If Marie had been knowingly reckless in an aircraft, there was no way the ATA would swallow it. This we *had* to hear.

'Well, OK, I'll tell you. I know *you'll* understand, Juliet, what with being a stunt pilot and all – but promise you won't *glower* at me, Anna! You know how prissy you can be!'

Anna's jaw fell open. She looked at me and mouthed, 'Prissy?' I shook my head to reassure her.

'It was the day you gals went to Cornwall. I met some RAF guys in town and we got to talking and they said they'd flown under this bridge in Bristol and I said "that sounds like fun" and they bet me a crate of champagne I wouldn't have the nerve to do it.'

I could see where this was going.

'So, the next day, I was taking a Spit to St Athan ...'

'Why is St Athan always involved when you mess up?' Anna asked, confused.

Marie stepped over Anna's question. '... and phoned them up and they went to the bridge to watch and I flew under it. That's it. No big deal.'

'No big deal?!' The exclamation was out before Anna remembered she needed to button it in.

'What?' Marie asked, incredulous. 'It was easy. It's a big bridge!'

I couldn't help but laugh. Anna was still open-mouthed. I put my hand under her chin and shut it.

'Anyhow, somehow the boss found out, so he hauls me into the office and chews my ass over it for half an hour – I mean, seriously, what is it with this damn country that no one can mind their own damn business any of the time!?'

Marie surprised us then by bursting into tears.

'But I don't care about any of that crap.' She looked up, her wretched face a complete mess. 'It's Jimmy. I've lost him.' Her bottom lip started to tremble.

'Won't you see him again?' I asked, resting my backside on the arm of the sofa next to her.

She shook her head and blew her nose.

'He's being posted – abroad. He can't even tell me where he's going – or won't.'

Anna took her hand.

'It'll blow over,' Anna said. 'You'll see. I don't know about the Jimmy, thing, but as for the ATA, hanker down here with us and wait it out. Give it a couple of weeks and they'll be begging you to come back. They need you more than you need them!' Anna looked up at me for support. 'Don't they, Juliet?'

But I sensed that Marie had begun to make other plans. She was a rich American socialite and could do what the hell she liked and Marie simply didn't respond well to the discipline of the ATA. For Marie, the ATA had been a fantastic, dangerous, distraction. A place where she felt she was doing her bit for the war *and* having the time of her life while she was about it. But in losing Jimmy (a man Anna knew nothing of and I had believed to be nothing more than a fling rather than 'the one') the light had gone out from her deep blue eyes, her sparkle had diminished and it was clearly time to look for a new distraction, because Marie was like a shark – oh, a wonderful, loving shark – but a shark nonetheless. She had to keep on swimming, keep on being entertained, or she would die.

'What are you going to do?' I asked.

She took a moment to pull herself together.

'I've been asked to go back to the States for a while – just for a month or so – to do a recruitment drive for the

ATA, see if I can't persuade a few more guys and gals from the old flying clubs to come over, lend a hand.'

'But I thought you been fired? Why would you help them?' Anna asked.

Marie shrugged.

'Oh, they're not so bad and I don't suppose I've been *fired* so much as ... redistributed. To be honest, I'm ready for a bit of a change.' – *I knew it* – 'And the god-awful food and clothes over here are killing me! This war is all just so ... depressing.'

Anna slumped back into the sofa. Her eyes filled with tears. 'But it won't be the same without you, Marie. Who'll take us up to London now?'

Marie took both of our hands.

'Hey! I'll be back here before you know it,' she said, throwing her fabulous smile in Anna's direction. 'Those sonofabitches won't keep me out of the game for long. I'll get my ass back in a damn Spitfire before you know it, you just see if I don't.' She squeezed our hands. 'We're the Spitfire Sisters, aren't we?'

Marie left two days later. She never did buy that motorbike. We had a last, fun-filled night of impromptu singing and dancing at the Bugle Pub, ending with *We'll Meet Again* and Anna's favourite, *Somewhere Over the Rainbow*. which made us all cry.

We cried a great deal that night and we cried because we knew it was the end of an era, that despite her promise to fly the Spitfire again, Marie would move on for good. It was simply her way. And there was something else too, a sense of things beginning to draw to a conclusion.

She wouldn't let us see her off at the station – said it would ruin her make-up. Instead Marie hugged us at the door and with the parting words of, 'I love ya, you crazy sonofabitches.' She walked away. Nothing at Hamble was ever quite the same once Marie left and little did we know, things were about to get much, much worse.

Chapter 32

Juliet

An angel in the cockpit

The weather conditions were marginal as Anna and I sat chatting with our fellow pilots in the mess, grounded by the weather, waiting for the cloud base to lift, killing time. Anna was thrilled that we'd been tasked again to deliver two Spitfires to Predannack and was particularly anxious to go. Bill, Anna's new boyfriend, was still flying with his squadron and would be waiting for us on arrival, so long as we arrived that day, because the following morning he was being posted to another squadron in Scotland. Anna, standing at the window literally watching the clouds roll by, insisted we were to get airborne the moment the weather started to improve, which wasn't like her, she was always the cautious one – overly, sometimes. But I wanted to delay our departure, even if that meant Anna would not see Bill. Yes, it was usual for ATA pilots to fly at the edge of the weather envelope, but too many names had been rubbed off the chalkboard by now, fellow pilots who had fallen to the perils of flying in bad weather and I was determined that our names would still be written on the board at the end of the war.

I pointed to a poster on the mess wall at a copy of the top three rules for ATA flying and read two of them out loud to Anna:

i) Bad weather flying strictly prohibited.
ii) No flight shall be commenced unless at the place of departure the cloud base is at least 800 feet, and the horizontal visibility at least 2,000 yards

Nevertheless, an hour later, the cloud base lifted to seven hundred feet and the visibility improved to 2000 yards with the forecast of a cold-front clearance moving in from the west. Anna grabbed her kit.

'Come on, Foxy,' she said, excitedly tapping me on the leg. 'Remember the ATA motto, Juliet, *anything to anywhere!*'

Reluctantly, I also began to gather my things, but I refused to fly on her wing. If we hit a bad spot of weather it would be difficult to retain the required visual references to stay in close formation, especially if she began to make unpredictable turns in attitude and height while trying to navigate around low cloud, so we agreed to depart twenty minutes apart.

Anna went first. She dashed out of the ops room and

blew a kiss in my direction, grabbing her flying jacket as she ran. But it wasn't her jacket, it was mine, which had my father's compass in the pocket. I couldn't fly without it.

I dashed out after her. She was already in the cockpit, the canopy pulled back, going through her checks, the rotor blade not turning yet. I climbed on the wing.

'That's my jacket,' I said, but she was already strapped in. She began to unstrap. 'No, don't worry. I'll fly in yours, but I need my compass. It's in the right pocket. Sorry, I know it's ridiculous, but I never fly without it.'

She reached through her parachute straps and delved into the pocket.

'And don't forget,' I shouted above the noise of the airfield, taking the compass, 'if the weather closes in, turn back.'

'It won't!' she said, smiling. 'And anyway. It's time I was a little more confident, you said so yourself.'

'But not in bad weather, Anna. And remember I'll be twenty minutes behind you, so if you turn back, watch out for me coming the other way!'

She *shoo*'ed me off the wing. 'I won't be turning back. I'll see you there.' She pulled on her helmet and goggles. 'And don't worry, I'll be fine.'

I kissed her on the cheek. 'Stay safe.'

'Safe? In a few hours we'll be dancing in the mess hall,' she said. 'Now off you go.'

I watched Anna let off the break and open up the throttle.

She waved as she taxied past me and I couldn't help but remember another smiling woman waving at me from another aircraft in another field, many years before.

It was a terrible flight.

The slight rise in the cloud layer at Hamble had been no more than a sucker's gap and by the time I hit Devon, the low cloud, mist and rain hit me. But where was Anna? Which way had she turned?

I considered my options. In an ideal world I would keep clear of the high ground of Dartmoor and skim over the sea towards Cornwall, with the hope of the promised weather clearance hitting me sooner rather than later. But the south Devon coast was heavily defended against attack from the Luftwaffe and it would be too risky to head towards the coastal defences at Plymouth.

For the first time in my entire flying career I had absolutely no idea what to do for the best. I descended lower and lower, trying to stay below the cloud, skimming church steeples and looking out in desperation for a decent navigable landmark, such as a river or a train line. If forced to climb into the cloud, goodness only knew if I would ever find a gap to descend through and without instruments, or a radio or any kind of training of flying blind, I would either run out of fuel or fly straight into the cloud-covered ground. Either way, I would crash.

My worst nightmare soon became a reality when the visibility became so poor I had no option but to climb into cloud. It was like playing blind man's bluff, but with the added pressure of certain death if I walked in the wrong direction. I checked my fuel gauge over and over again. With my detour away from Dartmoor well under way to the north, I realised that I no longer had sufficient fuel to make it to Predannack. I looked at my father's compass and checked my general direction of flight. I was heading north west. And then I remembered the lesson that the RAF pilot had given me in the ill-fated dance hall that time, a lesson in instrument flying. I recalled his instructions, to straighten the aircraft using the artificial horizon and mark my last known point before becoming disorientated. RAF Chivenor was in North Devon, I knew, and if I continued to head in a north-north-westerly direction, I would hopefully come across some better weather and either head to Chivenor or find a suitable field to land in. If I didn't, my fuel would run low and I would be forced to descend through cloud.

I flew on for another fifteen minutes watching the fuel gauge as it slowly wound down. For a moment I began to shake so violently that I was hardly able to keep my hands steady on the controls. I looked out of the canopy at the pillow of cloud engulfing the aircraft and wondered if this was what drowning felt like. But then, the most calming sensation of peace came over me, as if the Spitfire was under the control of another force altogether and the clouds that had acted to suffocate now seemed to swaddled me into a safe embrace.

With absolutely nothing left to lose, I closed my eyes for a moment, took a deep breath and allowed my hands to lift from the steering column and for a few seconds, handed my fate to nothing more than chance – but it was more than that. I had the feeling I was no longer alone – that another presence was in the cockpit with me. I felt such an overwhelming feeling of being flooded with love that I would not have cared right at that moment if I'd crashed and died. I was already in heaven.

The moment of peace didn't last for long. Suddenly shaken awake as if from a wonderful dream, I regained control of the aircraft and allowed my beautiful Spitfire to fly in the direction she had settled of her own accord, the direction I'd been gifted when I had simply sat back, believed and let go.

Less than five minutes later, the blanket of grey began to disperse and gave way to whiter, wispy clouds. I banked hard to the left and to my absolute relief saw land, roughly two thousand feet beneath me, and ahead of that, the North Devon coastline. RAF Chivenor, my chosen diversion airfield, would now not be difficult to find.

From that moment on, although I'll never know who or what flew with me, I never in my life felt completely alone again.

The ground crew at RAF Chivenor were surprised when a Spitfire appeared through the clouds. They were even more surprised when a woman opened the canopy. I explained the circumstances of my arrival and asked to be pointed towards two things – a toilet and a telephone. My only thoughts now were of Anna. Had she turned back to Hamble? Had she diverted to another airfield, or had she, by some miracle, made it to Predannack?

I phoned Hamble and asked if Anna had either returned or checked in. She had done neither. With fear rising in my belly I phoned RAF Predannack and prayed to almighty God that I would be told of her arrival there.

I wasn't.

I sat in the met office and hovered over the phone, berating myself constantly for bending to the pressure to fly. It took several hours for the news to be confirmed, but eventually it became clear that Anna never made it to Predannack, or to anywhere, in fact. By late evening the news reached Hamble that a gunner on a Royal Navy Frigate operating just off Plymouth had seen what might have been a Spitfire appear through low cloud and fog off the starboard bow. It had ditched into the sea. He thought he'd seen the pilot bail out. The captain of the frigate ordered a search to be conducted, but after several hours of scouring the Channel for any trace of an aircraft or a survivor, the search was abandoned and the aircraft and pilot declared lost.

With all other ATA aircraft accounted for and with no RAF squadron aircraft losses reported, there could be no doubt that the crashed Spitfire was Anna's, and that my wonderful, kind and beautiful friend, was gone. I wrapped myself in her jacket and wept.

Losing my parents to a flying accident had been unbearable, but with the help of the Lanyons, despite the odds, somehow I got through it. But a part of my soul disintegrated the day I lost Anna. For weeks all I could do was replay the day, picturing what might have been if the course of events had run differently. The what-ifs were agony. What if I had agreed to fly in formation? What if I had followed my conviction that the weather had not improved significantly enough to risk the flight? What if I had never taken her to Lanyon – she would never have met Bill and would not have been desperate to see him. What if his squadron had not been deploying the next day? But the biggest what if of all, was this: what if, on the most important day of my life at an airfield called RAF Upavon, Marie and I hadn't persuaded Anna to fly the Spitfire when she clearly didn't want to? The answers all led to only one outcome – my darling Anna would still be alive.

But that was the problem with accidents, if we could only foreshadow them we could very quickly break the chain of events that lead to disaster.

But it was too late.

It was always too late.

A hardness crept into my soul that hadn't existed before. I flew harder and longer than ever. I was living in a fog of grief and the only scrap of tenderness left in my heart was for Edward. With Marie gone, I dreaded going back to my home in Hamble. Anna floated around in the ether waiting to be grabbed onto. Every room contained a multitude of memories. But now, knowing that the memories could never be replayed in real life, recalling our time together at Hamble no longer brought happiness, but a deep and desperate sadness that suffocates the heart when it finds it necessary to endure the loss of an interconnected soul. Anna was an angel. She was a good woman with not one ounce of badness of selfishness in her. There would never again be any woman in the whole world who I would admire, adore and love so deeply. I have missed her every single day of my life.

Chapter 33

Katherine
Christmas Eve

Yvonne intercepted me on the way to Juliet's room, guiding me into the manager's office. She sat me down.

'Juliet dictated this to the night manager in the early hours,' she said, handing me a letter. 'Listen, I know you had the best intentions,' she continued, with quite a kindly tone for Yvonne, 'but I think the trip out yesterday was too much for her.'

I opened the note.

My dear Katherine.

Thank you so much for yesterday, it was wonderful day, wasn't it? I'm so sorry but I'm not feeling particularly well tonight. A kind of hushed daze seems to have overwhelmed me and I think it's best if I rest tomorrow. As you know there are three more ammunition boxes out there. I have written down the locations, attached to this letter, and I wonder if you might take a trip out on your own, see if you can find them? I hope and pray the compass is in one of them, but that search is beyond me now and if you don't find it, please don't worry, I know I'm going to have to let it go.

Sam has messaged to say that he is on his way home and I hope – more than anything I have hoped for in my life – that he is able to take me flying, which is another reason for resting up today, because I need the energy to fly, one last time.

I'll rest up now and save my energy for the big day!

With all the love in the world,

Juliet.

'Would you like a cup of tea?' Yvonne asked as I stared blankly out of the office window, my glazed eyes skimming over the expanse of lawn and down towards the sea.

I smiled, put my hands on my knees and stood to leave. 'No – thanks, Yvonne. I'll be getting on my way.'

She put a hand on my shoulder, her face was the picture of pity.

'I think you probably realise now that Minack was a bad idea, but don't feel badly,' – so this was the tack she'd decided to take – 'But if you don't mind, we'll keep her inside from now on and make sure she's taken care of properly, get her back up to strength. Perhaps it would be best to let her stay here for Christmas Day, I'll explain it all to Mr Lanyon if you like.'

I paused at the door and smiled.

'I don't feel badly about yesterday. Not at all. Even if she'd died at the Minack – even if her wheelchair had gone careering down the steps and she'd plummeted head-first into the sea – she'd have loved every minute of it. Juliet was – *is* – an Attagirl! I'll be back tomorrow with Mr Lanyon to take her flying.' I opened the door. 'Goodbye, Yvonne.'

The remainder of the day saw me walking miles and miles along the coastal path looking for the ammunition boxes. And I found them, too. One at Kynance Cove, one at the Lizard and the final one under a twisted oak on the banks of the Helford. Despite the dank morning, the mist cleared by eleven only to be replaced by a delicious Cornish blue sky.

It was a wonderful day. A day of adventure and promise, of retracing Juliet's footsteps. I wished I'd met her twenty years ago, when we could have talked for hours and I could have picked her sharp brain about so many things. I wanted to tap into her experiences. Juliet had moved on to consider bigger, more universal questions in her later years and I wondered, was this out of a genuine scientific interest on her behalf, or did she simply want to prove to herself that heaven really did exist – and that Edward, in whatever form, existed too and really was out there waiting for her? I also wanted to ask, how can you tell about love? How do you know who to walk through eternity with? What if I moved on with someone new, only to meet a smiling James at the pearly gates and have to tell him that

I'd fallen in love again, that my love hadn't been reserved only for him, after all? I sat on the cliffs at the Lizard, with a box stuffed with yet more twenty-pound notes sitting next to me, and remembered our wedding vows, *to love and to cherish, till death us do part.* And Death *had* parted us, which left me, what? Released from the agreement? Free?

My day of coddiwompling ended just before sunset with an hour at Fenella's. We needed to finalise arrangements for the Boxing Day party and I wanted to talk to her about Juliet, too.

I took my usual place at the kitchen table and waited to be fed.

Fenella, sporting yet another Christmas jumper (a chirpy-looking snowman with little flashing lights), dropped an un-iced Christmas cake onto the table in front of me with a thud. The cake had an inconsistent texture on the top, like it had been … nibbled. Fenella, muttering something along the lines of, 'The little beggars have been at it again,' took a bread knife out of the drawer and rather than cut me a slice, put the cake on its side and carefully sheared a centimetre off the top of the entire cake. Fruit and crumbs were swept onto the bin leaving a much-reduced cake, in height at least, sitting on the table in front of me.

'I daren't ask, but I'm going to have to,' I said as she cut a couple of slices. 'Why did you cut the top off?'

She waved the knife, dismissively. 'Oh, I forgot to cover it when I went to bed last night, and the mice have been at it. Not to worry, they've only got little teeth, and even if they pee'd on it, the pee wouldn't penetrate much more than half an inch down, so it's fine.' She handed me a slice on a patterned china plate. 'Eat up!'

The conversation turned to Juliet.

'The thing is, she keeps talking about endings,' I said, taking a mouthful. It was delicious. 'It's as though everything she's doing is quite consciously the last time she'll do it, like she knows she's going to die very soon. But how could she know that? Do you think she's ill?'

Fenella glanced up from her cake.

'When you reach one hundred years of age, Katherine, I'm sure every day feels like it may be the last.'

'Yes, I know. But this is different.'

'It probably is,' she said with a comforting smile, 'but don't you go thinking or worrying about it now. That's the last thing she would want you to do.'

I nodded.

'Has she got to France yet?' she asked.

'France? No.'

Fenella refilled my teacup with a knowing glance.

'You'd best get reading, then,' she said. 'Because if you think her story has been exciting so far, you just wait till you get to the next bit, and also ... well, let's just say things might become a bit clearer for you.'

I declined Fenella's offer to spend Christmas Eve playing skittles in the pub. I wanted to be alone tonight, to have the time to finish Juliet's story, and I so desperately wanted to find the compass, too. But this seemed increasingly unlikely now.

As the sun set over the islands, I prepared the lounge for a cosy evening in – candles, firelight, the memoirs and Lottie's shawl– and poured a glass of wine. But before settling on the sofa I remembered the pile of vinyl records stored away in the sideboard. One of them had a label stuck to it. *Our song* was all the label said. I smiled. It was *We'll Meet Again*. I ran a hand over the cover and imagined Edward, all those years before, at Christmas, taking the record out of the sleeve, polishing it, perhaps, before placing it on the turntable and taking Juliet in his arms. Their whole story had weaved in and out of Christmas, and it was her birthday, too, after all.

I heard the church bell chime five times and wandered through to the kitchen to turn the lights off before settling into the lounge for the evening. I stood in the darkness and looked through the window towards the harbour and smiled at the sight of the Christmas lights draped along the harbour wall. Tourist roamed the village, now, and amongst them – finally – there were quite a few children, wrapped in coats and bobble hats, looking on in wonder at the display. There were a couple of market stalls too, all thanks to Fenella, who was selling mulled wine and chestnuts, she never missed a trick, that one.

But that was their world tonight, and mine ... mine was somewhere else entirely.

Chapter 34

Juliet

A surprise visitor

Two weeks before Christmas Edward telephoned to ask if there was any possibility I might make it to Cornwall before the New Year. He sounded edgy and Edward never sounded edgy. I wasn't particularly hopeful of bagging an ATA delivery to Predannack as my marriage to Charles could no longer be used as leverage. It also seemed wrong to request leave when the continued pressure on the ATA to deliver was immense. My commanding officer had a different idea and called me in for an interview.

I was, she felt, flying on the edge of absolute exhaustion since Anna died, pushing myself too hard and by the look of me, not sleeping well or eating enough. I was offered two weeks' rest and recuperation and for once, I didn't argue. All I wanted was to be back in Angels Cove with Edward, to be held in his arms and to never let go.

On 19th December the duty pilot handed me my flying chit in the morning with a smile on her face. 'Deliver this and then you're done,' she said. 'Happy Christmas!' I looked at the chit in my hand – a Spitfire to Predannack! This was it, one last flight and finally, after all those months of heartache, I was going home, not to Lanyon, but to Angels Cove – to Edward.

True, flying to Cornwall evoked a number of heart-breaking memories, but the Spitfire was a beautiful aircraft to fly and as I banked over the cove towards Predannack, I looked down at the angels and smiled. It was my first genuine smile since Anna had gone.

My smile did not last for long.

Predannack had become a busy and important air station – an air station that the Luftwaffe were keeping an eye on. As I banked over the cove and began my final descent into the airfield, I saw a trace of bullets fly past my port wing, followed rapidly by another trace, a couple of which managed to hit my underbelly. I glanced over my right shoulder to see a German Messerschmitt sitting on my tail. ATA pilots were not taught how to evade attack, but from somewhere, the aerobatic skills developed during my flying circus days kicked in and having only taken what I believed to be a scratch, I was able to roll the aircraft to the right, then pull hard over into a loop, successfully placing myself to the rear of the German.

With no ammunition to fight back, a decision needed to be made. Should I attempt to outrun him or try to land at Predannack. The German made the decision for me. He ran! He bloody well ran and disappeared out to sea as quickly as he arrived. It had simply been a cheap shot from an armed reconnaissance aircraft.

I took a deep breath and repositioned for Predannack. With a mile to run and at four hundred feet I pulled the lever to lower the undercarriage but the wheels did not lower. I tried again. Nothing. The mechanism must have been damaged by the last round of bullets.

I levelled off at two hundred feet and overflew the airfield waggling my wings. This was a sign to the control tower and the engineers that I was in trouble, but they must have surely guessed this already. I saw engineers running out of the squadron building to take a look as I flew past. A red Verey flare was fired as I turned downwind, presumably to warn me about the lack of undercarriage. I flew a circuit of the airfield and passed over the runway again – as slowly as possible without stalling. I needed to make another decision: should I bail out over the sea or land on my belly at Predannack. Bailing out was not an attractive option. I would have to gain height before bailing in order to have sufficient time for the parachute to open, but even if survived the bail out, I wouldn't survive the cold of the sea for long if there was no boat nearby to haul me out.

The decision was made. I would land wheels-up at Predannack.

I positioned myself for a long approach on finals and

patted the Spitfire affectionately. 'I'm sorry, old girl,' I said, 'but this isn't going to be pretty. We're in it together now.'

Three hundred feet, two hundred feet, one hundred ... feather, flair, gently, gently ...

And then I was down. Sliding along grass and then concrete. There was nothing for it but to close my eyes, just as I had done once before when lost in cloud above Devon, and brace myself as she slid across the airfield, hoping to God we didn't burst into flames. I waited for the inevitable stop, which, when it came, came with a bang.

Three men pulled me from the cockpit. One of them was Edward Nancarrow. He saw the whole thing as it evolved – the attack by the Messerschmitt, my evasion and subsequent crash. There was blood on Edward's coat, I noticed, as they pulled me well-clear of the wreckage and laid me on the grass, waiting for the ambulance, which arrived moments later.

'You're bleeding, Edward,' I muttered, not aware of my injuries at the time.

'Don't worry about that now,' he said, supporting my head in his hands, his eyes full of love and tenderness. 'Just hold on, my darling. Hold on tight.'

I closed my eyes and passed out.

I was beyond lucky, that day. My injuries were significant enough for hospitalisation at Predannack sick bay, but not serious enough for my life to be in question. A bullet that penetrated the cockpit had punctured my left arm, hence the blood, and I was also heavily bruised and concussed from the impact. But fear and adrenalin make for a powerful painkiller and I hadn't even noticed much more than the pain of a scratch on my arm as I positioned the Spitfire for crash landing, but the wound was relatively deep and required surgical attention.

Two days later I went home. Ma was adamant that I should go Lanyon, but Lanyon wasn't home to me, not anymore. Home was where Edward was – at Angel View. We didn't worry about the repercussions (I was still officially married to Charles, after all), because all I wanted was to lay in his arms, in his lounge, in front of the fire, look across at the angels, and thank them every single day for bringing me home safely.

It was potentially a scandal in the making – Charles Lanyon's wife holed up with the mysterious American – but it was a scandal I was prepared to face.

And then there was Lottie.

I had written to her to explain about Edward, to say how much I loved him – had always loved him – and that Charles knew and had given his blessing. I received a perfunctory response. Lottie said she didn't mind about Edward, she was still grieving her husband after all and had never had serious designs on the man, but she was shocked and disappointed that I hadn't confided in her, my oldest friend, that there was a secretiveness about me that disappointed her since I'd met Anna, who had obviously replaced her as my confidante and all round best friend. Having no idea how to respond to this letter, I fell silent until I wrote again later, to explain that Anna had died. This had merited a response from Ma Lanyon and from Lottie, too, who had both written individual notes expressing their sympathy and their fondness of Anna.

But I had had no real contact with Lottie for many months until that day, Christmas Eve, 1943, when, at ten a.m. we heard a knock. Edward opened the door and the cottage was suddenly filled with the sound of my favourite Christmas carol – *Silent Night*. Lottie was holding Mabel, who was dressed in layers of hand-me-down clothes and sporting a bright red beret on her head.

Despite the bruising and shortness of breath, I pushed back the blanket with my good arm, got to my feet and rushed to the door. Mabel was holding a Christmas present. I tried to interrupt the singing in an attempt to hug them both, but Lottie held up a gloved hand to stop me – Mabel was determined to finish the carol.

I knew by the look on her smiling face that I was forgiven.

Lottie stayed at the cottage for an hour of chat that was surprisingly easy-going. We waved them off from the door and watched as they wandered down the lane towards the harbour, hand in hand, singing Christmas carols and swinging arms as they went. For a moment, I almost forgot that the war still raged on our doorstep. For a moment.

It was mid-afternoon when Edward asked if I felt up to a little walk. As I wandered slowly down the lane, leaning on Edward for support, I thought he would point us in the direction of our little beach, but he didn't. Instead, we turned into the village and five minutes later, opened the picket gate that led into the churchyard.

Edward gestured towards a pew half way down the aisle on the right. We sat for quite some time, holding hands in silence, staring at a stained-glass window above the altar that showed the side view of a magnificent winged angel. His long hair flowed over his wings and he was looking upwards, towards an omniscient, unseen figure.

The angel held the same expression a child might have when looking up to a parent when desperate for an answer. His hands were clasped together in prayer.

'The expression on that angel's face says it all, really, doesn't it?' Edward said, looking ahead and holding my gloved left hand in both of his.

'Yes,' I sighed. 'I'm afraid it does, rather. It's worrying really ...'

'What is?'

'Well, if the angels are confused and looking for guidance, what chance do us mere mortals have?'

Edward turned to me. His face bordering on excitable – feverish.

'Ah, but that's why this picture is so wonderful, Juliet. We all – every single one of us – need guidance sometimes. But no one – not even God – can tell us what to do in every given circumstance. I think God is smiling at the angel, saying nothing in answer to his question but simply offering love, because if this war has taught me anything it's that in the end, love really is the only answer. We just *have* to keep believing in love.'

'Do you believe in love, Edward?'

Rather than answering my question, he took my face in his hands and kissed me. When he sat back into the pew, he glanced up at the window again. His words took me by surprise.

'I have to go away tomorrow.'

I turned to face him. 'But, it's Christmas Day tomorrow ...'

'I have no choice. Listen, don't be cross, but I've taken the liberty of arranging for you to stay with Lottie ... at Lanyon. No, please don't argue. I asked Lottie not to give the game away earlier.'

'Can't you delay, just for a day?'

He shook his head. 'I'm afraid it can't.'

'But why can't I stay on at Angels View? Lottie can pop in from time to time ...'

'You can't possibly stay on your own, you're not fit enough.'

I sighed. He was right.

'How long will you be gone?'

'The thing is, I'm not sure when I'll be back.'

'Are we talking weeks or ...'

He shook his head again. 'More like months.'

A rush of panic swept over me.

'Don't go, Edward. Please. I'm begging you. Become a conscientious objector, you believe in love, you said so!'

He smiled.

'Why not?' I went on. 'I'm being serious. I'm frightened. What with losing Anna, and now ...'

He put a finger to my lips to silence me.

'You need to rest. Oh, and I've got a favour to ask, by the way.' He picked up his hat and brushed an invisible fleck off the brim with the back of his hand. 'I need to find a poem to learn before tomorrow.'

'A poem? But you're dreadful at remembering poems.'

He laughed.

'I know.'

'Why do you need a poem?'

'I can't really explain, it's something to do with messages, but I need a relatively short one that I can easily memorise. Nothing too over-the-top.'

I picked up a prayer book that was resting on the back of the pew in front of us. It fell open at a page marked by an insert of a loose leaf of paper. The paper had a prayer typed on it. I began to read it aloud.

'The Prayer of St Francis,' I began. 'Do you know it?'

Edward shook his head. I began to recite.

'Make me a channel of your peace. Where there is hatred, let me sow love ... where there is doubt, faith. Where there is despair, hope ...'

I glanced up towards the angel and smiled my thanks before handing the paper to Edward.

'I do believe that this,' I said, 'is for you.'

Unable to fight off the tiredness after our walk, I slept, waking mid-afternoon to find Edward smiling at me, sitting on the floor by my side, his dog, Amber, sleeping on the hearth rug next to him. It was a picture-perfect moment of complete contentment and I wondered if such perfect moments can only be found when the recipient knows that the situation is temporary. We took Amber for a last walk to the beach and watched the sun slowly dip behind the islands. As the last arc of golden light disappeared behind the horizon, surrounded by twilight, Edward delved into his coat pocket and took out an envelope. He handed it to me.

'For you,' he said, before tenderly brushing his lips against mine.

'What is it?' I asked, trying to open it with one hand. He took the envelope, opened it and handed me the card. He had made me a birthday card. There was a just enough light left for me to read his words inside.

Happy birthday/Christmas my darling Juliet.
I wrote a poem while you slept, after all. But this one is just for you.
Whatever happens, keep believing in love, my love,
Always, Edward.

'*Where Angels Sing*, by Edward Nancarrow,' I said, swallowing back the tears. 'A poem? For me?'

He nodded.

I glanced up. 'You actually wrote one, you, yourself?'
He nodded again.
'Yes, Ma'am, I did! And it took me a whole ten minutes.'
I laughed. 'That long? It must be an absolute master-piece.'
'Oh, it is.'
I began to read, but soon realised what the poem was a message of love, just in case he didn't make it home.
'Oh, Edward,' I said, resting the card on my knee, 'it's lovely, but you mustn't think that you won't make it back, in fact you must believe that you *will*! Promise me – promise you'll keep believing, promise me you believe that you'll make it back! Belief is half the battle with this kind of thing – that's how I feel when I'm flying all the time – that I'm invincible, and somehow, it works. But only if you truly believe. You must believe, Edward.'
He turned to face me.
'No one wants to survive this war more than me. I want to come back to this little wonderful cove more than anything – *anything*, Juliet. But this push has to be all or nothing. But I have to tell you – have to be completely honest – that the chance of me making it back, it isn't great, but what I have to do has to be done. Has to.'
'But ...'
He raised his hand.
'I want you to promise me three things.'
My tears were flowing freely now.
'Go on.'

He stroked the dog that sat loyally beside him. 'First, look after Amber for me. Take her to Lanyon, she loves it there. The guys up at the house have been minding her for me, but it's not the same as having a proper home.' He leant down to kiss his beloved dog. 'She's probably got two or three good years left in her and I want to know she'll be loved.'

My heart broke. 'Oh, Edward. Of course, I will.'

'Second, always be as you are now.' He laughed. 'My brave and daring coddiwompler. Be the woman I met that day on the cliff top, the stunning adventurer who leapt out of her plane, devil may care, travelling with absolute purpose – purpose to be thrilled, to be excited, to live life at the edge of living. That's the woman I met and that's the woman I hope you will always be.'

I laughed through the tears.

'I'll try my very best.'

A sea breeze had picked up and was playing with my hair, brushing it across my eyes. He gently tucked several strands behind my ear.

'The third one is easy,' he said. 'I want you to promise me you'll live until you're a hundred.'

'What!? A hundred! But that's crazy! How on earth can I promise that?'

He shrugged, knowingly.

'It's like you said, if you believe something will happen, half the battle is over. I'm absolutely certain you will survive this war, Juliet, and I want everyone who survives it to live long and very happy lives, because if not, what did all the others die for?'

He jumped up and held out his hands, looked down at me and smiled a bright and contagious smile.

'One hundred, ya hear now – promise me!'

I stood and put my hand on my heart the American way,

'I promise to try to live until one hundred, or at least I'll do my very best to—' I decided to lighten the moment '—and when I do, I'll take the old Tiger Moth up for a spin on my birthday and fly around and around the angels until I see you, waving up at me!'

He laughed. 'It's a deal!'

He took the poem from my hand, placed it in the envelope and handed it back.

The early evening sky was illuminated tangerine red and wispy cirrus clouds kissed the edge of heaven.

'Keep this safe,' he said, taking my hand and the letter in both of his. 'And remember, when you're one hundred years old exactly, let yourself drift away into Neverland and go to the far side of the island,' he pointed to the middle angel, 'to that one, there, the one we went to that day we took old *Mermaid* for a spin, and I'll be waiting for you, and it can be our own island, our home, for eternity.' He looked deep into my eyes. 'I promise you, Juliet, I'll be waiting for you.'

I broke down. He was being serious. This was it. The poor, poor man genuinely believed he was going to die. And if Edward was going to die, what on earth was the point of me living?

That evening was the best and worst of my life. We held each other close by the fireside and danced to the Vera Lynn hit song, *We'll Meet Again*. Amber never left his side all evening. She loved this enigmatic stranger, this American, this Austrian, this Edward Nancarrow, this Felix Gruber, or whoever else he might be, Amber didn't care. With every morsel of her body she simply adored him, and so did I.

Chapter 35

Katherine

Another surprise visitor

I lay the manuscript down on the sofa beside me and sat for a moment thinking of Juliet. Not Juliet of the 1940s, but Juliet as she was right now, asleep perhaps, or maybe sitting her chair, awake and remembering.

In need a little air, I wrapped Juliet's shawl around my shoulders, slipped my feet into a pair of Wellingtons left by the door, stepped outside and looked down towards the harbour. The Christmas lights were turned off now, but the village didn't need any extra sparkle tonight. The almost-full moon shimmered across the water, reflecting a silvery road through the middle mount of the angels, which – to my absolute delight and enchantment – had been given a single cross that remained lit, positioned on the crag on top of the island.

It seemed to be the perfect moment to pour out a glass

of wine and play some music and try to behave a little more festively – it was Christmas Eve, after all – and maybe tonight I could break my embargo on love songs, if only in memory of Lottie, the incorrigible romantic. I flicked through Juliet's record collection and smiled when the wartime songs Juliet had occasionally referenced popped up, including, *I'll Be Seeing You, Hold Me in Your Arms a Little Longer, Baby* and *Yours*.

With my wine glass for a partner, I danced slowly around the room to the slow, evocative song, *Yours*. I played the song twice more and I was just smooching around the room in my Scottish tartan pyjamas, pretending to be Vera Lynn, when my phone pinged. Uncle Gerald, no doubt. His timing was always perfected to the exact moment when I need to be brought down to earth with a thump.

But it wasn't from Gerald. It was an email from Sam Lanyon.

Hi Katherine.
Happy Christmas!
Quick question. Is that white wine you're dancing with, or champagne? If not champagne, don't worry, I have some!
See you VERY soon.
Sam

What the ...?
I glanced through the lounge window and saw nothing

but the moon and the sea and the little cross on the island.
I emailed back.

Hi Sam
Wine, I'm afraid. Did the elf grass me up?
Katherine

Almost immediately there was a knock at the door.
He was here. He was actually here.

I glanced at my reflection in the hall mirror – mascara
stains and bead head. I spat on my pyjama sleeve and
wiped my eyes before eventually opening the door.

And there he was.

Standing in front of me wearing his Navy flying suit with
a bottle of champagne in his hand and an infectious smile
on his face (his beard was surprisingly sweet, actually) was
Sam Lanyon. And I have absolutely no idea why – maybe it
was the emotion of Juliet's story, or the noise of the party
that had clearly spilled out of the pub and onto Noel's front
garden, or the half bottle of wine I'd just worked my way
through – but right then and there on the doorstep, just
as Vera Lynn nailed her final lines, I gave this man, this
complete stranger who had gone through hell and high
water to get home for Christmas to make his Grandmother
happy, a welcome home hug. And for the first time in a
very long time, knowing that I was safely swaddled in
this stranger's house in this peculiar little village, a village
protected by mermaids and angels, I didn't feel alone.

Chapter 36

Juliet

Matthew Wilkins

A note for my Grandson:
I began my story by stating that I would write of love, not war and I hold fast to that statement. But I ask you to remember that we were living in a time when conventional rules of society had all but disappeared. I also ask that you try not to judge me when you read on. Everything you read in the following pages I did for love – not only a love for Edward, but a love for a free world, too, and for all those who had given the ultimate sacrifice.

On with the story we go!

Having said an emotional goodbye to Edward from the haven that had become his little cottage on the morning of Christmas Day, I waited with Edward's beautiful dog at my side for Lottie to arrive to escort me back to Lanyon.

It was one of those perfect, crisp days, but when I closed my eyes, I could not stop re-living my crash, and all the fruits of Arabia could not have sweetened the taste of blood or lessened the acrid smell of my beautiful Spitfire as she lay burning at Predannack. Lottie arrived promptly at ten. She had brought Jessops and a horse and cart. With our previous quarrel forgotten (or, if not completely forgotten, put to one side forever) we headed up the hill away from the cove and back to a house that felt like a prison to me.

I settled into my old room, allowed Amber to sleep on my bed, slumped down next to her, tried and failed to finish *Gone With the Wind* and wondered, with Lottie busy at work all day, how on earth I was going to endure the coming weeks of having no one to talk to or to play with at Lanyon. Charles had gone, having recovered sufficiently to return to a portside desk job with the Navy. We had said our goodbyes on such amicable terms, it would not have been uncomfortable to spend time with him at Lanyon. But it was academic, Charles was not at home.

I was just about to return to my book when a pretty little face – a face that glowed with the personality of a sincerely beautiful soul – appeared at my door. It was darling Mabel, who had been sent by Ma Lanyon (who had been the first to remember that the family would do well to keep me – and my money – on side) to see if I would like to join her and Pa for a cup of tea and a bit of bread and butter. Pa had brought some cheese home from one of his tenants and maybe, after tea, Mabel suggested, we might have a bit of a play in the garden with the dog, if I felt up to it. My melancholy melted immediately and I realised I needed to buck up.

'Yes, Mabel,' I said, prising an equally depressed dog off the bed. 'That is a fabulous idea. Amber and I would love to play.'

I spent two months recuperating at Lanyon, and thanks to my new pals – Mabel, Amber and Margaret Mitchell (*Gone with the Wind*) – they were not wasted months. I often watched the house from the garden, watching the comings and goings of the SOE and noticed that Pa Lanyon often ventured into their territory. At first, I thought his visits to the other side of the house were from an estate management perspective, but the regularity and duration of the visits spoke of something else. Pa, I decided, had become part of it all, whatever *it all* was.

Then, one miserable afternoon. Mabel, Amber and I were playing hide and seek in the house when Pa appeared at the foot of the stairs and asked Mabel to report with Amber to cook, who had a surprise treat for them. He asked me if I would mind nipping into the other side of the house to meet a friend of his, who was also a friend of Edward's, who was also the man who ran the whole operation at Lanyon.

His name was Matthew Wilkins. He had a pronounced limp and a kind smile. I took a seat in his office while he talked in general terms about flying – he'd been a pilot himself, he said, early in the war, but an accident had brought an end to all that. He asked me about my own flying career, what type of aircraft I had flown and if I missed my life in the ATA since the accident. Yes, I said, I had. So much so, in fact, that I planned to return to Hamble next month to resume flying duties with the ATA.

But Matthew had another idea, he needed my help, he said. He wanted to recruit me into a small team of aviators, aviators who were given very specific and very secret, tasks. This was when I finally found out the truth about the operation at Lanyon. Yes, I already knew of their involvement in clandestine operations – had gathered as much from Edward – but in my wildest dreams I had not imagined just how significant the whole set-up was.

The SOE had been established at the beginning of the war with the sole purpose of working with local resistance movements in Europe and subversively wreaking havoc behind enemy lines – espionage and sabotage were the staples of their work. But the operation at Lanyon was even more than the training and inserting of agents behind enemy lines. Pa Lanyon was also the head of a group of local men trained at Lanyon and known as the 'Stay Behinds'. The southern coast of the whole of Britain was a siege line – the closest point between the Nazis and their ultimate goal, Britain. And although Hitler's planned invasion had been postponed because of the allied success in the Battle of Britain, plans had been made at home to facilitate a number of men who would act, in the case of invasion, as stay-behind saboteurs. Such stay-behinds would be hidden from the Germans in secret bunkers along the Cornish coast. As the Germans invaded and the siege line moved up the country, they would work behind enemy lines to sabotage the German occupation from within. It seemed odd, imagining German boots on British soil, but this was the reality of the time. The men recruited for such stay-behind tasks knew they had signed up for a suicide mission and Pa Lanyon was no exception.

But Lanyon gave yet more to the war effort. The men under Matthew Wilkins' command also worked with a secret organisation that ran flotillas from Falmouth and the Helford River. Such flotillas comprised of commandeered fishing boats from France (especially Brittany) and Cornish fishing boats (re-rigged and coloured to act as French boats), requisitioned to operated covertly between Cornwall and France to transport evacuees, escaped POWs and SOE agents, back to Britain. The men who operated these boats – once ordinary, untrained, local men – also dropped and recovered secret messages. With every port along the French coast fortified by the Germans, who shot suspected spies on sight, theirs was a ludicrously dangerous operation, but no more ludicrous and dangerous that the job Matthew Wilkins had in mind for me.

He asked Pa Lanyon to leave the room – a room that had once been Pa's office – took a dossier out of the desk drawer and placed it in front of me. My ATA photograph was paperclipped to the front. He sat forward in his chair and in a measured, calculated manner, began to speak, glancing towards the file.

'It's the way things are, you understand.'

I shrugged. 'Makes no difference to me. I have nothing to hide.'

'Perhaps not, but you have built up quite a reputation.'

'Good or bad?'

'Oh, very definitely good – superb, in fact. You're one of the most naturally gifted pilots the ATA have ever seen. It must have been frustrating not to have been allowed to join the RAF.'

'Not really. I love flying for the ATA.'

'Yes,' He picked up my file and flicked through it before landing on one particular page. He looked at me a smiled. 'I see your father ran a flying circus—' he raised his brows '—amongst other things. Quite the entrepreneur. He left you a considerable fortune, all in all. Did the Lanyons ever ask where his money came from, the bulk of it, at least?'

'He was a businessman. I never asked how he made his money. After I was born, he was only really interesting in the flying circus – that and his family.'

Wilkins nodded, took a packet of cigarettes out of the top drawer, opened the packet and offered me one across the table. I shook my head. He took out a box of matches, lit his cigarette, took a long, satisfying drag, exhaled and sniffed.

'I'll get to the point, Juliet,' he said, resting his cigarette on an ashtray. 'You are exactly the calibre of pilot I've been desperate to find – a flying ace, a risk taker, but at the same time, a hardworking, level headed operator. Your evasion of the Messerschmitt over Predannack was superb.' I sat expressionless, waiting for him to finish. 'I need a small group of pilots exactly like you – skilled, calm under pressure. Your mother was French, I believe?'

I nodded.

'—and you know France well and are fluent yourself – you even look French.'

'Mr Wilkins, what is it that you want me to do, exactly? Please don't sugar coat it. Just tell me.'

He took another draw on his cigarette.

'I want you to train with a small group of pilots who fly Lysanders out of an airbase in mid-Devon and then, when you're ready, I need you to fly for me, doing secret pick-up and drop offs – from here, most likely. The Lysander will be your own aircraft and no one will be party to your trips but me. You'll have a small team of trusted engineers staying here and working on the aircraft with you but they won't know where you're going, or why. You're familiar with the Lysander?'

It was a fairly straightforward, high wing, monoplane.

'Yes, but—'

'The aircraft will be painted black. You'll fly covertly to France at night, into secret locations hidden from the Germans, often retrieving or dropping agents, that kind of thing. A fixed ladder has been added to the rear cockpit on the port side, to get the agents out and in quickly. You'll be in and out in minutes.'

The ladder wasn't a concern. The destination, however, was.

'Fly directly into France? But that's crazy. A blacked-out aircraft can be heard, if not seen. The whole thing sounds utterly suicidal.'

He scratched an eyebrow.

'We'd give you the same training we give to RAF pilots who are already doing the same job, and we'd give you the skills you'd need to escape and evade, although it would be very unlikely that you'd be required to put these skills into action, of course.'

I began to shake my head.

'Take a day to think about it and come and see me tomorrow.'

'I'm sorry,' I said, pushing my file back across the desk towards him. 'And I know you must be desperate for suitable pilots, but what you're offering isn't for me. I'm afraid you've been given an overly-inflated opinion of my flying skills. Doing a few loops and rolls in a flying circus does not qualify me for this. I may not even have the stomach for flying when I get back. I'm not sure how I'll feel.'

I stood to leave.

'Is that because of the crash at Predannack,' he asked. 'Or because of your friend, Anna.'

I refused to be ruffled, even though the thought of Anna's death ripped apart the inner workings of my heart.

'The answer is no, Mr Wilkins. I am not the man for you.'

He stubbed out the remainder of his cigarette and also stood.

'But I didn't want a man, Juliet. I wanted you.'

I headed towards the door.

'Well, it's your decision. All things considered, I suppose it's perhaps best you're weren't allowed to fulfil your dream after all.'

I stopped with my hand on the door handle.

'Dream? What do you mean?'

'To fly in combat. Isn't that what you always wanted to do? RAF pilots do not have the luxury of choosing their missions, Miss Caron, they fly when and where is necessary. Whatever the danger. Go back to the ATA or stop flying completely and sit the war out at Lanyon. I'm sorry to have wasted your time.'

I knew this barbed comment was aimed to rile me but it didn't work. My flying with the ATA had been treacherous at times and I had lost too many friends to worry about taking his words about my failed RAF dream to heart.

'You're probably right,' I said with a saccharine smile while turning the door handle. 'I would have been useless in the RAF. I may have chipped a nail.'

He shot from behind the desk to stand in the open door. He was grinning now.

'Are you always so unrufflable?'

I smiled.

'Only on Tuesdays.'

He laughed. His eyes danced. 'But my God, Juliet. Can't you see. This is exactly why you would be perfect for our operation. Please – *please* – reconsider.'

I shook my head.

'I'm sorry. I would help if I could, but it's not for me.'

He bowed as if defeated and stepped away from the door, but as I turned to leave saw that he had saved his most powerful ammunition till last.

'I understand that you're a close personal friend of Edward Nancarrow ...'

I stopped in the doorway and looked at him.

'Yes, I am.'

'Do you understand the importance of his work, Juliet?'

'He's never really told me what he does. But now I've learnt about your operation, I'm guessing he's an agent.'

'I mention him because he would also be coming back from France that way – by Lysander. It's becoming increasingly dangerous to get agents back by boat. Edward is a hunted man in Europe. The Nazis have had a price on his head for some time.'

'Why are you telling me this?'

'To sway you, clearly. Because I have a feeling that although you won't do this for King and country, you'll do it for Edward. And I need someone to go and get him, but I want it to be someone wholly unconnected with any

aspect of the operation so far. Edward is in great danger.
We have a mole and I can't trace it. Could be anyone.'

I took a deep breath but I did not smile.

'When do I start?'

I started immediately. My training took six weeks. It began
with escape and evasion training and how to cope under
torture if captured. It wasn't fun, but it was necessary. I
was taught how to kill silently with a knife, how to make
Molotov Cocktails and work a luger pistol. I also became
a dab hand with a grenade.

I hated it.

Then I was shipped to an airfield in mid-Devon and
joined a small team of male pilots who cared not one jot that
I was a woman, which was refreshing. Our particular arm of
the organisation was so secret that most of the military had
no notion of its existence. I took a couple of days getting
back up to speed in the cockpit before being kitted out with
a selection of French personal items – clothing, cigarettes,
shoes, jewellery and, most importantly, a new identity. My
first name remained the same, but spelled Juliette, and my
surname, already French but no matter, had to change.

My new identity was that of a milliner from Brittany.
My parents had been chicken farmers. They were both
dead. I now lived with an Aunt on a farm, in Plouvein.
Wilkins had done his research well. This was the place of
my mother's ancestry and I knew it well. I was given the
address of my fictional aunt's farm and told to make my

way there if I ever had to bail or abandon the aircraft on the ground. It was my safe house.

And then the flying began in earnest, mainly to Brittany. I did not fly frequently, but when I did fly the preparation was thorough and the pressure immense.

Edward did not return home that month, or for several months and I realised how easily I had been duped, but by the time I realised this, I was in too deep. After just a couple of trips to France I realised the importance of the work and was awed by the bravery of the many men and women (parcels, we called them) who I either dropped or collected.

A few months into my new job, Wilkins took me into his office for a private chat. Edward was injured and holed up in a safe house. They needed to get him back – tonight. The weather conditions were not ideal, but Edward's safety, even in his safe house, could not be guaranteed. And then he told me the truth about Edward Nancarrow–Felix Gruber. Before the war, Edward had worked for a major oil company and was well-travelled and multi-lingual. He was trained in guerrilla warfare and had begun the war by rounding up German spies in the South West of England, spies who were on the Class A list. As the war progressed, he had travelled often to France working with the resistance against the Nazis and to destabilise the Vichy regime.

But there was more. Wilkins was certain that Edward had discovered the secret locations of the V1/V2 rockets, but the information was so sensitive it was kept only in his head. But now, word was out that he was injured and Wilkins wanted me to fly to France, tonight, to bring him home. I only flew during a two-week period in any month, in line with the moon, a much necessary navigational aid when flying at night without instruments. The moon was waning on this particular night, on the very cusp of when I – or any of the other Black Squadron RAF pilots – would wish to fly such a sortie.

Any pilot will tell you that some flights – some days – feel uncomfortable from the off. Even during the planning stage, the sense of unnerved apprehension cannot be shed. Yes, I always felt apprehensive before flying any of my missions to France, but this was something else. I had felt the same way before flying on the day my Anna died as I felt it now. The route, the weather, the moon phase, were all far from ideal. Then there was an unserviceability for the aircraft engine on start-up and it all felt wrong. And yet, blinkered by my desperation to bring Edward home, I was determined to go.

I spent the afternoon memorising maps and the latest intelligence on coastal flak defences. I prepared my kit and waited for the all-clear to be sent from France to Wilkins to confirm that the pick-up was a 'go'. I also studied photographs of the field the agent who was escorting Edward had planned for my landing. I knew the time for the RV and number of passengers – one.

I was ready.

After a far from relaxed dinner, I sat quietly and attempted to gather my thoughts. Wilkins appeared at ten p.m. to give me the special code that would be flashed by the resistance agent from his position in the field prior to my landing. Together we waited for a message come through from France to say whether tonight was a 'go' or a 'no go'.

It was a 'go'.

Wilkins immediately contacted the BBC for a message to be passed during their French Language broadcast. This was our way of letting the agents, who listened to this broadcast via secretly stashed wirelesses – usually while hiding in an attic or a barn – that the pick-up was on. My code name, invented by Wilkins, was 'The Angel' and the message for Edward simply said, 'The angel is coming.'

At midnight, with my fake French papers stashed down my bra, my escape and evasion kit (French money, concentrated food tablets, beret, women's shoes), thrown into the hold, a map of Brittany printed on silk and a cyanide capsule kept inside a purple velvet pouch sewn into the lining of Anna's flying jacket, my pistol in its holster and my father's compass in my pocket for luck, I said my goodbyes to Wilkins, put on my flying helmet, jumped into the Lysander and slid the glass canopy shut. I went through pre-take-off checks, primed the engine and started her up. While allowing the engine to tick over until the oil temperature was 5 degrees centigrade, I tested the flying controls and brakes and chocks, opened her up to 1,800rpm, changed the propeller to course pitch before returning it to fine pitch and checked the magneto switches. Checks complete, I taxied to the grass strip that had been prepared for me at the back of Lanyon, waved my final farewell to Wilkins from the cockpit, let out the throttle, raced her down the field to 80mph, pulled back on the stick, lifted the Lysander away from the airfield and headed out over the Channel.

With only the sliver of a moon and my father's compass for company, I tried to ignore the fact that a vast and lonely sea (and German fighter aircraft) were only six thousand feet away from the belly of the aircraft and brushed my fingers over the compass now and again for courage and for luck. With no radio aids to fall back on I was flying purely by eye, dead reckoning and fixing my position using airspeed and heading while taking wind variation into account. I set a straight and steady course across the channel, heading for my first check point on the French coast and all the while keeping a lookout for German fighter patrols.

It wasn't romantic, or adventurous, or any of those things one might associate with war and covert operations. It was, quite simply, petrifying hell.

Despite the blackout in France, I could just about make out the darker shade of grey of the land from the lighter shade of the sea. I had been given sufficient intelligence by Wilkins to plan the best route into France to evade enemy flak and on previous trip I had successfully evaded any enemy contact, but tonight, just inside the French coast, a coloured tracer curved up towards me, then curved away. I kept my course and somehow kept my nerve. The flak petered out and I felt my shoulders relax a little. Thankfully, the moon gave enough light to mark out towns and woodland and knew from my planning that it was time to descend and turn to a higher definition map to navigate precisely to the rendezvous field.

The procedure for landing was this. The agent on the ground would set up an L shape of lights on the field. The lights were nothing more than pocket torches attached to sticks. The agent would turn one light on at first. As I approached, I would flash a code with my landing light, pick up a reciprocal prearranged flash from the agent's torch (indicating once more that it was safe for me to land), then the remaining torches would be turned on. If no Morse signal was sent from the ground (or if the signal was corrupt) then I would not land, but turn tail and fly home. On landing I was to keep the rotor running and spend no more than three minutes on the ground. The agents had been trained to find suitable fields and describe them by wireless ahead of time. The pilot had to simply trust that field would be suitable for landing – no ditches, low walls or trees.

At eight hundred feet, just as had happened with my previous flights into France, I saw the light. At that moment, the fact that the passenger waiting anxiously in the field for our rendezvous was Edward, was not relevant.

I surged my engine, flashed the bright landing light and, while nearing ever closer to the ground, waited for the secret code to be flashed back at me. It came, the remaining lights of the L-shape came on and I made final preparations for landing.

But the landing itself was where my luck ran its course. The field was rough, full of drainage ditches and completely unsuitable for landing, but in the dark it was impossible to see just how unsuitable the field was. The aircraft was fitted with a super-strengthened undercarriage, but even my wonderful Lysander could not possibly withstand the brutality of such deep ditches. I had slowed on the ground to about 20 mph when the aircraft stopped abruptly as the nose pitched forwards into a ditch, tipping the aircraft to an angle of about forty-five degrees with the tail in the air.

I was too stunned to move at first but then survival instinct kicked in. I slid back the canopy and scrambled out. My poor aircraft was trashed, disgraced and dishonoured.

A man dashed towards me as I jumped down onto the grass. I ripped off my helmet and shook my head.

'You fool!' I shouted in French, forgetting momentarily the need for silence. 'How could this field ever have been suitable for a safe landing.' I turned towards the Lysander. 'And look at my aircraft! Look! Look at it!'

The man did not answer immediately, but stared at me. I had seen this look before. It was the confused gaze of a man trying to understand how it could be that a woman would be flying such an aircraft. He came to his senses.

'I checked the field this morning,' he said. 'The farmer must have ploughed the ditches this afternoon. I'm sorry.'

I put my hand to my head and felt something wet. I was bleeding. But I had others concerns right now. I needed to grab my survival bag, torch the aircraft and run. Two men approached. One was holding the other, helping him to walk as they struggled across the field. The weaker man, I saw as they approached, was Edward.

'Juliet?' he whispered, still leaning on the other man. 'But ... how?'

'I came for you, but ... I'm so sorry. The field ... the ditches ...?'

The man who had approached me first spoke directly to Edward in a rushed whisper.

'We need to get you out of here.' He turned to the other man. 'Julien, take Edward to the next safe house. She's right, we need to torch the aircraft. I'll stay here and see it's done.'

Edward spoke. His voice was weak.

'But, Juliet? No, I can't leave her.'

My resilience rallied.

'Go, Edward. I know this area. I'm strong. You know I am. Please ...'

Edward was simply too injured, too frail, to argue. He held me close and whispered into my ear.

'We've been compromised. Run alone and evade in the opposite direction before heading to safety. Tell the agent you've been told to head to Spain, to try for a boat out of Santander. Don't trust him. Make sure you're not followed to the farm.'

351

He turned and disappeared into the darkness. I grabbed my survival bag and threw it in a hedge, away from the aircraft.

'You know how to torch an aircraft?' I asked.

He nodded.

'You'll have to shoot the fuel tank. Do you have a silencer on your gun?'

'Yes.'

'Good. Get on with it.'

No dog barked and no church bell sounded to pierce through the silence. As my poor Lysander began to burn, we ran to the hedge where I had stowed my survival bag. I took out my French overcoat, beret and shoes. The man turned to me.

'The Germans will be here soon. Give me your jacket and boots,' he said. 'And your helmet, too. They need to burn with the aircraft.'

My boots were my ATA flying boots. They had been with me through so many adventures, Anna had even worn them. And my jacket ... it was Anna's and Pa's compass was in the pocket. I handed everything over except the jacket.

'Not this,' I said.

He threw up his hands but I was adamant. I would bury it away from the aircraft, but I wouldn't tell this man that.

'I'll go with you,' he said.

I shook my head.

'No,' I whispered. 'I'm better alone. I'll head to Spain.'

'To Spain?! But ...'

I trusted no one and all I could think was, what if this man was the mole, the double agent? What if he was working with the Germans and knew about the ditches all along? No agent worth his salt would have picked this field for a landing. No, I did not want him to know the location of my safe house. I'd planned my initial escape heading away from the field that afternoon with minute accuracy (due west for two and a half miles, reach a farmhouse, then north west). It would not be a problem to find my way there alone, even in the dark.

We shook hands.

'*Bon nuit*,' I said, shaking hands one final time.

'*Bon nuit*, Madam. And may God be with you.'

'And with you.'

I did not head straight for the farm, but headed in the opposite direction before circling behind a beech hedge, only to begin again in the right direction once I was sure that the agent had gone. There was a copse at the end of the hedge with the diggings of an abandoned fox den or a badger lair beneath it. I kissed my father's compass, stuffed it into the inside pocket of Anna's jacket, forced the whole thing firmly into the den, turned tail and making sure I kept low, close to the hedgerows and trees, ran.

It was dawn when I knocked on the door of Ferme de Bray, which lay just a few miles from the crash site. A woman in her sixties answered almost immediately, her expression blank.

'Madam Bisset?' I asked.

'*Oui.*'

'*Bonjour, Madam. Je suis, Juliette.*'

She nodded, opened the door wider and stepped aside.

'*Entrez, ma nièce.*'

I was led into the kitchen and immediately introduced to Monsieur Bisset – a calm and carefully spoken man with a spectacular bushy beard and hands like dinner plates. There was no time for refreshment or pleasantries. After being shown to my room – set up with photos of my fake family, a reading book with a page turned at the corner and a few clothes – Madame Bisset, now Aunt Cecille, took my muddy, soiled trousers and handed me stockings and a skirt to wear. Monsieur Bisset, Uncle Paul, cleaned my shoes.

I was shown to a room in the farmhouse – my milliner's workshop – and after gratefully feeding on a simple breakfast, was briefed on the workings of the farm, on my new family's history and invited, finally, to sleep. The Germans may come, they said. But they were optimistic. My Breton accent was second to none, my papers were perfect and my fake family history watertight. I had taken the identity of a woman – their niece – who really had been forced to leave her parent's chicken farm and had come to Ferme de Bray to work as a milliner. The real Juliette – who had just lost her parents and was niece to the Bissets, had, in fact, recently escaped to England on a boat via Falmouth to work for the Free French under De Gaulle in London, not that the Germans knew any of that.

And so, for all the world to see, I was simply a young French woman, living on her uncle's farm in a remote part of Brittany. But the Germans did not come. If my suspicions were correct and the agent on the ground had tipped them off, they were looking in a different location entirely. I did not mention Edward to my hosts and they asked me no questions. I stayed a month, working on the farm, only ever speaking French and playing the part of the loving niece. Monsieur Bisset would walk into the village from time to time, but no one came to visit and I stayed at home.

Then, one evening, Monsieur Bisset pulled a dresser away from the back wall and unscrewed two floorboards. He delved into the recess and retrieved a hessian sack. The sack contained the component parts of a wireless radio. Madame Bisset built the radio and tuned into the BBC French service. As the service closed the newsreader said, '*Les roses fleuriront cette année*' – 'the roses will bloom well this year'. Madame Bisset shook her head when she heard this.

'Tonight? No.'

Monsieur Bisset nodded. I saw tears rise in her eyes. 'But how? Where is she to go? She is safe here, no?'

The wireless was put away with haste before anyone spoke further.

'Prepare yourself, Juliet,' he said, pushing the heavy dresser back to its place against the wall. 'You are leaving tonight. Soon, in fact.'

Monsieur Bisset rested a reassuring hand on his wife's

shoulder and spoke over her head, looking at me directly across the table.

'You are going home. An aircraft will come for you, shortly after one a.m.'

He opened a curtain and glanced out of the window.

'There is a good moon and clear skies, but we must pray the mist does not gather in the valley.'

Madame Bisset stood. 'Come,' she said, her body sagged with weariness. 'Let's get you ready.'

I rose and followed Cecille up the stairs to my room.

I said the word over in my head – home.

On the one hand I was delighted, but there was still the matter of Edward. Where was he? I thought of our brief meeting on the night of the crash and recalled my suspicions about the agent who had chosen the fated field that night, thereby sealing the death of the Lysander. If I was ever to ask a question about Edward, it was now.

'Cecille,' I said, 'I wonder, do you know if the parcel I was supposed to pick up on the night I landed is still in France? I was worried, you see, that the pick-up had been sabotaged by the agent ... because the field was not at all suitable ...'

I trailed off. Cecille shook her head.

'I doubt that is possible, Juliette. I know that agent. He is a good man.'

'I'm sorry,' I said. 'I didn't mean to question, or to criticise, it's just ... it's been playing on my mind. My aircraft crashed into a drainage ditch, you see, and he said they must have been ploughed that day, but how did he not see the ditch and call off the drop?'

Cecille's hand rested on my shoulder.

'I will mention it to my husband,' she said. 'You will be home soon. Try not to worry.'

'And also,' I pressed awkwardly. 'The agent I was supposed to take home that night. He was injured. Do you know what happened to him?'

I dreaded the answer but Cecille shook her head. 'I'm sorry. I do not know.'

At eight-thirty p.m. Madame Bisset handed me a thick woollen jumper to put on under my coat and kissed me on each cheek.

'Safe journey, *mon petit*.'

I threw my arms around her while her husband looked on.

'Thank you,' I whispered through her hair. 'I'll pray for your continued safety every single day of my life until this terrible nightmare is over. Promise me you won't take any unnecessary risks.'

She stepped back, breaking our embrace.

'I cannot promise that, Juliet.' She took her husband's hand. 'I'm afraid we must continue to fight ... to do whatever can.'

I nodded my understanding, put the jumper on, fastened my coat and headed outside with Monsieur Bisset, who led me two miles across fields to a barn where he handed me back my pistol. I hid alone in the dark until a second agent appeared, who guided me a further mile across the Breton countryside to a dug-out under a hedge. He covered me in bracken and said, 'Wait here.' I asked for how long. 'A while.' came the answer. 'Don't move,' he said. 'Even when you hear the aircraft, don't move.'

It was the longest wait of my life. I had no papers with me now. If the Germans caught me, I would have no cover story. Just after midnight, I heard a reassuringly familiar sound filter through the darkness – it was the sound of a Lysander, and to my absolute delight, I heard the pilot power the engines twice, just as I had done, as a signal of his arrival.

The aircraft landed. I still dare not move. But then the bracken was pulled away revealing the silhouette of a man whose right arm was in a sling. His whole body was backlit by the moonlight. The profile seemed familiar. I climbed out of the hole and looked at the man more closely.

'Edward?' I whispered, hardly daring to believe.

He smiled.

It was Edward! He was alive and we were going home. I threw my arms around him, being careful not to press against his injured arm. He whispered an unexpected question in my ear.

'You have your pistol?' he asked.

I looked at him in the moonlight.

'Yes, why?'

'Can you kill a man, Juliet?' Shocked, I looked around and saw the Lysander in the next field, a hundred yards away, beyond an open interconnecting gate. 'I can't do it. My right arm is broken and my left hand is damaged. The agent tonight is working with the Germans. He's the man who arranged the field on the night of your drop. We brought the RV forward an hour to trick him. He's by the aircraft, now. When we approach him, don't even hesitate, kill him, Juliet. All future drops will be compromised if you don't.' I nodded my understanding. 'Cock you weapon now so that he doesn't hear it.'

We ran to the aircraft, and a moment later, I shot a man, at point-blank range, through the head, without hesitation.

Edward spoke to the pilot who powered the engines and taxied the aircraft a distance from the body. He then took a grenade from his backpack.

'You've been trained how to use this? he asked.

'Yes, but ...'

'Empty his pockets, all of them.'

I hesitated, looking down at the body.

'Quickly, Juliet,' he barked.

I found identification papers, a knife and money. Edward took the papers and instructed me to put the knife and the money back in the man's pockets. He then took his own French papers out of his pocket and told me to put them in the pocket of the man's jacket. He then handed me the grenade.

'Put this by his face,' he said. 'There's a thirty second delay. Let me get to the aircraft, then pull the cord, run as fast as you can and climb into the aircraft behind me. Do not look back.'

I set the grenade and ran to the aircraft and clambered up the ladder just as the grenade exploded behind us.

The Lysander could carry two passengers, who sat facing backwards, directly behind the pilot. I reached up and closed the canopy while the pilot, not waiting a second longer, began his take-off run. I remembered Wilkins' instruction at Lanyon. 'Three minutes, Juliet. That's all the time you have to pick-up your parcel and turn the thing around. Any more than that and you leave everyone behind and fly home.'

Our pilot had waited at least seven minutes in the field that night. Grateful beyond words, I made a note to myself to thank him profusely on our return, but then rested my exhausted head against the canopy and watched France dip away beneath us. In silence and while scanning the skies for enemy patrol fighters, I held Edward in the moonlight and thanked the Lord for sending another angel to fly us home. To my astonishment on landing, I saw that the name of that angel, was Wilkins.

We took Edward directly to his cottage after landing. Pa Lanyon had lit the fire and left bread, cheese and wine on the table. Edward's dog was there too. Wilkins came into the house with us, to be met with a barrage of criticism from Edward (once he had calmed the dog down who was crying and wailing at his return) who was furious with Wilkins for recruiting me as an agent-drop pilot. Wilkins simply winked at me and shrugged.

I stayed with Edward for three weeks during his recuperation at Angel View. His broken arm mended quickly enough, but it was expected that two of the fingers on his left hand would never function properly again. There were many questions to be asked about the failed Lysander trip and I wanted answers. I got them.

It seemed that Edward's advice not trust the agent with either my name or the destination of my safe house in Brittany had been an inspired one. Edward knew that his network had developed a leak – a mole – but couldn't decide whom, amongst his team, was the double-agent. He had begun to suspect the man, whose name I never knew, never wanted to know, just before the pick-up. So much so that he had instructed the other agent that was with him that night to create a dug out, similar to the one I had hidden in, with water and blankets and a little food, in a neighbouring field and if the pick-up was subsequently compromised (as it was) then Edward would not run, but hideout for a couple of days. On seeing my Lysander crash into the ditch, Edward was certain the mole was probably the agent, what he did not expect, however, was to see his beloved Juliet jump out of the cockpit. He said it was the most distressing moment of his life, because he knew he was too injured to run with me, but had to hope and pray I had heard him when he said to run alone. Edward and his trusted companion had slipped away and headed to the dug-out, leaving the man to torch the aircraft and me to run.

I asked why the man hadn't just told the Germans the time of the RV, surely that would have been a simpler way – to simply hand Edward over. He explained that it was better for the agent to make it look like an accident and have us all rounded up by the Germans once they saw the burning wreckage. That way he could stay working for both sides – trusted by the résistance and working for the Germans. In the past the man had done amazing and daring work for the Allied cause, which was why it was difficult to believe that he would compromise them now. This was why the timing of the next RV was brought forward an hour. No one knew of this plan except for two people – Edward and Wilkins. Monsieur Bisset had simply been told to get me to the dug out early. Absolutely no one was trusted. Once the message had been passed that I was on the move, Edward had informed the man that he also wanted to get moving early, knowing that it was too late to get a message to the Gestapo or the Vichy police. He also knew I had a pistol and he knew, when it came to it, that I had the gumption to kill a man – I did not know whether to take this as a complement, or as a terrible failing in my character.

But the pride in Edward's eyes when he talked to Wilkins of my escape from the field on that first night was a fine thing for a woman to see. All the same, he was adamant that I must stop piloting the secret drop offs in the Lysander.

I said nothing. It was time to allow Edward to rest, catch his breath, walk on the beach, and above all else, be shown just how much I loved him. In those three weeks we were for each other the light and the dark, air and water, sun and moon. But in my heart, I knew that it wouldn't last forever and that if Edward could go back to France, he would. He would never give in.

It was during our walk to the beach one morning that we had almost a carbon copy conversation of the one we had had on Christmas Eve, only this time, I felt exactly the same way too. There was no such thing has having felt as though one had done one's bit ... the fight simply had to continue, over and over again, whatever the personal cost, until it was done. Many so-called ordinary men and women felt this way too. Churchill referred to them as the unknown warriors, whose deeds would never be recorded, but without them – all of them – the war would never be won.

Edward took my hand and ran his thumb over the tops of my fingers. We were sitting on our boulder again, looking out at the islands.

'I have to go back,' he said.

I'd been waiting for this moment.

'Yes.'

He turned to me.

'But you understand why, this time?'

I nodded.

'I start flying for Wilkins again during the next suitable moon phase, which is at the end of next week. They're delivering another Lysander to Lanyon for me to fly.'

He bit his lip and paused before answering.

'You don't have to do this, Juliet. I can see why you want to keep working, but you could do that more than adequately in the ATA. Go back to Hamble. They would snap you up, there, you know they would, and you loved it once.'

'So, there's one rule for you and one rule for me ...' I nudged him playfully.

He smiled.

'Not at all. You're a brilliant pilot and I can see why Wilkins is desperate to get you flying again – a French-speaking female stunt pilot? You're a dream come true for his operation, and if I wasn't so desperately in love with you, I'd want to recruit you as a ground agent for my own operation, too, you're perfect. But please don't do this, Juliet. Go back to Hamble, go deliver those big bombers you used to love flying.'

I shook my head.

'I'm sorry, Edward, but I can't do that. Not now I've seen what it's like first hand, seen how life is in France, seen the fight that goes on day after day after day by ordinary people, I can't walk away. Wilkins needs me – your organisation needs me. And I don't know why, but I just know I'll be fine. I've always known it. Remember the last time we sat here? You said you wanted me to live to be a hundred years old and you know what, I really do think that I will. So, don't worry about me, just keep doing what you're doing and keep yourself safe and I'll be here, waiting, when you get back.' We looked across the ocean. 'There's a whole load of people just over that sea who are desperate for us to keep fighting. We can never stop this, Edward. Not until it's finally done.'

'You'll fight them on the beaches, eh?'

I smiled. 'If I have to, yes, I bloody well will!'

At that moment Edward took a small box out of his pocket and turned to face me. He opened the box, took out a ruby ring and with tears rolling down his face said,

'I know you can't just yet, but one day, will you marry me, Juliet?'

I took the ring without hesitation and kissed him tenderly through the merging of our tears.

'Oh, Edward, I'd love to.'

Two weeks later, on the night of the next full moon, I flew Edward to a remote field in northern France. He jumped out, another agent climbed in and without waiting to say goodbye, I turned the aircraft around and climbed away. Just a few days later Edward Nancarrow was captured in Paris and tortured by the Gestapo. Incredibly he was not shot as a spy, but sent to Dachau, a concentration camp in Bavaria that specialised in the incarceration and torture of political prisoners, Jews and homosexuals. All I could do was to keep flying and pray for the war to end.

Chapter 37

Katherine

Tied with a red ribbon

The fact that I looked like rat-shit and that Sam had bags under his eyes the size of Gambia and could barely speak he was so tired, did not in any way dent the rest of the evening. It should have been awkward, two strangers bunking up in a cottage together, but it wasn't. We sat in front of the fire drinking champagne, catching up like old friends, talking about Juliet and Edward, and going through all the memorabilia I had been collecting around the house but with the proviso that Sam did not divulge any of the details the closing chapters in Juliet's story – the best Christmas present I had ever had.

I told him all about Fenella and Percy and Noel and how we'd (they'd) saved Christmas in Angels Cove for all the little children, which meant, given all the shenanigans, that I hadn't had the time to decorate the cottage. I confessed that the elf was probably quite disappointed in me.

To cheer the elf, despite the late hour, Sam clambered into the loft reappearing with a couple of plastic boxes full of Christmas decorations. We chatted while rummaging through the boxes until I came across something wrapped carefully in tissue paper. I recognised it as the miniature painting of the cottage Edward had done for Juliet, framed and still tied with a faded red ribbon.

I fell silent.

'They were so in love,' I said, the little frame in my hand.

'They really were.'

I wanted to know how it ended. Did Edward survive the war. Did they live a long and beautiful life together? I hoped so. But as Sam's surname was Lanyon – not Nancarrow, or Gruber, even – I was worried that if I asked the question, my hope for a happy ending would be dashed. One more day of wishing for a happy ending wouldn't hurt, would it?

'Sam, sorry but can I ask ... do you think, this flight tomorrow ... it's just, she's put her engagement ring on, the one Edward gave her, and ...' I stalled. How to say what I was thinking. Would Juliet survive it? Was she actually hoping to die, to meet Edward on the far side? The more I read on, the more I wondered ...

Sam smiled.

'I know what you're trying to say. I'm going to pretend to myself that I haven't read her memoirs. However tomorrow turns out, I'll deal with it afterwards. She's one hundred years old – one hundred, Katherine,' he said, softly. 'Living at Lanyon, it's a prison to her. She's not happy, I know she's not. And she's always been so very very happy all of her life. Joyful, even. I love her too much not to let her go, if that's what she wants. Although goodness only knows how she would actually do it – maybe she's planning to jump out over the islands, I wouldn't put it past her.'

My eyes filled with tears. He smiled through his own damp, sparkling eyes.

'Listen, tomorrow is a day for celebration – her birthday. The biggest birthday ever! Now ... let's drink this champagne and you can tell me all about that damn apostrophe problem of yours!'

Chapter 38

Juliet

A promise for Lottie

I lived on at Lanyon, working closely with Wilkins. It was odd – just a year before, Lanyon had seemed alien to me, a cold, uncomfortably large house belonging to a bygone era. But for all that had gone before – the lulling into a ridiculous marriage to shore up a crumbing empire – the family did love me. Charles, Lottie, dear little Mabel, Ma and Pa Lanyon, they were all my family and love – when received and given in whatever form – was surely better than no love at all. And with the thought of Edward's imprisonment at Dachau rattling around my brain, I needed all the love I could get.

It was during my flights into France that I felt most connected with Edward, and as I crossed the channel in the moonlight I would visualise sending my love direct from my heart to his, through a long strand of interconnected love, my heart with wings, flying across France to Bavaria, where I knew without question it would find its way to Edward and give him the support and strength he needed to carry him through the most horrifying days of his life.

By June 1944 the allies were on the offensive and the liberation of France was just weeks away. Hitler expected the Allied attack to come through Calais, via the narrowest part of the English Channel, but he was wrong. On 6 June the Allied invasion of France began – D-Day – when 130,000 troops landed on Normandy beaches. The liberation of France and the beginning of the end of the Second World War had begun. My thoughts that day were with my wonderful friends, the Bissets, and I hoped and prayed that they had survived to see this moment. It was a day to be remembered, a day of incredible bravery and sacrifice, and yet in years to come, I would remember D-Day for a different reason entirely, a personal one.

Lottie Lanyon spent D-Day at work. Still in the WAAF and working in the Mechanical Transport Section at RAF Predannack, she regularly drove aircrew and senior officers to and from the train station, or wherever else they might need to go. We spent the evening before D-Day together. Mabel was playing in the garden with Ma while Lottie, Amber and I walked the cliff path from Lanyon to Predannack and back again. It was a balmy summer evening and a light, warm breeze floated across the cliff tops. We sat on a craggy outcrop above Angels Cove at the end of our walk and watched the sun being slowly swallowed by the sea.

'I'm so sorry about Edward,' Lottie said. 'Awful for him – and for you, of course.' Lottie took my hand. 'You must miss him, Juliet.'

'I do,' I said. 'Every single moment. But having you, and little Mable ...' at that moment, Amber nuzzled herself under my arm '... and yes, you, too – having you all around, it all helps. Whether or not the troops will liberate Europe in time to save Edward is a question I don't even want to think about.'

'So, *don't* think about it. You've always had such strength. Such belief. I've envied you of that. Don't stop believing now.'

I nodded but couldn't hold back the tears. Lottie placed her arms around me and held me tightly, rocking from side to side as if comforting Mabel. 'We've both had our share of heartbreak, haven't we, old thing? And poor Charles, too. Did you know he's coming home on leave next month?'

I took a handkerchief from my pocket and blew my nose.

'Yes. I heard about Florence. Poor woman. Charles must be devastated. I think he really loved her, you know.'

'He did,' Lottie said softly. 'He did. And to be killed on a hospital ship, too. It seems nothing is out of bounds. Just terrible.'

I thought of Anna.

'Do you remember when Anna and I came to see you

in Yorkshire? You were so low and so frightened. I was worried about you.'

Lottie began pulling out long strands of grass from the cliff top.

'I'm sorry, it wasn't fair,' she said. 'But I was overwhelmed with such black feelings then. I couldn't see straight.'

I took her hand again.

'I didn't mind. And you know, I will always love Mabel every bit as much as I'd love one of my own. She's such a dear little thing.'

Lottie smiled and hugged her knees to her chest. 'She really is. When I tuck her into bed night, I jump in next to her, just to hold her close, to make her as real as I can. And I know I squeeze her too tightly, but she just murmurs, "I love you, Mummy" because she knows that I'm the one who needs reassurance at bedtime, not her.'

'And how are you feeling now, Lottie? Can you see a bright future for you both?'

She squeezed my hand. Her golden curly hair brushing across her face. She smiled. It was the brightest smile I'd seen from Lottie Lanyon in a very long time.

'Do you know, I can! And it's as bright as the brightest star! I always thought my happiness was dependent on being desperately in love with a man. That I needed to be looked after by him – to be married – to feel secure and content. But I don't feel that way now. Working as a WAAF has done wonders for me. Really helped me to see how capable I can be, truly.'

'Well at least the war has done one good thing then.'
She stood and held out her hands to help me up.
'You know, I really think it has.'

The very next day, allied troops crossed the channel and
fought their way to victory across the beaches, a victory
that would eventually lead to the liberation of France and
the end of the war. But Lottie Lanyon never knew any
of this. While driving from Redruth train station back to
Predannack, having picked up a senior RAF pilot who
was heading to the base to begin a new tour of duty, on
Cornish lanes that were only ever designed for carts and
cows, at the exact point where Ma Lanyon and crashed
six years before, Lottie's car came head to with an Army
truck. Lottie was rushed to the medics at Predannack, who
fought to save her life. Four hours later, holding my hand
and fighting desperately for a life she had hoped would
be as bright as the brightest star, she asked me to make a
promise to her to look after Mabel one final time.

'The poem, Christina Rosetti, *Remember*,' she murmured,
half in, half out of consciousness. 'Tell it to Mabel ... tell
her, no tears. I want her to be happy and tell I love her,
love her with all my heart. Look after her, Juliet.'

I buried my face in her hair and through a million tears
of my own, promised her that I would. Moments later, dear
Lottie Lanyon passed away and another shining beautiful
star was extinguished forever.

Chapter 39

Katherine

Sam's grandmother

I had returned to the manuscript only briefly while Sam pottered in the kitchen rustling up a late supper. He walked into the lounge with a smile on his face and a tray of cheesy nachos in his hand to find me staring at the last words. I was devastated.

'Oh, no,' he said, noticing the manuscript in my hand and tears streaming down my face. 'Who died now?'

'Lottie! Lottie died! I can't believe it. How absolutely awful. Life was just so cruel back then, so cruel. How on earth did they find the strength to carry on?'

He sat down beside me and offered a nacho, which I took and dipped in sour cream. It was always best to feed grief, I found.

'Did you know Lottie was my grandmother?' he asked.

The nacho paused halfway to my mouth.

'Grandmother? But I thought Juliet ...'

He rested the tray on his knee.

'Juliet *is* my grandmother – my adopted grandmother. I'm Mabel's son.'

'Mabel's. Oh, I see. But then, what happened to Mable?'

His eyes glistened.

'She died ten years ago. Cancer. I ... Juliet ... well, we were all devastated. My mother was such a kind, beautiful woman. Juliet brought us both up as her own.'

'I'm sorry. I thought that as your surname was Lanyon, Juliet perhaps got back with Charles ...'

'No, that never happened. I was given the Lanyon name to keep it going. I'm the last one.'

'And what about her own children?'

'Juliet? She never had any.'

Just then we heard the sound of distant voices in song through the window.

'That'll be the church choir,' he said, heading to the door. 'They always gather to sing on the harbour before heading up to the church for midnight mass.'

He opened the door. I wrapped Lottie's shawl around my shoulders and we stood in the moonlight and listened. In a moment of strange synchronisation, I realised they were singing Edward's poem, not the one he had written for Juliet, but the one Juliet had found as a loose leaf in the Bible, the one he had memorised for the passing of coded messages – the peace prayer of St Francis.

We listened as they sang.

Melanie Hudson

Make me a channel of your peace,
Where there's despair in life let me bring hope,
Where there is darkness, only light,
And where there's sadness, ever joy.

I suddenly had a desperate desire to get outside. To run with the wind.

'Would you come for a walk with me?' I asked. 'I don't know where and I know it's late, but I just feel like being in with the crowd, suddenly. Do you mind?'

He didn't answer but grabbed our coats from the hallway.

'Mind? I'd love it.'

I closed the door behind us.

'It's strange,' he said, as we headed down the hill towards the choir. 'But I've got the strangest feeling you might be a kindred coddiwompler, after all.'

I laughed just as the church bell rang twelve. I glanced up the hill towards Lanyon.

'Happy birthday, Juliet,' I thought, drenched through with melancholy. Happy birthday.

Chapter 40

Juliet

An old friend returns

On 24 August 1944, the Americans entered Paris and suddenly everything changed, although my own life had already veered into a different direction, and one that did not include flying. With the retreat of the Germans, there was longer the requirement to fly covertly into France and so my wartime flying career came to an abrupt but welcome end. It was time for me to take on a new role entirely – that of guardian and mother to dear Mabel. I would never try to replace Lottie, but I would try to bring as much joy and love into that little girl's life as I could possibly muster.

Wilkins returned to a job in London but kept in touch and I took comfort in the knowledge that he was doing everything he could to trace Edward.

On December 15th Wilkins telephoned to say that he was returning to Lanyon and he had a surprise for me – two surprises in fact – and could I pick him up at Penzance station the very next day? Having finally learned to drive by now, I said, yes, of course, and took Mabel along for the ride.

My surprise came in the form of a glamorous lady who stepped off the train ahead of Wilkins. I was standing further down the platform holding Mabel's hand tightly, scanning the carriages for Wilkins when I saw her – all mink coat and bright red lipstick. And when our eyes connected through the steam, I had to put my hand to my mouth to hold back a scream. It was Marie and she was running down the platform, her arms flung open, to greet me.

The hug was long and told of a thousand unspoken words. Words that were too painful to say out loud. Marie stepped away from me and took my face in her gloved hands. The tears ran for both of us.

'I should have been there,' she said. Wilkins eyed us nervously as he approached down the platform, carrying two suitcases.

I shook my head.

'I can't talk about it, Marie. It's just too hard.'

'I know. For me, too.'

I took a deep breath, rallied, stepped back and held her arms at a distance. 'But look at you! You look amazing. What on earth are you doing here?' I turned to Wilkins, not waiting for Marie to answer. 'Is this my surprise?'

'It certainly is,' he said. Looking a little coy.

Coy? Wilkins?

'I hope she's not a disappointment.'

I beamed. 'A disappointment? I'm absolutely thrilled! But I had no idea the two of you were even remotely acquainted?' I glanced from one to the other as we stood on the platform, a river of passengers walking around us.

'We weren't, not until a month or so ago. And when Matthew said he was returning to Cornwall for a visit I couldn't believe it was *your* Lanyon he was headed to, so I invited myself along too for a little visit, just a couple of days. Is that all right, Honey?' Marie asked, her eyes glistening with a mixture of excitement and tears.

'Yes, of course. But tell me, how on earth did the two of you meet?'

Marie threw a side-glance at Wilkins. He caught it and bounced it back. 'Oh, we met through work ...'

'Work? I can't keep up. Are you flying for the ATA again?'

Marie shook her head. 'No, that ship has sailed. I'm doing something else now, I'll tell you about it sometime. No, Matty and I bumped into each other at an embassy party and ...'

Matty?

'*And* ... it's a long story that's best told over a cup of tea, I'm parched,' Wilkins interrupted, picking up the cases again. He turned to Mabel. 'Hello, little one,' he said. 'Cold, isn't it? What say we all nip into town for a nice iced bun?' Mabel nodded wildly. 'Is that little tea room still going on the Causeway?' he asked, turning to me. 'The best scones in England, I'd say.'

'I think so.'

'Let's go there, then. My treat. You two can catch up while Mabel helps me with the crossword ...' he winked at me 'I didn't get to do it on the train. I don't think Marie drew breath since Paddington! Americans, eh?'

Marie tapped him gently on the arm. 'Hey! I'm a Yankee tourist now, remember? I can't help but gas away!'

Mabel giggled and another glance passed between Marie and Wilkins that hinted at more than a professional relationship, but surely, I must be mistaken? Marie and Wilkins? Together? But no, it couldn't be. He wasn't her type *at all*.

He was.

And the surprises kept coming. Marie took off her gloves in the tea room to reveal a sapphire engagement ring. Speech eluded me. It didn't elude Marie, whose thousand mile an hour conversation made up for the both of us.

It seemed that Marie had returned to London in August on invitation from a chap she knew from the 400 Club (who also worked at the Home Office) who knew she had a degree in Maths and an incredibly sharp mind, and asked if she would report to the Government Codes and Ciphers School to lend a hand. Marie said yes, but I didn't know any of the detail of this until long after the war had ended, at the time all I was told that she was using her maths degree to help the Government. But I always suspected she was doing more. After all, Wilkins worked for the SOE and if she was running in the same circles as him, then her work would probably be something top secret. I knew not to pry.

After tea, we wrapped ourselves up again and took Mabel for a little stroll. Wilkins played with Mabel in the park while Marie and I looked on from a bench.

'She's a real sweetie pie,' Marie said, nodding towards Mabel. 'It's good of you to take her on,' she added, 'especially now you're divorcing Charles. Are you sure it's not going to be too ... restricting for you?'

I waved at Mabel who looked back for reassurance as she ran across the park, laughing.

'I want to do it,' I said. 'It seems to be the most natural thing to do now the war is coming to an end – and please God, let it come to an end soon.'

'Will you stay on at Lanyon or start again, somewhere new?'

I took a deep breath.

'Stay at Lanyon. Someone has to, Charles seems to have no interest in the place and his parents are not what they were. But it the long term, I don't really know, not until ...' I paused.

She took my hand.

'Until you know about Edward?'

I nodded.

'Matty told me what happened. The poor guy. But listen, that's what we've come to talk to you about.'

I turned to face her on the bench. Such conversation

deserved face-to-face conversation, not sideways meander-ings. 'About Edward, you mean?'

'We were going to wait until we got back to the house to tell you, but now seems as good a time as any. He's been traced.'

'Traced?' I put a hand to my mouth. 'Oh, my God. He's ...' I daren't finish the sentence.

'Alive? Yes, he is, Juliet. Edward is alive. He escaped!'

Having been able to use his old network to see him safely from Bavaria into France, by grace and by God, malnourished and having been beaten almost beyond recognition, Edward crossed France to safety. But he was ill. By Brittany he could travel no more. His old contacts in the Résistance stepped in to care for him and those carers, not surprisingly, were in the guise of Monsieur and Madame Bisset. Typhus was suspected and the couple were doing all that they could to care for him, but the prognosis was not good.

That evening I asked Wilkins if he could find me a Lysander, to bring Edward home. He couldn't. Frantic, I spoke with Pa Lanyon in the hope of finding a fishing boat that was planning a trip to Brittany, but there was none and he would not be able to get me there until after the New Year, but if I was planning to bring Edward back by boat, I should probably think again. No captain would want Typhus on his ship.

That evening, I left Marie to the capable hands of the

Lanyons and ran across the cliffs to Angels Cove in the rain. I wanted to be at the cottage, to hold Edward's things near to me and hope for a miracle. But rather than head straight for the cottage, I ran to the church and prayed. I looked up at the angel and begged – begged for inspiration. It was only while staring at the stained-glass picture of the beautiful questioning angel that the solution came to me and I could not for the life of me understand how I had not thought of it before.

The rain stopped. I dashed back up the hill and ran into the field, sprinted to the barn, threw open the doors and there she was – my bright yellow Tiger Moth, waiting for me. A little dishevelled, yes, and in need of a great deal of love and care before I could even think of getting her airborne, but get her airborne I would and I knew just the woman who could help me.

Marie extended her stay to help prepare the Tiger Moth for the biggest flight of her life. Wilkins arranged for the fuel to be delivered – the 20th of December being the date we worked towards for my departure. But the weather was not on my side. A thick mist descended that spread from the tip of Cornwall across the Channel to France, but the next day was expected to be brighter. It was.

At eight a.m. I pulled on my old ATA uniform and a flying jacket and headed off across the fields towards the barn. With Marie by my side, something of our old ATA pioneering spirit kicked-in and as we crossed the fields, my helmet and goggles in my hand, we could almost have been at Hamble again.

Almost.

'Anna would have loved this,' Marie said, vocalising my own thoughts as I opened the barn doors.

'She would.' I turned to Marie. 'I wish ... I wish we'd never ...'

'Never persuaded her to get her ass into that Spitfire at Upavon? Me too, honey. Me too.'

Nothing more needed to be said.

We took a wing each and pushed the Tiger Moth out of the barn and into the field. A cold north-westerly shook her as I climbed in. I put on my helmet, goggles and gloves while Marie, standing on the footplate, wrapped Ma Lanyon's warmest blankets around my legs. She kissed me on the cheek.

'Safe trip, darling Juliet.'

I took a deep breath and smiled.

'I'm a Spitfire Sister,' I said. 'An Attagirl! I'll be just dandy, as you lot say over the water.'

Marie gave me a last hug before jumping off the footplate and walking to the nose.

She turned the propeller.

'Contact.'

'Contact.'

And before I could even think, I turned the Moth into wind and after waving goodbye to Marie and the Angels, set a straight course for Brittany, not worrying about keeping an eye out for German fighters this time.

Chapter 41

Katherine

Christmas Day

The final flight

Juliet was sitting in her chair staring out of the window, dressed and ready for the day and listening to a Christmas choir on Classic FM when we arrived at Lanyon the next morning. I hovered at the doorway, allowing Sam time to enter the room alone.

Sam and Juliet embraced. Juliet began to cry.

'My boy,' she said, her delicate arms thrown around his neck. 'My darling boy. You made it home. You made it home ...'

'Happy birthday, Grandma,' he said, his voice shattering into a million pieces of raw emotion.

They held on for a few moments before Juliet pushed herself onto her feet and turned to face me with a wonderful broad smile.

'Right then,' she said, brightly. 'Let's get the party started, shall we?'

After knocking back a neat shot of Fenella's Christmas Spirit and spending half an hour in the communal lounge accepting birthday cards and good wishes and wishing staff and residents a very merry Christmas, Juliet – that brave and enigmatic hero I had grown to admire and love so quickly – was duly bundled up into every warm item of clothing she owned and with a final wave to the crowd, and wearing Anna's flying jacket and her flying boots for luck, she brushed off Yvonne's offer of a wheelchair and walked out of Lanyon, arm in arm with her Grandson, her silk scarf the exact colour of the morning sun, blowing in the wind behind her.

Sam sat in the back of the car with Juliet while I drove to Predannack. The conversation was light and excited. The gate to the airfield was not manned, but it was locked. Sam jumped out and unlocked the gates. I took a moment to glance across to a plaque attached to a large standing stone by the entrance. It was a Second World War plaque of remembrance. It read:

This memorial honours all ranks and nationalities that served here during World War II.
While casting your eyes on this memorial, spare a thought for those who flew from here and failed to return, many have no known grave.

386

"Like a breath of wind, gone in a fleeting second, only the memories now remain."

I felt my throat tighten.

Never before had a war memorial hit me so personally, the reason being, of course, that unlike a memorial in a park or on a busy town street I may have skirted past hundreds of times before, this time I knew an intimate part of the story.

Juliet had offered the Tiger Moth on long-term loan to a local flying club several years before, in the knowledge that they were the best people to care for and maintain her beloved old aircraft now that flying was beyond her, the only proviso being that she and Sam were to have unlimited access to fly whenever they liked.

Which was why, despite it being Christmas Day, grateful to Juliet (and also in complete awe of her and to celebrate her birthday) two members of the club were waiting at the hangar when we arrived. They stood proudly next to the aircraft, offering a salute to Juliet as we pulled alongside.

Sam jumped out of the car while I waited and glance around. The airfield itself bore no resemblance to the airfield Juliet would once have known, during its wartime glory years. Most of the buildings were long gone, or had been left to rot away, and it was now nothing more than a shabby satellite landing strip – a graveyard of Nissan huts and abandoned aircraft of yesteryear.

It was a surreal moment, seeing the Tiger Moth for the

first time, sitting on the concrete, the bright yellow paint shining in the winter sunshine. And she really did shine today of all days, on this most beautiful day to fly.

I slid into the back seat of the car to chat to Juliet while Sam prepared the aircraft. Juliet took a small knife out her handbag. She handed me the knife and pointed to a part of the lining.

'Would you open it up – here – for me, please, Katherine?'

'You want me to rip it? Why?'

'You'll find a little velvet pouch in the lining. It's got a pill in it, from the war.'

Her tone was purely matter-of-fact. My eyes widened.

'What?! But that's ...' I couldn't say the words.

Her voice was sure and her eyes were firm. 'Please, Katherine ... before Sam gets back.'

With tears resting on my lids I began to pick away at the stitching.

I wanted to say, 'Don't do this, Juliet. Let's all get back to Angel View. We'll have some lunch and forget all about it.' But as I looked at her, I knew that Sam was right to not ask but to give her whatever she wanted, to let her go. And what Juliet wanted now, was to find Edward, just as she promised she would. And as I glanced up to look at Sam carrying out his final checks on the aircraft, I knew for certain that he knew what Juliet had planned, too. It was written in his body language as he spoke to the men from the club, because despite his smile, a tangible sadness echoed from every pore.

The stitching came away easily and I delved into the lining. I didn't find the velvet pouch, not at first, but I did find something else – something smooth and cold and round. I removed it from the lining. Juliet's hand flew to her mouth.

'Oh, my word!'

We beamed up at each other.

'The compass?' I asked, knowing the answer.

Juliet nodded, holding the little gold trinket close to her chest.

'Thank goodness,' she whispered. 'Thank goodness.'

Juliet opened the back of the compass, lifted out the central casing and rested it on her hand to show me the inner workings – which were lined with diamonds.

'The Caron legacy,' she said, closing the casing one final time. 'Give it to Sam for me – later on.' She opened her handbag and took out a book. 'And give him this, too. It was Lottie's.'

The book was *Gone with the Wind*. Juliet opened the back cover. Lottie's favourite poem, *Remember*, had been written on the inside by Lottie, all those years before.

Juliet placed a hand on mine.

'*Better by far you should forget and smile, than that you should remember and be sad.*'

I nodded my understanding and slipped the compass into my own coat pocket before glancing across at Sam. I wiped my eyes and sighed.

'I'm just popping over the rainbow, Katherine, that's all,'

she said, softly. 'It's where all my old friends are, and it's time to join them now. And about the pill, don't ever tell anyone you knew, that you saw it, not even Sam. I'll just be an old woman who had a heart attack while doing the thing she loved.'

Ashen and feeling sick to my core, I nodded.

She took the jacket from its resting place on my knee and pressed her hand inside the lining. Her hand reappeared holding a little purple velvet pouch. Without looking inside, she put the pouch inside one of the jacket pockets and with a final herculean effort, put on the heavy jacket and opened the car door. She turned to me and as she did so, removed the ruby ring from her engagement finger. She handed it to me.

'For Sam,' she said. 'Just in case he ever marries again.'

I nodded, unable to speak.

'Oh, and I've left you a letter,' she said. 'It's in my room in a box with some photographs.'

She stepped out of the car.

I jumped out of my door and rushed around the car to take her arm as she crossed the apron to the Tiger Moth. Struggling to stand and with her hand resting on the old wooden airframe, she closed her eyes and took a very deep breath. A few moments later Sam appeared by her side and she opened her eyes.

'Time to fly?' she asked. Sam handed her a pair of goggles and a leather flying helmet. He placed his arms around her gently, both of them seemingly never wanting to let go.

Eventually he stepped back to face her. His eyes shone with tears. 'You're sure you want go?'

Juliet nodded and glanced around the desolate airfield. 'I'm sure.'

Sam lifted Juliet into the seat and tucked her up with blankets and before I could run after them and beg Juliet to change her mind, the sparkling Yellow Tiger Moth was speeding along the runway, and as I lifted my hand to cover the glare of the midday sun, I saw Juliet waving at me wildly from the front seat, her bright yellow scarf trailing behind her.

Chapter 42

Katherine
Boxing Day

A letter from Juliet

Fenella and I walked slowly along the beach in silence, trying to settle the events of the previous day in our heads, when my phone pinged.

Gerald. Had to be.

We're back! George is still a bit weak but fine. Don't be sad about Juliet, she was a wonderful woman who led an incredible life – a life she wanted to be celebrated, not mourned, just in case you're feeling low. What a way for her to go, too – flying! X

A second text came through moments later.

By the way, what decision did you come to about the apostrophe?

I turned to Fenella.

'You look like someone just died!' she said.

I laughed out loud and elbowed her gently in the ribs before burrowing my face in my hands.

'It's that bloody apostrophe. I was intending to come up with something last night, but with all the goings on after the flight, I completely forgot.'

She shrugged.

'I told you. Forget about it. It's not your problem. Don't worry about it.'

My phone pinged again.

Your big speech is at five p.m. (wear something nice – and maybe a bit of lipstick?)

I showed Fenella the text.

'I can't let him down. Hey, I meant to ask, how did the gin go down?'

'Oh, fabulous,' she said, lowering herself onto a boulder. 'I'm going to turn it into a proper concern, you know. You'd never believe what the Londoners will pay for it if you put it in a fancy glass and cover it in flavoured tonic, and I was thinking we could go into business. Me and you?'

I couldn't believe it.

'Really? But ...'

'If I live as long as Juliet, I've got loads of time left – and you never know, I may even get myself a new dog. Stay a little longer, Katherine. Enjoy yourself, get to know a few more people.' She winked. That would be the gin again. 'I mean, you never know what might happen. We'll convert the back room for you into a little bedsit, if you like?'

My mouth gaped. I closed it and put an arm around her.

'Oh, Fenella. I'd love to, but I'm not sure I'd make a very good gin distiller – or house guest. But I have been dreading going back to an empty house, truth be told.'

'Well, forget about the gin. Why don't you stay on for a month and we'll see?'

I hugged her. 'Thanks, so much Fenella. It'll be great! Just don't keep feeding me up all the time, or I'll be big enough to pull a plough!'

She nodded.

'Yes, I suppose you could do with shaving off a couple of pounds.'

We both glanced up the beach at the sudden sound of footsteps crunching on shells. Sam was walking down the beach towards us. Fenella nudged me.

'Although, that one likes his women with a good pound of flesh on them.'

I glared at her. 'His grandma has just died!'

'Just saying. He's a catch!'

A grain of sand suddenly rubbed in my shoe. I adjusted my foot to free it.

'It's a letter from Juliet,' Sam said, sitting down on the

rocks beside me and placing an envelope on my lap. Fenella made swift excuses to leave.

'I got one, too,' he said. 'She dictated them to the night manager at the care home. I read mine this morning.'

He handed me the letter with a smile. I stared at it.

'If I open it, I may possibly cry.'

'Don't worry, I've shed buckets this morning. Open it, you won't be disappointed.'

25 December

My dear, Katherine

It's two a.m. and I wanted to write you a note, partly to thank you for being such a wonderful friend to me this week, but also because I've been thinking about the apostrophe question and I think I have the answer for you. But before that, there is something else I want to say.

You said you would have loved to ask me lots of questions, as if, because of my age, I have developed a kind of sage-like wisdom you could tap into. But I'm afraid that despite my years, I really do not feel very wise and having given it some thought I realise that only have one piece of advice to give to you, and it was given to me by a committed coddiwompler a very long time ago – simply believe in love, my love, and everything will always be all right.

Now then, you were worried about where to put the apostrophe. Here is what I think, and it all boils down to a question of possession. I'm certain that our little cove has been visited by angels many times. Edward believed this to be the case too. But the angels never stay, they simply do their work and move on. Also, these angels don't have wings, or harps or other such nonsense. They are nothing more than ordinary people who don't realise they have been given little tasks to do. I have noticed over the years that quite a number of people have been drawn to Angels Cove when they needed help. And so, the cove really does belong to the angels – to lots of them. But to add an apostrophe would be to indicate ownership and I really don't believe that angels need such a thing. It is simply a Cove of Angels as it always has been and always will be – in other words, Angels Cove. No apostrophe. I hope that helps.

The only thing left for me to say is that I hope you'll live a life where you want nothing more than to wake up every day with an overpowering urge to have a wonderful day. You asked about Botox. Well, all I would say is to remember that the most beautiful woman in any room is the woman with the most joy in her heart, not with the fewest wrinkles on her face. Wrinkles are beautiful badges of honour – they represent all the fun and laughter and tears in your life. Iron out the lines and you iron out your life, and that is something I would never do.

With this in mind, I bequeath to you five thousand pounds. Spend the money as you wish, but my wish is that you use it to learn how to fly. The Attagirls shared a very special empowering secret – that every woman should know how to fly – there is truly nothing like it, and there is no better time for you to learn than right now.

With much love and grateful thanks,
Juliet x

Flabbergasted at the bequest, I handed the letter to Sam.

'She was right about the apostrophe,' he said, placing the letter back in the envelope. 'Why don't you read the letter out loud at the meeting this evening? Juliet was adored in the village. They'll go along with her suggestion, I'm sure. In a way, it saves face for everyone. No one in the village will think the other side has won. It's perfect.'

I took a very deep and relieved breath.

'Thank you, Sam. That's exactly what I'll do.'

He surprised me by reaching into his pocket and taking out a velvet pouch. He opened it to show me. There was a pill inside, but time had caused it to crumble to nothing more than dust.

I gasped.

'But ...? I thought ...?'

Sam shook his head.

'I found it in her jacket this morning. She died naturally, Katherine, just as Edward said she would, and I'm almost certain it happened as we flew over the angels.'

'That's incredible. And I'm so pleased,' I said. 'It was her choice, of course, but I hated the thought of her leaving her life that way.' I nodded towards the pouch. 'What are you going to do with it?'

'Most of it has disintegrated, but I'm glad you asked, because ...'

He took a pair of surgical gloves out of his pocket and walked a little way into the lapping sea. He dipped his arm into the water to pick up two pebbles and crushed what was left of the pill between the two pebbes before allowing the flow of the water to wash the dust clean away.

'I was wondering,' he said, returning to my side further up the beach, 'Would you like to go for a walk?'

I jumped up.

'Where?'

'No idea.'

'I'd love to, but before that, I have some things for you too, from Juliet.'

We returned to the cottage. I sat by him at the kitchen table and handed him the ring box. He opened it.

'It's the engagement ring, from Edward. She wanted you to have it.'

Sam smiled and nodded, doing his best to hold back the tears.

'And there are bags and bags of old twenty-pound notes, too, and a copy of Gone With the Wind – it was your grandmother's.'

I handed him the book.

'I wondered where that was,' he said, lifting the book to smell it.

'It has a poem in the back, written in by Lottie.'

'Yes, I know. *Remember,*' he said.

'Exactly.'

'But the most important gift ...' I opened an ammunition box to take out the compass. 'Is this one.'

His face brightened.

'The compass! You found it!'

'It was in her flying jacket. There was never the right moment to give you any of these things yesterday, it all got so busy, after you landed, you know ...'

He opened the compass to look inside.

'She loved this old thing, not that it's worth much, but it's priceless to me.'

'Not worth much ... may I?'

I opened the catch the way Juliet showed me and revealed the diamonds.

Sam's jaw dropped.

'I had no idea ...'

'It's your inheritance – the Caron jewels.'

Gerald, Percy and Noel gathered around me like expectant fathers when I arrived at the hall just before five. The hall was packed. I couldn't for the life of me understand where all the people had appeared from, but I assumed many of the crowd must be tourist who had arrived early for the party, where they were very pleased to find Fenella peddling her newly-branded gin – The Tipsy Angel.

Gerald began the event with a quick speech in remembrance of Juliet before handing over to me, his niece, the professor. I read Juliet's letter and concluded that Angels Cove should stay as exactly as it was – Juliet had said so, after all – and not one person argued with this hypothesis. Gerald shouted, 'Good show, well done,' from the back of the hall and went back to drinking gin. Talk about fickle, or storm in a teacup. I was almost disappointed at the lack of unrest.

But then the party really started and I quickly forgot about the apostrophe along with everyone else. Fenella had decked the hall proudly and her efforts were a triumph to the phrase – cheap and cheerful. The local charity shop had loaned out china cups, plates and glasses and what with pots of tea and little cakes and sandwiches, dilute squash and bunting, other than Fenella's 1940s hairstyle, pinafore and lipstick and Percy's wartime tailored suit, it was more like a 1970s Jubilee street party than a wartime gathering, but it didn't matter and at least the music was bang on the money.

Fenella had borrowed Juliet's gramophone and wartime selection of records from Sam, which created the perfect ambience, and soon the children were doing the boogie-woogie to Glen Miller while their parents looked on, pissed as farts, on knock-off gin.

Suddenly overcome by melancholy, I took a seat at the back of the hall, happy to watch and from somewhere, remember my promise – a promise to the megalith to take an offering in return for my wish – for Juliet to find her compass – which, to my great relief, had been granted. I thought of the ammunition box, and the ruby engagement ring. I looked down at my own engagement finger, at the wedding ring. I would borrow Fenella's car tomorrow and take my offering, the only gold I had. It was time.

I was just gawping wide-eyed at the only couple who were genuinely able to jive and had taken the floor like a couple from *Strictly Come Dancing* when the music changed.

A woman's voice – a beautiful deep, smoky voice – rang out, singing one of Juliet's songs. It wasn't a record this time, it was live music.

The band from the pub had taken to the stage and when I glanced up I saw that the woman singing, was Fenella.

Well I never!

A clean-shaven man appeared in front of me, blocking my view of the stage. He seemed familiar, but different. It was Sam, I realised, and although he was looking like he hadn't slept in a week, he also looked rather lovely.

'You were dancing to this two nights ago, when I arrived,' he said, glancing towards the band. 'Which means it's kind of our song, and I was just wondering – if your dance card is free, of course – if you would do me the honour of dancing with me?'

I smiled up.

'My dance card is most definitely free, Mr Lanyon, and I would love to dance with you.'

I took his hand and that moment had the definite feeling of another hand slipping away, and for the first time in three years, I didn't reach out in a panic to take it back.

By ten thirty, the evening came to a natural close and after helping Fenella clear the room, we headed down the road.

'Did you finish Juliet's story, yet?' she asked, folding my arm into hers.

I shook my head. 'No, not yet.'

We ambled down the narrow little Cornish lane, past the pub and the school to the harbour and stood outside of her front door. We glanced up towards Juliet's cottage. The lights were on.

Fenella gave me a hug and simply said, 'Yours.'

I pulled away and laughed.

'Mine? What is?'

'It was the name of the song, you nincompoop.'

'What?'

'The name of the song – *Yours*.'

'You've lost me now.'

'One day,' she said, fumbling in her handbag for the door key, 'when you try to remember the first song you danced to ... remember, it was *Yours*.'

We hugged again but I didn't let go this time.

'Thank you for looking after me, Fenella. I love you.'

She sniffed. Pulled away. Nodded her 'I love you too' and shuffled through the door.

'Now get yourself up to that cottage,' she said, 'He shouldn't be on his own tonight. I'll see you when I see you. Drink some wine, play some songs – do what Juliet did?'

'Which was?'

'*Live*, Katherine!'

She closed the door behind her and left me standing in the street. I heard the radio in her kitchen sound out through the old cottage window – *It's Beginning to look a lot like Christmas* and you know, I really think it was.

I walked up the lane to stand in front of the old cottage that had begun to feel like home. Sam opened the door with a warm smile, beckoned me inside and my time in Angels Cove ended, almost, as it began. With a glass of whiskey in one hand and a memory from Juliet in the other – the very last one.

Chapter 43

Juliet

Christmas 1944

Going home

Flying over the French coastline felt so very different this time. For a start, it was daytime and easier to navigate, but previously, as I had looked down from my viewpoint, six thousand feet above, I had felt an overwhelming sensation of heading towards a world shrouded in oppression and sadness. A world where, across this patchwork of fields beneath me, lay pockets of deeply unhappy people, forced to live-half lives in absolute fear. Nazi occupied France had seeped into the aircraft like a noxious gas, and didn't dissipate until I was back over the channel again, heading for home.

But now, although the war on a global scale was not yet done, here at least, in this little corner of France, those crucial axioms of liberty, equality and fraternity, could once more be celebrated, and as began my final descent towards a Brittany field in winter, I no longer noticed the harsh concrete of the German coastal defences beneath me and no longer imagined a Gestapo agent hiding behind every wall, but noticed church steeples and pretty farmhouses, instead. And even though we were surrounded by the detritus of winter, the sense of oppression had lifted, and was replaced by the indefatigable traces of the beginning of new life.

It took less than fifteen minutes to run from my landing field to Le Ferme de Bray. I landed close by this time and headed directly down the road, no longer evading the Germans, excited but nervous at the thought of seeing Edward again.

I ran into the familiar farm courtyard but suddenly paused for a moment, because quite unexpectedly, at seeing the farmhouse again – the dovecote, the ancient slate roof that dipped in the middle, the shabby green window shutters, the cobbled path leading to the old oak door – I began to cry. During my stay I hadn't noticed the beauty of the place, so caught up was I with anxious thoughts. But now, looking on, for the first time since my father died, I experienced that feeling of being home, because home, I realised, really is where the heart is, which is why more than one place can feel like home at one time, because the heart really is capable of being flooded with love when it comes across the right people, capable of leaving a little piece of itself in the corners where love lies waiting for you to come home.

The door opened. Cecille stepped out. Neither one of us rushed to greet each other at first, but simply stared. We both needed that moment, to soak each other in, to look on at the other, to allow the euphoric feeling of knowing that despite everything, we had each survived. She held out her arms and like a lost child running back to its mother, I ran across the yard and fell into her, only to feel Monsieur Bisset wrap his bear-like embrace around us both a moment later. And for a moment my happiness was whole, absolute and complete – for a moment.

Edward was upstairs, in bed. How he had survived the journey across France was both a mystery and miracle to Monsieur Bisset. But once embraced at the farm, a fever had taken hold and he had collapsed into bed. A doctor had been sent for and the suspected diagnosis confirmed – typhus – a shocking disease spread by lice that had run like wild fire through the dirt and deprivation of Nazi concentration camps.

His clothes were burned to eradicate the lice, but the local doctor could not source the medicine needed to combat the disease. I should prepare myself, Cecille said, for the sight of a very sick man.

But no words could have prepared me for the sight of Edward today. During my flight to France I had played out a completely different reunion in my mind's eye – a scene that cast me as the rescuing heroine, with Edward, understandably a shadow of his former self but very much alive, walking down the lane to greet me, before wrapping me in an embrace and declaring that he would never ever again let me go.

The third step creaked as I knew it would as I edged upstairs alone, leaving Cecille at the foot of the narrow curving staircase, looking up, her eyes full of concern and tears. I tiptoed along the landing and rested my hand on the door handle. Edward – my Edward – was behind this very door.

The body beneath the sheets was so emaciated it barely made an outline. Wearing one of Monsieur Bisset's frayed nightshirts, Edward could have been a child dressed in his father's clothes. One arm rested above the bed sheet. I took the wooden chair that always sat against the wall next to the window, placed it at the side of the bed, sat down, took Edward's hand in mine and waited.

Half an hour passed by until he stirred, but when he did, a trace of the vibrant, dynamic man I once knew, flashed briefly into his eyes.

'Juliet?' he breathed, desperately trying to sit up, his frail arms outstretched, trying to grab a hold on me.

I leant forwards and allowed my face to brush against his.

'Yes, my love,' I whispered. 'I'm here.'

'I knew you'd come,' he said, over and over again. 'I knew you'd come.'

Yet more tears ran freely down both of our faces as we embraced. I sat forwards in my chair and held his hand. His eyes rested on my face but then took in my flying jacket.

'You flew?'

I nodded, wiped my nose with the back of my hand. 'In the old Tiger Moth, but ...'

I couldn't continue. Edward's eyes betrayed his acceptance of the truth.

'Take me home, Juliet,' he whispered. 'As soon as you can. Today if possible.'

I shook my head.

'You're not well enough for an open canopy flight. You'll freeze.'

He ignored my answer by smiling.

'That's how I always imagined you, you know, in the Tiger Moth. In Dachau, when I ... I tried to remember you – I imagined you that day, in the field, with the cows.' He lifted a hand to stroke my face. 'Just like a pixie queen. I loved you from very first moment.'

The tears began again.

'It was exactly the same for me too,' I whispered. 'There was only ever you, Edward. There will *always* only ever be you.'

'Take me home?'

My upper body fell forwards into a broken heap of sobs across him on the bed.

Edward stroked my hair.

'There's something I've been wanting to tell you,' he said. 'Remember that day we sat in the church together, when we wondered what the angel in the window was asking God?'

I pulled myself up to look at him and wiped my eyes. I tried to muster a smile.

'I remember.'

Edward tried to sit himself up. I took the cushion from my stool to rest behind his head.

'The thing is, I met him, on the beach. I met the angel, Juliet.'

Edward's eyes suddenly burned brighter. I wondered if delirium was setting in.

'You met him?'

'Yes, incredible, but there he was,' Edward explained, struggling slightly to catch his breath. 'He was on the beach– the same face, long blonde hair ... we spoke. Water ...'

'Water? Oh, yes. Sorry, darling. I'll hold it. Here you are.'

He paused to take a sip. I waited.

'What did he say,' I asked. 'The ... angel.'

'We talked about so many things. It was wonderful, Juliet. I can't tell you. But listen, he said, I wasn't to worry about you, when I was gone. He's going to look after you. Never be scared, my love because there really *is* an angel at the cove. There really is. And he's watching over you.'

'But, Edward ...'

'No, I know it seems crazy. But I *know* it.' Edward took my hand. He was excitable, feverish. 'You once said to me, you *have* to believe – and that's what I'm saying to you now. You *have* to believe – in us. Our time may not be now, but we *will* not be apart, not really, and one day, we'll be together forever.' He started to cry. His tears were impossible to describe. Pain, joy, but most particularly – love. But not just a love for me, but a universal kind of love. As if he finally understood – everything. 'The poem,' he said, closing his eyes and resting back into the pillows. 'Never forget my poem. I'll wait for you.'

Reluctantly leaving Edward to sleep, I returned to the kitchen and wept into Cecille's arms. I wept for all that we had lost, rather than all that we had won. I wept for Edward, for me, for Anna, for Lottie, for the stranger whose blooded head had rested on Marie's knee that day at the dance, and for Mabel, too, the little orphan girl who I knew would be sitting in the drawing room at Lanyon playing with Amber, watching the skies as I told her, waiting for me to come home.

Monsieur Bisset sat in his chair smoking his pipe, the reassuring smell of his tobacco calming me into a rested haze. I explained about Edward's wish to go home. They did not try to persuade me to stay, but at two p.m. Monsieur Bisset put on his coat and stated that he would be back by nightfall – that he would arrange everything to enable Edward and I to leave first thing the following morning. He said his goodbyes with a smile and closed the door behind him. I grabbed my coat, threw open the kitchen door and ran after Monsieur Bisset as he read-justed his hat and headed out of the farm gates towards the road.

'Monsieur Bisset,' I shouted. He paused at the gateway until I caught up.

'I'm sorry to hold you up,' I said, catching my breath,

'but I wondered if you could point me in the right direction, I need to find a field, you see.'

'Oh?'

'On the night I arrived, the first time, I crashed into a field not far from here, do you know it?

He nodded, confused. '*Oui.*'

'I wonder, could you perhaps tell me how to walk there. I came here by quite a convoluted route across the fields that night, and there's no way I could retrace my steps now. But I left something ... something very special to me, nearby. I buried it in a fox burrow, in a copse, and I'd very much like to see if it's still there.'

He smiled his understanding. 'I'm going by that way myself,' he said. 'Walk with me, if you like?'

After dashing back to explain my plan to Cecille, and after having her green beret pressed into my hand, I walked with Monsieur Bisset down the bare-branched Brittany lanes, side-by-side with a man whose courage and kindness I could never repay. He talked of the relief of finally being able to walk freely – to actually enjoy a walk – to listen to the birdsong, to imagine the rising sap deep within the avenues of twiggy trees, to talk openly and freely with a friend without fear of oppression, but most importantly, he could now leave the house knowing that his wife was safe. He talked of the joy of being free to wonder in life's simple things again, and just as I would be eternally grateful to him for my freedom, so, too, would he be eternally grateful to the men and women of the allied forces who had never given in, who had fought on and eventually given the French their freedom too.

We reached the field within the hour. The skeleton of the burnt-out Lysander was still there, albeit robbed of any part that was remotely salvageable after the fire. The deep drainage ditches were clearly visible. I stood for a while, remembering. Monsieur Bisset, reading my confused thoughts, placed a hand on my shoulder and said, 'We will lose the light soon. I must leave you now if I'm to arrange everything for tomorrow. Look for your things, and get yourself home. Don't dwell too long in the past.'

I nodded.

'Thank you.' I took his hand in mine and squeezed it. 'Thank you, so very much, Monsieur.'

It took me just ten minutes to find the copse with the fox burrow and by some small miracle, in a hole beneath the roots of a beech hedge, there was Anna's jacket. I delved into an inside pocket for my ultimate prize and felt the familiar coldness of gold brush against my fingertips.

My father's compass.

I fell to my knees and pressed the compass to my chest. It wasn't just about my inheritance – a inheritance hidden deep within the inner working of the face – but about years of wonderful memories. Memories locked up inside that quirky old thing, now returned to me. I open the face and saw the needle sitting in a neutral position. Had the time come to ask my first question? I heard my father's voice: 'You already know the answer to any question, Juliet. There's never any real need to ask.'

And I did know.

I put the compass in my pocket, tucked Anna's coat under my arm and ran the whole way back.

The following morning, after having spent every possible moment by Edward's side – either reading to him while he slept, or sleeping on a mattress by the side of his bed – Monsieur Bisset prepared Edward for the journey. Monsieur Bisset, blessed with the silent strength of three men, carried Edward down the stairs wrapped in layers of coats and clothes that he had either donated himself or acquired from neighbours the previous evening. He carried Edward out into the courtyard and placed him in the cart. A tired old mare snorted her approval and with Monsieur Bisset at the reigns and Cecille and I seated either side of Edward – holding his hands and steadying his weak and lifeless body – we travelled in silence on the short journey to the waiting aircraft.

As if handling a baby, Monsieur Bisset lifted Edward into the front seat of the Tiger Moth, kissed him on both cheeks and without ceremony or displaying her grief-stricken emotion – just as I had asked her to behave – Cecille returned to the cart, flicked the reigns and waited from a safe distance on the lane to watch us depart. Her husband stood by the nose of the aircraft, waiting for the signal to turn the propeller.

All that was left was for me place a helmet on Edward's

head and goggles over his eyes and strap him in. Standing on the footplate, I leant across Edward and allowed my face to brush his as I secured the straps. Despite my resolve to keep my emotion at bay for the flight, the tears would come.

Edward found the strength to lift an arm free of the blankets. He touched my face and smiled through his obvious pain.

'On the far side,' he said. 'Don't ever forget.'

I looked into Edward's eyes.

'We're just going coddiwompling, that's all, over the rainbow, this time.'

I rested my forehead against his, kissed him one final time and climbed into the aircraft. I gave Monsieur Bisset the signal to spin the propeller and the familiar sound of the Moth's engine filled the still winter air. I knew that Edward would hear the engine and smile, because I knew he would remember that I had once called the sound of flight the sound of freedom, and today, more than ever before, that was exactly what it was.

It was a calm flight on a cloudless winter's day. We headed out across the Normandy beaches and crossed a channel of water that had acted as the most precious and effective moat history had surely ever seen. As the Cornish coast edged closer, my heart sensed that he had gone. Part of me wanted to go with him – to the far side. All I had to do was to push down on the stick, never pull up and the whole world would slip away. And I was sure for a moment that I would. I saw the faces of all those I had lost – my parents, Anna, Lottie and now Edward and I wanted to join them. But then I felt the familiar shape of my father's compass through my jacket pocket and I was transported to a field in Oxfordshire where a young girl was chatting happily to a journalist. 'It's instinct,' she had said, 'It's just a case of knowing when to pull up.' And although I could barely see to navigate through a cascade of tears, when I saw Lanyon appear through the haze in the distance, I thought of Marie and Wilkins, and more especially of Mabel who was playing in the garden with Amber, waiting for me. And that's when I heard Anna's voice, she was singing to me – *Somewhere Over the Rainbow*. And at that moment I vowed to remember all of it – every amazing, horrifying bit of it. I would live my life to its absolute limit – for Edward, for all of them – in the certain knowledge that one day we'd be together again, that he was waiting for me, on the far side, where the angels sing.

And that is where my story ends. As it began. In a bright yellow Tiger Moth, flying high above the angels, with Edward.

Acknowledgements

My heartfelt thanks to the following: my wonderful editor, Charlotte Ledger, who guided me with tenderness and tact through the writing of this story. To Frankie, Becky and Caroline, who keep me going with endless encouragement and enthusiasm. And especially to dear departed Mary Ellis, whose wonderful autobiography, *A Spitfire Girl*, was the inspiration for Juliet's story. I have so very many questions and I wish so much that I had met her.